BIBLE STORIES
for
SECULAR HUMANISTS

by

S.P. SOMTOW

DIPLODOCUS PRESS
LOS ANGELES • BANGKOK

BIBLE STORIES
for
SECULAR HUMANISTS

published by
Diplodocus Press • Los Angeles • Bangkok

Main Office
48, Sukhumvit Soi 33, Bangkok 10110, Thailand

Some material in this book has previous appeared in various anthologies.

Hardcover
ISBN: 978-0-9860533-6-8

Trade Paperback
ISBN: 978-0-9860533-7-5

FIRST EDITION
1 2 3 4 5 6 7 8 9 0

DEDICATION

Organized religion loves to teach
what you are not allowed to do.
I love to teach that you can do anything.
reach any star, touch any truth.
And so it was that I didn't get around to teaching you
that you shouldn't hurt me.
And you did.

Nevertheless, I know
you learned your lessons well,
and that inside,
you know the truth,
and that when you are ready,
you will understand,
like Dorothy,
that you have always been home.

DISCLAIMER

Just to be sure you realize it:

This is a work of *fiction*. I made it all up.
In the unlikely event that any sentient being,
animal, human, or divine, feels a certain
similarity to their own lives in this book, rest assured
that it is entirely coincidental.

It isn't true.
I made it up.
I do this for a living.

Contents

... and perhaps this little piece from
Iniquities *magazine will help to*
set the tone for our little odyssey through
the dark underpinnings of the Judaeo-Christian mind....

Theology for Secular Humanists

a column from *Iniquities* magazine

In my last couple of columns I talked about distant lands and exotic climes — demons in Bangkok — farting in England — shamanism in Southern California. I thought I'd spend time in this, the third issue of the ever-more-popular *Iniquities,* to discuss profound philosophical problems a little closer to home. Having recently escaped — by about 1/10th of a second — being crushed to death by a hit and run driver, I've been spending a lot more time recently meditating about death, and about the transience of existence.

Not that I don't think about death all the time — after all, I *am* a horror writer! — but I generally only think about other people's, not my own. And anyway the death we horror writers deal with is metaphorical; as with the tarot card named Death, we use death to mean transformation as often as we use it mean actual, physical, one-way-ticket death.

The other main component of literature — indeed, all art — is, of course, sex. Sex and death are what it's all about, and the thing that disturbs people most about horror — the thing that stands most in the way of its respectability as a literary genre — is the fact that in the horror medium we are able to actualize the equation of sex and death in a far more blatant way than can be done in other literary fields.

Of course, writers whose works are not generally relegated to the ghetto of horror can be just as blatant as any of us. One has only to examine the works of Shakespeare to find such sentiments as the following, from *Romeo and Juliet:*

> *"O happy dagger,*
> *This is thy sheath! There rust, and let me die."*

Bearing in mind that, in 16th Century English, the word "die" had the double meaning of having an orgasm, we can see that Shakespeare's really being pretty damn blatant about how Juliet's suicide is really all about the equation of sex and death. Of course, if one of the modern splatterpunks had been writing this scene, he might have phrased it something like this:

"Looking at that dagger reminded Juliet of Romeo's throbbing dick inside her, pumping her until she was ready to explode with ecstacy. 'Give it to me, baby!' she murmured. 'Fuck me until I'm swallowed up in the great big lubricious cunt of death!'"

Or — to take another example from that endless cornucopia of examples — how about the scene where Othello strangles Desdemona, then crawls toward her hapless corpse for one last kiss?

> *"I kissed thee ere I killed thee. No way but this:*

Killing myself, to die upon a kiss."

Once again, the old bard really knew that sex and death go together as surely as do "things" and Coke. I imagine, if one of the present bards of gore were to write this scene, it would go something like this:

> *"Othello cradled Desdemona in his arms. Rigor mortis had not yet set in, and she flopped in his muscular embrace like a Cabbage Patch doll that had seen too much service in the marital aid industry. 'I done killed you dead, white bitch,' he crooned huskily, 'but now I know you didn't screw around with no motherfucking Italian captain. Well, you dead, and ain't nothing I can do about it now. But just looking at you, lying there, with your baby mouth all soft, it sure do make me horny. Oh, baby, let me come on you one more time. Yeah, let me come all over you and you don't even have to move, 'cause Ofello he about ready to croak heself.'"*

Perhaps it should be explained to any of the "loud" horror writers who happen to be reading this article that I am not, of course, parodying any of them individually — just creating a kind of "virtual reality" hypothetical horror writer of somewhat limited literacy — in order to demonstrate that that the passage from the sublime to the ridiculous is not a quantum but a continuum — that all of us, from the Master on down, deal with the sex and death thing in ways that go all the way from the transcendently metaphorical to the messily physical.

I started thinking very seriously about sex and death one day a couple of weeks ago when a friend of mine, a teenage kid who occasionally hangs around my house, started asking me some serious questions about it. It must be noted that this kid doesn't usually draw me into philosophical discussions; he's generally more interesting in such teenage preoccupations as "scamming," "racking", and "tagging," which, to the best of my knowledge, may be roughly translated for those over thirty as "heavy petting," "shoplifting," and "writing on walls". Today, though, he was inclined to be serious, and he came right out and asked me (as the resident guru of the house), "Somtow, why do people believe things that are so obviously bullshit?"

"What do you mean?" I said. "Have you decided to take up a career in politics or something?"

"No, I don't mean like, the P.T. Barnum kind of thing, putting things over on people, selling them snake oil ... I mean like, the Bible and shit. I mean, how could someone live in the belly of a fish? How could like, people really believe that these naked dudes talked to a snake and ate an apple and ended up getting kicked out of the celestial Club Med by a dude with a white beard? I just don't understand. These things are just totally not true, and yet people just believe them and you can't argue with 'em."

Well, one thing was clear: Alex must have been spending the weekend with his deeply religious grandparents, and it wasn't really my place to countermand their solicitude for the poor boy's soul. But the problem of faith was not the only thing his question set me thinking about.

Most of the horror writers I know are not fundamentally religious people. Some of them may believe in *something,* but they are also people who like to question, who are always into challenging the bases of their own beliefs; if not atheists, they tend to be at the very least agnostics. And yet the imagery of religion — its metaphoric content — not only Judæo-Christian but also that of more ancient or more exotic religions — figures very prominently indeed in the work of horror writers. This is especially true in the case of supernatural horror, since the supernatural presupposes a supernatural cosmology, and that cosmology is necessarily buttressed by the trappings of religion. Vampires and werewolves come replete with

Catholic paraphernalia; so, at a second remove, do zombies, since the voodoo that creates them is a West African religion seen through the distorting lens of Catholicism. Satan goes around fucking innocent women and engendering the Antichrist so frequently in fiction that his multitudinous offspring threaten to outnumber the extant fragments of the true cross.

But even in psychological or realistic horror, there is a tendency toward demonization, so that the terror the reader feels at the exploits of some serial killer or bogeyman often becomes a supernatural terror — a religious terror.

Why, if horror writers don't generally, as a class, subscribe to Judæo-Christian (and other) mythological systems? And why are many readers willing to accept these systems as true, at least temporarily, during the course of a work of fiction, even if they'd never in a million years set foot in a church, and have surely never considered the theological ramifications of original sin?

As I said, I didn't want to upset the kid's grandparents, so I decided to try to steer the conversation into calmer waters. "Alex, those stories *are* true," I said. "But there's more than one kind of truth."

"What do you mean?" he said.

I could see that there really were no calm waters in this particular sea, but I was still trying to avoid religious controversy. Murmuring a secret prayer to St. Bruno Bettelheim, I said, "Fairy tales, for instance. They use a language of symbols to tell us truths about ourselves that sometimes we're not ready to face if someone just told them to us bluntly. You may not think *Little Red Riding Hood* is true, but in a very real sense, it is."

"Huh?" he said, mystified.

"Well, think of a girl who's just had her first period. She's starting to think all kinds of exciting and frightening new thoughts about sex. The red riding hood she's wearing shows us she's going through puberty, because it's the color of blood ... and the dark forest is —"

"Oh my God," said this fourteen-year-old boy, who only required one little hint to see the whole picture vividly. "It's about her father, isn't it? The wolf, I mean. She thinks he's gonna rape her or something. And he tricks her into getting into bed with him, and —"

I marveled at Alex's ability to see right through to the core of this fairy tale. I'd only shown him the first stepping stone, but he'd managed to figure out the whole thing: that this children's story explains, in symbolic terms, an all-too-common domestic situation, and, by making the girl victorious and restoring the grandmother to life, it also shows the girl that she can and will wander off the beaten path one day ... when she's ready.

"No one ever told me this before," Alex said, "thanks." I thought I was off the hook, but he went on, "But that was only a fairy tale, and nobody really believes those literally anyway. Come on, dude, you're like, evading the issue. Tell me why Adam and Eve is true and *then* I'll stop bugging you and go back to playing Tetris on my Gameboy."

"So tell me what you think is wrong with the story of Adam and Eve," I said. I didn't want to launch into an explanation of how most biblical scholars believe that two different authors are responsible for the first eleven chapters of *Genesis*. "P", the boring one, wrote Chapter One, transcribing it almost word for word from the Babylonian creation myth, and specifically saying that God made lots of men and women all at once; "J", who wrote the story of Adam and Eve, had a more poetic view of the universe. (One controversial new theory attempts to prove that "J" was a woman.) But I didn't think that academic theories would really help this young man's dilemma, which was the old Socratic problem of the nature of truth.

"Well," he said, "apart from the fact that it's bullshit anyway — I mean, I *do* know about evolution — how could it be true that God would kick these dudes out of paradise just for making a dumb mistake that anyone would make? And just because they made that mistake, we're like *all* full of sin and have to be saved by Jesus, even though I sure never had a bite of that apple? If God really existed, he wouldn't be such a dick." (Alex was, without knowing it, quoting almost directly from Euripides.)

I thought about something my friend and collaborator, Brian Yuzna (who directed *Bride of Re-Animator)* frequently talks about. He's really fascinated by the fact that amoebae don't have sex, and they don't die. An amoeba version of *Re-Animator* would probably be pretty dull.

So I said, "Well, think, Alex. You're stuck in a beautiful garden with everything you could possibly want. You're there for all eternity with the most beautiful girl in the world, and she's always naked. All you have to do is not eat the apple to stay there forever. What would you do?"

"What use is a naked girl if I don't even know she's naked?"

"Exactly. Do you remember what was in the apple?"

"Knowledge."

"And if you *knew* she was naked, what would you do?"

"I'd fuck her," he said.

"You've just explained the whole story," I said. "People have this burning need to know things. Not just mad scientists, everybody. And the price of knowledge is sex — and death. It's human to want to know things, and it's human to want to make love, and it's human to die. Before they ate the apple, they weren't really human, because they didn't have those things. The story doesn't say that it's a bad thing to be driven from the Garden of Eden. It celebrates the fact that human beings want to know the truth and are willing to pay the price. It's a story that describes what it's like to be a human being. I mean, let's face it — what would you do if you were living in a perfect place, and your parents did everything for you, and you got everything you wanted, and you'd never grow old ... as long as you had to stay in that one place forever?"

"Shit! I'd leave."

"Exactly. Sooner or later you have to give up being a child. You have to learn that your parents aren't perfect. You have to grow up and leave home."

I saw something that pleased and moved me greatly then: I saw the light of understanding in Alex's face, and I realized that he would never again dismiss those Bible stories as untrue.

And that, I realized, is also true of all us horror writers who profess a certain militant and iconoclastic irreligiousness. We continue to draw on the imagery of those very systems of belief which, we loudly claim, have lost their power over us. But they have not. Horror fiction is, at root, a profoundly religious genre — perhaps the most religious of all branches of literature — and it speaks to that gut sense of awe, that pre-logical child within, the only part of us that still sees the universe in terms of absolute good and evil.

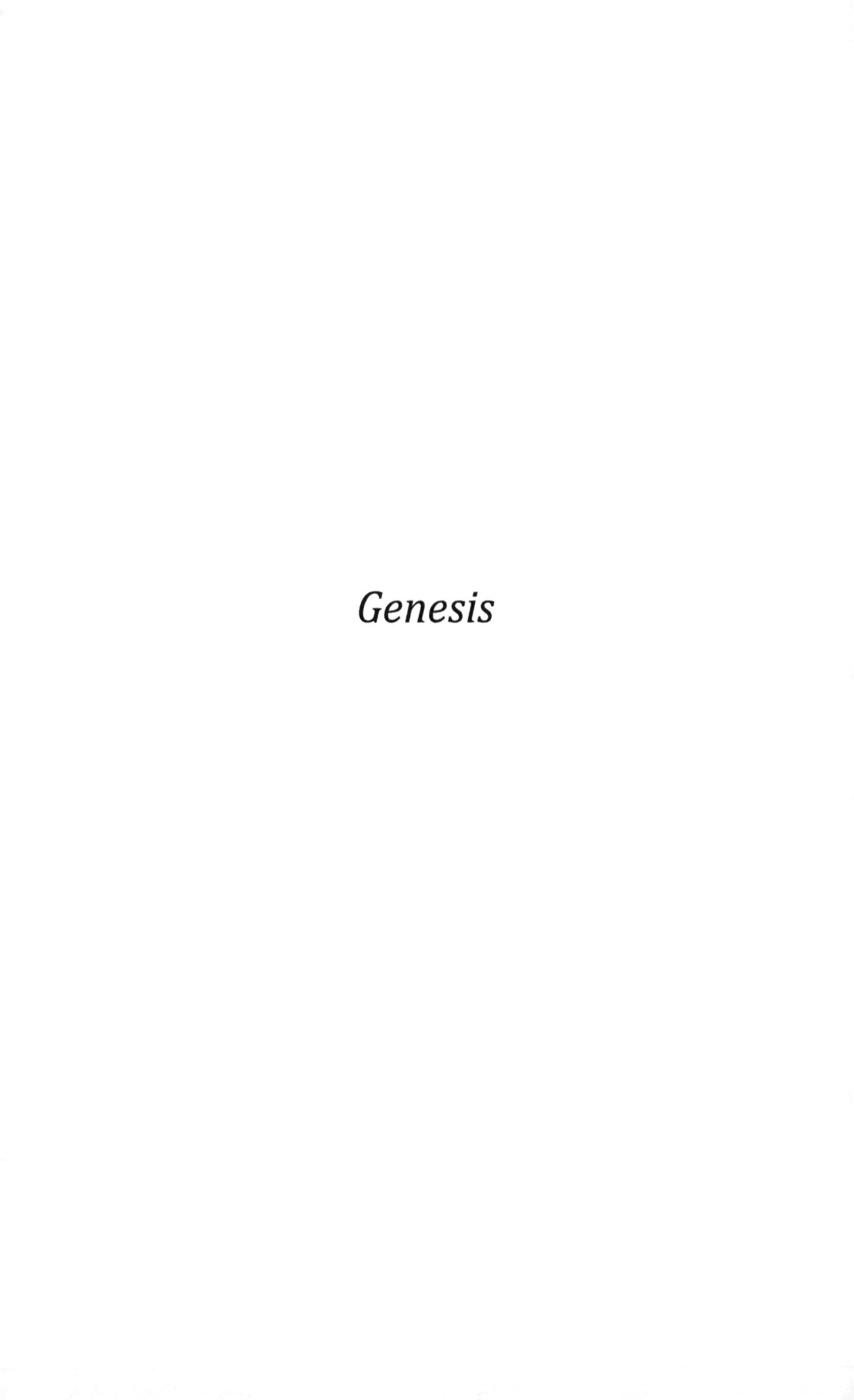

Genesis

I'd like to briefly introduce each story; this one
won an International Horror Guild Award and was
nominated for the Bram Stoker Award.

I have always been bewildered at the story
of Lot and his daughters. I have always wondered
why someone like Lot was entrusted to
find "good men" in Sodom.
I have always wondered what they did in Gomorrah.
I have always wondered why no one thought that
there was anything wrong with what Lot did;
but then again, it's all about context, isn't it?

The Qur'an doesn't talk about
Lot's curious domestic arrangements; the book
of Genesis is so casual about it that one almost forgets
to notice that the daughters do not even receive
the acknowledgment of being named,
an indignity they share with the sisters of Jesus.

What we do, as novelists, is connect dots,
fill in blanks, ask questions. In this book, I connect the
dots in many uncomfortable ways, and yet,
I assure you, the dots themselves are all real.
Who decided that a certain pattern of stars
was a waterbearer or an archer?

People like me.
People who make things up;
for in so doing, we sometimes unveil a kind of truth.

Brimstone and Salt

And what, you ask me, did they do in Gomorrah?

It's a reasonable question. We all know what they did in Sodom. They sat around buttfucking each other until God, in his wrath, rained down fire and brimstone, and blew the place to kingdom come. Everyone knows that, right? It's all there in the bible. An angel told Lot that if he could find ten righteous and upright men in all of Sodom and Gomorrah, the twin cities would be spared; Lot couldn't, and that was that. Boom. Apocalypse. Mushroom cloud hanging over half of Mesopotamia.

Of course, Lot's own righteousness was pretty questionable; the bible tells us that he screwed his own daughters, so he was probably not the very best judge of character. One wonders what gave him the right to pick ten honest upstanding citizens out of that double den of iniquity.

As usual, alas, the good book has it all backwards; and we must, in fact, look elsewhere for the facts. Ask me anything. I know. I was there.

Don't laugh, Mr. Big-shot Shrink. You run a tight support group. Melvin the Multiple's pretty damn entertaining, and Mildred's regressions to her four-year-old closet of satanic abuse are truly *Hard Copy* material. Nothing to complain about there. Maybe Jack-in-the-box, who doesn't do a fucking thing except rock back and forth, isn't that much of an asset to the group, but on the rare occasions when he does talk, he goes wild. One of these days I'm going to get Entertainment Tonight in here for you, but for now, we just have each other, don't we? As if that weren't enough.

I've been watching you guys go at each other for three weeks now. You know I haven't said anything. I've sat, and I've watched, and maybe you people think that my hundred bucks an hour are wasted because I haven't had the chance to spill my guts all over the plush white carpet of your elegant art deco office. Tonight, my friends, you're going to get your money's worth. This is one child abuse survivor support group that's never going to be the same.

Melvin, you had such a hideous time when you were four years old that your mind fractured into a dozen personalities. I've had a thousand.

And not because of one cruel stepfather — because the entire world hurt me. To survive, I've become a thousand people over the years. Oh, Melvin, you have me beat on one thing — all your people are inside your brain now, fighting among one another. My personalities came one at a time. Each of them grew up, grew old, and died, yet I went on.

As for Jack, rocking back and forth — I like you. You had a narrow escape from a serial killer when you were seven years old, so you don't talk much. Look into my eyes. I'm a lot worse than the one you escaped from. I've dined on the kind of man who made your life a living hell. I'm a serial killer's serial killer.

Mildred: maybe you were a victim of that satanic abuse bullshit, and maybe not. False memory syndrome is a big thing right now, and your last analyst is being sued by half her ex-patients. I don't really believe it personally. You think you hung out with Satan? Satan was a personal friend of mine, back in the days when he *was* somebody.

So here I am. Just a visitor, in a sense, although I too am a survivor of what happened to all of you; I just happen to have survived a few thousand years longer than any of you have. Don't laugh, Mr. Shrink; I am not delusional. I am not suffering from any psychosis, though, after all these centuries, I probably ought to be. I'm not some rich bitch paying through the nose in order to play elaborate mindgames or live out arcane fantasies, two evenings a week.

I am a vampire.

I am Shoshana, the youngest daughter of Lot.

I am probably the oldest incest survivor in the world.

You want the support group confession to end all support group confessions? You want a night to remember, full of spectacle, bloodshed, debauchery, greed, insanity, shame, lust, angst, orgies, belly-dancers? Hold on to your horses, my friends. Tonight, after five millennia or so, I finally feel like talking. And you, my friends, are a captive audience. Not because I compel you to stay, but because we of the ancient kindred possess a seductive glamour that makes it nearly impossible for you to resist us. You fear us, but you desire us too.

Look at me, Mr. Big-shot Shrink: am I not beautiful? Is it the moonlit pallor of my complexion, the lurid carmine of my lips, the dusky splendor of my shoulder-length hair? Or is it perhaps the sensuous contralto of my voice, or my indefinably foreign accent, or the bizarre way that I lisp sometimes, as if the air had been trapped in my lungs for decades at a time, because I don't seem to need to breathe? Surely it's not the way I dress — about four centuries out of style — passing for gothic chic in today's strange, alienated youth culture? I am, you know, forever young. And I do mean forever.

Maybe you want to know, if I'm really this immortal creature of the night, why I need to be here with you at all. You're beyond all this, you tell me. You're not even human. Psychiatry is about helping human beings come to terms with their humanity, is it not? If you're really a vampire, presumably you don't have to worry about such mundane things as night terrors, bad dreams, neuroses, obsessive-compulsive behaviors.

But you have to understand that before I changed into what I am today, I once was human, and the bad thing my father did to me started long before I even knew vampires existed....

It was at Ur that my father first came to me in the middle of the night. We had come for the funeral of Enkidu, the king's lover. Our people had long since been displaced from the land we called Eden, the fertile valley of the Tigris and Euphrates, by a technologically superior people, smelters of bronze, builders of cities; the desert had become our home. We lived in a manner not much different from the Bedouin tribes today; but in theory the King of Sumer had suzerainty, and now and then it was necessary to send an official mission to the court. A formality, really. Abraham, the patriarch, didn't need to come himself, so he sent Lot.

My sister and I came with him, sharing a camel. We were not important. They didn't even lodge us in the palace, but allowed us to set up our tents in walled garden that had once been part of the royal harem.

As one of the lowliest of the subject peoples, my father was not even granted an audience with Gilgamesh. But on the morning of the funeral, they gave us a perfunctory tour of the city. We were a convoy of litters, each one carrying a visiting party from some distant outpost of civilization, and they were doing their best to impress us with the splendor and spectacle of their superior culture. But everyone was in mourning, so there wasn't much to see. The marketplace was closed, and all the houses shuttered; from inside came the constant sound of weeping. The king had decreed that anyone caught not acting suitably doleful would be impaled.

The only action within the city walls was at the temple of Ishtar, which couldn't very well be closed down. Our palanquin moved slowly past it, and our guide, a minor functionary of the court named Turak, lectured us about sacred prostitutes. I had no idea what he was talking about. But my father covered our eyes with his fat palms.

"Abomination, abomination!" he murmured. "Don't look!"

"But father," I said, trying to pry his fingers off my face, *"you're* looking. In fact, you've got that look in your eye. The one that usually gets you in trouble."

My sister Rachel was a lot less defiant than me. She turned her back on the temple and squeezed her eyes tight shut. But I got in a good look. It was a spectacle! There was a ziggurat in the midst of a plaza, and it was all limestone, shimmering in the sun. On the front steps of the temple sat women of all shapes and sizes. Most were young — some as young as me, even — but a few were haggard and hideous, and there were one or two leviathans among them. They weren't wearing very much. Except for their makeup, that is: they were kohled and rouged and powdered until they looked more like statuettes than human beings.

One of the women winked at me and beckoned with a languid hand. She was, I thought, very beautiful. The thick layer of makeup made her seem quite unreal. My sister saw me gawking and poked me in the ribs. "Don't let abba catch you staring," she whispered.

"But he's staring himself," I said.

"He's a grownup," she said. "Not like you."

Turak was explaining to us bumpkins, in an self-important drone: "When a girl reaches the age of her initiation, she must come to the temple of Ishtar and wait to be deflowered by the first man who desires her...."

"What's 'deflowered', abba?" I asked my father.

He slapped my face.

My sister began giggling. "You'll soon find out," she said.

My father grew very red. "Faster," he said to the litter-bearers. "Faster. We don't need any of this heathen nonsense." And he flailed at the nearest one with a little lead-tipped flagellum. The slaves marched a little faster. They narrowly avoided a six-palanquin pileup with a little fancy footwork. The streets in Sumer were narrow, the buildings leaning inward, mostly in that white adobe style you still find in places like Tunisia.

Enkidu's funeral was an obstreperous affair, with bevies of women beating their breasts, and slaves, animals, ex-wives and catamites of the deceased being drugged and buried alive along with him. We, the visiting diplomats, watched the whole thing from a specially erected pavilion. We caught a glimpse of Gilgamesh, the god-king, but he was wearing a golden mask of grief, so we couldn't be sure if it was really him or whether it was some priest, subbing for him so he could sulk in his private apartments.

As is customary at funerals, the last clod of earth shoveled over the dead (and the half-dead) was the signal for a different mood, a kind of desperate merrymaking. There was a banquet to be held in the throneroom, and yes, there were plenty of dancing girls and all sorts of food and drink. Gilgamesh didn't bother to show up.

My father drank deeply of the wine, which was cooled with snow that had been brought down by runners from mountains, they said, a thousand leagues away. He was in a foul mood. Ambassador though he was, he wasn't being well treated. And the incident at the temple of the goddess seemed to have put him into a severe depression. My sister was deep in conversation with some Akkadian prince, which didn't please my father either. I loved my father, and I hated to see him this way. So I took it upon myself to sit by him, to fetch him a fresh beaker of wine now and then, and to cool his brow with a piece of damask dipped in spring water.

Turak, our erstwhile guide, had taken a shine to my father, for some unearthly reason. Perhaps it was because he was being snubbed by everyone else at the party. In between gnawing off great mouthfuls of leg-of-lamb, he insisted on informing us who all the guests were. Not that I really had any idea what was going on.

A long time after sunset, when half the guests were already sprawled out snoring on pillows stuffed with rose leaves, there was a brief commotion. Conch-trumpets blared. My father rubbed his eyes and bestirred himself a little. Several acrobats and fire-swallowers entered the throneroom, followed by slave girls strewing flower petals.

I overheard some of the guests talking:"The impertinence! Getting here this late, how can they get away with it, not even showing up at the funeral itself," and other gossip that I didn't understand. It was at that point that the mystery guests entered the throneroom.

One was a young man dressed as a woman, his hair delicately hennaed, his eyebrows brushed with kohl. "Abomination!" my father whispered, and tried to cover my eyes again; but I was able to peep through his half-separated fingers, and I thought the man-woman was really very goodlooking. "Such a creature has no right to exist on this earth! It is an abomination; it should be stoned to death."

"Nonsense," said Turak. "You Hebrews are so provincial. That is the King of Sodom, you ignoramus.

Their priest-kings take the form of the Sacred Hermaphrodite out of respect for their god, who possesses both sets of genitalia; he is said to have impregnated himself, grown himself inside his own womb, and at length given birth to himself."

"What arrant superstition," said my father.

"You think your little tribal thunder-god, whose name you don't even dare utter, is any more believable?" Turak said, laughing. My father simply fumed.

At that point, I took a good look at the other guest. She had long black hair that went all the way down to her knees, and it was artfully draped around her body. To my amazement, I realized that it was the only thing she was wearing, apart from her earrings. Her skin was as pale as the snow on the mountaintops on a moonlight night; her hair was blue-black, like a raven's feathers. Her eyes had an unearthly glow about them, and when she smiled something glistened in her mouth, shiny and pointy-sharp.

I found myself staring at her. Amazingly enough, she appeared to be staring at me too. I saw her whispering to some confidante, perhaps trying to find out who I was.

I did not have to ask; Turak was already explaning. "The Queen of Gomorrah," he said. "The less said about Gomorrah, the better."

I went on staring at her, and I thought I could hear her voice inside my head, murmuring of cool springs and fragrant gardens, telling me of a land of eternal starlight, or perpetual night.

Later in the evening, I found her seated next to me. I didn't see her move across the room. She touched my shoulder. Her hand was icy. She said, "You are beautiful, daughter of Lot. You are wasted on these ill-mannered nomads. One day you should come to my city. Then you'll know what love really means." And she smiled, and I turned to see my father scowling.

That was the night my father stumbled onto my pallet, his breath sour with alcohol and vomit. That was the day he caressed me with gnarled hands, tossed aside the coarse woollen covering, and lay next to me, touching me in places where no man had ever touched me. I lay awake, but dared not open my eyes. My father started to speak in a harsh, strained whisper: "Oh, Shoshana, I'm a wicked man, I'm a man who's drawn to abomination and darkness, but you shouldn't have stared so hard at the sacred whores of the goddess you bitch cunt whore look what you're making me do you bitch oh, oh, Shoshana, I can't help myself, you're such a fucking bitch you cunt you whore...."

Oh, god, it got worse. He ripped open my sleeping robe. I felt something hard drive into my body. I felt torn up somehow. I knew I was bleeding. I couldn't help crying out. My father whispered, "Go to sleep, go to sleep, nothing's happening," and at that moment he began to shudder and — most heinous of all — began to utter the sacred Name of our tribal thunder-god — "YHWH!" he cried out. "There, I've done it, just as I do it every night with the other bitch, and you haven't struck me down, you haven't turned me to stone, you haven't seared my abominating body with a lightning bolt, YHWH YHWH YHWH," and each time he screamed out that word he thrust deeper into me and once I opened my eyes and I saw that his eyes were the eyes of a madman and I thought to myself, This is the worst worst moment of my life and I wish I could go away far far away....

It was in that moment that I saw, in my mind's eye, the face of the Queen of Gomorrah, saw her thin-lipped smile, saw her eyes grow wide and bloodshot, and heard her voice inside my head again, speaking of endless night. And I was comforted.

In the morning, there came gifts to my father's tent from the court of Gomorrah: a pound of salt for my father, and a terracotta doll for me. My father made me smash the doll in little pieces. "It's a graven image," he told me. He divided the salt into several pouches and put it away in a cedarwood chest.

"Salt, after all," he said, "is the most valuable thing in the world. It's only because of salt that the people of Sodom and Gomorrah can be so arrogant, so blatant in their public disregard for propriety and godliness."

Nothing was said about the happenings of the previous night.

So far, it was all very 90s. The drunken father sneaking into the bedroom, the silence the morning after, the blame being cast on the child, even my father's little attack of Tourette's syndrome while he was violating my innocent person. Nothing, you say, has changed in five thousand years. But that is not quite true.

We had no support groups in the Bronze Age.

We had no runaway hotlines, no battered children's shelters, no psychiatrists, no *Hard Copy.* I had no way of knowing that my fate was not unique. My mother was dead, and there was no one else I might consider talking to; my sister was moody and self-involved, and seemed to have a boyfriend in every oasis, despite my father's efforts to keep her chained to the hearth.

My father's visits became more frequent.

I think I was about ten years old, although we measured time differently in those days, not being tied, as the city people were, to the cycles of moon, sun, and river. Our tribal god had rejected agriculture in favor of the hunter-gatherer lifestyle — that's why my great-uncle Cain had been exiled from the fold — but that's why our people had become so backward, wandering the desert instead of living in shiny cities, lacking a real notion of the passing of time. But I did grow taller, and my father grew crazier.

One night —

It was after one of my father's nocturnal visits. It was full moon night and I suppose I couldn't stand the pressure anymore, so I ran out into the night — a bitter cold night as many desert nights are — wearing only a shift of Egyptian linen. The stars put me in mind of the Queen of Gomorrah. It was bitterly cold, and I hid from the wind by snuggling against a line of tethered camels, comforted by their toasty, rancid body odor.

Presently, I saw that the patriarch's tent was aglow, and that shadowy people were moving around inside. I got curious. I crept along, lifted the tent-flap, and crawled among the sheepskins that were draped over everything. There were voices, and they were coming from deep within.

Flickering light, too. Around me, Abraham's wives and concubines huddled together for warmth. I moved toward the inner tent, conscious that I was doing something very wrong, very unwomanly; the Hebrews were perhaps the most chauvinistic culture of that period, and we girls were certainly not allowed to trespass into the holy of holies.

The patriarch was sitting on a woven reed mat, and my father was with him. In the background, surrounded by veils, were the emblems of our tribal thunder-god, which few had ever gazed upon and lived, which had been ours ever since the big flood.

I watched them, knowing that I'd probably get a severe whipping if I was caught — Dr. Spock had not yet informed the world's parents about how traumatizing it might be to beat your children — and I saw the patriarch in a foul mood, rubbing his beard and now and then glancing askance at the holy of holies, as though afraid it might emit a thunderbolt at any moment.

"I've been hearing voices again," said Abraham. "Voices from, you know, behind there." He pointed to the sacred veils.

"What are we supposed to cut off this time?" said Lot. "Our dicks?"

I narrowly avoided giggling. My father was returning to Abraham's recent vision in which our god told him that all the men would have to slice off their foreskins as a sign of servitude to him. Well, it could have been worse; some gods require the sacrifice of one's firstborn, and others expect female clitoridectomy; I hoped that idea had not occurred to the patriarch.

"No, no," said Abraham. "It's Sodom and Gomorrah. We have to teach them a lesson."

"So what is the Lord God planning to do?" my father asked. "Have us take over the salt mines?"

"Our Tribal Deity," said Abraham, "is going to blow those twin cities off the face of the earth as a punishment for their iniquity." He said it as casually as you or I might talk about snuffing a candle. That's what made him the patriarch, you know; he could make the grandest of concepts seem almost trivial; crossing Sinai was like crossing the street.

"Quite right," said my father. "Nothing but abomination. Should have taken care of it during the flood."

I hadn't realized that our patriarch's voices were now claiming responsibility for the great flood that almost wiped out Mesopotamia a few generations before. I wondered whether they'd be taking credit for creating the universe next.

Don't gape, Mr. Bigshot-Shrink. The world was a lot different then. Monotheism was still in the future. Every little society had its own god in those days, but no one had gotten around to claiming that other people's gods didn't even exist. That was a level of theological abstraction to which we hardworking nomads had yet to aspire.

"I want you to go to Sodom," Abraham told my father. "Scout the place out. I've told the Lord God that if you can ferret out ten worthy men in all of the twin cities, I'd like him to spare them the cataclysm."

"Good move," Lot said. "That way you don't lose face if — heaven forfend — no cataclysm actually takes place. Ten honest citizens won't be hard to find."

"True," said Abraham. "And while you're there, learn all you can about the salt business. You know, we're not going to be a bunch of desert-faring nobodies forever. One of these days, I see us taking over every city in the world — running the banks — the entertainment industry — taking charge, the way a Chosen People ought to take charge." I gasped. Another of his childishly simple, earth-shattering concepts. Talk about ambition! "Take your daughters," the patriarch continued. "Settle in. Keep an eye out for anything unusual. You'll be guests of the King of Sodom, so you'll have diplomatic immunity. Try to keep kosher if you can. And whatever you do, don't go over to Gomorrah."

"Why not, patriarch?" said my father.

Abraham leaned over and whispered something in Lot's ear. My father's eyes hardened; in the sooty light of the oil lamp he looked crazy, the way he looked sometimes when I sneaked a peek at him and saw him lumbering over me, sweating, in the night.

And once more, I thought of the Queen of Gomorrah, and wondered whether I would ever see her again.

Ur had been a dull city, all white and featureless. Sodom was beyond belief. Sodom had a night life — torchlight burning until the wee hours, taverns overflowing with wine. The salt mines had made the upper classes rich. People had slaves for everything. Even the public punishments were ostentatious — beheadings were accompanied with psaltery music and dancing girls, and whippings were performed by trained flagellants, wearing dark robes and golden goat masks. Nothing so simple or so interactive as a stoning.

Salt permeated the city. Their food was over-salted. The water held a hint of brine. Even the heaps of camel dung in the streets were encrusted with salt crystals. Salt caked the alley walls; you always saw a few dogs licking at the limestone.

Abraham had told us our host was to be the king, but at usual we were palmed off to one of his lower-echelon retainers; we were lodged in an apartment in the mansion of one of the royal salt accountants, who measured the salt into earthenware containers and employed a staff of six to tally the amounts on clay tablets. They went through a lot of tablets a day, and once I visited the archive, with itsstacks of cuneiform-covered documents. Being a girl, I could not of course read — those were chauvinistic times — but it was fascinating to stare at the little wedges, and wonder what they meant.

Gomorrah was dark as Sodom was colorful. Separated from its sister city by a narrow stream so briny from the nearby salt mines that no fish could live in it, Gomorrah was permanently in the shadow of a thundering mountain — the only active volcano in the region. The city's walls were black basalt; Sodom's were limestone. When any of the inhabitants of Gomorrah emerged, it was only at night. Sometimes they showed up at one of the nightly orgies which, as visiting diplomats, it was my father's tiresome duty to attend; but they never ate, and they never drank wine.

I suppose it was only inevitable that I should become obsessed with the idea of Gomorrah.

In the first place, I had been very strictly brought up. I knew nothing of fleshly things — strange to you, maybe, considering my father's now almost nightly invasion of my most private world — but think about it. We didn't have sex ed. in those days. I assumed, in my subservient way, that I'd been a very bad girl, and that I was simply getting what I deserved. It's not that surprising that I should become more and more drawn to that which was forbidden.

My sister Rachel, on the other hand, seemed to blossom in this place. The more my father came to me by night, the less depressed and moody she became; it was hard not to think there might be some causal connection between those two things. She took belly-dancing lessons from one of the king's minor concubines (contrary to popular belief, buggery wasn't the only form of sex they practiced in that town) and soon became the life of the nightly orgies. My father never even bothered to scold her, though often, after she'd been particularly exhibitionistic, or ate too much barbecued pork, he would come home and beat me senseless with cedarwood cane he kept especially for that purpose.

I remember the cane well, because it had a curious knob in the shape of a dog's head, and it had come all the way from Troy. I also remember it because of some of the painful uses to which my father put it in those wee hours of the morning, sometimes not even bothering to anoint it with camel fat beforehand.

I don't want to dwell on it, but I think it's fair to say that I wasn't having a very good time in Sodom. If you check your Torah, the book of Genesis claims that "it" only happened once, that I got my father drunk, and that he never noticed a thing; well, that's what you get when the history books are written by male chauvinist pigs.

I started to wander the night.

It was safe to leave the apartments as soon as my father left my side; within minutes I would hear him snoring. My sister had taken to staying out all night, painting her face, and indulging in all the other Sodomite activities; my father no longer really gave a shit. Wandering alone in the streets, a young girl who had yet to even have her first period, I was self-conscious at first. But I found that if I kept to the shadows, if I darted quickly from alleyway to doorway, from pillar to gatepost, few ever noticed me. Sodom was a tolerant city.

One night, I found the pit of discarded slaves....

It was by the eastern gate, the closest point in the city to Gomorrah. It was the stench that first attracted me. There was a temple dedicated to their hermaphrodite god by this gate, and a cloud of frankincense smoke, billowing out of the front portal, almost masked the odor of rotting corpses. The steps of the mini-ziggurat were lined with vultures. There was no one on the street, which was strange; in this town, no matter how late at night, you always ran into some drunken partygoer quirting his litterbearers, or a prostitute primping in a doorway.

Past the temple stood a low wall, and when I looked down I saw them: emaciated bodies heaped up, arms and legs and bony faces, staring eyes; in the bright moonlight the eyes glittered like polished onyxes.

Have you ever seen some of those holocaust photographs? This was just the same. Except that no one thought it particularly immoral. I gazed, but I did not condemn. We all had slaves. I was impressed at the quantity of the dead, the conspicuous consumption of the society. I was too young to feel much pity. But presently I heard the clatter of a cart, and I ducked behind a statue of Ishtar that overlooked the pit. An old man was pushing the cart, which contained a fresh load of corpses. He dumped them unceremoniously over the side of the wall, and left.

I heard a noise. Someone — or some creature, perhaps a jackal — was prowling through the piles of corpses. I heard the patter of its feet. Yes. Definitely an animal. It sprang from heap to heap, sniffing, searching for something in particular. I'm not afraid of jackals; they are cowardly creatures for the most part. He stopped now and then and howled. He listened. I froze. He ran up a body that was tilted up, arm hugging the lip of the wall, and now he was on the other side of the statue, a little upwind of me; I hoped the wind would not change.

Then it was that the eastern gate creaked open, and there came through the portal a palanquin completely draped in black. The litterbearers were all Nubians, and their loincloths and headbands were also black. I shrank back in my hiding place. The eyes of the Nubians were glazed, as though they had been drugged or in some magical trance.

They carried the litter to within spitting distance of where I was. I crawled between the statue and the wall, between the breasts of Ishtar. I tried not to breathe. The jackal was suddenly right next to me.

It snarled. I was trapped between the goddess's breasts. I could smell its hunger. It was salivating, shuddering. I didn't want to scream, but when it leapt up onto me and began tearing at my garments, I let out a startled whimper. Because there was something about the jackal that was a little like my father — the look in his eye, a faint whiff of desire — we did not know then about pheromones, Mr. Shrink, but we could certainly feel their effects. That animal was embracing me in a parody of what my father had done that night, itself an obscene parody of love.

When the jackal bit me on the breast, I did scream, and then I felt powerful arms pulling me out, felt the sharp stone graze my elbow, found myself suddenly face to face with the Queen of Gomorrah.

The jackal was whimpering. I saw a deep red scar on its back, and the queen was handing her gold-handled whip to an attendant. "You should know better," she said to the jackal. "Roaming the slave-pits at night! Stupid, stupid, stupid."

In the moonlight, losing my terror, I saw that there was something human about the jackal. It was cowering from the queen. At length, it slunk away. She turned to me. "We meet again," she said, as though she had been expecting it all this time. "I see you have been bitten. Are you ready to come to Gomorrah?"

"My lady," I said,"the patriarch forbade us —"

She laughed. The sound was like the clatter of clay pots. I felt a certain comfort in that laugh. I dared to look her in the eye. I saw myself, twin images of a girl in those eyes, and I thought: How young I look, how vulnerable, how sad. And I knew she was thinking the same thing.

"You mustn't let men do all your thinking for you, Shoshana," she said. "Men see everything in black and white, and always in an adversarial relationship. Good and evil, man and woman, life and death. There are, you know, twilight areas where opposites intermingle, shadowlands you might call them. Sodom is such a land: in Sodom, the distinction between man and woman is blurred, and that's what your father calls abomination. But in our kingdom, it is the line between life and death that is crossed, you see."

"What do you mean?" I asked her."How can something be both dead and alive at the same time?"

She touched my hand. Cold, cold, cold; I had touched a dead man before, and I knew that cold. "My daughter," she said softly, and I thought she was about to weep.

"I cannot weep," she told me.

"Do you read minds?"

"No," she said, "but after the passage of a few centuries, one learns to guess what humans think; their emotions skitter across their faces; you can smell their thoughts, sometimes before they even think them."

"Humans?" I said. "You speak as though you are not one. Are you a goddess?" I knew that the gods took human shape sometimes. Our own god used to take long walks in Eden with Adam and Eve, our forefathers.

"I am more real," she said, "than any goddess."

She lifted me to my feet — in my confusion I had fallen on my knees before her, as though she were that very goddess she claimed not to be — and caressed my cheek, my hair; her hand moved slowly down to the wound in my breast, an ugly welt that showed through the tear in my sleeping-robe.

"Oh," she said, and her icy fingers tensed a little, "I see that the vile creature has already ... embraced you. That was not according to my plan ... but never mind. It's time you visited Gomorrah."

She enveloped me in her arms. I flinched. Her skin was bitterly cold. I buried my face in her bosom, heedless of the burning iciness that seeped into my pores, that seemed to invade my very veins. Even this cold comfort was better than my father's hot embrace. She kissed my brow. It was as though she were branding me with the imprint of her frozen world. I knew then that I loved her. That was what I had felt when I first looked on her face, long ago, in the city of Gilgamesh.

"Did you like that kiss?" she asked me. "Is this what you have longed for, secretly, in the middle of the night — to be sucked into a world deeper than death, colder than the grave, darker than shadow?"

"I don't know," I said, "but I know it's got to be better than the world I know." And she drew me by the hand and led me to her palanquin; a slave made a back for me to step up; I reclined against cushions made of human skin, stuffed with the feathers of exotic birds; and I lay in the darkness and let the queen kiss me, again and again, not even crying out when her kisses drew blood.

Thus it was that I share "d the palanquin of the Queen of Shadows, and came to the city of night, and learned the darkest secret in the world.

Things became a little better after that. My father remarried — rather, he purchased a plaything from the slave-market, and scaled new heights of perversion and sadism with her. I never found out her name, never attended the ceremony, which was a Sodomite one in any case and therefore not actually binding on us. I suppose her name is of little interest; nobody thought it important enough to record in the Torah.

They left out my name, too, and I'm supposedly the ancestor of an entire race.

Gomorrah —

By day, a tomb. The basalt mansions, some carved out of the side of the volcano itself, were desolate. Volcanic ash lay over draperies, furniture, statues, dimmed the once-bright murals. The citizens of Gomorrah lay sleeping; some in a communal catacomb, a network of tunnels that burrowed into the mountain; others in splendor, in sarcophagi of granite or marble or pure gold. The houses were like tombs, their contents piled up; treasure-hordes were guarded by skeletons in armor; statues of gods and heroes lay in disarray; there was no food or drink, except for the occasional depiction on a mural. A smell of brimstone lingered in the air, perhaps because they had burrowed deep into the side of the volcano, exposing clefts that spewed out fumes of sulphur now and then.

By night, the court of the Queen of Gomorrah was lavish beyond all I had seen in Sodom. As the sun set behind the volcano, the courtiers would emerge from their hiding places. The megaron of the grand palace was cloaked with cobwebs and carpeted with dust; it was hard at first to get used to the darkness, but when I did, I saw that a different light suffused these creature's existence. The phosphorescence of their skin, the dust-motes scintillant in the starlight, the silvery radiance of the moon over burnished mirrors of bronze — the flecks of gold dust on their black cloaks — the crystalline intensity of their eyes — all these things illuminated a world that never needed lamp or torchlight.

On the third night, the queen led me by the hand to a garden in the heart of her palace. It was overgrown with blackened, twisted vines; here and there, a red rose bloomed; and in the center of the garden stood a mirror-still pool, bordered by four dragons sculpted from lapis and malachite. Incense spewed from their jaws, a bitter odor, mostly myrrh, I thought.

"Your father," said the queen, "has a god who speaks from behind a curtain, through the lips of a befuddled old man. Would you like to meet our god?"

"I've never met a god," I said.

She chuckled. "Don't be afraid."

She led me to the edge of the pool and told me to look into the water. The water was quite still. And now, the queen took a pebble from a little basin beside the pool, murmured words in a mystic tongue, and cast the stone into the water. "Now," she said, "repeat after me — Dracula, Dracula, Dracula."

"What does that mean?"

"It is a magic formula whose resonance opens up a gateway from the present into other times, other places."

She cast the stone into the pool. I repeat the words; they rolled richly off the tongue; they were words of power; I shivered, trying to blame it all on the cold, for Gomorrah was a cold city, even in summer.

The water shimmered in the moonlight....

Then, kneeling over the edge of the pool, I started to see things. I saw a man on horseback, dark-haired, with a drooping mustache and a helmet of some unfamiliar metal. He looked out at me. I heard him whisper in my head: Greetings, daughter from the distant past.

"Who are you?" I cried out. "What kind of god are you, that condescends to speak even to an unlettered girl?"

I am your people's future.

"My people?" I said. "You hold the destiny of the Hebrews in your hands? But I thought that our tribal thunder-god —"

He laughed. "There are a people even more chosen than your own," said the god. "Believe me. You are the ones who will influence all the events of the future. Nations shall rise and fall; empires, religions, and races shall came to power and be overthrown. But behind all these great events will be yourselves — the eternal ones — the ones who have embraced the world of darkness."

I turned to the queen in disbelief."I don't understand," I said. "What is he telling me — that I will live forever?"

"If you take good care of yourself," said the queen. "We are not gods precisely; we can't change the laws of nature; there are ways to kill us. But there is no reason you shouldn't survive for a thousand years."

"The way people used to," I said, "before the great flood."

She laughed again. "How superstitious you are," she said at last.

"Images in pools — isn't that some kind of heathen superstition?" I said. "Our patriarch says we shouldn't trust gods we can see and touch, but only the invisible one behind the curtain in the tabernacle."

The queen said, "Let me tell you something of our god, then. He is not so much a god as a visitor from the future. The word of power came to me in a vision long ago, when I was still mortal. In his time, he is some kind of great king, a *voivode*. He is feared. He impales his enemies by thousands and dines while watching their death-throes. A great mage captured his spirit in this pool, so that we can speak to him through the chasm of time; to him, in the time beyond, it seems as though he is dreaming. Because to him we are figures of history and legend, he knows more about us than we do ourselves; to us, he can serve as a kind of oracle. If you want, ask him a question about your future ... it will come to pass, I promise you."

There was really only one thing I wanted to know. But I was afraid to say it out loud. I have not divulged my shameful secret to anyone until tonight. Oh, I wanted the god to tell me whether my torment would ever end, but to do so I would have had to confess that this torment existed. So instead I asked about something I cared far less about. "Are there," I asked the god, "ten upright men in all of Sodom and Gomorrah? My father is on a mission —"

Dracula glared at me across the gulf of time. *Your father,* he said, *is wasting his time.*

I said, "You mean that he might as well pack up and go home, that he won't find what the patriarch has sent him to look for?"

No, daughter of Eve, he said, *I merely mean that his search has become irrelevant. There are some things even the gods have no control over.*

The queen took me by the hand once more. "Talk to me while I bathe," she said, "and I will tell you more."

We went into an inner chamber hewn out of the basalt, and there she commanded an attendant to draw her bath, which was a curious thing; for there were twelve young women chained to columns, and the attendant bled each one into an earthenware pitcher, and emptied its contents into the tub. The victims were drugged, perhaps; they stared dully ahead, not seeming to care that their lives were being siphoned away from them. She stripped, stepped into the frothing blood, and began languidly to scrape herself with a lump of pumice.

I sat beside the bath, handing her cloths and unguents as she requested them, waiting. One always had to wait with vampires; they have so much time on their hands; they do not move that fast, unless it is to attack, immobilize, and drain their prey's blood. I tried making light conversation. "Among our people," I said,"when a woman has her monthly bloodletting, she takes a ritual bath, a *mikvah,* to cleanse away every trace of blood ... but you are doing the opposite...." She only smiled.

"Don't chatter," she said. "Enjoy the profound silence of night."

I listened. The room was quiet, save for the groans of dying slaves. The walls were thick. At first I heard nothing more. Then I realized I was hearing more than I had ever heard before. Somehow the acuity of my hearing had increased. I could make out individual crickets. A nightingale halfway down the mountain. I thought I could hear the grass grow ... and yes ... if I really listened ... there, there, my father's drunken snores, and the quick, sharp breathing of his Sodomite woman.

Finally, she said, "The god is right. You see, Shoshana, our mages have been studying the mountain for some years now, and we are certain that it is on the verge of erupting — in a matter of days."

So it had nothing to do with divine retribution at all.

"But what will you do about it?" I said. "Will your people pack up all your belongings and found another city somewhere?" If, indeed, the inhabitants of Gomorrah knew that they were going to be buried under tons of lava, why didn't they seem remotely worried?

"Oh, some of us undoubtedly will leave," said the queen, "but for most it will be at best a minor inconvenience. The mountainside is honeycombed with tombs. We will sleep a little longer than usual, perhaps, but what is a century or two, or even a millennium, to those who must contemplate eternity?"

"What about the Sodomites?" I said.

"Why worry about them?" said the queen. "When your farm's burning down, are you going to waste your time rescuing the cattle? There'll be other prey."

I still couldn't believe this, couldn't grasp the long view that the vampires took of history. The queen smiled sadly. She touched my cheek, my forehead. She was no longer cold; the blood had warmed her body almost to burning, and I winced; but then, when a rivulet of blood dribbled down toward my lips and I tasted the smooth salt fluid, I felt something I'd never felt before. Orgasm only hints at its intensity. I shuddered. The warmth shot down my throat and seemed to rush directly into my arteries. I could hear my heart pumping, could hear the river of blood as it gushed through the capillaries of my brain.

"YHWH!" I cried out. I was shocked at my own perversity. To let the sacred name pass my lips ... yet there was no thunderbolt.

"What's happening to me? Have I become a vampire?"

"You are not completely changed, my daughter. But a time will come when the daylight will cause you grief...."

"The blood! The blood!" She gripped my wrists now and drew me into the tub of blood with her. She caught me in the slippery embrace of gore. Blood seeped into every orifice of me. I was on fire. The room careened about; everywhere I saw the lifeless eyes of the chained slaves. I could not tell terror from ecstasy. With a slender finger she traced on my young breasts the outline of an apple. With her other hand she plunged down to my most secret places, touched what only my father had touched before; but he had not sought to kindle any flames in me. The queen's deft fingertips skirted my nether lips, snaked upward to caress a certain mound that made me tingle and finally quake and scream, and I profaned the holy name several more times, heedless that if one of my people heard me I might well be stoned to death; I no longer feared death; I knew that the woman who held me in her arms was death, that death was a new way to say love.

Before dawn, I went once more to the oracle of Dracula. I threw in a stone and repeated the magic formula, and once more I gazed into the visage of the impaler from a future time.

Daughter, he said, *I dream of you again.*

"Show me this future they're talking about," I said. "I suppose it's too late for me now, there's no going back, I don't know if I've chosen wisely, but —"

The water rippled softly. The moon was obscured by the mountain. Incense rose from the brazier. Through the wisps of smoke, in the undulating water, dimly lit by candlelight and starlight, I saw vague images. I saw the volcano burst, the city buried, the people screaming in the streets. I saw new cities, always new cities, bigger, shinier, dirtier,more and more crowded. I saw wars that spanned whole continents. Death was everywhere. Dracula's own victims cried out from their spikes. I saw my own people driven from their homeland time and time again — from Egypt, from Judaea, from Poland, from a thousand places with unpronounceable names; I saw them die by millions; I saw a weapon that killed more people in a single hour than the entire population of our known civilized world; and I knew at last the truth of the legend of Adam, my ancestor and the patriarch's; that man is a fallen creature, that our god is infinitely wrathful, destructive, and uncaring.

The only light in the world's future came from a place of ultimate darkness....

I saw the Queen of Gomorrah emerge from a thousand-year slumber, shatter her igneous prison, break out of the walls of obsidian. I saw her in the night, her skin luminescent in the starlight. I saw vampires everywhere — though I could not know what the scenes represented then, I now know what I saw — Auschwitz — Hiroshima — London in the Black Plague — Naples during the cholera season — vampires. Standing watch at the foot of a cross where a man was tied up and nailed alive; ruling in the courts of Egypt and England, Constantinople and Kazakhstan. I saw vampires dancing in the neon night of a thousand cities. I saw vampires in theaters and opera houses, vampires in darkened cinemas, vampires feasting on the numberless hordes of humans who populated an exploding world. I even saw myself. Yes. Sitting in an art deco office of the future, pouring my guts out to a roomfull of strangers. No, I didn't understand any of these visions. It was a kaleidoscope of alien landscapes.

Daughter of Lot, the dark god whispered in my mind, *do you like what you see?*

I couldn't answer. I was bursting with new emotions. All my life I had hungered for something without even knowing that I hungered. The taste of blood lingered on my lips. I felt fulfilled. I wasn't just some insignificant female anymore. I had a destiny.

Two messengers were at my father's house the a few days later. The Septuagint calls them angels, but *angelos* just means messenger in Greek; those Greeks do have a knack for fancifying the mundane.

They came from the patriarch, who was encamped in an oasis nearby. It was a day of tumult and festivity, the annual ceremony of their god-king's sacred marriage to himself, which was also the city's fertility ritual, signalling the commencement of spring. Drums, conch-trumpets, harps and dulcimers could be heard coming from every direction. People jammed the narrow streets; palanquins rammed into one another; merchants jostled one another as they peddled shish kebabs and wine.

A parade was streaming past our apartment; we sat on a balcony, watching it go by. Abraham's messengers were young men, twins, and very attractive; my sister Rachel had been making eyes at one of them all through breakfast, and now my father's wife was winking suggestively at the other as she broke bread and poured out salt.

In honor of the hermaphrodite god-king, it was the custom for the men and women of Sodom to cross-dress. It was not unlike the *mardi gras* in New Orleans; drag queens everywhere, and music pouring from every tavern; the only difference was the constant death-gurgle of the sacrificial victims from altars all around town, for the sacred hermaphrodite god was propitiated by the flaying alive of dozens of young boys and girls, mostly culled from the children of the slaves who worked the salt mines. The flayed skins were hoisted up on poles and carried aloft by dancers; the smell of death mingled in the hazy air with the tang of salt and the odor of sweaty bodies.

Abraham's messengers weren't particularly disturbed at the bloodshed per se; you have to understand that this was before our tribal god banned human sacrifice.

The patriarch's wife, you may recall, bore a child at a very advanced age; it was naturally incumbent upon Abraham to sacrifice his first legitimate son, but one of those revelations from heaven conveniently intervened — that's how it is when you have a direct hotline to the Lord God — and soon everyone was denying that the Hebrews ever practiced human sacrifice at all.

It was the scale of human sacrifice that appalled the two messengers — I mean, this was their first time in the big city — and the stench was making it hard for them to keep their breakfast down. They complained loudly about the abomination of it all, and my father chimed in now and then in hearty agreement.

At that point, a group of revellers stopped beneath our balcony and started hooting and whistling at the two messengers. The celebrants were drag queens to the *n*th degree. One wore a flounced skirt in the Minoan fashion, with fake breasts made from two large conch shells; another was dressed like an Egyptian, with a wig, blackened eyes, a chain of scarabs around his neck that rested athwart another pair of artificial boobs, these ones made from gourds; a third was actually in the costume of a Hebrew matron, which is to say that she was very plainly and concealingly attired.

It was the pseudo-yenta who cried out, "Who are those handsome young studs up there in the apartments of the Hebrew ambassador?"

"Send the fresh meat down," said the one in Egyptian garb.

"Yes," said the Minoan, "we want them for the sacred fertility orgy."

"Is it true you Hebrews are all circumcised?" said the yenta. "Show us yours and we'll show you ours, honey!"

Lot cried out, "Abomination! You would practice your craven lusts even upon the angels of the lord?"

They hooted and jeered, and the messengers looked suitably embarrassed, and Lot got up and did what every good Hebrew does when confronted with abomination; he rent his robes and howled. I was glad he did not put on this exhibition too often; with the amount of abomination in this town, he would have had to spend all our barter goods on clothes.

At length, the procession moved on. At noon would come the solemn nuptials of the god-king. I wanted to go to the palace to watch, of course, but my place was at my father's table, waiting on the guests hand and foot; even now, I was oiling their feet as my father discussed the salt business and how our people might want to get a piece of the action.

"What about the patriarch's ten upright men?" said the first angel. "How's that going?"

"Oh, it'll be fine," said Lot. "I got a list from the king's treasurer of the most honest men in the city — they pay their taxes, are faithful to their wives, and don't indulge in any more abomination than absolutely necessary — so we can easily pick ten at random."

"Good," said the second messenger. It was the politically correct thing to do, to satisfy Abraham's mysterious voices while simultaneously managing to do business.

"Daughter," Lot said — I honestly think he could not remember my name at times — "Hurry up and finish drying the guests' feet; you're so slow — are you sick?"

"No, father," I said. "It's just the sun. For some reason, it's really hurting my eyes. I think I'm burning up."

"Not even that hot," my father said. "You'd think she'd never been reared in the desert at all, she's become so spoiled by their soft city ways," he went on, but it was true that I was finding the sun almost unbearable, and I was glad that I was able to crouch under the shadow of the breakfast table. "I'll write a note to the patriarch," he said, "and tell him the ten good men are no problem; he can call off the apocalypse. The Sodomites will no doubt be very relieved," he added, winking.

I don't know why I even opened my mouth. Girls are supposed to be seen and not heard. But I had a acquired a new self-esteem during my visits to the Queen of Gomorrah. I piped up. "Father, the volcano is going to blow any minute. I don't think you'd better find any upright citizens in this town. You wouldn't want the Lord God to make a mistake, now, would you?"

"What?" my father screamed.

"I know," I insisted. "I've been to Gomorrah. I've spoken with the Dracula oracle, the voice from the future. You've never spoken with any god; you just listen to whatever Abraham says; every little whim he has is the word of YHWH."

My father gasped to hear the sacred name pass my lips, and the two messengers looked very sheepish. My father's wife, knowing nothing of Hebrew customs, just looked bewildered.

It was my sister who shrieked, "You stupid little girl. Don't you know you can be stoned for saying —"

"And who's going to stone me?" I shouted. I got up, hurled the basin of expensive oil at the wall, quickly backed into the shadow of the doorway, away from the sunlight. "It's not like there's a couple of hundred tribesmen here to pick up rocks. I mean, look around you.

These people are *civilized.* They don't go around stoning people just for saying YHWH."

My father slapped me resoundingly. I tasted blood. And that taste rekindled my memories of the night I spent in the Queen of Gomorrah's bloodbath; instead of cowering and backing down, I got right in my father's face. His breath, stinking of wine and garlic, brought back a flood of memories of traumatic nights, and I shrank back, but only for a moment. I looked him right in the eye and said, "YHWH, YHWH, YHWH, father, I don't see any thunderbolts descending from the sky; if that was true, you'd be burned to a crisp by now."

That was how my father found out that I'd been conscious all those times, that I knew what he was, knew him to the core. He exploded. He started to slap my face over and over, and finally he shoved me through the doorway into the apartment. "Go to your room," he said, "and you will receive neither food nor water until you are ready to apologize."

"Go fuck yourself," I said to my father.

He just gaped. I started to laugh. For the first time I felt that I had power, real power; that I was a real woman and not some defenseless child. I could just imagine what the two messengers were going to tell Abraham when they got home.

By sunset, my father was more drunk than he had ever been in his life. I could hear him shouting and throwing things, and cursing at the messengers. With my attenuated hearing I knew everything that was going on; heard the wine splosh out of the jug, heard my father's heavy breathing, my sister giggling, my father's wife pacing back and forth in confusion.

I lay on my pallet, brooding. At length, my father stormed into the bedchamber. He saw me in the half-dark, thought I was asleep.

"Bitch!" he shouted. "Whore! I'll teach you your place. You think that you're a woman now? You think you can defy me, little girl? You think that because I've neglected you of late, I can't come right back and give it to you all over again?"

He hulked over me. Seized me by the shoulders. Out of force of habit, I squeezed my eyes shut, waiting for the invasion of his touch. Sweat ran over my shoulders, slicked my narrow breasts. He shook me. His fingernails drove under my skin and I could feel blood welling up, and the smell of my own blood maddened me.

I bit him.

He raised his hand to slap me down.

At that moment, the volcano began to rumble.

There came an eerie red glow through the window-slats. I caught a whiff of burning sulphur. I opened my eyes. I didn't care anymore. My father looked defeated, spent, consumed with inner torments I had never seen before. He let go of me and crumpled down to the floor.

Then he left the room. I heard him shouting. "Rouse the messengers! Tell them to get word to Abraham that ten good men could not be found in Sodom! Get our camels — we're getting out of the city!"

He did not even bother to summon me. But I crept out of bed, and I too began gathering up a few pots and some fresh bread out of the oven, and a basin full of salt. My sister and I worked feverishly together with a new kind of solidarity. I knew she had heard everything in my room; she had a newfound sympathy for me. "You too, Rachel," I said softly.

"Yes, Shoshana; me too."

And we embraced; it was the first tender moment we sisters had shared in many years.

In the streets, the drunken revelry was still going on. Only a few were surreptitiously marching in the direction of the westerly gate. The volcano, I suppose, had rumbled before, without much effect. But now, as I looked eastward toward Gomorrah, I could see that the mountaintop was coated in brilliant vermilion, and that smoke was funneling up toward the moon.

My sister and I and my father's wife sat in a cart; my father drove the camel; the messengers, riding a chariot, were disappearing into the distance. We reached the gate; the gate-slaves opened it; we entered the plain; we moved on without speaking.

We were only about a mile away when the explosions began.

"Don't look back!" said my father to us all. "The abominations are being wiped out! Great is the Lord God, the Lord of Hosts! Holy is he, the Lord of Sabaoth! Don't look back or you too will be consumed!"

We were traversing a ridge now. Below us were the salt mines. Slaves were still working them by torchlight, and overseers still stood with whips. The ground was quaking. We hastened. Our camels grunted.

"I have to go back," said my father's wife. "You think I want to live in a stinking sheepherder's tent for the rest of my life?"

"You'll die!" my father said.

She leaped from the oxcart and began running down the slope, toward the salt mines. Behind her, Sodom was in flames. The sky was black with ash. The lava was hurtling down the mountain now. The twin cities glowed. Even from this far I could hear the screams.

If we didn't hurry, we too would be buried alive. My father urged us on, but I stood and watched her. I knew that I was not wholly human, and that even if I was buried in the ashes I would find a way to come back.

I saw the earth open up. I saw the mines collapse. Slaves blowing into the air, arms, legs, decapitated heads flying. I saw Lot's wife, standing there with her arms outstretched, gazing at Sodom, saw the hail of salt and brimstone descend upon her, whiten around her, turn her into a statue in mid-scream. I felt my sister grab me by the arm and drag me back to the cart. Heard the wheels clattering, felt the cart bumping over the stones; at length, when the plain evened out a little, the rhythm of the cart put me into a deep sleep, and I dreamed of the Queen of Gomorrah, and of nights of blood and shadow.

We lived in a cave. My sister and I were pregnant; I died in childbirth and they walled me up in that selfsame cave and returned to the tents of the patriarch; by then the story of Sodom and Gomorrah and grown to — dare I say it? — biblical proportions.

Why, then, am I here? Listen. I've ridden into battle alongside Vlad the Impaler, stalked the catacombs of Rome for lost Christians, gorged myself on the battlefields of Waterloo and Gettysburg. But always I was haunted by my father's face: not only the face of rage as he violated me on countless nights, but also the expression of helplessness and defeat on the night I finally overcame him. I was alone for a thousand years, and then I encountered the Queen of Gomorrah at a party in Antioch; she smiled, we talked of old times; but you know, we had drifted far apart in that thousand years. Since then I have known crowned heads and white trash, presidents and slaves, and I feasted on their blood. But buried deep within me ... somewhere ... there's an angry little girl.

For a hundred bucks an hour, I want someone to hold her, soothe her, wipe away her tears. For a hundred bucks an hour, I would like to learn yo weep again. I've lived with this so long I don't know what I'd do if I could be cured, but I think the time has come for me to try.

Can you help me, Mr. Big-shot Shrink? Can you hold Shoshana's hand? Can you read her a bedtime story?

Can you love her?

Protoevangelion

I was asked to write a story about the qabalah.
I think I was the only non-Jew permitted into the anthology,
in itself a rather flattering thing.
The editor said, 'But I want your qabalah *story to be*
about Jesus.' But of course there are many more
dots to be connected in the gospels
than in almost any other works that purport to
be biographies.

Apart from the amazing fact that I
now had an excuse to use a Phoenician font in a story, doing
this allowed me to speculate and to
use interesting episodes from the
Infancy Gospels, which were of course
expunged from the Bible during the
Council of Nicaea along with
so many other interesting things which would have
shed so much light on the thoughts and minds
of people in the first few centuries A.D.

I am not sure that the anthology it was
written for actually appeared. so the first time
this story was seen anywhere was
in a German translation in the book Untergang von
Eden. *It's quite a rare one and I guess now it will*
upset a few more people....

A Different Eden

I am an old woman in Ephesus, sitting alone in a small house paid for by strangers. It is a small house, but it is real stone; I am an old woman, but they call me ageless; they call me mother to the world; they call me the daughter of the morning star; but I am just an old woman sitting alone in a small room, looking out over the alley, where the pilgrims jostle each other and are cheated by peddlers on their way to see the hundred-breasted goddess.

Years ago, in Jerusalem, while the pain was still fresh, a man named Paul came to see me. He was starting a new religion. He needed my endorsement; for in his pantheon I was to become the mother of God. He had crafted a new theology of such grandeur and such outrageousness that he believed it would sweep the world.

In vain, I told him true things about my childhood, and the birth of my son Joshua. I even broke terrible oaths of secrecy and revealed to him some of the mysteries that only women are allowed to know — I told him of the spring rites on the hillside, of the Roman centurion who might have embraced me in the guise of a horned god, of a secret flight to Egypt. But even this knowledge did not give him pause. He would keep telling me that the new religion was not one of literal truth, but of the truth concealed; that the truth he was fashioning was so much more true than this world of illusions we live in.

"The earth from which my perfect man, my Adam, is fashioned," he told me, "is a different dust; it's today's dust, you see, Hellenic and Roman and Judaean; my Adam will speak to people; I can sell him. I know about selling; I've sold tents."

I was not convinced. "My son was messiah of the month ... and so were many others. He said many beautiful things. And now he has been dead a while, and the utterances have become the empty wind; some remember, some distort, some forget."

But Paul told me how he had seen my son in the clouds, in the lightning; my son would have been bemused at such an image of himself. I insisted that there was no magic here. Even then, I felt old, withered as the parched desert, drained of all feeling.

"Somewhere," Paul said, "there *was* magic."

"Where? Not in Nazareth, where they soon made mincemeat of my son's fanciful tales of a superhuman father. Not in Alexandria, where we lived like dogs, always hiding, always insecure; not in Cornwall, not in Galilee, not in Jerusalem, where they nailed him to the tree of death."

"You've left out something, Miriam."

"Perhaps there *was* a place of magic," I said, "but it wasn't even in the real world ... the real hard world we know ... the Roman world. It was beyond. Far beyond. Outside the known world, anything can happen; there are no rules. But now, as you see, we are back on earth."

"But you're wrong there. There's no rigid wall between paradise and the flesh. There was once, but it's leaking now. Anything is possible."

"It did not really happen. It was a dream."

"Who is to know that the world of dream is not reality, and reality but a shadow of the dream world?"

"Sophistry. You've been living with Greeks too long. Even your Aramaic has a twang to it."

Then again, hadn't my son lived with Greeks too long?

"All right," I said. "I'll tell you."

Why should it have surprised me? In Alexandria, we spoke Aramaic to my son; he answered us in Greek. Alexandria, a Greek city in an Egypt ruled by Rome, had its own kind of Jews; they considered themselves better than us. In Alexandria, even the Torah was in Greek, and those who sheltered us thought us uncouth for lapsing into the mother tongue. Joshua did not grow up with sights and sounds a proper Jew knew intimately: the screaming of a thousand lambs on holy days, the smell of their blood sluicing down the gutters of the Temple... the tramp of Roman boots on cobbled alleyways ... the arhythmic thud-plop of a whore being stoned. We were always on the move, always being shown the door if we displeased someone; soon, I knew, we would run out of friends, or of friends of friends.

It was Joshua who was the problem. Now, as I sit out my last days in Ephesus, I hear rumors about his childhood ... they are writing what they call "infancy gospels," fanciful anecdotes about his childhood. There's a story about him being teased by other children, killing them and resurrecting them for a lark ... breathing life into clay pigeons, too. And irritating a schoolmaster by knowing too much. There's always a kernel of truth to the stories. For example —

When we were staying at the house of Samuel the Mapmaker, a client of Joseph's cousin the Arimathean, I came from the market to find Samuel's son David pinned to the floor of the atrium, and my son pummeling him in the face. I ran to him, pulled him away, but he writhed and punched at the air. David was unconscious.

"Let me go," Joshua screamed. I couldn't hold him even though he was just a child.

"What's wrong, what's the matter?"

"He told me my father's a Roman with antlers," he shouted. "He said I was spawned on a mountain top. He said that a demon raped you."

David lay motionless. And Joshua began to cry. Hysterically, appallingly. Then the doorway opened and I saw Samuel and my husband by the mezzuzah. And Joshua, just as abruptly, was dry-eyed, unrepentant.

David lay motionless on the mosaic stones, black and white, which spelled out words in Greek. Samuel ran to his son's side. David did not speak, and he stared unblinking at the patch of open sky. A fountain whispered; caged birds trilled.

"You've killed him," Samuel said to my son.

Joshua shook his head. "Not for long," he said. Wild-eyed, he left my side and knelt down beside the boy. "You can quit fooling now," he said. "Come back, come back from the dead."

Abruptly, David sat up. "You're a freak," he said softly. Pointed his finger in Joshua's face. Joshua backed away. Held out his hand for mine. Not to ask for solace, but to steady himself.

"Don't tell lies about my father," he said. His whisper hid an utter desolation, as though he were an angel cut off forever from the sight of God.

"I think," said Samuel, "that you people had better leave my house."

The boy was unmanageable. He was unruly. He made no friends, and so he found imaginary ones; he would stand in an atrium, talking to the wind, and he also had a habit of talking to statues of gods — Egyptian, Greek, Syriac, it didn't matter. If there was a shrine to Horus on a street corner, he'd strike up a conversation.

One day, my husband beat him for speaking to Priapus. Joshua was quite passive, did not cry out; that angered my husband all the more.

"There is only one god you are allowed to speak to, Joshua," he said when he was done. "You will remember that now."

"I'd speak to him if I could," Joshua said, "but he never shows his face to me. All the others do."

My husband wanted to go back to Judaea. "Look at your son," he would say. "He's gone pagan; half the time he runs around without any clothes on. When I teach him the Torah, he ignores me. One day he will have to become bar mitzvah, and I dread to think how he's going to botch that. He needs to be with proper Jews."

"You're consumed with guilt, Joseph, because you don't love him."

Joseph could not answer that, for he knew I could see through his posturing.

My son was only ten years old then; I told Joseph there was plenty of time. My husband was miserable in Alexandria, a severe man among hedonists, a learned man among dilettantes; and Joshua was heading toward trouble. There were gangs of idle youths in Alexandria. There were potent herbs to be smoked, wine to be drunk, and the Greeks believed that sex was little more than an itch to be scratched, which they did often, and with whatever person or creature was to hand.

My husband was not a modern man; he wanted nothing better than a woman of quiet modesty and an obedient son; he had neither of those things. Joshua was sullen, always angry. I wanted to much to tell him how special he was to me, how special his birth was, how even our fugitive status was born from his special quality; but I could not.

One night my husband and I argued until late. Joshua had not come home for supper. "I'm going to go look for him," said Joseph, "and in the morning we'll pack up, and leave for Nazareth."

"What about the danger?"

"Danger? it's been almost ten years."

"We shouldn't go back," I said. "Not unless there's a sign, a messenger."

"Messengers don't come to disobedient wives and wayward children," said Joseph.

"Only to the unbending, I suppose."

He raised his hand to me. I flinched. He stopped himself. He was not a cruel husband; I'll give him that; among the devout, wives are whipped for far less than impertinence.

"This is impossible," he said. "It's all wrong, everything is wrong. I'm a learned man among people who don't want to learn. This son of yours is recalcitrant. And you're not a dutiful wife."

It was an old argument. But that night I felt feistier than before; I wanted to argue back. "I'm as dutiful as can be expected," I said.

"Behind my back, you think of those women's rites. And the goddess who is abomination, whose statue stares down at us everywhere in this city. And the horned man in the hills." Which was a mystery of which no man should speak.

"No one forced you to marry me."

"You've given me no children," he said.

"In this place, Joseph?" I said. "In time. When we're home again, I'll give you sons."

"It's intolerable," he said. "This alien place ... being shunted from stranger to stranger ... and never knowing where Joshua is, whether he's talking to harlots or idol-worshippers or —"

"I'll find him," I said.

"In the night? Alone? A woman? In this iniquitous city?"

"I'm strong, Joseph," I reminded him. "Didn't I bear a child, without a midwife, in a cave? Didn't I walk with you to Egypt, with a child and our worldly possessions strapped to my back? If there's iniquity out there, I think I can resist."

"There's something that protects you. A demon, I think."

"Then my demon and I will go out into the street."

There was no demon. But there was a goddess.

I pushed my husband aside and went to find my son. It was not hard; my son loved to consort with the lowly. If it wasn't the alley of the lepers or the beggars' corner, it would be the street of the harlots, which ran from a Temple of Venus all the way to the wharf, where the drunken sailors prowled.

This was no Hellenic Aphrodite, coy and enigmatic, but the Babylonian Venus whom we call Ashtaroth, the earth that swallows up the sky's seed and spits forth life. In Judaea, the men worshipped the father whose name cannot be spoken; the women safeguarded more ancient truths; those truths, I fear, will die now that the Jews are scattered. I did not fear the Goddess; I was not afraid to walk along that street. Even the men who strutted and preened there were afraid. They do not want to acknowledge that before Eve, the obedient, there was Lilith, the elemental.

Joshua was a man-child who did not fear these women's brazen sexuality, and had no need to cast it to the ground and conquer it.

He was deep in conversation with one as I approached. They leaned against the temple walls, each one more painted than the next. The moonlight pierced the fronds of the date palms, and the women's faces were criss-crossed with shadow. The air sweated attar of roses; insects buzzed; clouds of incense billowed from braziers between the paws of stone sphinxes.

I couldn't help eavesdropping. The one he was talking to was a little one, perhaps no older than I was that night of the hillside rites of spring. She was telling him how sore she was, how she had bled, the pain she was feeling, "as if," she was saying, "I was a terracotta doll, broken, and no one knows how to mend me."

"Maybe I can," my son said. He looked her in the eyes; he had a look that said, *I can draw your pain away.* And he held her hands; not in arousal, but how you might hold the paw of a wounded animal. "I can't always mend things," he said, "but I'm getting better. One day I'll touch a person's hurt and just suck it into myself. And the pain will be gone."

"Is your father a doctor?" said the prostitute. "Usually these skills pass, you know, father to son."

"His father is a rabbi," I said, stepping from the shadows, "and a very frustrated one right now."

Joshua didn't look at me. He continued to hold the hands of the daughter of Lilith between his hands. Finally she said, "I think I'm feeling better now." And she broke away. It was too intense for her, perhaps. She ran off, and my son turned to look at me. But only for a moment; then he looked at the ground. I did not merit the soulsearching gaze that any common whore could receive from him.

Joshua of the penetrating stare, Joshua could to drain away a sick man's pain with a single glance ... this Joshua was not for me.

"Your father says it's time to go back. Time for you to take your Torah seriously; time to become bar mitzvah."

"He's not my father," Joshua said. "Besides, we've been waiting for a sign."

"You shouldn't be dictating to us; you're a child."

"I know, and you've let me run wild," he said; verbatim, one of the Carpenter's lectures. "You don't believe that."

Sulking, he started to walk away. He was exasperating. Especially when he was right.

"Still, there's no sign, and we're out of time."

"There's been a sign. Today. An angel came." I noticed he had slipped into his Aramaic the Greek word for a messenger.

"What messenger?"

"You know him, mother." He turned to look at a small shrine to Caesar. A young Roman was wringing the neck of a pigeon to lay on the altar; another was sprinkling incense on the brazier; such common sights in Alexandria, scarcely worth noting; yet he watched, intent.

From the shadow of the temple wall a man emerged. Old. Sunken. Bearded. His white robe was in tatters; his skin was dark, and on his brow there was painted a scarlet curlicue, like a half-formed eye. It was his voice that was unmistakable; for he had a curious lilt, and his Greek was full of circumlocutions.

"You are knowing me, Miriam, I think," he said. And I remembered that we had called him Balthasar, because his true name was a tonguetwister in an alien language.

"But ..." I said . "Your silks, your jeweled turban...."

"Gone now, gone. But you know, I am having gained wisdom as I lost in sartorial preeminence."

"When you came to the cave, my child was just a baby. Some people called you a king."

"And some still may," he said. "But kings lead; I am a follower. I go where the stars lead me. And now, here I am. I have been sitting on a street corner, interpreting dreams and reading minds; parlor tricks really, waiting, waiting for a child on the brink of manhood, I child I once deemed worthy of frankincense."

"What do the stars want you to do with my child?" I asked him, for I knew he could only mean Joshua.

"My beautiful young prince," said the king, "ah, like me, you now resemble a pauper on the outside."

"Mother," Joshua said, "he says that in his kingdom there's an orchard where miracles happen."

It only occurred to me later that my son, who was stubborn about speaking Greek, had used a Hebrew word for orchard; he had called it "paradise."

"Mother, he wants me to go on a journey with him."

"So does your father," I said. "He wants to take us home."

"But I'm telling you, Mother, before I go home I'm going to find my real father."

And that, you see, was a Quest without a Golden Fleece; for I knew that he could never find a father who would satisfy him.

When I first moved into the house in Ephesus, I planted a tree in the middle of the little atrium garden. The tree was in memory of my son. I watered the tree with my tears. But the tree grew slowly....

I did not think my husband would countenance another journey, especially one whose destination we did not truly understand. But after our quarrel of the previous night, which had kept our hosts awake, it seemed as though we were about to be shunted to another family again; and so he acceded. We did not know how long the journey would be, or even whether it would be by land or sea.

"Perhaps," my husband told me, "this journey will heal us."

Joshua said nothing.

"Perhaps," my husband told him, "this journey, wherever it may take us, will throw you and me together long enough for us to read the Torah together, so that by the time you have to go to the Temple you will not make a complete fool of the Carpenter."

And again, Joshua said nothing.

But at dawn there came to the door a strange woman, veiled from head to toe in blue silk. She held a flute in her hand, and before my husband could ask her name, she held up the instrument, which seemed to play of its own accord. The melody was subtle; it twisted and turned; it was haunting, yet somehow you could not quite remember it from phrase to phrase. The woman's garment rustled though there was no breeze, and in the music of the flute you could hear the rushing of a mountain storm; I knew the sound well; it was the sound of my child being conceived, on the hill's side, in the high wind, in the circle of spring.

This is a vision, I told myself. I could see that my son and my husband did not see what I saw at all.

And when I looked a second time, she was gone; in her place was King Balthasar's charioteer, in full Indian battle raiment, his quiver on his back. And I knew that was all my husband saw.

But I had seen the Goddess. I knew it must be she. Men make a fuss about how men's secret wisdom must be hidden from women; but women are better at concealment. Most men have no notion that women have a secret cosmos, secret gods. My husband was such.

Though the woman's face was covered, she turned to me, and I felt that she must be smiling.

She did not speak, but merely pointed the way with her flute. Outside the door, there was a cart, covered with a woolen awning woven in fantastical designs such as the Persians love to devise. The Indian mage, still in his torn clothes, his hair still matted and filthy, bowed to us; he placed his palms together is a gesture of greeting.

We climbed into the cart; inside, it seemed far more capacious than it had on the outside. Woolen rugs canopied us and made walls; there seemed to be several chambers inside the vehicle.

Our host climbed up to greet us in his ornate Greek. "You will of course be forgiving of the humility of these surroundings; the stars bade me make haste; I could not summon an appropriate conveyance in time."

"And will you soon tell us where it is that the stars have asked you to take us?" Joseph said. "Some idea of how long we must travel would also suffice; and you know that we are Jews —"

"Who may not eat what others eat," the king said. "Do not be concerned, Joseph who is called the Carpenter. The place where we will go was built by Maya, the Lord of Illusion. You will eat and drink the empty air, and you will dance on the wind. The journey will take as long as it seems to take, yet it will be over in a single breath."

Joseph said softly, in the Ancient Tongue, "In thy sight, a thousand years is but as a single day."

My son sat up; it was if he had never heard the Psalms before.

My husband asked again, "But where is this place, this castle of illusion?"

And Balthasar answered, "Within."

And he opened the front-flap of the cart, and said to his charioteer, "Time to go."

I heard the flute music again. I heard the rushing of the wind. I felt the rumble of great wheels against the stone streets of the city. But we could not see outside. And presently our host retired to another chamber inside the vehicle, and my husband told me to absent myself, because it was time for him to teach the Torah to my son, and I should not be there lest I hear things that a woman should not know. So it was that I slipped out through the flap, and found myself sitting beside the driver, who was whipping the horses into a frenzy; the landscape flew by so quickly I could barely make it out; I saw great sphinxes, giant pyramids, oases, Cyclopean walls, ziggurats, and perfumed gardens; each time I blinked, another vista opened up.

I could hear my husband from within; when he recited the Torah, his voice had the resonance of a shofars and the pounding rhythm of a great drum.

He was speaking of the creation of the world, how the breath of God had but to touch the waters of chaos, and there was light; the words of the Torah thundered from him, and I was moved.

But then came my son's piping voice: "Father, I've heard that story in the marketplace. A tall man with a terraced beard recited it to me. The only thing that was different was the name of the creator: not Elohim, but a mother-thing named Nammu, and then Ki-An, and then Enlil."

Joseph said, "You are not to interrupt me. The Babylonians may also have such a story, but their is but the imperfect mirror of ours. We have the one true god; their god is like a fractured mirror; in the broken glass we can see many gods."

"But," Joshua said, "*Elohim* is plural. If it means God, why does it say 'the gods'? And if *they* can call Enlil and Nammu by name ... why can't we?"

"God is all things at once," Joseph said. "Plural in singular, many in one, and that one unnameable, everything and nothing. Can't you see, it's just your imperfect command of the Old Tongue that confuses you?"

"Am I confused when I'm only pointing out that a word is plural?"

"Don't answer questions with questions."

The wind roared louder, and I could hear no more. But presently the charioteer turned to me, and it was no longer the charioteer but the woman I had seen earlier, veiled in blue. I said, "Do you think his real father would teach him differently?"

She said, "Do you mean the centurion?"

But she knew that I did not.

We passed through searing desert; at nightfall we reached an oasis ringed with palms. Camels were tethered, and there was a palace of tents; fires kept out the evening chill, and from within the tents came the sound of timbrels and psalteries and belled feet stamping. As we approached, the camels sank down on the sand, and a dozen painted girls emerged from the main entrance to the tent, prostrating themselves. More emerged; warriors, sages, musicians; all feel to the ground.

I naturally assumed that it was the Indian they were bowing to; but when I looked behind me, I saw that he too was on his knees. And it was Joshua, descending the rickety steps, who was receiving these people's obeisance. When Joseph emerged and saw, he was immediately in an ill humor.

"Tell these people to get up," he said to the king. "He must learn that we prostrate ourselves only to God."

"Indeed," said Balthasar, "he must learn it." Was there a hint of irony in his voice? He snapped his fingers, and the worshippers immediately rose to their feet and went about their business. "We will rest here awhile," he continued, "and refresh ourselves."

The tent-flap was pulled open; now the entire clearing was filled with raucous music. The floor was covered with the finest carpets, and as we entered, slaves washed our feet. The king motioned us to recline on great cushions stitched from old kilims and stuffed with rose-leaves; so as not to intrude on the men, I sat further off, next to the ensemble of musicians, all female, all veiled. Slaves poured tea from tall bronze vessels with serpentine spouts. Though there were elaborately dressed dignitaries present, I had the feeling that this entire place had been conjured up for our eyes alone, a particularly vivid mirage.

Balthasar said to Joshua: "So, what did Joseph teach you on your way to this place?"

"He was telling me about the creation of the world," my son said, "but there were things that didn't sound right."

"My son's mind is like a fishnet," Joseph said, "and he has snared creatures with claws and tentacles along with the fish with scales and fins that are our proper diet."

"We will tell you another story tonight," said the king.

And I saw that the woman in blue was standing amidst the orchestra, holding her flute aloft, and from an inner chamber of the tent there came twenty-two dancers. Their eyes were kohled, their hair in delicate black ringlets; they wore veils and their ankles were bound with bells. Their veils fluttered as they moved.

The music grew louder; the drums pounded in the rhythm of an agitated heart, and the plucking and piping became frenzied. I watched my husband. He was entranced ... who would not be? ... aroused. He drank deeply of the proffered wine, the wine-jugs cooled in a mound of packed snow that must have been brought from a thousand miles away.

The dancers were beautiful. They leaped; as their veils shifted, I could see the taut musculature of their thighs ... there was something almost manly about them ... their eyes darted, quivered, circled in a synchronized choreography as elaborate as the dance itself. And I realized that they exuded a sexual power ... that it touched me ... it was their maleness that affected me, even as their feminine qualities had stirred my husband.

Now there were cymbals and timbrels, harps and lutes, and panpipes and flutes wailed above the clanging. The veils were flying, weaving patterns in the flickering firelight. You could see more flesh. The dancers moved with such precision they seemed like cogs in one of those Roman mechanical marvels, those contraptions that keep their public baths flowing or their catapults wound up. They climbed over each other, fell apart, reassembled their bodies into writhing creatures with many arms and legs.

The audience, was enraptured; they did not move; they seemed, indeed, to have fallen quite motionless; it occurred to me once more that they were not entirely human, but put there only to make this vision more complete.

The music swelled; there was a shuddering climax as all the dancers mounted one another to form a whirling, precarious human rope; then, it seemed, they climbed up a ladder made entirely of themselves, while the shortest dancer, a child perhaps, twirled on his toes on the head of the dancer beneath. It was dizzying; it was ingenious; and then, with the music so cacophonous that it could no longer be called music, it was over; the rope tumbled to the ground and the dancers were in a heap, and the veils, tied end to end, were being whisked into the ceiling by an assistant hanging from the tent-poles.

They were near-naked now, these twenty-two men ... or were they women? Their breasts were so tightly bound with a flesh-colored cloth that one could not tell, and for the parts below, a loincloth of the same hue was wrapped so cunningly that one could see no telltale outline of gender.

A gong sounded, and the dancers melted into the shadows. The feast continued into the night; I retired to the women's quarters, and thence to the chamber they had apportioned to my family, to find that a pallet of sheepskins had been spread out for me. A bondswoman was folding clothes and putting them away in a carved cedar chest.

In the distance, a harpist played, and sang some saga in a long-dead tongue. Again the voice seemed neither man nor woman.

"Woman, do you know —"

The slave turned to me. Her face was veiled, but her very gaze perfumed the air. "Yes," she said, "I do know."

"Were they men or women?"

"Neither, my lady. They belong to a caste of sacred man-women; they may originate as men or women, but they take great pains to fashion themselves into something in between."

"Why?" I asked.

She held up bronze mirror and began to comb my hair. I had rarely been so pampered, and I allowed myself to luxuriate.

"But you already know why," she said, and I knew her voice at that moment, and I was honored — and afraid — because a supernatural being was acting like my slave. "They seek to emulate the perfect state of humankind, before there were men and women, before the war between the sexes."

It was true. I'd realized the answer before she even spoke. I wanted to question her more, but she vanished in a flurry of glittering dust. And so I prepared to sleep, and waited. And heard voices outside the door-flap. My son was arguing with my husband. Their voices were shrill, and the substance of their argument esoteric. "Abomination, abomination," my husband was shouting, and my son was speaking of how Adam was, perhaps, at his creation, a hermaphrodite, since his femininity had not yet been extracted from his side and breathed into a second handful of dust.

When they came in, they must have realized I had overheard some of their arguing. Because the things they spoke of were not for women to hear, they stopped, and looked at each other, and looked away; in the sooty glow of the chamber's one oil lamp, their faces held a sullen menace.

"I was right," Joseph said to me. "This trip is bringing me closer to my son; we argue now; before, we never spoke at all."

Joshua did not speak until my husband was asleep and snoring. When he was sure Joseph would not wake up — what with the wine and the dancing girls — he said to me, "Walk with me a while, Mother."

The night and I were young, and my husband was an old man, crotchety, dogmatic; I wanted to breathe the desert air, so I went with my son. The guards at the door of the tent-palace were the same holy transvestites who had danced for us. They made obeisance to us, their palms held together, inclining their necks.

In the moonlight, my son said, "Why is he so angry all the time?"

"Because you won't treat him as your father," I said.

"But he's not," he said.

"At least he's trying to be," I said.

"He's a strange man," Joshua said. "He knows so many facts, and yet he only wants to put them together one way."

"He doesn't mean to be cold to you," I said. "It's just that —"

"I'm a bastard," Joshua said. "I wish you'd stop lying to me about the special circumstances of my birth, about angels and portents and wise men's gifts —"

"But one wise man came back," I said. "And you were the one who called him an angel."

"Joseph says he's a messenger from the dark goddess whom women worship in secret."

"But he agreed to come on this journey."

"Because he doesn't want to know that he's afraid. But I do know. He's an open book. More open to me than his Torah, anyway."

And though he was the one who invited me to walk with him, he sped up and moved away from the encampment, in the direction of the desert. In the distance, there were dunes, stark in the moonlight, slowly shifting, sifting in the chill wind.

I caught up with him. "Joshua —" I said. I put my hand on his shoulder. But he brushed me away.

"Maybe if I stand out here long enough," he whispered, "my father will come and talk to me."

"Joseph's asleep," I said.

"Yes," Joshua said, "he is." And he turned from me, and walked further into the expanse of sand, his gaze fixed on the moon.

"You'll catch cold," I said, but I knew he wasn't listening anymore.

The tree in my atrium in Ephesus has ten branches. I've kept it very carefully pruned, so the branches are evenly spaced and the foliage has room to spread out. It's the only thing that lives in that atrium garden; everything else I've planted always dies, so I've taken to letting the stonemasons dump their failed statues here; there's a few Cupids, one of Jupiter, and many abortive Dianas of Ephesus, with her many breasts, she is tough to get right.

Sometimes one of the Christianoi will come and see me; Paul's propaganda war to make my son into God seems to be working; I've heard them whisper to each other, "Look, look, God's mother." And they tell me the tree symbolizes the crucifixion, and they exclaim, "Lo! the tree flourishes, and all around it the statues of the ancient gods have been smashed; our new order is sweeping away the old." They do not know, of course, that no one smashed those statues, least of all some supernatural power; these gods were never killed, because they were never born; they are trapped in half-formed stone for all eternity.

One day that tree will be full-grown, and the ten branches will be ladder to the bosom of God.

At least, that's what they have told me.

This was a journey of the spirit. I cannot tell how much time passed, or if time passed at all. On the second day, the sound of my husband instructing my wayward son was quickly wearying, and I crawled out to the front once more to sit beside the charioteer who was to me the goddess. I smelled the sea as soon as I emerged. The sun was bright; the wind had a briny moisture to it.

I had stepped out onto the deck of a ship, but such a vessel as I had never seen on the Sea of Galilee. Where the horses had been, there were wave-crests like row after row of white-maned steeds. Beneath us, I could hear the drumbeat of a hortator, and I could he the rhythmic slap of the oars against the ocean. The prow of the ship was a many-breasted woman with blue skin; although she was made of wood, her eyes were living; I knew now that the vessel, like the horse-drawn cart, was an extension of the goddess's body.

A servant brought me a tray of fruit. Like the musicians and the dancers in the oasis, this slave seemed both male and female.

There were pomegranates, figs, and quinces; grapes, dates, and apples. The servant kneeled before me, holding out the platter; I reached out to touch the fruit, and then I thought again.

The pomegranate is the fruit of the dead; the secret wisdom of the women has taught me that the leaves and the seeds of the pomegranate are what binds the souls of the dead to the world beneath. And I thoight too of the quince, which some claimed was the fruit of the knowledge of good and evil. I wondered if the other fruits had darker meanings, too.

"Is this fruit forbidden?" I asked the servant.

She only said, "Nothing is forbidden, my lady, unless you yourself forbid it."

At that moment, I saw King Balthasar emerge from below decks. He saw me and said to me, "Remember, Miriam, you are being a traveler in the realm of Maya now; nothing is real."

I still did not feel I should eat the fruit.

"You're going to see terrible things now," he went on. "But remember ... it's illusion."

Even as he spoke, I saw my son and husband in an animated conversation some distance away, leaning over the side of the ship. Halfway to the horizon, two whales were breaching the waves, the sun glancing off the slick skin. They were coupling. I had never seen whales in the throes of passion before; the one lay on her back, the other mounted her, and the pair swimming at top speed to sustain the stability of the position....

And far away, against the horizon, there were jagged boulders, a blue-green mist, the vaguest outline of land....

Out of nowhere, a storm unleashed itself. Rain pelted down. There was thunder and lightning, and the androgynous crew members were rushing about, scrambling to get below deck. I had no time to think. The ship heaved, I staggered, my stomach churned ... I feel to the deck. Brine sluiced the planks. Salt flooded my nostrils. I was spluttering. Trying to grab hold of anything. I could see treasure chests floating into the sea ... silks and jeweled goblets bobbing up and down and ... the wet wind lashed at us. The ship righted itself, and I heard shouts of: "The Carpenter ... he's fallen overboard ..."

The storm was already subsiding, harsh sunlight bursting through chinks in the cloud cover. The crew were climbing back up now, tying things down, staring at the ocean ... and as I rushed to towards the stern I could see my husband in the water, furiously trying to swim toward a plank....

And there was my son. "Don't worry, Mother," he said. "I'll bring him back." And he smiled at me, a smile of such utter calm that it chilled me. Because though the wind was dying, the waters were still turbulent, and the sailors still in panic over a tempest that had lasted but a moment.

How could Joshua bring him back? Joseph was being carried out further to sea. And the seamen were throwing down ropes, but no one wanted to leap in after him.

Except my son. He stripped off his Grecian chiton and his head covering, and leaped naked into the sea. I had never seen my son swim before. In Alexandria, he had stuck to the streets, not the sea. But even now, he did not swim.

He fell very slowly, as though riding the wind.

He landed on his feet on the waves.

And I thought, *He will not suffer thy foot to be moved....*

With great deliberation, carefully placing one foot before the other, like a temple dancer on a tightrope, he moved towards his stepfather.

I heard others whispering, "He's walking on water."

But I could see, just below the surface, the dark, unmoving outline of leviathan. The sea water sparkled in the sun; his bright eyes shone against his olive complexion; he seemed as strong as fullgrown man as he pulled his stepfather from the ocean.

The crew were gathering now, and someone cast down a rope ladder; and it seemed that on the instant that Joshua and my husband alighted on the ladder, the monster of the deep sounded, and a moment later the pair of whales was to be seen afar off, and a strange music filled the air, keening and thrumming at the same time; it was, Balthasar assured me, a song the whales sang often, and always to the glory of God.

A few moments passed; Joseph looked at Joshua as a sailor threw a garment over his shoulders.

At length, my husband said, "Well, at least you're dressed like a Jew now."

"I'm trying to please you," Joshua said.

Joseph said, "Then don't walk on water; you'll catch your death."

"I didn't walk on water," Joshua said. But I knew that the others had all witnessed a miracle; only I had seen how the monster of the deep had interrupted his lovemaking so that my son would not dash his foot against the sea.

"And don't argue with me anymore. There's a time for debating, and a time for listening."

"I'm listening."

And I saw, then, that though neither of them could speak of it, there was a kind of love between the two of them. I did not think they would ever come to admit it. They would not even look at each other.

And now, almost tripping over the robe that was far too long for him, Joshua turned to me; wordlessly, still wet and shivering, he fell into my mother embrace; but even close to me he was wary, unyielding.

And suddenly we came upon those shoals that I had seen at the very edge of the horizon, and King Balthasar was urging us inside.

"I don't need to go in," Joshua said. "I'm not afraid."

"Go in anyway," said the king. "We're about to be shipwrecked."

The ship foundered on a massive rock, and I heard a groan as of splintering timber, but with a curiously human quality to it....

At this point in my narrative, the man who was about the create a new religion on my son's dead bones broke in. "You don't have to go on," Paul, Saul, whatever his name was, said to me. "I've heard enough. There's nothing I really need in what you're telling me."

I smiled. "Ah, but there is," I said. "It's all there, every bit of pagan symbolism you need to make your religion palatable to the Gentiles."

He paused then, because he knew I had seen through him. He wanted a story from me that he could spin into a perfect arc of godhead, with the bitter widow as golden Isis suckling the crucified rebel as shining Horus; me as the Great Mother ploughing the blood of my son and lover into the soil to bring forth the harvest; he wanted to ship me off to Ephesus to replace the hundred-breasted huntress. Which, in the end, came to pass.

Paul said, "I want something more powerful than reality ... I want truth."

The kind of distinction the Greeks love to make, and which quite staggers those of us who speak less dissembling tongues.

The beach we foundered on was India. Not the India of history, where Alexander the Great had stumbled upon the far boundary of the universe, and turned back from the edge to encounter only drunkenness and death; this was, perhaps, an India of the mind. Though Paul would no doubt draw many comparisons to Alexander; for Alexander, too, was a god's son, a messiah of sorts, dead in his thirties.

From the impact of the ship against the rocks to the time we stepped onto the sand was mere moments. It seemed to me that the ship fell apart in two halves, and the halves dematerialized into the burning air, and there had never been a ship at all. Instead, there was a white elephant, caparisoned in cloth of gold; atop its back was a howdah cunningly carved of wood, with caryatid columns and a roof made from the images of many-headed demons.

The elephant knelt, and the king led the way, mountain by way of gilt steps that were wheeled up to the creature's side by attendants.

Seated on the elephant's neck was the woman in blue.

"Your journey will soon be over, Joshua," the king said to my son, who, since his adventure with the sea, was ever more withdrawn, huddling in a corner of the howdah, hugging his knees and staring at the ground as it swayed beneath us. "Look, Miriam; do you see the castle?"

I saw only snowcapped mountains, impossibly tall, impossibly far.

"No, you don't see it yet," said the king. "You see only the Himavant, and high Kailasa, dwelling place of the gods. Open your mind, Miriam ... let the illusions in."

The elephant was climbing a steep path, pausing now and then to roll a fallen tree trunk out of its way. We traveled for what might have been days; time was a flexible thing in these countries past the known world's edge.

The mountain still seemed impossibly far. We stopped at a waystation in a clearing. Sandalwood incense filled the air, and there was a temple in the same ornate style as the elephant's howdah. Priests in white robes and turbans wandered haughtily about. There was a statue of a goddess with a hundred arms, wearing a necklace of skulls, her feet trampling on corpses.

"There's your demon Ashtaroth," Joseph said to me. "The man-killing she-beast. It seems that she rules here."

I did not argue with him; I knew it would be useless. I gazed at the statue. I knew that the goddess had a thousand names; she was Persephone, queen of darkness; she was the mother of the spirits that visit men in the night and drain away their seed; she was Lilith; she was the goddess who had been the consort of the most high once, and who was now condemned to rule over dirt and shadows; in this country, at least, men acknowledged her power.

We resumed our journey at dawn. The road grew wilder. We passed a surging river lined with temples; men and women bathed in its waters, and the dead were burned in pyres there, their ashes cast onto the waters. We passed ascetics, naked old men covered with filth, some standing on one leg, some with their cheeks and torsos pierced with metal rods, all bone thin; we passed some sitting cross-legged under trees, their eyes closed, gazing as it were upon some inner vision; we saw men whirling themselves into frenzies, women dancing among monkeys; we saw men prostrating themselves before oxen, and everywhere the many-armed demons, towering over shrines, guarding palace gates, painted on walls; and always the lady in blue drove the white elephant forward, tapping its neck with a silver goad.

"This is a desolate place," my husband said. "Abomination everywhere. Men who imitate women, men who worship beasts. I thought Alexandria was a second Sodom, but this is beyond imagination."

Joshua was still huddled in the corner of the howdah, staring at emptiness.

"Look at what it's done to our son," Joseph said. "This journey is killing him, filling him with terrible ideas, destroying his soul."

And I marveled, not only at what he said, but that this was the first time he had said *our son;* and I knew there was a kind of magic at work.

So I simply said, "We'll be home soon."

I think my husband would have embraced me if we were not in a small open chamber perched on a lumbering beast. I put my hand out to steady myself; he held onto it, and, perhaps, squeezed it; I was not sure. I thought: He does love me, underneath it all, though I've put him through so much. I wanted to put my arms around him, but I knew he would think it immodest of me.

We stopped again. This new encampment was a place shrouded in mist; moisture seeped into our lungs; scarred rocks emerged from the roiling fog, and here and there a shrine stood, its offerings mouldy and half devoured by wild animals. The mountains were still just as far away as before.

We took shelter in a cave. But it was nothing like the cave in which I held my newborn child. This cave was covered with murals depicting the exploits of strange gods. Gold leaf was peeling from wooden beams; the scent of incense was everywhere; and there were statues of a man, cross-legged, his hair aflame; whose eyes held a rare serenity. And then, in niches in the cave, there were live men too, anchorites I guessed, in the same cross-legged attitude. Their eyes were closed. Like many we had seen on the road here, they seemed to be gazing inward.

"Who are these men?" I asked the king.

"They believe that the world is an illusion," he said. "They are trying to end that illusion. They are thinking that if they are perfectly still, they will touch the still center of the cosmos, and when they have become as nothing, they will be everything."

There were bats and monkeys in the cave, too; the bats perched high up, sleeping, like black furry roof-tiles; the monkeys scurrying, peering, chattering, stealing the offerings to the gods.

Balthasar took his place upon a throne of rock, with incense braziers at his feet. Vassals brought food; other servants spread out pallets of straw for us in shadowed crannies of the cave. Joshua seemed at last to have become impatient. He wasn't in a corner rocking himself back and forth now. He was pacing. Finally he asked the king about his father. "Who *is* my father, then? Why did he send *you* to me? Why is it taking so long to reach him?"

The king said only, "You will be reaching him, Joshua, when your soul will tell you you are willing to reach him."

"Riddles! You're as bad as Joseph. You told me there would be an orchard at the end of this journey. You told me my father would be waiting for me, and I would finally know who I am."

"No riddles, my beautiful young prince. You do not know the answers because you do not want to know them."

And in the night, with the moonlight streaming in through high fissures in the cavern's roof, I could not sleep; and I saw that neither my son nor my husband were sleeping either. I lit an oil lamp and wandered listlessly; the cave was labyrinthine.

In the hollow where the king dozed on his capacious throne, the walls were painted from floor to ceiling. These were the gods and demons these people believed in; each one had many heads and arms. A great ape yawned the moon and the stars. A goddess dancing across the clouds wielded the lightning. And directly behind the throne, there was painted a golden door, and on either side of the door were depicted Greek letters — alpha on the left, omega on the right. It did not surprise me that there was Greek here; perhaps the murals had been painted in the days when Alexander the Great ruled all the world.

Next to the door was depicted a golden chariot, even in the light of my flickering oil lamp it seemed to shine of its own. Next to the chariot stood a god, his skin completely blue, holding a flute. His face was the essence of manliness, yet it held a feminine beauty as well. His eyes sparkled. I found myself staring at that face; for it was a face I seemed to recognize, though I could not imagine whence.

Presently I heard voices; it was Joseph and Joshua deep in conversation yet again; I could hear the stark music of the ancient tongue, and I knew that Joseph was making another attempt to teach my son the meaning of the Torah. Because I knew that my husband would find it unseemly, I ducked behind the throne, pressed myself against the stone, tried to will myself into invisibility.

Joseph was speaking of the first words of the Torah. "Every word, every letter," he told Joshua, "encapsulates a myriad hidden meanings. For example, we say in Aramaic that in the beginning God created heaven and earth; but does the text really say that? No — the word *bara,* 'created,' comes second, not third, do you see that? God could be the object as easily as the subject. So what created God? Surely only God can have created God. And then the word *et,* the accusative particle that precedes the words for heaven and earth — how is that written but as *aleph* and *taf,* the beginning and ending of the alphabet, which by extension means the entire alphabet, the key to all creation?"

Joshua said, "But what about the question I asked before? About how the text doesn't really say 'God' at all, but 'the gods'?"

"God is an axiom. You can't argue with an axiom."

"But when God said, 'You shall have no other gods before me,' he didn't say that other gods don't exist."

"Demons," said Joseph. I saw his shadow in the lamplight, huge and not unlike a demon itself. Joseph turned a corner. And saw me. "Miriam!" he gasped. "You know you can't listen to men's talk."

Fury welled up inside me. I thought of the torment of childbirth, the dickering between Joseph and my parents over my soiled chastity, the trek across the desert with my baby on my back ... "Your thousand interpretations of the meaning of those words," I said. "I know one that you haven't thought of."

Joseph looked at me as if to say, "How could a woman understand?" But he didn't say it out loud. He stood there, in front of the painted doorway, challenging me.

"The word *bara* has no gender," I said. "And the world *elohim* might be plural. What if the real meaning was, 'In the beginning, *she* created the gods?"

"Blasphemy!" my husband scoffed. "That's bound to happen when a woman meddles in the affairs of men."

But Joshua said, "Don't speak to my mother that way," and ran at him full tilt with his fists out.

"Don't hit your father!" I shouted.

"He's not my father!" Joshua screamed at the top of his lungs. He started pummeling at Joseph with his fists. He was hysterical, lashing out, punching the air. My husband stepped aside and Joshua was banging at the painted portal and the plaster was flaking away and —

There was a crack as of smashing wood. Joshua's fists broke through the wall and all at once he was sucked into the mural ... I screamed ... the wall closed up around him and —

He was gone.

And so was the image of the golden chariot and the charioteer.

My son — flesh and blood — absorbed into an illusion — and yet it had the logic of a vivid dream — and I was not afraid. It seemed to me as it should have been. I heard, from within the rock, a muffled laughter ... the happy laughter of a child ... something I had not heard in the real world for many years.

"This is too much," Joseph cried, and he began pounding on the painted door with his fists. I thought I heard the hollow resonance of old wood, but nothing gave way. I went up to the wall. Put my finger on it. It was flat, but I definitely touched the texture of wood; I tingled. A glow seemed to emanated from the door and envelop me in a cold blue light.

My husband stepped back. "Have I married a witch?" he whispered. And quoted the words of scripture: "Thou shalt not suffer a witch to live."

"Don't kill me, Joseph," I said softly. "I don't know what is happening. I don't understand anything."

"Your demon-goddess is manipulating you," he said. "Even if you don't know what you're doing ... you're her puppet."

It was at that moment that the room filled with light, as though a thousand torches had been lit. I turned. There were the hermaphrodite servants of the king, and each one held aloft a flaming sword. As though for the first time, I saw the cavern whole, with niche after niche of anchorites in deepest meditation; they were all awakening now, yawning, stretching their limbs as though they had been in a millennial sleep. And there was the king himself; he had stepped down from the throne, and stood between me and my husband, no longer clothed in the tatters of an ascetic, but in the full splendor of his kingship, his hair topped by a jewel-encrusted turban, his robes of peacock-hued silk, a pectoral jewel like a massive diamond eye.

"Where have you taken my son?" Joseph shouted.

Balthasar smiled. "I took him nowhere," he said. "This was always his journey, not mine; I am but a messenger. You may follow him, if your heart is steady and your will is sure."

"I can go anywhere he goes," he said. "I raised him, I taught him right from wrong; he belongs to me even if not in the flesh."

"Then go to him," said the king.

As Joseph turned to the door, I saw that the Greek letters had burst into flame, and the lines of fire were transforming themselves into Hebrew: and the Alpha was twisting itself into א just as the Omega was becoming ת. But the door would not yield to him. He banged until I could see the blood oozing from his clenched fists, and yet the stone did not give, though now and then there was a telltale creak, as though the fabric of reality were willing itself to shift but was not quite able to.

"Joseph, Joseph," said the king, "you are in a cage that you have been making of your own accord. You must let go your conscious self. If the Torah is a great edifice, you have given it brick by brick to your wife's son, and each brick you have illuminated with skill and even passion; yet a temple is not wrought from bricks, but from the soul."

And it was then that my husband wept. He had never wept in my presence before. He wept, I think, because he knew every word of the Torah, yet he did not know the word that could open one child's heart.

"Miriam," said the king to me, "do you want to know who Joshua's father is?"

"No," I said firmly. And so saying, I consigned to the abyss my memory of the masked man with the antlers, the handsome centurion named for a were-leopard of the night, and all that spring ritual on the hillside.

As soon as I said *no,* the letters began to glow again, and this time they metamorphosed into blue bolts of lightning that formed an even more ancient script, thus: 𐤀 and 𐤕 And I knew them for letters that people had used a thousand years before ... the people of the Great Goddess, who had occupied the promised land before the coming of my people. They were the first and last letters of the Phoenician alphabet. And so there were three magics at play: the magic of earth, of the past, of the mother, my magic; the magic of the Greeks, whose civilization would influence the future; and the here and now, the eternal present, Joseph's magic.

The past and the future could enter the gateway; the present could not. And I understood why: Joseph's kind had already been driven from Eden. My kind had remained there, had never truly entered the world. And Joshua's kind had yet to be.

There were three Edens behind that door. Three choices. Three human conditions.

If I stepped through it, I would not see what Joshua saw.

King Balthasar said, "You and your husband, Miriam, were not invited to this feast. But Miriam, as you are a woman, and as you are all women, and as you are the woman beneath the sky, she whom the rain makes fertile and who brings forth all the good things in the world, you may if you open your inner eye see all three Edens."

I put my husband's hand in mine.

I saw: a creature both man and woman, split in twain, the two halves always seeking each other out; I saw passion. I saw the man and the woman making love in the orchard. I was the man and I was the woman. His penis was the sword of flame. His arms were the enfolding branches of a great tree that encircled the world. He leaped out of my body as leviathan breaching the deep.

My lips were the fruit of knowledge. My hips were the gates of desire. My eyes were the stars, and my hair the nurturing night.

My husband groaned as I clenched him hard inside me, and the waters that flowed from every opening in my body were the waters of creation, the waters on whose face God breathed; and my husband loved me for six days, six eternities in the mind of the almighty; and on the seventh day, he stared into my eyes as he held me, and his gaze held a terrible despair, the despair that all men feel when they have conquered what their heart has always desired ... for all men, after the explosion of pleasure and contentment, soon begin to sense an unease, a feeling of "Why was there not more?"

And with that single look, I understood why Joseph could not return to Eden.

Man who is born already possessing the perfection of what could be possessed will still ask "Why is there not more?"

That was why he had been driven from Eden ... or rather he had caused himself to be driven from Eden ... because it is human to quest for the ever-unreachable, to reach for the ever-untouchable. To taste paradise, yet never be allowed to return — this was the source of all man's creativity, man's genius. I understood my husband now; I understood men.

If he returned to paradise, he would no longer be human.

The vision faded; I sat with my back to the garden door, my husband sleeping in my arms, smiling, content, it seemed, for the first time since we had left Nazareth.

And so I rose, and left my husband sleeping; and the king, who could not himself enter, held open for me the gateway to my Eden.

Immediately, a wind caught me. It carried me above the clouds; I saw the world spinning below, saw moons and stars whirl over me; I was riding some kind of chariot through the sky, and the goddess stood before me, whipping the steeds into a frenzy, before I could catch my breath, I was dropped down on a hillside in Nazareth, the place of the women's rites. It was night. I knew the place. I had arrived at a moment in my own past. I was so young then ... it was not long after my first bleeding. But inside my own mind, I was also an older woman, seeing with the eyes of experience ... I was seeing the time of my innocence with the hindsight of having already tasted the fruit from the tree of knowledge....

Dancing in the dark. The stars wheeled overhead. The moon wept blood. On this hillside, we women chanted and banged our drums and spoke in a secret language men cannot know. Our song was as ancient as the hills; these trees and boulders had heard this music in a time before there were Jews in Judaea.

Within the circle of women there stands a creature, a man, I think, a man or a tree. His face is masked in foliage. A deer's antlers sprout from his forehead. His arms are spread out, cruciform. As the mist roils across the stony ground, I find myself being drawn toward him ... reeled in, almost, like a fish from the sea ... and I see the man's eyes ... *my* eyes. He embraces me. He laughs. *My* laugh. He hugs me hard in his arms, his arms sinewy and sinuous; his arms are the branches of a great tree, they are serpents, constrictors, they are flaming clouds; he sucks me into his embrace ... I cry out ... for as my lips seek out his lips, as we stand locked in a sensual coupling, I know those eyes at last ... the eyes that have looked away all these years ... the eyes that would never meet mine, though they gazed freely at the lowliest beggar ... my son has come to me as a raging firestorm from the sky ... my son has planted himself within me ... yet this is no abomination ... there is no incest when a god engenders himself.

And my son divides me in two. I am like the Red Sea; I am a channel for the chariot of fire to race skyward.

At the center of the orchard there is a tree whose roots penetrate deep into the heart of darkness, and whose topmost branches caress the very face of God.

The chariot disappears into the face of the sun. I am alone.

A terrible sadness comes over me; it is the sadness a woman feels after childbirth. But soon, I know, my spirits will soar. I will come down from the mountain all alone, but I will always know now that I don't need a man to complete me. The wind was chill, but soon the sunlight will warm the air, and I dance. I am woman. I am the world.

In the third vision, I am the woman in the serpent. The serpent has wrapped itself around the tree of life. The serpent has one hundred breasts, and from each breast there pours a river. Is this how my son sees me? As the dragon who guards the great mystery of his birth? I do not have time to ask myself more questions, because my son has come into the orchard. His charioteer is an angel with blue skin, clothed in the sun.

My son leaps from the chariot. His sword is forged from the tears of the stars. There is the tree; from every branch hang fruits ... fruits like jewels, like scrolls, like trumpets. I must protect the treasure. No one can steal the golden apples of the gods.

My son charges towards me, sword outstretched. From the heavens comes the music of seven shofars, and the branches of the tree are lashed together with liquid lines of light.

I am the dragon. I must protect the treasure.

"Why have you come?" I try to speak gently, as a mother, but from my throat there issues a draconian roar;

the earth itself rumbles at my footfall; sulphurous flames belch from my throat.

"I've got to kill you," says Joshua. "Can't you see that? I don't want to, but it's destiny."

"But I'm your mother," I say, and I slither forward to embrace him in my scaly arms, I offer him sustenance from my hundred breasts, but he plunges the sword into me. Over and over and over, until I am bleeding in a hundred places, and the rivers that run from my breasts run red.

Blood fountains up. It is more crimson than polished rubies. The wounds are burning. It touches the sky. The blood turns to air. I am dissolving into nothingness.

"You are my mother," says Joshua, "and I won't forget how much you loved me. But it was written that I would slay the dragon darkness, and climb to the top of the tree, and gaze upon my father face to face."

I try to cling to him, but I am melding with the rays of the sun, the emanations that stream from the tree of life. I am dying, I think, but in the midst of dying I realize that I am becoming one with everything; I am the air, the tree, the earth, the sun; I am knowledge; I am death.

I see the charioteer now. He is a giant. His name is Krishna. He is but a fragment of God, even as I, the slain darkness, was another piece of divinity. He stretches out his hand to hold the tree steady.

Because I am the air, my son is breathing me into his lungs. Because I am the sun, I warm him. The charioteer gives my son a leg up. My son springs skyward, branch to branch, climbing hand to hand on the twenty-two filaments of light that link the branches; up there, at the summit, he will pierce the canopy of clouds, he will see God.

My son lay sleeping for many days in the palace of King Balthasar. I tended him. The king assembled provender and made arrangements for our return. After a day, Joseph too began to help me, squeezing a rag dipped in snow-cooled water on my son's forehead, touching him gently, realizing for the first time how precious he was to him.

I was away from Joshua's side when he awakened. I was sitting at a window (for Balthasar's palace was many stories high, and perched on a mountain ledge) watching dancers with gold and purple saris swaying to the sound of flute and drum.

As I watched, I noticed the mist clearing ... the mist that had draped the palace since our arrival ... and I saw for the first time how green the valley below was, how emerald-clear; I saw the king's city straddling the mountain side, with stately columns, an agora, domes and gardens and fountains and statues.

Joshua was mumbling something. I turned. Joshua said, "Father." And he put his arms around my husband's neck, and Joseph hugged him, I think for the first time; he hugged him and he wept. It was not a moment for me to intrude; I stayed out of sight, as a mindful woman should; but like all women, I saw more clearly, saw what they don't see.

Joseph did not say, *This is the first time you have called me father.* But he knew it, and it melted his hard heart.

Joshua did not say, *I am giving myself to you of my own free will, knowing that one day I must face another destiny; we all have roles to play in a vast cosmic drama, but for now, I want to be a child, I want to be loved as a child, made much of; it will be over all too soon.*

But his silence said all those things, if only my husband would listen.

Joseph said, "Let's go home now."

Joshua said, "I've climbed to the top of the tree of life, and I've seen what is there ... it's nothing, Father."

Wasn't that what the anchorites in the cavern were trying to find: the Nothing at the core of the coiled cosmos? I heard the words behind Joshua's words: *God is everything; God is nothing.* And I knew that he had received that illumination that had eluded the ascetics with their fasting and their self-mutilation, and the meditators in their niches, staring at eternity.

"Thank you for teaching me, Father," Joshua said.

"It was only my duty," said Joseph. "You will be a man soon; it will be time for me to take you to the Temple, so you can impress the priests with your knowledge of the Torah; it's almost time for you to be bar mitzvah."

"Father," said Joshua, "I will tell them all that I have received."

Only I noticed that, though they were speaking our mother tongue, Aramaic, Joshua had used a strange word from the old tongue for "that which I have received" — he had called it *kabbalah.*

When I finished my story, Paul took a long gulp of wine. I don't think it was what he expected. "You know the rest, I'm sure," I said. There is a garbled version of Joshua's bar mitzvah gone mad in those Greek biographies that circulate among the Christianoi. He did preach the wisdom he had received at the summit of the tree. He preached, and no one understood him. And they said, "So this is the kind of incoherent theology the Carpenter has been teaching his son." And after, I bore Joseph sons and daughters, and he became ever more estranged from my enigmatic firstborn; and he never did say aloud the words I heard so clearly in his mind, on a mountaintop in India: he never did say *I love you.*

And my son and I spoke even less. I had seen his vision in which he slew the mother-dragon; and I think he had seen mine, seen that we shared that which cannot be spoken of; even though it was in a dream, and in a country of dreams, there are truths too deep to be spoken except in dreams.

I wanted Paul to leave me alone; I was not done mourning. Crucifixion, you know, negates man's very humanity. There is no dignity in it, though perhaps, in future generations, when it is no longer practiced, men will come to see in it some mystic quality.

"So you see," I told Paul, "there's nothing here for you; mysterious hallucinations, vivid dreams, that's all there was. And when we returned to Nazareth, there was no more magic."

"Nonsense, Miriam," he said. "Everything you've told me is wonderful. Now I feel as if I'm waking up from a transcendent vision, trying to grasp the images before they fade away ... trying to hold on."

"I don't even know if it really happened," I said.

"It'll need editing, of course," Paul said. "But you can trust me to extract the truth out of this chaos of myth and symbol. I mean, forgive me, Miriam, but you are the vessel, not the drinker; you are the platter, not the fruit. There's no dragon left in you; your son has slain the past."

My husband had feared the she-demon in me, whom he sometimes called Ashtaroth, the goddess of lust; the Christianoi would defang this devil and take away even her womanhood; that was part of what Paul meant, I think, by "editing." He would extract from my son's life a shining arc of sin and redemption; as a woman should, God's mother would sit in a corner of his church, and speak only when spoken to.

Why not? If we are to believe the ascetics in the country beyond the edge of the world, the ultimate truth is a great nothing. Joshua told my husband that he had ascended to the top of the tree, and there had found nothing. Nothing meaning *nothing,* or nothing meaning *that which is so beyond absolute that nothing can describe it?*

Now I am an old woman in a small house in Ephesus, waiting for death. From time to time I visit the Great Mother in her Temple here, one of the world's seven wonders; she is a hundred cubits tall, and I am a little woman, and very frail now; but there are days when I do have the hubris to call her "sister".

Years ago, long after my interview with the man who called himself Paul, I arrived in Ephesus and bought this small house with money that my sons and daughters had collected for me from people I did not know. I planted a fruit tree in the center of the atrium. The tree stands tall now, amid the statues of vanquished gods. One day its ten branches will be mighty enough to support my tiny frame; one day its topmost branch will stretch all the way up to the end of the sky.

That day, I think, I'll climb that tree, climb all the way to God.

Passion

I had assumed in my narcissistic, writerly fashion that publishing the story that you're about to read would cause me to be dragged out for a public stoning. The editor of this anthology, who commissioned this story, told me he wanted something 'as shocking as possible.' I wondered whether people would get past the 'Oh my God, this story depicts Jesus as a gay vampire,' moment and actually see some of the serious contemplation about how a new religion might come into being.

Once again, though, there's nothing in this story (well, maybe the vampires) that isn't part of some unchallengeably 'traditional', if unorthodox, Christology. From the boyhood visit to Cornwall much enshrined in British mythology and even in England's national hymn, Jerusalem, *to age-old speculations about Paul's relationship to Timothy ... there is really nothing new in the story. Except the spin.*

And the vampires.

Beloved Disciple

First off, I never fucked him.

I know, I know, Your Holiness, Your Eminences, Monsignor, distinguished fathers of the Roman and other churches; some of you are going to be disappointed. I've heard that there's even a church named in my honor, the Church of the Beloved Disciple, with the implication that I'm the patron saint of homosexuals, which is all very flattering, especially knowing how many of you reverend fathers suffer from certain... proclivities which you hypocritically practice even though they are forbidden in your religion.

Not that it never occurred to me. For in any other country in the Empire or beyond, it would have been perfectly natural. But this was Judaea, and Joshua barJoseph, Jesus to his Greek friends, was very, very Jewish: no pork, no graven images, and no buggery.

He was so pure that I don't think he ever even masturbated. But he had a passionate hankering for all those things that make a man immortal: philosophies, ideas, poetry. And a hankering for me, too, since I was what, at the time, he was not: I was, so to speak, the real thing.

I am immortal. I am a vampire.

He was a dreamy boy — no more than a boy when I first met him, though old enough to turn a few heads in Cornwall — for the Celts, when it comes to boys, were more Greek than the Greeks, as you would know if you read Caesar's *Gallic War* unexpurgated.

Cornwall, you protest! Jesus was never in Cornwall. Oh, but you surely know William Blake's poem:

And did those feet in ancient time
Walk upon England's mountains green?

As late as the nineteenth century there still lingered some memory of the truth: that Joseph of Arimathea, one of the most influential men in Judaea, owned shares in a Cornish tin-mine, and had become rich from the manufacture of bronze; that he once had occasion to bring young Joshua to distant Britannia, the most barbaric outpost of the Empire.

Joshua's father was another Joseph, a rabbi of the Essene sect, so learned and so diligent that they nicknamed him The Carpenter. His mother, Miriam, doted on his little brother James, and ignored him. They were, in modern parlance, dysfunctional.

I learned all these things when I was in Cornwall for the winter solstice.

The solstice was a marvelous thing. You cannot imagine what you have lost by turning your backs on the paganism you so shamelessly plundered for the trappings of your own religion. You still burn the yule log. But the Celts burned living things: virgins, children of particular purity and beauty, lambs, chickens, cattle, all imprisoned within monstrous wicker statues, so tall they dwarfed the trees, the houses, even the menhirs or votive monoliths that the Celts loved to erect in honor of Bridget, their great goddess.

This was, you understand, before the rampant Romanization of the area. I visited it less than a century later and found a health spa, a marble shopping mall and slave market, next to a temple to the God Vespasian. The Old Religion had become unfashionable. I see you're smiling, Your Holiness; the same thing seems to have happened to your own Old Religion.

But not to digress, the solstice was a wonderful time for hunting humans, and on the night of the great sacrifices I was mingling with them, sniffing the night air, redolent with the fragrance of excited blood. Bloodlust was blowing in the wind. Druids strode among the populace, and so did I, in the same white robes, a wolf in wolf's clothing.

The feet of the wicker men were already aflame. They held the lowlier life forms; the humans, lashed together inside the statue's chest and head, would have ample time to reflect on their mortality. Most seemed resigned, though a few screamed and tried to free themselves, much to the merriment of all. I moved through the throng. There was snow on the ground, but the heat from the wicker men was turning it to mush. Boars were roasting on spits, and tourists were being fleeced by cunning vendors into buying any number of sacred stones, elixirs, mistletoe love charms, and the like. Among those tourists was a small group of Judaeans; and one, apart from the others, was gazing intently at the holocaust, almost as though he were feeling the victims' suffering with them. This was the boy called Joshua barJoseph.

I could single out the peculiar scent of his blood, even in this chaos. It was a sweet blood. In today's all-too-scientific parlance, you might say that I detected a complete absence of adrenaline; his was a terrifying kind of inner calm, almost as though he were already one of us. It was this calm I found most beautiful about him. I wanted to make him kindred to me. I did not want to feed on him, and then abandon him to the worms and fishes.

I do not breathe, and so it was I was able to stand behind him, quite close to him, without his noticing. I wanted to hold off the moment of attack, to savor the fragrance of his blood, as a mortal lover longs to delay his climax till he can bear no longer.

At last I could no longer rein myself in. The sacrificial victims were on fire. Smoke billowed through the crowd. Blood, I thought to myself; blood, blood. I coiled, prepared to pounce.

"Don't," the boy said.

It suddenly occurred to me that he had known I was there all along; perhaps he had even been toying with me.

"I have a sense about these things," he said, and turned to me. Looked me over with his soulful, serious eyes. "Joshua," he said. "And you... I suppose you have many names. I'll call you John."

"All right."

"You're not a druid at all, are you?"

"What am I?"

"I'm not sure, really. I think you're sort of an angel."

"Hardly. I'm what you might call a fisher of men. You often talk to angels?"

"My whole family does. They're always at the house. An angel told my mother she was going to get pregnant with me, you know. Other people laughed when she said it was an angel; they said it was a Roman centurion named Pantera. Another angel told my father he should marry my mother anyway, but he still doesn't like me."

"You're here without them."

"Yes, I made a scene at my own bar mitzvah, got into a big argument with some learned men, so they sent me away with Uncle Joseph to cool off. Wasn't a scene, really. All I said was that the whole of the Torah could be boiled down to a single sentence — 'Do unto others what you would have them do unto you.' Rabbi Hillel says that all the time. I was just quoting him. They don't call *him* a dangerous radical."

"I'm assuming this Rabbi Hillel is a learned, venerable scholar rather than an insolent pipsqueak like yourself."

"I keep trying to go about my father's business, but I never seem to get it right."

"So they don't think you should be a rabbi."

"That's right. They want me to get into bronze, like Uncle Joseph." The Roman occupation had made Joseph of Arimathea a very rich man.

We did not talk for a while. The wicker men were fast being consumed, and the Celts were rolling around drunk and indulging in the usual debaucheries. The druids were droning an interminable paean to the sexual forces in nature, and I needed to slake my thirst. A suitable prospect ambled by at just that moment. I entranced her with a look, sipped a little from the nape of her neck even as she stared into empty space, seduced by my eyes, which seem to mortals like an yawning void. Joshua watched me, alarmed and fascinated. "You're a strange kind of angel," he said at last, as I let the woman go and she stumbled into the crowd. "You're beautiful, and that in itself is dangerous. The way your skin sucks in the moonlight. It's probably really cold, as cold as the moon."

"Yes." If only he knew how cold. I have stood in the country of the midnight sun. But what I am is a thing more desolate still. "Tell me about that sense of yours," I said. "Most people are completely clueless about what's lurking in their very midst."

"Well," Joshua said, "I just make myself go very still, and then it's like I'm outside myself."

"Samadhi," I said.

He started. "What language is that?" Almost as if he had heard it before.

"A language of India. It's something ascetics know how to do... leaving their own bodies, turning themselves into creatures of pure spirit, floating above the world. Only they have to meditate for years first."

"Oh!" he said. "You've been to India!"

"Occasionally," I said. I did not tell him how long ago.

"So have I," said the boy. And he told me all about it. I'm not sure how much there was to it. It was all so mythic: the massacre of the innocents, a flight by camel across a great desert, then forests, palaces, sages, teeming cities; and him so young through all of it, he could not possibly have remembered so much. I think he was told some of it, surmised some, imagined most of it. He had the gift that all great leaders have; he could take the wildest fancies and make them palpable.

Before long, I was telling him some of my own adventures in India. Encounters with hermits in the jungle. How I once sipped the blood of a maharani as she rode to a tryst with a secret lover on the back of an elephant. How I had sat at the feet of the Buddha and heard him tell me that the world is only a dream. He came alive as we talked. I was almost convinced he had been there.

"You see," he said, "we do have something in common."

"More that something." For he had seen the void, and he had not been afraid.

From that moment on, I wanted to make him my beloved disciple, to teach him the ways of love and death, to be his guide through the labyrinth of night. But he had other ideas. "One day," he said, "they'll hold this festival in my name. But I think I'll get rid of the human sacrificing." Even then, Your Holiness, he was suffering from what has come to be known as a messiah complex.

A bearded man, richly attired in the Hellenistic fashion, his head covering the only indication of his Judaean origins, called out to Joshua: "Let's go back now, Joshua. This place reeks of pork."

Joshua surprised me by putting his arms around me, and his lips to my lips, also in the Hellenistic fashion; I held him a little longer than was seemly, but only because I wanted to savor the pure still fragrance of his blood;

perhaps, though, he mistook my meaning, for he then said, "I'd love to, but you see, I'm Jewish; we're not allowed to."

He stepped away from me, a slender, shadowy figure that soon blended into the crowd. A hint of that strange fragrance hung in the air, for the fires had died down and the celebrants mostly passed out from too much partying. I wandered among them for a while, feeding here and there. But their lust-drenched blood was too rich, too ripe.

He's only a minnow, I told myself. I've tossed him back in the river. But I couldn't shake the suspicion that it was I who had been let go. Who was fishing whom? It depressed me so much, I went to a cave in the Himalayas and slept for thirteen years.

When next I saw him, he was in his thirties. I, of course, had not aged.

"John," he said. I hate the name John. You will note that I have contrived to omit it from that gospel. But Joshua had changed. Getting dunked in the Jordan by his cousin the mad guru had caused him to undergo what you might call a religious experience. The messiah complex was in full swing, and he'd caught a bit of the infallibility bug, too, Your Holiness. Yet he was no fool. He knew me at once. Even though night was falling, and thousands of people had gathered to hear him preach.

I had braved the twilight to come and see him, cowled and caped like Mr. Death to protect myself from the dying sun. He had been preaching all day, mostly, it seems, a rehashed rendition of Rabbi Hillel's doctrines; but there was a healthy dose of Buddhism in it too, the whole non-violent "blessed are the meek" angle, half-remembered from the stories I had told him about India.

Like a guru in Benares, he was surrounded by disciples, fetching him wine, bread and fish, sitting at his feet so that not a pearl could escape.

They stared at me, with my pallid mien, my unblinking gaze, the fact that I do not breathe except occasionally, for a touch of verisimilitude. One of them, tall and bearded and reeking of fish, was about to shoo me away, but Joshua barJoseph silenced him with a barely perceptible flick of the wrist. I smelled the strange tranquility of his blood. I knew at once that this was the memory that had drawn me back from the sleep of the dead.

"Now I'm old," he said, laughing, "and you're the callow boy. You'll have to be my beloved disciple this time round." We both laughed, but the companions didn't. I made them uncomfortable. "Peter," he said to the tall one, "don't you know an angel when you see one?"

Warily, the disciples looked me over. One of them — I could tell from the family resemblance that this must be James, the favored younger brother — said, "Is he Jewish?" They were eating, you see. It wasn't as rude as you might think; dining with goyim violates one of their innumerable *mitzvot*.

"Don't be such a brat, James," Joshua said. "Haven't you been listening? I've changed the rules."

"You're such a fucking egotist," said James. "No one minds your being the messiah — everyone and his mother's the *kwisatz haderach* these days. But you start saying 'I've changed the rules' and people are going to think you're crazy." He wouldn't eat another bite, but the others were less fastidious.

"I'm not crazy," he said slowly. "There's got to be five thousand people camped out here tonight. They need something. I'm giving it to them. There are miracles. The blind can see. Today" — he looked straight into my eyes — "you've seen the dead walk." Peter poured me a krater of wine. "He never drinks wine," Joshua said, and made me laugh again, and baffled the others even further; grumbling, they turned away from us and began debating some arcane aspect of the Torah.

"We've got to talk," said Joshua to me. He got up suddenly from the rug they'd laid out for him. He gripped my hand. The coldness of my flesh didn't make flinch. I didn't feel his blood quicken. Only the preternatural calm. He led me a little further uphill. It was sheep country here, crags protruding out of sparse vegetation; the moon was rising now, and you could see all the followers, bundled up, dotting the slopes and on down into the valley; the sheep analogy felt particularly poignant. "I've been... well... waiting for you to come back," he said.

"What for?" I said.

"You're still the same. The childlike eyes. You don't need to breathe the air. You are an angel. I know I wasn't wrong when I was a boy, in Cornwall, at that awful sacrifice."

"Maybe a dark angel."

"You have to help me, John. I'm the captain of the ship, but I don't know which way to go, and I don't recognize any of the stars."

"Rabbinical teachings are hardly my thing. You haven't tried asking your father?"

"Which one?"

"Touché," I said. Inside the head of this brilliant, radical rabbi there was still the angry little boy, uncertain of his parentage, whose mother saw angels where others saw centurions.

"I've been suckered into this whole messiah scheme," he said, "but I'm all wrong for the role. I don't understand politics. I've never led an army. I don't even believe in an independent Jewish state. Have you heard of this guy Herod Agrippa? Now he'd make a fine messiah. He's had military training... and he went to school with everyone who's anyone in Rome, so he knows the enemy... speaks Greek like a native... plus he's got royal blood. The messiah's supposed to have royal blood."

"Genealogies can always be faked."

"Yes, but—"

"So why don't you just endorse him?"

"Yes, but... well, I know it's hopeless. The Romans are the greatest nation on earth... well, the *only* nation on earth. No messiah has ever succeeded before... it's essentially a losing proposition. Unless...."

He had no intention of asking my advice at all. He was bouncing ideas off me. Well; we cast no reflection, you see. That's because we are *your* reflection. We hold up the mirror to your dark souls. Chew on that one, Your Holiness. I stood beside him, on the hilltop, overlooking the sea of sheep, showing him his true self in my vacant eyes.

"Unless," he went on, "the redemption of Israel is really a metaphor for something much bigger, something cosmic. Unless the kingdom is not even of this world. Do you follow me? Like the world you come from, the world of shadows. That's it, you see. If I build my church on reality, then I'm building it in the sand, and Rome is the infinite sea."

"What are you saying?"

"Nothing really. Except...."

"Except?"

"Can't you stay, this time? I know I can't turn back the clock to that time in Cornwall, and of course I'm just as Jewish as I was then, so I don't do abominations, but... you're the only one who understands. There's more to life than... you know, life."

Had I been human my heart would have raced, my hormones would have started to hum, because Joshua was on the verge of admitting that he loved me, even though he couldn't quite bring himself to suck my dick. He still didn't quite get it, Reverend Fathers. I was going to have to use the direct approach. You never have much time, with humans. You blink and they're dead.

"I'll stay, but you're going to have to give me something," I said.

He sighed.

"No, no, you fool," I said. "I only want a little blood."

"Wouldn't be kosher," he said. "But I guess you wouldn't care about that. Well... why not? The whole world's going to be drinking my blood soon enough."

He pulled back his right sleeve and offered me his wrist. I knelt down, worried a little scab with a fingernail, then sipped it, one drop at a time. It was something to savor. That otherworldly calm seeped into me. A memory of my mortality surfaced for a moment. My mother's milk. I had not thought of mortality in a thousand years. For a moment I almost thought my heart was beating. As I drank, he stared out over the sleeping congregation. His eyes shone in the moonlight. Some humans become aroused when I feed on them, and cry out as in orgasm; he only made himself go far away.

Finally, faintly, I heard him say, half to himself, "They crucify you through the wrist; did you know that? A lot of people think it's through the palms, but that would just rip right through."

And that, Your Holiness, Your Eminences, Reverend Fathers of the Church, was the extent of the Beloved Disciples's carnal knowledge of the Son of Man.

It took some time for Joshua's followers to get used to the idea that I was there to stay. Judaea was a pretty tense place, a messiah under every rock, political activists railing in every street corner, and the Romans sitting around crucifying people almost at random. I wasn't a spy, and I wasn't one of the peasants, and I was surely no theologian. But it was necessary, for various numerological and historical reasons, to have twelve apostles, and Joshua always got his own way.

I was there for it all: the miracles, such as they were, though you people have become a lot slicker at these things; the triumphal entry into Jerusalem, carefully stage managed so as to function as an elegant *midrash* on selected passages of the Tanakh; I was there for the passover shabbat, wherein Joshua made no mention of his body and blood, such pagan concepts being quite distasteful to him; and I was there for the awful climax and its bathetic denouement.

After they dragged him away, the apostles called an emergency meeting at Joseph of Arimathea's house. Joshua's parents were conspicuously absent, as usual; but there was another Miriam, an ex-prostitute, who was Joshua's first and most devoted groupie and could not be kept away. Joseph — a liberal — didn't mind having harlots in the house, though he did draw the line at publicans.

"It can't end this way," James said. It was as if, having been the family's darling all his life, he couldn't stand the thought of being permanently one-upped by Joshua's martyrdom.

"So what do you suggest?" said Peter. "We can't very well storm the dungeons; we'll all end up getting strung up." He stared shiftily about; on his way to the meeting he had denied knowing Joshua three times. The fetor of his fear permeated the chamber. They were all stinking drunk, except for me.

I sat in the shadows, thinking of other things. Between mortals and immortals, love always ends in an unending longing. I wished we could have gone to India together. Or even to the world on the other side of the ocean, which I had heard about from a sage whose skin was the color of wine. I relived our first meeting again and again. Their lives rush by so fast, I thought. Larva to chrysalis to butterfly to putrefaction.

It was Joseph of Arimathea who said, "But it's so simple. Let John bring him back from the dead."

They all looked at me, looked away, drank deeply; I said, "It's a gift that can't be taken back. And he has never asked me to make him immortal."

"We need him," Peter said. "You can see that. We're like a chicken with its head cut off. If he comes back, everyone will see that the God of Abraham, Isaac and Jacob is more powerful than idols of stone and brass."

"When's the execution?" I said.

"Friday," said Joseph of Arimathea, who, being a man of influence, had a tendency to know these things. "The Romans'll give him a fair trial, but there's really no way they can let off someone who's being openly called King of the Jews."

"But his kingdom's not of this world!" said Thomas, who never believed anything he was told.

"The Romans," I said, "are completely literal-minded. That's why they own everything."

"It's politics as usual," said Joseph, "and Pilate has to protect his own ass back home. Can't blame him, really." But he was on the verge of tears. I've often wondered whether it was not he, rather than the legendary Pantera, who stuck it to the rabbi's fiancée; for he loved Joshua far more than the other Joseph ever did.

It was Joseph who convinced me, not the squabbling, self-righteous rabble who called themselves his apostles. No, I take that back, Your Holiness. It was I myself who convinced me. Perhaps it was selfishness. But you, Reverend Fathers, have never faced eternity. You just wouldn't understand.

Oh, but you preach eternity from your pulpits. Eternal bliss, eternal damnation. Fleecy clouds and fiery brimstone. You don't know what the fuck you're talking about. After the first few hundred years, every color becomes gray. Every song is a single note. Every mortal is another scurrying piece of vermin, and all that is left is the ache that can never be slaked, and the loss than festers forever. You are fools to say forever so lightly. A long long time, my friends, is not forever.

"I'll do it," I said softly. "But somehow, we have to get him to drink my blood."

"Is it kosher?" said James. No one so much as looked at him for the rest of the evening.

Humans can never get used to crucifixions, but for me an almost clinical detachment was possible. In their own way, the Romans bent over backward to accommodate the practices of their wayward subjects. Usually it takes days for the victim to die, but the Judaeans had a religious taboo against leaving corpses hanging after sunset (or was it only on Saturdays?) so they had compromised by using novel techniques for speeding up death: the flogging and the nails were, grotesquely enough, designed to shorten the agony. That was Roman knowhow for you.

The "display" crosses you see in religious paintings were not a common feature of these operations. Actually, criminals were strung up only slightly above eye level; you could look right into their faces, even spit in their eye; and people did. Public executions bring out the worst in mortals. You all know that Joshua barJoseph was crucified between two thieves, but actually the whole hillside was crammed with crosses; under Roman law, virtually everything was a capital offense.

It was afternoon, and so I almost didn't make it there. But about three or four o'clock it became preternaturally dark; a nightingale began to sing outside the room at Joseph of Arimathea's mansion where I was lying. I came to suddenly, bewildered because my sleep seemed so short. There was no one in the house. I made my way to the crucifixion hill.

In the tribal north, there had been at least a sense of elation and celebration about the wicker men. Here there was nothing of the kind. Here only beggars and lepers lurked about, and a few idle curious; the Roman soldiers, jaded, went about their business, nailing them down and stringing them up. Unrecycled crossbeams lay on the dirt; the smell of stale blood clung to them, mingled with the scent of fresh-gushing blood which permeated the hot, dry air.

I made my way through the forest of the dying, and at length spied Miriam — the whore, not the mother — standing almost at the summit of the hill, where three recent crosses formed a sort of triptych of suffering. The smell of Joshua's blood was faint, but it still held that eerie calm. I went up to Miriam, told her we had to go through with the plan.

She said, "Wait. His mother's here."

Then it was I saw another woman, one who had remained conspicuously absent throughout Joshua's ministry. She looked up at her son now, and I do not think she wept.

And I too looked, and did not weep, but for another reason; I cannot.

It was going to have to be done soon. And still I was unsure, because, Reverend Sirs, it takes more than an invitation for a man to enter my eternal kingdom — not a sprinkle of water over a baby — not a few murmured phrases. To borrow a cliché of your modern pop psychology, Joshua had to want to change. I was almost sure I had seen that longing in him, at our very first meeting... but might it have been something else?

I watched for a sign. His agony beggared description, but then all agony does, in the end, doesn't it? They had crowned him with thorns. Blood caked his forehead. There were flies. Vultures, too. The *causa poenae*, tacked to the cross, read "*Rex Iudaeorum.*" He gazed back at me, his eyes already beginning to dull. In his mother's eyes I saw... disappointment, perhaps. She looked at Miriam the prostitute and for a moment I thought she was going to claw her eyes out. Then she saw me.

I do not look Jewish. I am clean-shaven as I was in life, which the Judaeans considered a sign of Hellenistic effeminacy. I have a certain clarity of complexion, a glow;

all vampires do. That is why the ugliest of mortals becomes beautiful once he has heeded the call of night. I could tell that she did not admire my otherworldly looks; rather, she instantly assumed the worst — that I must be the masculine counterpart of Miriam the whore. She looked at me, and her dying son, and I could just imagine her thinking maybe I was the reason her Joshua could never settle down and have kids.

Then Joshua gasped, "Mother, he's your son now. John, kiss your new mother." She gaped at the outrageous insinuation. I wanted to tell her it wasn't what she thought it was, but I daresay it would have made even less sense to her. Just like human beings, to stoop to a bit of domestic bickering at a moment like this.

I was surprised that he could still speak. The process of crucifixion is actually one of asphyxiation, of the body slowly sagging and collapsing the lungs. The power of speech soon goes.

"I'm thirsty," he said.

A small detail was marching uphill, pausing in front of each cross to smash the criminal's legs. Without the anchor of nailed-down bone, the body caves in on itself and squeezes the life right out of itself. Another practical Roman solution to the Jewish taboo about corpses being strung up past nightfall. No time to lose. I found a sentry, nodding off against a boulder. I shook him. "Let me give him something to drink," I said. I dropped a silver denarius in his helmet. He grunted, let me borrow his javelin for a moment; I pierced my left wrist with a fingernail and squeezed out enough blood to wet a sponge, held it up to his lips; blood trickled onto his tongue, which was already beginning to protrude.

When he tasted blood, something about him changed. Was it the touch of the first breath of eternity? Softly, he said, "It's done." But what was done? Surely not his crazed master plan for establishing the perfect Jewish society,

God's kingdom on earth? Or was it an acceptance of his vampiric destiny? Only the night would tell.

He closed his eyes. The darkness gathered. But I left swiftly, for these unnatural darknesses have a way of lifting, and I did not want to be stranded in sunlight even on the short distance from the execution site to the tomb that Joseph of Arimathea had prepared — a luxurious tomb, for he had intended it for himself.

Once inside the tomb, I waited awhile; in time, my circadian rhythms, interrupted by the unnatural darkness of the afternoon, forced me back into slumber. I slept more than twenty-four hours; when I go out by day, even in darkness, my body needs a little longer to repair itself.

When I awoke, he was hunched on the lid of the stone sarcophagus, tearing the bloody linen off himself. "I'll get that," I said. I ripped away more pieces of his shroud. His wrists were regenerating nicely, but there was a deep puncture in each one, wide enough to stick a finger through.

"What did you do to me?" he said. "What have you made me?"

I said, "They begged me, your apostles. And I've seen it in your face. You want this. You've looked eternity in the eye before, Joshua, and it didn't scare you."

He didn't answer. He was staring at his hands. They were white as the limestone sepulcher itself. Yes, I knew he was no longer mortal. There was no source of light in the tomb, and yet he saw with the eyes of night; and for those who see as we see he himself was light, cold, phosphorescent, pale.

"This isn't what I had in mind, John," he said.

"Don't call me John anymore," I said, and instead cried out my own true name in the language of night, which only the dead can speak. In that instant he knew his true name, too, which cannot be spoken here.

I sensed his confusion, sensed also the incipient pangs of the great hunger; and slitting my wrist once more with my fingernail I gave him sustenance, becoming mother to him as well as midwife. He did not complain that the blood violated his dietary taboos; he knew already that to cross into our world is also to abandon the very concept of god. "I was hoping to be resurrected," he said. "But at the last minute I despaired; I tried to pray but all I could hear were the words of the psalmist about having been forsaken by god; that's true, isn't it? Instead of god, you came."

"And once you called me an angel."

"You still are. *Angelos*: messenger. But who sent you? That's what I can't figure out. Is this how we're going to defeat the Romans... by turning Judaea into a kingdom of the undead?"

"Just the sort of harebrained grand scheme you'd come up with. Get the long view, Joshua. You already have defeated the Romans. Do you know how old I am? I was old when the citadel of the Hittites was plundered and razed. Where are the Hittites now? A few scratches of cuneiform in other people's history books. Where are the Trojans now? The Minoans, the people of Thera, the Carthaginians? I've already defeated them, because I'm still here, remembering the taste of their blood, and they are dust. If you ask me a question, and I pause till the fall of Rome before I answer you, it is only a blink. The mortals cannot see the grand spectacle of their own lives; they cannot be as passionate as we, nor as pitiless. Don't you feel the thrill of it?"

"If you say so," he said.

But perhaps he didn't. I recalled the odor of his blood. The tranquillity that had so intoxicated me... it had survived the transformation. Why had I been lecturing him about the sweep of history? He had felt all of that without even having experienced it, even as a mere mortal. It occurred to me that perhaps it was not my blood that had brought him back from the dead. Maybe he was some kind of natural vampire, self-creating, self-sufficient. I had never encountered anything like that, but if you think about it, there's got to have been at least one vampire to start the whole cycle off..

This was a disturbing line of thought. So I said, "Well, Joshua, if not for the sweep of history, then at least knowledge. We've spoken of India, but there are other lands too... Cathay... there are some of us who have found a whole new continent to the west... there are more worlds to conquer than your Roman Empire."

"And we shall conquer them, my friend," he said. He had freed himself from his winding-sheet now. He embraced me, and said, "We'll find new worlds and fresh philosophies."

"You mean it?" I said.

"You know that I can't lie," he said. Such is the loneliness of eternity that I welcomed what he said without considering its ambiguity.

Your Holiness and others... I see that you are becoming heartily troubled by my narration. But it gets worse.

You all know the story of the empty tomb. We met up with the rest of the apostles at Joseph's, and a couple of other times. They all thanked me — somewhat perfunctorily, to be sure — for bringing Joshua back from the dead. Miriam and Joseph (the rabbi, not the tin tradesman) and the rest of that mixed-up brood went through a transformation of their own. Having shat on their wayward eldest all his life, they resolved to put him on a pedestal; the fat, spoiled little brother led the campaign to make Joshua's proto-Marxist precepts into the biggest new sect of Judaism.

A book of those down-home little parables and precepts was circulated underground — much like Chairman Mao's little red book — it's the "lost" book that biblical scholars —

which many of you, reverend fathers, are not — call "Q". I know, it was a cheap trick, using xeroxed pages of my personal copy of "Q" to cause this, ah, ecumenical support group to be convened, and, yes, I will present you all with the entire manuscript after I've had my say — but how else was I going to get your reverend asses all in one room and to believe in the authenticity of my tale?

In any case, you'll find that the scholars were quite correct: virtually all of "Q" is quoted at length in the four canonical gospels. You won't find anything new in it. The scoop, Reverend Fathers (oh, I do apologize, Sister, I didn't notice you amongst all the male chauvinists) is in what I'm telling you. I know you're all spazzing already, but please hold your sphincters for just five more minutes.

Something really, really weird happened next: Christianity.

Joshua and I were gone for, oh, twenty years or so. It was wild and glorious... the vampiric equivalent of a honeymoon. Yes, we went to India. We fed on pilgrims as they stripped to bathe in the Ganges. I did most of the hunting. Joshua saw the necessity of it, but was still queasy; he was still adjusting. We rode through jungles, were received by maharajahs, drank the blood of virgins, were venerated as gods in some cities, reviled as demons in others. Yes, we did set sail to what you now call America, so you Mormon elders may consider Mr. Joseph Smith's febrile imaginings, at least in part, vindicated. Joshua did not preach. Instead, he listened. He was like an empty vessel into which men poured what was best and worst in themselves. And I admired him for that, because in transcending mortality he had not lost compassion, which is usually the first thing to go. He grew in compassion, in fact. I had not known that was possible.

In time, we came back to the Levant, and it was in Ephesos, a town most famed for its huge gold statue of the Great Mother, that we first encountered Jesus Christ.

It was, in fact, in front of the famous statue (in Ephesos they call the mother-goddess Diana) that we first heard the name being bandied about. It was night and they were sacrificing — strange how that motif crops up again — and we were hunting. The place was a spectacle, all towering columns and clouds of incense and everything gold and ivory and the statue itself tall as a ten-story building. No babies being sacrificed here, though; we were well inside the civilizing boundaries of Rome. In the shadow of a fluted column, voices were whispering about Nazareth.

Joshua pricked up his ears. "They haven't forgotten me," he said, and smiled.

Good news. Baptism. The Kingdom of Heaven... the redemption of mankind... the resurrection... it sounded hauntingly familiar. There was a meeting later that night, we overheard. In a back room of a local synagogue.

The crowd was an odd one. I had never seen so many goyim in a synagogue, and they didn't cover their heads. There were women, too, sitting right alongside the men. A lot of riff-raff — slaves, the homeless, prostitutes — Joshua liked that. He had always gone down well with the proles, with that stuff about the first shall be last and blessed are the poor and camels going through needles' eyes and all that. One or two rich people, too. We blended right in; no one so much as stared at us.

The thing was as brilliantly stage-managed as a contemporary revival meeting. There were warm-up speakers, who gave testimonials about the efficacy of using the ineffable name of Jesus as a kind of mantra; Joshua chuckled a little at this, but as the meeting went on he became more and more solemn.

The keynote speaker was a man named Paul. Bit of a flamer, a Liberace type... a real-live Roman citizen, as he never tired of pointing out. The tale he told was an amazing one, a sort of throw-it-in-the-blender mélange of every popular cult in the Roman Empire. Jesus was the son of God (like Hercules) and that bitter yenta of a mother was transformed into an eternal virgin, much like the Great Mother herself who was worshipped at the Temple of Diana down the street. Like Adonis, Jesus had died at the beginning of the spring fertility rites and been resurrected on the third day. Like Odin, he had been strung up on a great tree. Adam's dismissal from Eden was no longer what everyone had always thought it was, a profound, poetic metaphor for the human condition, but a temporary inconvenience to which Jesus would soon put an end, especially since he was coming back any moment now to snatch up the faithful and punish the sinful. The whole of the Tanakh was just Part One. All this was gospel truth because Paul, formerly Saul, had once persecuted Christians ... and Jesus had come to him in a vision and set him straight.

Mixed in with all this fantasmagorical mythology were many of the homely parables and radical sociological viewpoints that Joshua had actually preached. It was very inspirational, very feverish, very much like a rock concert. Women were weeping and fainting and having orgasms; men were having attacks of glossolalia; cripples were tottering around and blind men claiming they could see while banging their heads on pillars.

As Paul's rhetoric climaxed with an appeal not to resist persecution — to welcome martyrdom as it would mean instant acceptance into the bosom of Jesus. Crucifixion, flaying, burning, being devoured by lions, all were but painful preludes to paradise.

It got better. Next came a magic ritual — a pagan parody of that sad last passover meal we had all had together, the night they came to take him away. They broke bread, and after a few incantations pronounced that it was Joshua's body; a flagon of wine became his blood. Such irony! It made me relive once more the moment I had first savored that blood, so innocent of inner turmoil. Eating the sacred body of the god-king was a custom as old as the Stone Age, but Paul had managed to trivialize even that most ancient and potent of metaphors. Fucking Roman citizen indeed. He certainly had their literal-mindedness.

"I can't take much more of this," I said, and we fought our way through the throng as someone bore down on us with a collection plate.

But suddenly Joshua stopped me. "We have to talk to him," he said. "This is insanity. We have to stop it."

"They're only humans," I said. "This will all blow over."

"But it's my name they're using," he said. "It's my name they're dying for."

"Your human name," I said scornfully.

"Yes," he said.

You know, we don't change all that much when we cross over to the darkness. Alive, Joshua had attracted me because he grasped eternity so completely; now that he was dead, I saw that his comprehension of mortality far surpassed my own. He had not been comfortable in their world, and now he had still not found his home.

I had to humor him. It was not in my power to douse this spark of difference in him; it was what I loved most about him.

Easy enough for us to blend into the shadows, to drift along the dusty columns until we found a back room, where a young man stood flexing in front of a polished shield. We stood behind this youth, too absorbed in his narcissistic endeavors to look over his shoulder — we cast no reflection in the shield, of course — and waited.

Presently we could hear a hymn being sung, fervently and discordantly, by the crowd outside, and Paul came storming into the room. We stepped back into gloom. Paul and the young man kissed passionately. "A strong showing tonight, Timothy," Paul said. "I think we've collected enough to hit the big time."

"You think we'll actually get to play Rome?" said the boy. The adoring gaze he had for the old man turned sour when Paul looked away, and I recognized the sullen mien of the street hustler. Definitely rough trade.

"Rome? Honey, we're going to *own* Rome!" said Paul.

Many theologians and sociologists have argued that St. Paul was a closet homosexual who imposed his misogyny on the misguided Christian masses; but let me tell you, Your Holiness — in spite of your recent encyclical — that civilized people in the first century were far too sophisticated to be hung up on such minutiae as sexual preference. Later. of course, when St. Augustine decided that sex was *dirty*...

We interrupted before the scene could become x-rated, materializing out of the shadows. "Paul!" Joshua said. "Do you know who I am?"

"No," he said, mystified. Timothy shrugged and went back to flexing.

Joshua held up his pierced wrists. You could see the smoky flicker of the wall torch through the holes.

"You're not," said Paul.

"I am," said Joshua barJoseph.

I stayed out of it. It was Joshua's fight. I lurked in the background. Outside, the hymn singing crescendoed to a cacophonous climax.

"Why are you doing this to me?" Joshua said softly.

"James and the others... they said you'd risen from the dead, said they'd seen it with my own eyes... thought it was the greatest new gimmick... but it's true, then. Dear me, who would have thought it?"

Joshua said, "I'm not Dionysus. God didn't come down from heaven to screw my mother. I'm not Osiris, come back from the dead to guide mortals beyond the grave. I'm not the Corn God, ripped in pieces to fertilize the earth and then reborn as king. I'm just a rabbi who hung out with hookers. I wanted my friends to become better Jews, to understand what the Torah's really trying to say instead of hiding behind their petty regulations."

"What good are the Jews? They crucified you."

"No, they didn't. The Romans did."

"They made them do it."

"You don't make the Romans do things. I broke a Roman law. I would not render unto Caesar something which belonged to Caesar — sovereignty. I wasn't talking about political sovereignty, but you know how literal-minded the Romans are. Why would the Jews have had me killed? For claiming to be the messiah? There's a new messiah every week, and they don't get crucified."

I had to speak up. "He has to blame it on the Jews," I said. "He's preaching to the Romans. Roman complicity in your death would be a real no-no. What do the *goyim* know about the workings of the Sanhedrin? As far as they're concerned, a bunch of swarthy, middle-eastern religious fanatics is capable of any depravity... even Deicide. Have to bend the truth a bit here and there, don't you, Paul?"

"The truth! And what, as Pontius Pilate said to you, Jesus, on the morning of your crucifixion, is truth?"

"He didn't say that," said Joshua. "He didn't even talk to me. He had a dozen other death warrants to sign that morning, and he didn't want to miss lunch."

Paul was fuming. "You're just like your brother James," he said. "I've built this majestic structure of powerful, rich images that trigger the imagination, that make men's spirits soar. I'm giving hope to the downtrodden and picking up a few denarii along the way. So what if it's a house of cards? So what if it didn't really happen that way? I've found the core of mythic truth in your tawdry little bio, and I'm going to make you the biggest thing since the invention of the wheel, you ungrateful insect. This new religion is going to take over the world. It's got everything. Tragedy and pathos, terror of judgment, the catharsis of forgiveness. It's the grandest religion yet invented."

"But I don't want a new religion," said Joshua barJoseph. "I'm Jewish."

After a while, Paul seemed to calm down a little. "I'll need to regroup a little," he said. "Maybe I can still salvage some of this."

While he guzzled wine, we told him some of our own adventures. We got drunk together... he and Timothy on a couple of kegs of Samian wine, Joshua and I from a pint of Timothy's blood which he obligingly let me draw... after I told him I could do it painlessly.

Paul became so drunk he even stopped speaking Greek. In tearful Aramaic, he told us searing childhood tales about his father whipping him for sucking off the stablehands. No wonder he preferred being Roman to being Jewish! No wonder he wanted to bring the gospel to the goyim!

That was what it all boiled down to after all. He wanted to be accepted, to be loved for what he was, this poor little sissy boy who had the misfortune to be born into the one culture where they stoned sissies. One could almost sympathize. After a while, indeed, one did. "Forgive me," Paul was weeping into his goblet.

"I forgive you," said Joshua.

"Thank you... thank you, abba," said Paul. I realized then that he wanted his real father to forgive him... that the source of the angst that drove him was his fear of having disappointed his earthly father... he had created in his mind a surrogate father, all-merciful, all-forgiving, to succor his own self-loathing. And Joshua understood all this... truly understood it... and felt compassion for this lonely little man... a compassion as deep as any love he felt for me.

I envied the world, because not even death had sundered Joshua from his love for it.

Paul invited us back to his home. "I want to hear more stories," he said. "I want to learn everything you can teach me. After all, you are my redeemer. You ought to have a hand in the religion, especially since it's all about you."

Very softly, Joshua said to me, "He just doesn't hear me."

But we went home with him anyway, and as dawn approached we bedded down for the day in a cosy wine-cellar.

Night fell and I rose from my dreamless sleep. I found my beloved disciple lying on the dirt floor, unmoving, in a pool of still, cold blood, with a stake through his heart.

Paul and Timothy had gone on to Rome.

And I too fled, for the inchoate feelings that raged through me were too much like my memories of pain.

He must have known. He had a sense about such things. He must have realized that Paul could not long abide the shattering of his great glass cathedral with the hammer of blunt reality.

He loved the world. He loved beautiful things, cities, trees, animals, and even more so, people. It must have pained him more than I can imagine, to choose to leave the world behind. Why, then? Was it that he could not face the prospect of his name being taken in vain by thousands, thousands who would become millions, billions? Did he sense that his homespun stories about shepherds and widow's mites and mustard seeds would become the official religion of the Roman empire, that that religion would plunge the western world into a Dark Age for a thousand years, that it would spawn senseless massacres, enslavements of entire peoples, wanton destructions of countless noble, ancient, beautiful cultures?

I don't know.

Your Holiness, Reverend Fathers, Your Eminence, and... yes, Reverend Sister... this is what I know.

He was good. I have never known anyone before or since who has truly deserved that adjective. He was brilliant. He loved, deeply and with complete commitment.

He possessed an absolute empathy even for the dispossessed. These qualities were in his very blood.

The blood of mortals is spiced with the hormones of desire and fear, but his was not. It was to other blood as a sparkling mountain stream is to the murky effluvium of a city faucet. It was the Platonic absolute of blood. It was pure. It was the holy grail of bloods, the true taste of which all other tastes are but an echo.

We are much alike, you who have hocus-pocused a million gallons of cheap wine and call it redemption, and I who have savored your savior's actual blood. We cannot believe he is gone forever. Love such as ours, we desperately think, can not stay unrequited for ever. The Absolute is by its very nature Eternal.

We live — you for a few heartbeats, I for all time — in the hope (the fear, too) that he will come again. He *must* come again.

The river of time is long. I know. Trust me. One day he will. Suddenly. Without warning.

Like a vampire in the night.

Acts

I love Romans.
I love hardboiled detectives.
I love zombies.

I think that people have written stories containing two *of the above, but never all three.*

I wanted to show how persecuting a religious minority could, under certain circumstances, be viewed in the context of its time as simply one of many elements in a thriving entertainment industry.

So in a way, this story is as much about Hollywood as anything else. I was living there when I wrote it....

Hunting the Lion

I have never liked eunuchs. I must confess a certain queasiness in their presence; in this I fear I am behind the times, and possessed of a kind of naïveté most unsuitable for one who practices the craft of the private detective in this modern world, this Ninth Century since the founding of the greatest nation on earth.

It was nevertheless a eunuch who was ushered into my triclinium at the hour of cena. I was drinking a goblet of undiluted Falernian and attempting to disentangle a dish of calves' brains sautéed in egg and honey, all the while dictating a letter to the steward of my Sicilian estates. I did not take kindly to being interrupted, but the creature whose presence now graced my dining room was not the kind of person one could ignore if one had any regard for one's political prospects.

He had the singularly inappropriate name of Eros. He wore a gold-fringed tunic dipped in purple (making up in ostentation for what he lacked in virility) and, when I showed him the couch, waddled towards it like an animated blood pudding.

"Rejoice," he said in his clipped demotic Greek, "O Publius Viridianus! I trust I find you in good health? Ah, but I see you are at dinner; perhaps I should come back at a more convenient hour."

"No hour could be more convenient," I said with practiced insincerity. I made to proffer the Falernian, then changed my mind and called for an amphora of Lesbian wine. Eros hemmed and hawed until I dismissed the scribe and whisked aside the arras to show that there were no spies. Even then he stared about like a caged beast. At last I said, "Come, come; I know you didn't come here to admire the murals. You just had your own house in Baiae done by the same artist, though I understand the mythological scenes you selected weren't quite as tame as the ones here —the rape of Ganymede, was it not?"

"How did you know?—but of course, such is your business—I imagine you've a thick dossier on me by now."

"You flatter me," I said. Not to mention yourself, I thought. "I am not nearly as omniscient as is rumored. Nevertheless, it delights me that I am deemed capable of providing service to no less a figure than the—third?—undersecretary of the—privy purse, is it?—division of Caesar's household."

"You will be well paid," Eros said. Wine dribbled from his lips. He took another swallow. There is nothing more unnerving than a fidgety eunuch. "That is, if you—ah—accept the commission." He emptied a purse full of gold aurei onto the dining-table. One of them skittered into the brain omelette. "An advance, perhaps." I did not look at the money, though I wondered where such a supply of gold could have come from, what with the recent debasement of the coinage. I did not imagine than many of the coins would bear the image of Nero Claudius Drusus Germanicus, our current God of State.

"You haven't told me what the commission is."

"Haven't I?" He looked around again.

"My good man," I said, "I think you can see from my surroundings that I do not lack money; why, the very idea of your offering me so much seems not a little vulgar—I no longer make my living by spying on the mistresses of the nobility, tracking down changeling heiresses switched at birth by inattentive nursemaids, children running away to join the foreign legionaries, and the like. Now and then, as a favor, I might essay a little investigation, but...."

"Name your price, Viridian! I've no time to haggle...."

I smiled. "There will be a price. I take it we are not speaking of some petty patrician whom it would be politically expedient to embarrass. You want me to hunt... nobler game. The lion rather than the jackal."

"Q. Drusianus Otho, to be precise," said the eunuch, his voice dropping to a whisper. "Now that I've revealed this, I may as well tell you that, should you refuse the assignment, I have been given authorization to order you to commit suicide."

Probably a bluff, I thought, shrugging. And even were it not, it would not do to appear overly concerned. After all, I am a real Roman and not some freedman's son...at least, not since I bribed a palace scribe 2,000 denarii to "purify" my birth papers. Pity I had to kill him afterwards, but one can't be too careful nowadays.

He immediately began to imbibe the Lesbian and, though I had not asked him to share my cena, to attack my homely brain-and-honey omelette with gusto. I let him eat while I pondered my prospective target.

This Drusianus was an influential man. He was related by adoption to the Imperial family and also, by the marriage of his cousin to the Lady Octavia, to the Emperor's discarded ex-wife and through her to the Julian Divinity himself—thus he could claim, which more justification than many would require, to be descended from the goddess

Venus on both sides. He was extremely rich—had served as editor of the games on a number of occasions, and owned both a gladiatorial school and a menagerie most noted for its abundance of lions—but had kept his nose remarkably clear of politics, apart from serving as consul once or twice. He didn't indulge in loose women or little boys—at least no more than was politically correct under our artsy-fartsy régime—and his home life was a model of uxoriousness and probity. A lion indeed, I thought. No wonder they want to bring him down.

"Why?" I asked at last, after giving Eros a chance to sit around quivering for a few moments. "He seems harmless enough. Why, he wasn't even part of the Pisonian conspiracy."

The eunuch pulled a little scroll from his tunic and handed it to me. It contained a poem that purported to be by Petronius, although I could tell by its stylistic infelicities that it was some second-rate imitator. The poem extolled the virtues of this Drusianus while castigating the Emperor's excesses; clever little thing actually, in a mindless sort of why—the sort of ditty one might compose while squatting in the communal shit-house at the public baths.

"If you don't mind my saying so," I said, "this hardly seems something to get all flustered about. The man obviously had nothing to do with this poem; what's more, it's abysmal. I can dig up dirt for you—you know my reputation for finding merda in unlikely places—and undoubtedly I will be able to discover something, however picayune, to bring about the downfall of this member of the Noble Order of Equites. But why bother? You know how expensive my services are; it is well known that I have many scruples, and that I charge by the scruple. How many scruples will I have to overcome to finger the most honorable man in Rome? More than this," I said, clapping my hands for someone to come and gather up the gold pieces scattered all over my triclinium table.

"But Cæsar is annoyed," said Eros. "And you know what he's like when he's annoyed."

And that, of course, was that.

I spent the evening scouring through my files on Drusianus. I knew him only by reputation—we did not go to the same sort of parties—and his reputation was amply backed up by my researches. His wife Volumnia had been one of the Christianoi for a while, but after being interrogated by the secret police had done the sensible thing and turned in all her contacts; I doubted it was anything more than an indulgence in the cult-of-the-month fever that infects our city in the summer heat.

I had a lot more information about Eros. Castrated though he was, he had slept with everybody who was anybody in Rome. He was a Syrian of some sort, born a slave into the household of one Polycrates, owner of a chain of brothels that promised uniform prices and service from Gaul to Gaza; as a boy had first attracted the attention of the Lady Claudia Procula, wife of Pontius Pilate, procurator of Judæa, by his acrobatic skill with his tongue; brought back to Rome; several bills of sale later, earned his freedom and ended up buying out his former master Polycrates, whereupon he lost his entire fortune in a venereal disease scandal, and ended up working for the imperial house under an assumed name....

Exciting reading, almost as good as an evening at Petronius's house.

Drusianus was editor of the current spectacle season. Opening day was tomorrow, the Kalends of August... auguries pointed to a steamy, hellish day. With the Great Fire and its subsequent Grand Spectacle only two years past, the games were bound to be lavish, but I did not doubt that Drusianus had paid for them out of pocket, without a qualm; he was not the sort of person who ever needed to ask the price of anything.

Perhaps the Lady Volumnia would be a likelier target; she had fallen prey to the treacherous Christianoi once; perhaps she was still tainted by the bloody Oriental rites they were known to practise.

It was time to don the first disguise of the evening.

I spent a few minutes propitiating the household gods by the hall entrance, lighting incense and wringing the neck of a small dove in expiation for the impieties I was about to commit. I took a last look in a bronze hand-mirror and had to admit that my handiwork was impeccable. I had built up my nose with a liberal application of clay, applied a false beard, put on a white robe and wrapped around my head a prayer-shawl such as the Judæans use.

Of course, it would not do to be seen after dark in this costume, here in the old-money south side of the Palatine, so I called for my litter, drew the curtains tight shut as though I was cloistered Greek matron slipping off to a night-time tryst, and proceeded downhill toward the seamy side of town. The bearers moved at a brisk trot and I was pleased not to have to quirt them. I avoided the great squares and took only back streets.

It was a quiet night—many had gone to bed early, doubtless anticipating the early morning commencement of the games—but now and then a link-boy ran down a passageway waving his torch to light the way for some drunken reveller, and once I spied, through the peephole I had made in the curtain, a group of centurions gang-raping a slave-woman against a bakery storefront. A lone graffiti artist scrawled "Arrius is a nefarious retiarius" along a wall while his friend pissed noisily alongside.

At length we reached a taberna by the Judæan quarter on the other side of the Tiber, and I abandoned my litterbearers there with a bag of copper and the admonishment that they were not to get too drunk or they would feel the lash on my return. The litter was parked in one alley, and from another alley I emerged in my Judæan garb, shawl about my head, mumbling to myself in what I hoped was a passable imitation of the Aramaic tongue.

The night life was in full swing. The tabernae were open; whores in whiteface walked the streets, as did young children with their tunicae hitched up above their buttocks; the smell of bread being baked for the morning rush mingled with the odor of animal blood running into the street from a slaughterhouse that practised ritual killing in the Judæan fashion. There was an all-night bank across the street—for the Judæans engage in moneylending at all hours of the day or night—and I went there to deposit my bag of aurei, for the Judæans are the only people in Rome with whom I would trust my money, and I have accounts under different names in Jewish banks from Rome to Alexandria, all earning a hefty rate of interest.

"Rejoice, Ioannes!" The voice was a resonant bass. Quickly, I allowed myself to flow into my persona: Ioannes of Damascus, physician, philanthropist, thrower of good parties—thoroughly Hellenized on the surface, thoroughly subversive at heart.

I was not surprised to find the banker, an Alexandrian by the name of Chrysolithos (he found his true name, David ben David, too ethnic for his social aspirations) still up, doing his accounts by lamplight; he was only too happy to take my money, and smiled as he counted it out.

"It must be a good life," he said, "this specializing in the diseases of the rich."

"The rich have many slaves," I said, affecting an expression of wounded piety, "and those who have nothing are most likely to need riches in heaven."

Chrysolithos cackled. "Converting the heathen is all very well," he said, "but I'm glad you're lining your pockets too...it's the Roman way, after all...."

"Roma terra opportunitatis," I said.

I pocketed the receipt and, looking furtively from left to right, made the sign of the fish in the air.

Chrysolithos immediately became defensive. "Look, you're not going to go on and on about *that* business again, are you? Ever since the secret police cleaned up the catacombs for spectacle-fodder two months ago, you won't find much—"

"I'm looking for the Lady Volumnia Drusiana," I whispered. "She's in terrible danger! Her husband has angered Cæsar—*anything* could bring about his political downfall—especially her involvement with *us*—"

"Don't say 'us', Ioannes, please! Oh, I know my wife talked me into this new age nonsense for a while, but—"

"By Jupit—I mean, by the blessed Paraclete!" I said. "Do you mean to deny your savior, as did Simon Cephas the fisherman? Reprobate! Do you still cling to earthly things when you should be thinking of the life to come?" I rather enjoyed giving that speech; I must admit that I was really getting into the role.

It was at that moment that the Lady Volumnia walked into the room.

I gasped, for she was every bit as sensuous as I last remembered her—her features delicate, her nose aquiline, her dark hair luxuriously bunned, her gazelle-eyes imbued with fragility and a certain coldness. Though she was past forty, her breasts had not succumbed to time, and the robe she wore was designed to reveal more than it concealed.

She looked at me guiltily—it was, of course, because she thought I was this Ioannes fellow, an elder of the banned cult to which she had once subscribed.

"Daughter Volumnia!—but what are you doing here?—at this hour, unchaperoned, in a dangerous sector of town?"

"I am not entirely unattended," she said. Behind her stood a black man of impressive height, clad only in a leopard-skin. I had not realized that Lady Volumnia's taste ran to Nubian gladiators; perhaps this was going to be an easier job than I thought. After the austerity of the Christianoi, she could not be blamed for wanting to have a little fun.

"This is Babalavus," she said, "a mage of the Iorubae, a tribe that dwell in the yet-unconquered regions where lies the source of the Nile."

I smiled. There's a charlatan on every block in Rome, waiting to hoodwink a credulous rich woman out of a few million. Such a charlatan, in fact, was *my* role that night. "Have you abandoned then, Volumnia, the faith of the Christianoi? Have you ceased to attend the love-feasts?" I had to know.

"Oh, Ioannes," she whimpered, falling to her knees before me, "forgive me for being such a weak woman! Would that I were a slave, and had no position in society to lose for belonging to a subversive religion! Then I would gladly go to a thousand love-feasts every night. Really, I didn't mean to denounce anyone in the faith, it's just that—well—most of them weren't really our kind of people anyway, so I suppose they were more or less expendable...."

I made the sign of the cross over her and mumbled a few nonsense words, hoping that she and Chrysolithos would take them for the Christianoi ritual of "speaking in tongues." It must have worked, for the two of them immediately placed their palms together in an attitude of reverence, their glazed eyes fixed on me like a pair of village idiots. By the Pudenda of Venus! How I hate these weird Oriental cults!

We stood for a moment in a sort of tableau of religious ecstacy, and then Lady Volumnia, all business, got up and said to the banker, "Listen, the reason I came is—I have to make a rather large withdrawal."

"Precisely how large, O Clarissima?"

"Well, you know I've no head for figures, but—well, two million denarii?"

"Such a sum might be rather difficult to come by in cash—"

I was all attention now, even as I stood there mimicking the servile unctuousness of a preacher of the Christianoi.

"Perhaps one and a half million—" said the Lady Volumnia.

"My Lady, you will bankrupt me! Of course, bearing in mind the substantial penalty for early withdrawal from your interest-bearing equity account—"

How well I knew this ploy of Chrysolithos's! By the time Volumnia received her money, she would end up owing him more than she'd ever paid in; such were the perils of high finance in a world in which our Emperor has melted down the very vestments of the statues of the gods to help eke out a currency that is, at best, half silver and half lead.

"I'll have to give it to you in gold, Clarissima," Chrysolithos said, "and of course, there'll be an exchange rate deduction...." He called for a slave to bring out some bags from his vaults.

Meanwhile, my attention was drawn to the mage Babalavus. He stood with his arms crossed, every bit the bodyguard. I would wager that he was not a Christianos, for the followers of that sect have a look about them, a strange cross between the hangdog and the insolent. They have a complete disregard for human life, even their own, for they believe that they will shortly be resurrected and the world will end in an apocalyptic conflagration. There was something distinctly unnerving about him, for he stared back at me and would not be stared down, even though it is customary for the lower classes to be a tad more circumspect in the presence of patricians. I could well believe that Lady Volumnia had taken him for her lover, though a million and half seemed a steep price to pay for the services even of so stallion-like a physical specimen.

Unless it was hush-money...a coverup...unless this were only the epigraph to a veritable epic of scandal in high places....

Then again, Volumnia and the Nubian*Nubian* were not exactly lovey-dovey; a practised eye like mine can almost immediately tell if two people are involved in a clandestine intimate relationship, but with these two I had the distinct impression that something else was going on...some darker secret.

"Please, Ioannes, holy man," Volumnia said, "do not be too harsh with me for my lack of faith! I have a plan that will redeem me in your eyes...that's why I need the money, you see...."

What a stroke of luck! She was going to incriminate herself. I would have no trouble at all arranging for her husband's political demise if I could uncover some kind of bribery scandal....

At that moment I felt a sneeze coming on. I knew that my clay nose would be turned into a projectile if I stayed for another minute. It was time to retreat. "May the Sacred Paraclete guide you and comfort you," I said in sacerdotal tones. "I must go now and tend to my lost sheep. Rejoice, O Volumnia Drusiana, Chrysolithos, and Babalavus!"

"Such a model of Christian piety!" I heard Lady Volumnia remark as I passed from the hall into the street. It was getting toward the ninth hour. Keeping to the shadows, I made my way back to my litter, rousted the bearers, and returned to an alley next to the bank to await the emergence of my prey.

An hour later—it was not yet dawn, but the sky was already tinted red, for in the summer the night hours are shorter—Lady Volumnia and her companion emerged from a side door, the latter slinging a jingling sack over his shoulders. Babalavus whistled and two litters appeared: a plain one and one bearing the minotaur-crest of the

Drusiani. Side by side, they made off down the alley, curtains open wide so I could see they were deep in conversation as they rode.

"Follow them!" I whispered to the head bearer. "And be as inconspicuous as you can!" We started to move. I peered through my peephole while wrestling with the elaborate garments and makeup for my next charade. It was good to be able to sneeze at last.

The litters moved slowly. It was easy to follow at first. Whenever they stopped, we ducked behind a convenient pillar or fountain. I did not think they were lovers now; else why would the Lady Volumnia be so brazen about being seen in public with this so-called mage, not even bothering to keep the curtains of her litter drawn?

Another alley now—a street of smithies—I could hear the clank of chains and the clink of hammer on anvil—and somewhere in the distance, a slave being noisily chastised. The mage looked at the moon, which, though full, was paling fast in the impending sunrise; a look of concern crossed the Lady's face...the litterbearers went into a trot, and a lead-tipped quirt materialized in her delicate little hand.

"Faster!" I said. "But stay out of sight!" My litter swerved to avoid a chamberpot that was being emptied from an upper window.

My quarry took a left turn and suddenly we were in a fish market. Though it was the dead of night, the square was bustling. Dozens of carts were lined up, with slaves and peasants hastening to unload their wares before the dawn deadline—for horse traffic is not permitted in the city from dawn to sunset—and the smell of fish and horsedung was overpowering. Already the cooks from the great houses on the Palatine were out in force, snapping up the best fish for the evening's orgies. I followed the two litters closely as they wove in and out of the stands. The litterbearers were moving briskly, purposefully. Suddenly they stopped in front of a stall and purchased a few fish. Lady Volumnia did not even bother to have them wrapped. She said something and the bearers began sprinting back downtown, toward the Old Forum.

It was harder to follow them now. The avenues were broader and there were fewer monuments to duck behind. We collided with a bevy of partygoers, garlanded, drunk, and singing lewd songs, and wove in and out of a procession of Cybele-worshipers on their way to the Temple of Magna Mater. A beggar tried to climb into my litter, and had to be shaken off. At last the two of them turned sharply into a narrow passageway. It was difficult not to be seen, and my front bearers were literally pronging the buttocks of the aftmost litter-slaves of the Lady Volumnia when our way was blocked by a old plebeian, wheezing as he tried to push a cartful of chickens out of a rut. I braced myself for a collision. It came.

I barely had time to take in the spectacle of the three-litter pileup. Chickens ran amok. A fishy projectile had landed in my lap. It was, I noted ruefully, the common pufferfish, hardly a delicacy, and poisonous besides. Lady Volumnia screamed as she attempted to disentangle herself from the Nubian, the chicken vendor, and the chickens, and litter-slaves were rolling about in the excrementa, their livery ruined.

Fortunately, I had already taken finished donning my next disguise, and when I emerged, veiled and forbidding, from the litter, the Lady and her Negro witch-doctor were both aghast to discover that they had collided with the litter of the Clarissima Julilla Juliana, the aged, prim, severe and intractable second high priestess of the College of Vestal Virgins.

It is one of my most convincing disguises.

"Dear me, my children," I said, brushing the pufferfish off my stola, "you really ought to watch where you're going."

Even my own slaves were impressed, and many of them quickly kneeled and began muttering every formula of aversion they could think of.

"O sacred one! Forgive me for profaning—I had no idea—" the Lady Volumnia began, and then suddenly, inexplicably, winked at me with a kind of nudge-nudge informality that suggested some kind of womanly conspiracy of concealment. Meanwhile, the black mage seemed to have gone into a trance, for his eyes had rolled up all the way into their sockets, and he was looking from side to side in the manner of a hungry lion, occasionally muttering the phrase *"Oba kosó, oba kosó."*

In the distance, a cock crew.

Lady Volumnia roused herself in alarm. A shaft of predawn halflight made the dust dance in the noxious air. "Hurry, Babalavus!" she said, trying to shake him out of his ecstacy. "We're losing the moon!" Turning to me, she said, "By your leave, Clarissima," and, bowing, added, "I will see you at the games, perhaps." Then she clambered back aboard with her pufferfish under her arm and, tossing a purse to the disgruntled chicken vendor, quirted her bearers uptown. Babalavus set off with equal dispatch toward the gates of the city. I could not follow both; besides, it would be undignified for a Vestal Virgin to go charging through the streets at night.

What was I to do? I bade my bearers run alongside Babalavus for a few minutes, doffed my robes and, making sure that I could be seen turning in the direction of the Capitoline, slipped out of the far side of the litter, now garbed in the loincloth of a common slave.

I ran behind Babalavus's litter. It was hard to keep up as we raced downhill. Past the rickety insulae of the impoverished, the many-storied slum buildings whose roofs leaned across the alleys and blocked out the twilight, where dirty immigrant children played amid piles of refuse...past dingy temples of unfashionable cults, where priests with scruffy tonsures prayed in empty vestibules in unfamiliar tongues...past whorehouses frequented by washed-up gladiators and slumming patricians...I could see where we were heading...a catacomb whose entrance lay just beyond the walls behind the intersection of the Appia and Nomentana.

I tapped the hindmost bearer on the shoulder. Ran up alongside him and showed him an aureus that I had had concealed in my mouth, and explained to him what I wanted. The other bearers, panting as the leader called out the rhythm, were concentrating so hard that they did not notice when, without skipping a beat, I changed places with the slave and—thanking the gods that it was still pretty dark—changed loincloths with him also, for the bearers were a matched set. I was counting on the mage having hired the litter rather than owning one, so that he would not notice me, for one hired litterbearer is much like another.

The litter stopped at the entrance and Babalavus stepped out. He was carrying an amphora under his arm which appeared to be in the shape of a human skull. He seemed already to be drifting into one of his trances. He called for a torch bearer. As luck would have it, that torchbearer was me.

We descended. The steps were steep. The stench of rotting plebeians filled our nostrils. I held the torch high for him but he seemed to need no light, for he moved about as one possessed, rocking his head from side to side and now and then springing like a panther. We went deeper. There were white flowers and mushrooms and strange herbs growing from cracks in the floor. Once he paused to pluck some leaves from the eye-sockets of a human skull. Always he sang to himself. Sometimes his voice was high-pitched, like a child's; other times he appeared to be answering himself in a mellifluous bass. Now and then he paused to gather his roots and flowers and to throw them into the skull-amphora.

I was beginning to suspect that this was no Christianos.

Dead bodies lined the walls. Some niches were occupied by two or three corpses. Some had been incompetently mummified; others were just skeletons; many were fresh, and bore on their limbs and torsos evidence of the torture that must, by law, be inflicted on all slaves who give evidence in a court of law. The odor was nauseating, but I had a rôle to play.

Babalavus danced and chanted a while longer, then stalked up and down a passageway looking for something. At length he selected the skull of a child and slipped it into his amphora. He motioned to me to go on up.

I was not displeased when we once more achieved the upper air. The sun was just rising now, and I could see, along the Appian way, the long line of horsecarts hastening to leave the city before their owners were arrested for disobeying the ban on daylight equestrian traffic.

It was a simple matter to change places with the slave once more—he had been waiting in the portico of a nearby temple of Mithras—and to slip back to my own litter, wherein, once safely ensconced, I could once more assume the apparel of the Lady Julilla. I had lost a few hours. Nevertheless I made it to the Temple of Vesta just in time for the ceremonial blessing of the hearth and was able to go through the motions of the rite without any of the other Vestals noticing either my excessive perspiration or my inappropriate gender.

As soon as it was over I retired to the chamber of the Lady Julilla—fortunately, I had a duplicate key—just in time to see a shadowy figure slipping out of her window.

"By the Sacred Mysteries!" cried the Lady Julilla, springing from her bed with astonishing alacrity for one of her years, and sprinting behind the nearest arras. "I have been profaned—my honor violated—"

"Relax, O Clarissima!" I said, as I sat down on a tripod next to the window. "It is only me." I squinted as I looked out, but all I could see was a rather corpulent figure waddling at top speed through the garden, now and then bumping into a stone Silenus or satyr. Once more, I hadn't arrivedquite in time to discover the identity of the Lady's paramour.

The Vestal—who, upon realizing it was only me, had come out of hiding and was now seated upon a couch, powdering her face and looking at me with hauteur—said, "Ah, Viridianus. I trust the morning service went smoothly?"

"Most smoothly, Clarissima. No one suspects that you are in your bedroom trysting with—"

"Be nice, O Publius Viridianus!" she said, peeling an apple. "You know very well that if I am ever discovered, my life is forfeit; the virginity of the Vestals is inviolable. But I've been stuck in this dump since the age of sixteen, and a girl gets to wondering what it's all about, if you know what I mean...you won't gain a thing by turning me in, you know that. I'm a Roman of the Julian gens, and descended from the goddess Venus; I know how to die properly."

"True, Clarissima, but a certain curiosity—" I glanced once more at the garden, but the priestess's fat lover had managed to escape.

"Curiosity was not part of our deal, Publius Viridianus," she said, relapsing into that sternness of demeanor for which she was well known. She pulled a bag of silver from under the couch and threw it to me. "Our arrangement still stands, I trust. I need you to impersonate me at the games as well today; I have...ah...a business meeting to attend to... a little matter of the Temple archives."

"As you wish, Clarissima," I said, noting with satisfaction that her plans jibed perfectly with my own.

I was, I confess, rather tired when I finally reached the Circus of Nero and staggered up to the Vestals' balcony. A venation was in progress, but the heat and the humidity had rendered the mob restless, and only the distribution of the lunchtime lottery tickets had been able to prevent them from getting ugly. There are only so many gazelles, wolves, jackasses, ostriches and hippopotamoi one can watch being slain on a sweltering day in August without being driven insane with boredom. The Vestals' balcony was only half full; after showing me the deference due my putative rank, my fellow virgins mostly gossiped or licked their snow cones or nibbled at a tray of succulent kebabs assembled from thrushes' tongues, finches' gizzards, and the like.

I was able to observe the editor's box at my leisure, since it was next to the Vestals' and separated from me only by a marble frieze.

There was my quarry at last, in full view, every inch the lion. Q. Drusianus Otho was reclining on a gilded couch, with slaves and dancing girls at his feet. Suckling pigs stuffed with figs and apples sat ignored on silver platters; oiled Nubians wielded impressive peacock-feather fans; a couple of centurions squatted, rolling the bones, under a makeshift canopy put together from three javelins and a cloak.

Sitting next to him was Volumnia, heaving prettily. Behind them stood the Ioruba mage. They weren't sweating one bit after the adventures of the previous night. I was not surprised to see that Eros was there too, looking shiftily about. He was the only one to show any interest in the suckling pigs.

There was another woman there too, with gold dust in her hair, her face powdered to the color of packed snow, wearing a king's ransom in purple silk, plucking idly on a kithara. She was singing, and everyone stopped now and then to applaud.

I was somewhat bemused when I realized that this Lady was none other than Himself the God of State, His August Divinity, L. Domitius Ahenobarbus to his friends, Nero-666-The Beast to his treasonous and godless detractors, many of whom were fated to perish before our eyes that very day. The aria he was singing was none other than the fiendishly virtuosic *Hecabe's Lament* from Euripides' *The Trojan Women.* I'm no critic, but there seemed to be a number of wrong notes in his rendition.

As the carcasses were dragged off, the Emperor launched into a rousing rendition of something of his own. I was thankful that I knew nothing about modern music; I could not tell the wrong notes from the right. I was however, saved from having to comment by the miraculous emergence of the face of Petronius Arbiter from the thighs of a voluptuous Celtic woman; he made some pronouncement, the Emperor nodded daintily, and everyone clapped.

I took out a wax tablet and began making notes as the Amphitheatron was being filled with water for a simulated sea-battle. I kept an ear cocked, for one of the occupants of the editor's box might well reveal something I could use.

What had I found out?

Imprimis: the tableau of glorious dissipation that was visible in the editor's box was a mere simulacrum; in fact, I was witnessing a vipers' nest of seething intrigue. Someone had written a poem in a blatantly inferior pastiche of Petronius's style in order to discredit Drusianus; Lady Volumnia, guilt-ridden over turning in so many Christianoi, had dug deep into her pockets to form an alliance with a bizarre African magician; Eros was watching everybody, hoping someone would fall from grace so that he could move up the ladder of power; Petronius was not long for this world, for I had been invited to his suicide party later in the week; the Lady Julilla—that is to say, myself—was fooling around and decidedly non intacta; none of the pieces were falling into place for me.

Had the Emperor really sent Eros to destroy Drusianus, or did the eunuch have his own agenda? Should I deliver the innocent patrician up on a platter, or was I risking my own downfall by essaying something that the Emperor had not, in fact, commanded?

Was it not entirely possible that the entire thing was a ruse, and that it was I—the knower of secrets—who was the quarry? Had one of my thousand disguises finally been seen through?

These are the kind of questions a detective must wrestle with daily, and I fell into a kind of rêverie.

A theological argument was now going on in the editor's box, and now and then a phrase penetrated my miasma of self-examination....

"Resurrection of the body!" the Emperor was saying. "What a curious concept. These Christianoi must be quite, quite mad."

"It is not as uncommon as all that, Divinitas,"—I recognized the resonant bass of Babalavus—"for amongst the Iorubae, and also the Kikongii, our neighbors, malefactors are often sentenced to become *nzambi*, the Living Dead...they are first poisoned with a powder whose active ingredient is the ground-up liver of the homely pufferfish...."

Pufferfish!

I came to all at once. Resurrection! and pufferfish! were the Christianoi poisoning themselves in the hope of coming back to life? Was not their sign of recognition a fish? And had I not last seen the Lady Volumnia climbing onto her litter with a brace of pufferfish tucked under her arm?

In the arena below, two ships were having at each other with catapults. In a humorous touch, the projectiles were neither rocks nor flaming brimstone, but political prisoners—Christianoi of dwarfish stature, each one bundled and trussed into a compact sort of a ball. Since catapultae are not really designed for hurling humans about, it was impossible to aim them. The crowd screeched and hooted as Christianoi crashed into the sea or brained themselves against the embankments. Now this was not only purest entertainment—full of human interest as the prisoners bobbed up and down, trying to extricate themselves from their bonds only to find themselves being devoured by the crocodiles which were now being released into the waters—but a practical thing too, since the flooding of the arena also functioned as a rudimentary air conditioning system, and the water was constantly being cooled with cartloads of Alpine snow.

I was really beginning to enjoy the show when a man was catapulted right into the Vestals' pavilion. His head struck the marble floor and his brains spritzed my robes, my wax tablet, and my eyelashes. Fortunately I had the presence of mind to scream in falsetto.

I had seen and heard enough for the day. "I have been profaned!" I cried. "I must return at once to the Temple of Vesta to be purified!"

I turned and made for the secret passageway by which the Vestals may come and go as they please without being subjected to the indignity of plebeian frottage. I was more upset than I wanted to admit to myself. I had seen the dead man's face, in the split second before the big splat. To my astonishment, it was the face of someone I knew—someone who ought have been able to afford to buy his way out of this unholy mess.

I was going to have to get myself a new bank account.

I was finally getting a moment to myself, taking a postprandial soak in my private tepidarium, when the nomenclator announced the arrival of Lady Volumnia Drusiana. She stalked into the bathroom and flung a purseful of gold at my head. The two Spanish masseuses fled in panic.

"Take this!" she screamed. "You vulture! You parasite! You open-sphinctered catamite!"

"The first two I allow, Clarissima, but really you do go too far in accusing me of—"

"Oh!" she turned away from me and began weeping copiously, and I availed myself of the opportunity to slip into something decent.

"There, there," I said, "let's hear all about it now." I escorted her to the library, where three of my scribes were in the process of reproducing Petronius's *Satyricon* in triplicate—for the novel makes a nice gift for someone on whom one has amatory designs. I shooed the scribes away and offered Volumnia a drink from the jug of best-vintage Lesbian I kept on my desk.

"You've got to help me!" she said, flinging herself onto the nearest couch. "My life is in ruins—my husband's political future has been horribly compromised—" She pulled a little scroll from her bosom. I was not surprised to see that it was a copy of the insulting poem that had been attributed to the Arbiter of Elegance himself.

"Oh, I've already read that," I said. "And a million and a half denarii won't be enough to overcome my scruples—"

"One and a half—! How could you possibly—" She stared at me, for in my demeanor and accent there was absolutely no trace of Ioannes of Damascus, the fanatical prophet of the Christianoi.

"Yes," I went on, "you were consorting with an elder of the banned sect last night, weren't you? One"—I pretended to consult my notes—"Ioannes of Damascus. And you were visiting the offices of another Christianos, certain Chrysolithos, did you not? Who is now—"

"Dead," she whispered. "I'm going to have to open another bank account."

There was a pause while I took out a tablet and prepared to take some more notes.

"Anyway," she said, "I don't have all the money anymore. He took a twenty percent commission, the poor dead soul! And there were other—expenses. I can only offer you what I threw at your feet—if you'll only call off the hunt. Don't say you're not after him—I was told this by no less a figure than the third undersecretary of the Emperor's privy purse!" So Eros was playing both sides against the middle! So much for him! "My husband, as you well know, is innocent of all wrongdoing. Never has a man been more loyal to his Emperor. It is I who have been weak, I who have gone from faith to faith, never finding certitude in this complex modern world!"

As she shrugged out of her clothes, I realized that there was also to be compensation of another kind. The Lady Volumnia, though not young, possessed a statuesque voluptuousness which certainly lived up to her name. She palpitated curvaceously against the harsh right angles of my shelves of papyri.

"My dear Clarissima!" I said, tossing down the last of the Lesbian. "This display of your not unappetizing charms renders me quite inarticulate," I added, stooping to litotes in my confusion.

She smiled. There was nothing for it but to bed her, on the instant, in the half hour or so before my next appointment. She clawed, whinnied, and bounced about with such enthusiasm and vigor that I was glad I had recently had all the lecti cubicularii in the house reupholstered.

Afterwards, I assuaged my guilt by leaving a nice juicy leg of lamb as an offering to the house gods.

It was time for me to return to the games, this time as myself.

Cæsar too was Himself by the time I arrived. Garbed once more as a man, wearing a towering diadem of solid gold and a floor-length purple robe embroidered in gold thread with suns and moons, Himself was enthroned on a chair of state, with the outrageously beautiful Statilla Messalina at his side. I was glad to see that he was getting over the apotheosis of the Empress Poppæa, whom he had accidentally kicked to death one drunken evening.

It was almost the hour of cena, and the day was cooling off; a Greek tragedy, put on at the Divinity's behest, had just been booed off the stage, and the stage manager had been forced to bring on some Christianoi as an entr'acte. They were being eaten by lions, but as no one ever pays much attention to last year's hits, they were being watched only by the most devoted fans of Christianoi-bashing.

I hastily paid by respects to the God of State. "Ave, Divinitas," I said, and quickly switched to Greek, for the Emperor hated the uncouth jangle of the vulgar tongue. "Rejoice, Autokrator," I said. "I didn't have the chance to pay my respects earlier...."

"Pity; you missed my new poem. I'd sing it again, but I'm not dressed for it anymore."

"I am crushed," I said. "But maybe I'll have a chance to borrow it from the Library; I know it's not the same as hearing it from your Divine Lips, but—"

"Poor little Viridian," said Nero. "As tone deaf as can be, yet he still attempts, in his small way, to sit at the feet of the Muse."

The reason I had come back to the games was because I was sure I was missing some vital piece of information. I noted that Drusianus and Eros were deep in conversation, and that Lady Volumnia and her curious magician were absent; Petronius, on the other hand, was leaning on the balcony, watching the Christianoi being eaten with profound fascination. I supposed that, since he was about to die himself, he was finding something in common even with this most tedious of spectacles. I was really looking forward to his suicide party; it's not every day that a patrician decides to go out in style.

Since Petronius was as good as dead, I decided I might as well whip out the scurrilous poem and show it to the Emperor.

"What do you think of this, Divinitas?" I said. "It—ah—came to my attention last week."

He took it from me, looked at the first few lines, and began to chuckle. I became uneasy. I looked at Drusianus, but he was still deep in conversation with Eros.

"What a terrible thing!" said Nero, looking deep into my eyes. "Who do you think could have perpetrated such blasphemy?"

"Well, it *looks* like Petronius, and yet there's something — ah—something—ah—" I wanted to protect Petronius from the imputation that he might have written this inferior piece of doggerel, and yet....

"Something—ah—something—ah—" There was a feverish glint in his eye, and suddenly I knew what I was going to have to say.

"It looks like Petronius, only far, far *better*, of course!"

I knew at once that I had said the right thing, for the Emperor beamed and threw me a bag of money. The old fox had written the thing himself—was doubtless disseminating it as a test of loyalty! Well, that certainly put paid to Eros' contention that he had hired me at Cæsar's behest.

"Far from being displeased at him," said Nero with his mouth full of peacocks' brains, "I am thinking of giving Drusianus some kind of political appointment...a consulship perhaps, or even a procuratorial position...I've even assigned a high-level member of my staff to...ah...act as his financial advisor...." He indicated the eunuch.

It dawned on me that Eros's financial advice was probably the last thing Q. Drusianus Otho needed. It was the eunuch's greed that had led him to try to pay me into effecting the man's downfall, that much was certain. I had taken Eros's money and owed him some kind of investigation; I had also taken the money—not to mention the lubricious fluids—of the Lady Volumnia, and I owed her something too. And who had turned Chrysolithos in? Surely not the very Lady who relied on him for all her banking needs at odd hours of the night.

The God of State lost interest in me, since I wasn't talking about the arts. He called Petronius over for a chat about Homer. I had to admire the poet's sangfroid; he gave absolutely no indication that he was planning to commit suicide, and I was sure that it would come as a complete shock to Nero, who hated surprises.

Idly I watched the next number, a small group of Andabatae. These are the lowliest criminals, who are given helmets without eyeholes and unwieldy weapons, and swing blindly at each other until all are slain— an incorrigibly tasteless entertainment, and fit only for the vulgar element.

The fight was drawing to a close, and slaves were removing the helmets of the slain and fastening hooks to their feet so that they could be dragged out through the Gates of Death. Now the sun was low on the horizon, and the few remaining wretches, staggering about, cast huge shadows against the sea of togas in the patricians' balconies. One could not see to clearly what was going on, but it chanced that a ray of flickering, sooty light, cast upon the arena by a Christianos who was being burned alive on a lofty display cross, fell upon the face of one of the dead Andabatae just as he was being hauled away.

It was the face of Chrysolithos the banker.

Surely I am imagining this! I thought to myself. I squinted; the red sunlight made my eyes water; yet still I could have sworn, by Jupiter and all the Immortals, that that face was none other's. There was even a great red smudge on his temple whence, earlier that afternoon, his brains had been spurting forth upon my virginal garments.

Chrysolithos had died twice in the same day.

Somehow—my detective's intuition assured me—the resurrection of the old Judæan banker was the key to the whole affair.

For was not resurrection also the crux (no pun intended) of the Christianoi religion? Did these people not believe so strongly in a physical afterlife that they had not hesitated to set fire to Rome itself, the quicker to bring about their prophesied apocalypse? Were they not so confident of this resurrection that they did not even mind being killed in the circus? Why, instead of showing the proper terror when being eaten by lions, they would stand around singing their catchy hymn tunes, completely undermining the public service aspect of their deaths. These people really believed in resurrection all right.

Well, what if they'd actually found a way to do it?

There was only one way to find out, and to do that I would have to slip around to the Gates of Death as soon as the games were done for the day.

Sunset over the amphitheatron: I was just in time to catch the imposing figure of Babalavus climbing out of a litter and speaking to the guards at one of the back entrances. I was in costume once more, impersonating Ioannes of Damascus. As soon as Babalavus was admitted, I crept up behind the two guards and, placing my hands about their necks, put them both to sleep with a certain nerve pinch that induces a temporary state of narcosis. I followed Babalavus down the dank staircase. He was too intent on his business to notice me.

There is no sight more depressing than the bowels of a circus. The stench of animal dung was everywhere; in the half dark one could make out the cages of exotic beasts. Cramped though the bestiaries were, the human prisoners fared even worse, for they were a far less valuable commodity. One could hear, from behind dungeon doors, the screams of the panicstricken and the frenzied copulations of those who knew this lovemaking would be their last. From some torture-chamber lower down came the crack of the flagellum, the squeak of the rack, the hiss of the red-hot iron on human flesh, and, of course, the ever noisome screaming.

Babalavus strode through labyrinthine corridors, turning this way and that with the confidence of one who had come here often. I followed. After a while he ascended some steps, and we were in a chamber with an egress into a back alley.

We had arrived at the hall of the butchers, where the criminals killed that day were being methodically quartered and shoved into large baskets by slaves. Arms, legs, heads, and buttocks protruded from enormous containers which were even now being loaded onto carts; the meat would be sold to various menageries around the city, for the wild animals at the circus itself had to be kept hungry.

The butchers worked quickly, but there was still a heap of some two or three hundred corpses, their feet still pierced from the hooks that had been used to haul them off the sand. Little boys were engaged in divesting these corpses of clothing, jewelry, hairpins, anything that could be recycled. Indeed, I thought, the entertainment industry has been hard hit by the Emperor's financial cutbacks!

Concealing myself behind the pile of dead bodies, I watched Babalavus bargaining with one the overseers. There were a few relatives hanging around, hoping to bribe one of the slaves into releasing their lamented for a decent burial; a sobbing couple rooted through the piles of body parts, looking for their son.

Babalavus took out a bag of gold and presented it to the overseer. Greed gleamed in the man's eyes; he turned, barked out an order, and presently a wagon pulled up to the entrance, and—as Babalavus pointed to one corpse after another—they were loaded onto the cart. I recognized Chrysolithos amongst the fallen. I thought I saw a few other Christianoi too.

This was no time for reflection. I had to find out what was going on.

Quickly, under cover of the wall of dead bodies, I disrobed, smeared myself with dead men's blood, plunged my arms into an open abdomen and pulled out a piece of intestine with which to drape myself...then, when no one was looking, I sneaked behind the busy butchers and managed to clamber onto the cart while Babalavus's back was turned.

As chance would have it, I had landed right on top of Chrysolithos. He was dead all right. They were all dead. It was a necrophiliac's dream come true; alas, this has never been one of my favorite perversions. More bodies were being shoveled on top of me. A woman's half amputated breast rammed into my mouth, almost suffocating me; blood oozed into my nostrils and slicked my limbs so that I slid back and forth like a fish at the market. The stench was unendurable.

When the cart began to move, things got even worse. Even now it irks me to recall the discomfort of our journey. Every rut, every cobble made the bodies slip and slither and marinated me in their bodily effluvia. I could see nothing, for there were at least three layers of dead people crammed on top of me. I could hear the voice of Babalavus urging the horses on and singing snatches of barbarian music.

At length we stopped. The bodies—myself among them—were unloaded one at a time. I concentrated on acting out my most demanding rôle, that of a corpse. I felt myself being lifted by the arms and legs. I made myself limp. They laid me down on a rocky surface. When I finally permitted myself to peek, I saw that I was lying in an immense morgue. The bodies of Christianoi lay in neat rows on the stone floor of what seemed to be a vast cave; it was one of the natural chambers into which the catacombs led, though I could not remember which one. To my surprise, Chrysolithos the banker lay not two paces from me, to my left; eviscerated as he was, he was not a pretty sight.

Suddenly, I heard a familiar voice shriek out: "By the Sacred Paraclete! It's Ioannes of Damascus! Oh, how could they have killed such a holy man?" The Lady Volumnia ran out from the shadows and knelt by my side, covering my face and chest with so many kisses that I feared that, in my nakedness, I would accidentally reveal my lust.

"Do not worry, my Lady." It was Babalavus, standing beside her. He was clad only in a loincloth. His face was hideously painted in whiteface with streaks of black and red. "If Shangó wills it, he will not be dead for long."

There were others like Babalavus in the background, some with drums and marimbas. Other Negroes clutched chickens and turtles in their arms.

From somewhere far away, I heard Christianoi psalms being sung. One of their love-feasts was taking place. It was cold, and it was hard to keep my teeth from chattering.

At last, the love-feast seemed to end, and Christianoi crowded into the chamber. Volumnia and Babalavus were handing out phials of some potion. At length, Babalavus addressed the throng: "O Christianoi," he said, "it has become necessary, for political reasons, for the Lady Volumnia to denounce some of you to the secret police in order to save her husband's career. You will probably be arrested before dawn, so that you be can be ready in time for the morning tableaux."

His announcement caused a sensation as some wailed, others complained, and others still cried out their jubilation at the propinquity of their redemption.

"Doubtless a number of you are afraid that the resurrection of the body will not occur as promised. That is why I have been invited to join you, and why I have prepared this potion. Do not forget, in your hour of martyrdom, to swallow the pufferfish elixir before going onstage! Otherwise the magic will not work...."

Several of the crowd began to voice their objections. Some complained that the blessed apostle Simon Cephas had made no mention of any pufferfish elixir. Others shouted that Babalavus was no Christianos and had no right to order them around. Like every other Judæan sect, the Christianoi love to quarrel over the minutiae of dogma, and do so even when death is imminent. At length, the Lady Volumnia appealed for silence.

"Please, my brothers and sisters—" she said. "Just do what he says. The police are even now making their way toward this catacomb. You're all going to die anyway, so you might as well be decent about it."

A chorus of *amens* and *hallelujahs* echoed around the cave. Then, at a signal from Lady Volumnia, there began an ominous music, all drums and high-pitched keening and grunts and babblings. Above it all I could hear the phrase *"Oba kosó!"* repeated over and over. I knew it must be a ritual formula of these Iorubae.

At that moment, Babalavus went into a trance.

He fell to his knees and began to heave and buck like an angry minotaur. His pupils vanished into their sockets, and animal cries emanated from his throat. Sweat poured down his face and torso.

"Behold! He is speaking in tongues!" Lady Volumnia shouted, though I knew very well that this was nothing of the kind.

Babalavus began to do a jerky sort of dance. He leapt over corpses. He made clawing gestures in the air, as though he were possessed by some jungle creature. The pounding went on. It was hypnotic. Suddenly he was holding the skull-amphora in his hands, and asperging us corpses with its contents—a foul-smelling concoction of herbs and blood.

Then he was joined by his tribesmen, whooping wildly as they sliced the heads off turtles and chickens and began to slop their blood liberally over us. It was becoming harder and harder to play dead. Soon I was going to have to sneeze, or cough, or—

Chrysolithos began to twitch! As the chanting rose to a deafening pitch, as the black mages pranced about and sprinkled us with foul fluids, all the corpses fibrillated wildly. I soon realized that I had better stand wiggling myself, or I would look out of place. I started to jerk about with a vengeance, and when the corpses began to stand up, each with a glazed look in its eye, I too scrambled to my feet and attempted to mimic their rhythmic swaying. Soon the corpses were all lumbering this way and that, each one with a look of profound bewilderment, as though awakening from a drunken stupor. Chrysolithos was going round and round in circles, as one who has been struck in the head with a poker.

I heard Lady Volumnia cry out above the uproar: "Behold the resurrection promised to you by the Christianoi prophets! Death is an illusion! You will not die in the arena tomorrow; as long as your body can be recovered in one piece, you will be brought back to life as good as new! Zombificati sunt!"

What kind of a word was *zombificatus*? It must been that we had been made into *nzambi*, the Living Dead of which Babalavus had spoken to the Emperor. But as I looked around me I could see that this resurrection was a far cry from that promised in the utterances of the Christianoi. These *nzambi* were hardly human. They gibbered. Intestines dangled from their ripped abdomens. Arms and legs were missing. Heads lolled. Sputum and vomitus dribbled from their lips, and brain tissue trickled from their cracked skulls. It was hard for me to appear as disgusting as they, for I had no wounds; but I shambled and gibbered and swung my arms aimlessly along with them, while trying to work my way up to where Lady Volumnia and Babalavus were standing so as to be able to hear what they were saying.

"You have done well, O Babalavus!" she was telling him. "I shall not forget how you allowed me to betray the Christianoi, thus salving my husband's reputation, while at the same time providing this supernatural means of assuaging my betrayal of the religion I hold so dear...."

A piercing shriek issued from Babalavus's throat. All at once the music stopped. We *nzambi* stood, waiting, a little threatening. The unzombified Christianoi backed away, terrified—who would not be?—and I do not doubt that many were reconsidering the most cherished tenets of their faith.

At that moment, bucinae blared. We heard the tramp-tramp-tramp of Roman soldiers. It was the Prætorians. They burst into the chamber so quickly that there was no time time for a stampede. The crowd were too stunned to scream. Which professional speed and detachment, the secret police clapped everyone in chains—living and dead—and marched us all back to the amphitheatron, flogging us for good measure as we staggered along the dim streets.

I was thrown into a cramped prison cell along with my *nzambi* companions. There were also Christianoi who were not yet zombificati. Most sat around praying to their God, but one or two were heard bitterly complaining that this death and rebirth was somehow now quite as advertised. One was even suggesting that, if they should survive their martyrdom, they should bring suit in the tribunes' court against the cult for making these false claims. I had no time for specious arguments or theological speculation. I had to get out of there before the morning spectacle, for I did not possess a phial of the pufferfish elixir which had, it seemed, to be imbibed shortly before death for the Ioruban ritual to work.

In the flickering torchlight, I could see that some of the *nzambi* were gnawing on each other's innards. It was entirely possible that one would not even survive until the show started. I stumbled forward to the portal, which had a tiny grille through which I could see one of the guards. I banged to get his attention.

"My good man! I," I said importantly, "am Publius Viridianus, private investigator. I was spying on the Christianoi on the Emperor's behalf; I have been apprehended in error. Release me at once!"

The guard peered at me. "Publius Viridianus, the most famous detective in Rome?" he said. "Try another one! You don't look a bit like him with your big nose and your straggly beard!"

I plucked off my false nose and thrust it in his face. He raised an eyebrow. "False nose, eh?"

I started pulling my beard off. "This is false, too. Look, hurry up, I don't want my cover blown; luckily the Christianoi are too busy arguing about dogma to notice our conversation."

"By the pudenda of Venus!" said the decurion. He called for the keymaster and in a few moments I was free, and had a good woollen cloak to cover my nakedness. It turned out that the guard was quite an intellectual, for he would not let me depart until I had autographed a scroll of my memoirs which I had been vain enough to have published the previous year, and which he just happened to be reading.

"On no account," I said, "must you reveal that I have been here tonight. I will ensure that you are amply rewarded—but if this gets out—" I made a throat slitting gesture.

"High political intrigue, is it, sir?" said the decurion. "I loves a good intrigue, by the Gods! Don't you worry about the reward, just you mention me in the next volume...it's Olus Dolabella, and you must remember to spell my praenomen the plebeian way, O-l-u-s, not A-u-l-u-s; it's a point of pride in my family you see, we've been spelling it that way since my great-uncle done divorced my patrician great-aunt, she was one of the Scipiones, you know—"

"Yes, yes," I mumbled, hoping that my litterbearers would still be waiting at the other entrance of the amphitheatron.

"Treacherous lot, them Christianoi," he continued. "What a stroke of luck we had this tipoff from the Lady Volumnia. I wonder what's in it for her! I understand these people"—his voice dropped to a whisper—"eats human flesh, they does."

"They do indeed," I said, shuddering as I remembered the sight of one *nzambi* nibbling at another's loose body parts.

He wanted to know everything about their foul practices and orgies. I persuaded him to shut up only by letting him keep my nose as a souvenir, and giving him the slip while he gazed at it in adoration.

It surprised me a little to see Eros wandering through the corridors, scribbling feverishly on a wax tablet. He did not notice me, for I hid myself in the shadow of an archway. He met Babalavus; they had a brief conversation; he handed the magician a bag of money and they parted company. Why was he up so early, and what was he doing here, so far from the offices of the Imperial privy purse? Ah, but of course—the Emperor had appointed him Q. Drusianus Otho's financial advisor. Naturally he would be at the games, checking the figures—how many Christianoi at so much overhead per victim, how many tons of hay for the elephants, that sort of thing. But why was Babalavus in his pay?

Interesting, I thought; very interesting.

The mosaic stones were finally beginning to fall into place. But I still had to figure out who was behind it all—who stood to benefit—who was manipulating whom, and why. I would have to go through another day of spectacle, disguised as the Lady Julilla once more, for only from the Vestals' box could I eavesdrop on everything that was going on in the Editor's Pavilion. Unfortunately, I wasn't slated to be her double that day; nevertheless, I figured that she would not mind, since there was nothing she despised more than carrying out the endless round of litanies and sacrifices that were her lot.

It was the tenth hour; in two short hours (and the night hours are shortest in summer) would come dawn. I urged my bearers to make haste.

It was simple enough to enter the Temple of Vesta and to take the secret passageway that led from the main courtyard to the private vestiarium next to Lady Julilla's bedroom. A dozen sets of ceremonial robes hung from hooks. The Lady, with her back to me, was already up and seated on a sella, pinning her shawl in place with a silver fibula. She did not hear me enter, for I am nothing if not stealthy. I crept up behind her and tapped her on the shoulder.

She turned around and, seeing me, screamed.

I managed to cover her mouth just in time. Her scream became a gurgle.

"Just what in the name of all the Gods are you doing here?" I said.

"I might ask the same thing of you," said the Lady Volumnia, for that was who it was. "To tell you the truth, the Lady Julilla asked me to—ah—impersonate her at a morning sacrifice, because she had another—ah—appointment."

So that was why Lady Volumnia had winked so knowingly at me the night our litters had collided! Thinking that I was that wayward old Vestal Virgin, she had assumed I was returning from some tryst! I could not help laughing. "I was about to impersonate her myself!" I said. "I never realized that she had more than one—ah—accomplice."

As I said this, I was taking a robe off the wall and getting into it. I put on one of Lady Julilla's wigs and, sitting down in front of the mirror, started applying the whiteface and dabbing kohl on my eyelashes.

"You really seem quite professional at it," said the Lady Volumnia. "Well, I'm pleased to learn that I'm off the hook today; I'm really to tired to pull off the charade."

"Up all night?" I said.

She clammed up.

"I know all about the zombifications," I said. She gasped. "Don't worry—I really see no harm in it—the Christianoi are criminals, and I really don't care whether they die once or a thousand times. And you know, it isn't really resurrection at all—the elixir seems to put them into a kind of catatonic state, and when they are awakened in the zombification rite they are not quite themselves anymore. But I'm not going to berate you for playing on the credulity of a bunch of losers."

"Thank you," she said. "I love my husband so much, O Viridianus! Even when I allowed you to possess this admittedly shopworn body of mine, it was because I love my husband and will stop at nothing to prevent him from coming to harm...you do understand, don't you?"

I murmured something appropriate about the power of conjugal love.

"I mean," she said, "I had a lot of fun at the Christianoi meetings, singing those tuneful hymns and chumming with slaves and riff-raff; there's something so *elemental* about the lower classes, you know. Of course, I had to betray them for the sake of my husband's reputation, but I was so plagued by guilt about it—"

"You're a very sensitive soul, Clarissima," I said.

"That's why, when Eros introduced me to Babalavus—"

So the plot was thickening even in the moment of its unravelling! Somehow Eros had engineered the whole thing...but why?

I explained to Volumnia why I needed to go to the circus in the guise of the Vestal Virgin. "Why don't you stay here," I said, "while I go into Julilla's bedroom and tell her I'll take her place today? I'll only be a moment."

She nodded, then kissed me for luck. I placed the last layer of veils over my head and crept into Lady Julilla's cubiculum.

"Lady Julilla, it's me," I said. There was no answer, but I fancied I heard a faint scuffling noise somewhere in the chamber. Perhaps it was merely a mouse. A single lamp burned by the Vestal's bedside. She was not in bed. Nor did I see any telltale bulges behind the drapes. It was a sparsely furnished room, as befitted its occupant's otherworldly vocation; a few busts of Emperors stared at one from marble pediments of various heights; there was a couch and a an altar for private devotions. Several fumigators spewed clouds of incense into the air, which added to the gloom. Near the window was Lady Julilla's capacious bed, wide enough for the entire Prætorian guard it seemed, canopied with veils of damascene.

I had no time to wonder about the Lady's whereabouts, for I heard someone scrambling at the open window, and I dived into the bed.

To my horror, a blubbery mound of flesh, perfumed to the gills and attired in the height of nouveau-riche tastelessness, came tumbling through the window, rubbed its backside, stood up, began to shamble towards me, panting like a hippopotamos with sunstroke.

"My beloved," it squawked. "I simply had to come. I could stay away no longer!" It was all too apparent that the Lady Julilla's secret lover was none other than the emasculated Eros, and that if I did nothing I would soon become the receptacle of his sacrilegious lust!

It was too late. Eros bounced onto the bed, arms outstretched, and I had to duck to avoid his proffered lips. "I've pulled it off," he gloated, "the impudent get-rich-quick scheme I told you of...soon it will all pay off...and then I'll be able to take you away, far from here...far from the long arm of Cæsar...beyond the reach of Rome itself! Yes, my darling; you have but to say the word and I am yours forever!"

I am no fool. I realized that I had to do was lie there, avoiding the eunuch's advances, and he would eventually cough up the solution to the entire puzzle. Once more I wriggled free of his grasp, making little whimpering noises such as I imagined the randy old hussy might make were she there to reciprocate the creature's passions.

"Oh, Julilla, you're such a tease," Eros said. He managed to get me in a kind of amorous wrestling lock, and his mouth descended on mine.

"You're so masterly," I said, "but I've got a headache."

"Headache—splendid!" he said. "I know how you love it with a dollop of pain."

Pain! Clearly the Lady Julilla's appetites had been rendered decidedly deviant by her years of abstinence.

"I have my flagellum right under my tunic, my dear," said Eros.

"Er...it's that time of the month," I temporized in my best falsetto.

"You adorable old minx," he said, "you know it hasn't been that time of the month in fifteen years...."

So much for that. I prepared to either give myself away or yield to his caresses. I allowed him to chase me around the bed for a while, and then said at last, in sudden inspiration, "Before we consummate our love, O Eros, tell me more of your brilliant machinations! You know how... aroused I get with talk of political intrigue...."

Eros let go of me. I clasped my hands, fluttered my eyelids, and looked as adoring as I could. I had guessed, correctly, that political gossip was, for the aging Vestal, the most stimulating kind of foreplay.

"It's chicanery at its most devious!" he said. "Syrian political savvy, Judæan financial wizardry—combined with the secret black arts of unconquered lands! I've hired a Negro mage to reanimate the corpses of hundreds of Christianoi, so they can be killed over and over again in the arena. And the Christianoi love it! They think it's their day of resurrection or something."

"But—what advantage can this bring you?"

"Women and mathematics simply don't mix, do they?" he said, and I did not remind him that his equipment was little different from a woman's. "Look, the Christianoi are reckoned into the expenses of the games at so much per head, based on the overhead amortization of previous games...do you follow?" I did not, but continued to listen raptly. "A certain sum is charged against the privy purse per Christianos for his execution; in other words, the execution, which would normally be carried out by the state, is franchised out to the editor of the games. Another sum is also charged to against the editor's accounts to cover the actual cost of execution; this is a pro rata share of the total costs of the executions, as calculated from previous spectacles, with allowance for the debasement of the currency and so on so forth. The upshot of all this is, a properly placed person—such as—ahem—the Imperially-appointed financial advisor to Q. Drusianus Otho—can, by recycling the Christianoi over and over, funnel money from both the privy purse *and* the editorial budget into his own —ah—slush fund, from which—"

"Surely you did not concoct so labyrinthine a scheme entirely by yourself, O Eros!" I said.

"Well, I did have help from a certain Judæan banker, one Chrysolithos—but luckily I was able to have him silenced—and to seize his estate besides," he said, grinning.

"Chrysolithos! Good heavens, my family banks with him."

"Oh, the bank will go on as usual," Eros said. "It will merely be serving other interests." He began stroking my neck. "But enough of this nonsense! Let us get down to the real business of the morning—"

"But wait! I am so worried for you...won't you get in trouble? What of Drusianus and the Lady Volumnia?"

"Oh, I've already taken care of *them*. Babalavus the mage has convinced that airhead that she's saving her Christianoi friends from death while simultaneously protecting her husband from scandal...I have that detective to thank for that, whatsisname—"

"Publius Viridianus."

"Yes—I have hired him to look for hanky-panky, and he will soon find that—because of the recycling of the Christianoi—that goody-goody prig's books will not be in order—he will have been found to have cheating the Imperial privy purse—at which point—zombificatus! And his vigilant denouncer will be in a fine position to—ah—take over the Villa Drusiana, which has the most splendid view of Vesuvius."

The gig was up. But just as I was about to whip off my disguise, the eunuch seized me in his surprisingly powerful embrace and planted his tongue firmly against my gritted teeth. If I attemped to speak, that tongue would surely gain admittance into that cavity whither no man—let alone a gelding—had ever gone before.

At that moment, however, Lady Volumnia rushed into the room and began pummeling the eunuch with her fists. I was so startled I almost bit off his tongue.

"Monster!" she screamed. "You told me that Viridian had been sent to discredit my husband—but you never told me you had hired him to do it!"

"Julli—J-J-Julilla!" he said, looking from me to Volumnia. "Volumnia!"

"You, my dear Eros, are ruined," I said, ripping off my veils and dropping my voice back to its commanding baritone. "You may as well commit suicide now, for the Prætorians will be knocking on your door by sunset."

"P. Viridianus!" he shrieked.

"Indeed," I said, as I wiped the kohl from my eyes.

The eunuch looked at his two accusers in some bewilderment for a moment. Then he said, "You'll never get away with this. I have the ear of Cæsar! He'll never take the word of a known Christianos and a two-sestertius detective over that of a trusted civil servant. I'll hire the best lawyers in Rome! By the time I'm through with you—"

At that momen there came a sound like the rumbling of an earthquake. We all stared at the bed. It was quaking. The bedposts were clattering against the marble floor. I heard the jangling of an untuned lyre.

At length, an imposing figure emerged from under the bed, clutching his instrument, garbed in a cloak of Imperial purple spangle with stars and moons.

We all prostrated ourselves.

"Divinitas!" we said.

"The ear of Cæsar, eh?" said the God of State, glaring at the gelatinous Eros. "Guards! Arrest this thing!"

And so, at the last minute, an extra number was inserted in that afternoon's games, between the Rape of the Sabine Women by trained jackasses and the battle between Pigmies and Amazons. The punishment would fit the crime—Eros was to suffer an undignified end, the application of a molten gold enema—but would be one that would only be appreciated by true afficionados, since it was hard to see and lacked spectacle.

Lady Julilla had been invited to share the editor's pavilion, as had the Divinity himself, who sat upon a gilded cathedra shaped like a rearing lion. I asked her if she regretted seeing her erstwhile lover's demise.

"Not at all," she said, biting delicately into a snow cone flavored with crushed berries. "He was a brute."

"But how did the Emperor come to be hiding under your bed?"

"Oh, he always does that. You see, the idea of a Vestal Virgin coupling with a eunuch excites him greatly; it is the closest he can come to being reunited with his mother, whom, as you know, he was forced to have murdered. So we came to a little—agreement. Were the God to couple with me himself, it would be a dreadful impiety and bring about the downfall of the Empire; but since Eros was a eunuch, strict propriety was observed."

Wonders would never cease. Despite her licentious lifestyle, the old bag had managed to remain entirely intacta and true to her vocation! She was, I had to admit, a Roman through and through, able to answer the most bewildering moral dilemmas with pragmatic solutions.

They were hauling away the last of the violated women, and Eros was now being wheeled in on an ingenious contraption that would allow him to spin slowly while he agonized, thus providing even the plebeians with a decent view of his suffering face. There was desultory applause from the audience; most were bored, waiting for the Pigmies and Amazons.

Eros was brought over to our box so that he could pay the customary respects to the Emperor before being killed. He appeared to have gone quite bonkers. "Rejoice, Autokrator!" he cried, and waved merrily at us. "Don't you worry—I'll be back!"

Perhaps a last-minute conversion to Christianity?

"I'm thinking of giving Babalavus your old job," said the Emperor. Then he took out his lyre. "You have been a very fine civil servant, O Eros, and afforded me much amusement besides." He winked at the Lady Julilla. "I shall therefore pay you the supreme compliment—I shall accompany your death with a song of my own composition."

He began to sing. It was very modern.

Lady Volumnia came sidling up to me. "Oh, Viridian," she said, "we're having a big party at our house tonight to celebrate my induction into the mysteries of Astarte—do come; my husband owes you a debt of gratitude and I have pledged to—pay it myself." She smiled seductively.

"The cult of Astarte—that's the one where the women give themselves randomly to passersby, isn't it?" I said. It was really difficult to keep this Oriental cults straight, though it did not surprise me that Lady Volumnia had already found a new one to amuse herself with.

Eros screamed. Politely, I looked away.

"I really can't go," I said. "I've a dinner party at Petronius's. In fact"—I looked at the sun—"it's almost the eighth hour now, and cena is at nine."

So saying, I turned my back on the entrancing if not unblemished Volumnia, on honest Drusianus and careful Julilla, and on our magnificent and fun-loving Divinity, and furthermore on the entirely satisfying excruciation of the eunuch Eros and the marmoreal splendor of the Neronian amphitheatron. I left the spectacle behind in order to spend a last evening with C. Petronius Arbiter, a dinner of classical simplicity and artful conversation.

What happened at that dinner is, of course, known to all men; after reading us his letter to Nero in which he catalogued the Divinity's many infamies, he caused his physician to open his veins and died as elegantly as he had lived. So famous is that dinner party that it eclipsed all memory of my exploits; and while the name of Petronius will live on, the scandal of Eros the eunuch, the titillating amours of the Lady Julilla, and the multiple resurrections of Christianoi by the art of zombification, are all things that, I am sure, history will mercifully forget.

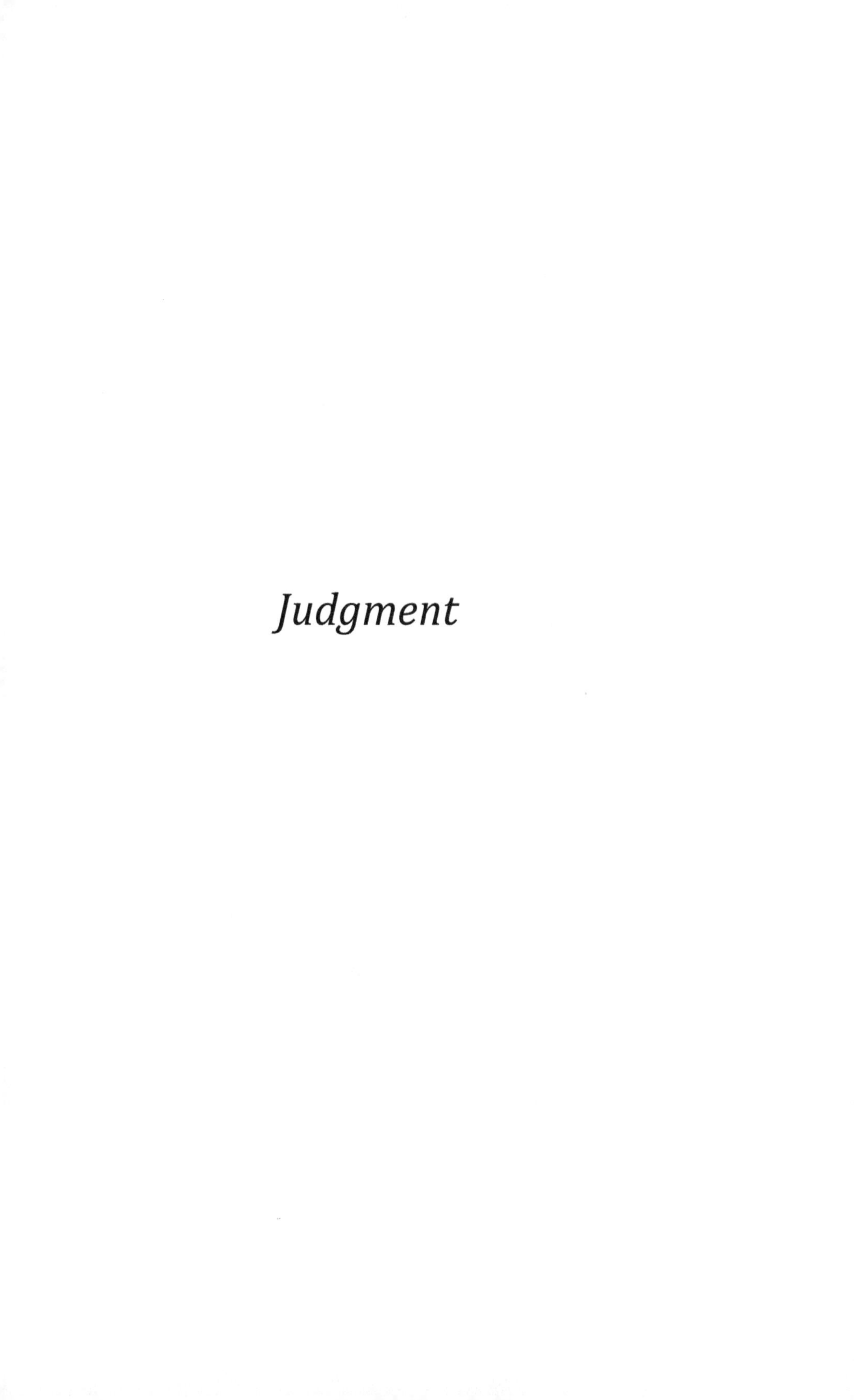

Judgment

This is story is a bit of a celebration because with it, I managed to break a bit of a seven year writer's block. In a sense, it wasn't a block at all. I managed to compose several operas and other vast works during this block, and yet for some reason the literary work was frozen. I discovered that a sleep disorder lady behind the problem. In moving to Thailand, it seemed I had also forgotten how to sleep.

In fact, many worlds intersect in the story. The music of Dufay was something I had been working on, and the mention of Gilles de Rais, the historical Bluebeard, harkens back to Bartok's opera as well as to Vampire Junction. *It also brings religion and science fiction together.*

I sent the story to Asimov's with some trepidation because I hadn't submitted a short story to anyone in something like fifteen years. To my amazement, it was as though I had never been away.

And the story also appeared in Locus Poll and Asimov's Readers' Poll nomination lists. I was incredibly grateful that the world I revisited still existed.

An Alien Heresy

I am not a heretic. I am a being from another world. I am lost. Send me home, I beg you.

You may say I am young to be an inquisitor, but in my brief existence in this world I have not remained unexposed to evil. For, in the Fourteen Hundred and Fortieth Year of Our Lord, I was a novice in the service of the Bishop of Nantes, and because I could scribe a fair round cursive hand, I was often called upon to set down confessions of such horror that it is hard to think of them even years later without a shudder; I mean revelations of deviltry, sorcery and heresy as would awaken doubt in the stoutest believer, and drive the purest of souls into the abyss of despair.

Thanks to that legible hand, I was appointed one of the scriveners at the trial of Gilles de Rais, called Bluebeard, and I was compelled to write down, dispassionately and accurately, descriptions of the mutilation of small children, onanistic rituals, and perversions I had never previously imagined. And when at last the Marshall of France came to be burned at the stake, I was asked to expunge some of the more lurid details from the record, for fear that the truth might give too much distress to future generations; and so my much-vaunted penmanship proved to be mere *vanitas.* What was torn from the pages, however, could not be expunged from our souls. We were scarred by it, and it still gives us nightmares.

Yet even that infamous trial would not prepare me for my encounter with the lost soul who claimed to have come from another world. It was only through my training and the sternest self-discipline that I would manage to survive the interrogation with my soul, to all appearances, intact.

The Gilles de Rais case was a dozen years ago, and now I was returning to Tiffauges, that cursed place where Bluebeard perpetrated his crimes. I was to investigate a new incident. It was a simple, open-and-shut case, just the kind of thing a junior inquisitor can handle in a week's work. His Grace the Bishop of Nantes used to favor me and often assigned me such routine cases, which help one to rise in the bureaucracy of the church and are not intellectually taxing.

These were the details: a fire from the sky. A strange man, mud-soaked, naked, seen by the river's edge. A strange man with strange eyes. Perhaps a demon; more likely a natural man, or a village idiot who had wandered back to the wrong village. I was either to quell their superstitions or, if necessary, act as the proper representative of the Church Militant.

Routine indeed. But of course no one wanted to travel to Tiffauges. I could feel the gloom long before I came in sight of the castle. Only three days by oxcart it might have been, but it felt as though I had left the world of men and entered a kingdom of ghosts. Beyond the hamlet of St. Hilaire de Clisson, it seemed that the sky became perpetually gray. Though it was already March, much snow still lay on the ground. The River Crûme was still part frozen, and, where it joined the Sèvre Nantaise, which is where the castle stands, ice clanged against ice.

When we arrived in the village, the sun was already going down. We were well stocked with provender, and we had brought all the instruments for the Question with us, in case nothing could be found locally. Ahead of me rode two knights, or rather a knight and his squire. I had not bothered to find out their names. In the cart with me sat Brother Paolo, a Roman musician and general note-taker, the dour-faced Brother Pierre, and the ever-smiling Jean of Nantes, a genial fellow, by avocation a barber, by trade a torturer. And I, of course, another Jean of Nantes — how many are there, I wonder? — who am called Lenclud.

A few hours' behind us marched the secular arm, a small detail of a dozen foot soldiers and a captain on horse; they would reach the village by midnight, perhaps, and would camp in the field.

My traveling companions had been garrulous all through the journey. Now, in the sunset, they could all feel the oppression in this village. No children played in the one muddy path that ran through the center, where stood a well. The huts were hushed. One, a little larger, seemed to pass for an inn. A bit of light came from within and there was had been noise, although the sound of our horses and oxen seemed to still it.

"We should press on," I called out to the knights, our escort. "It's barely one league to the castle."

The chateau had been abandoned since the trial, but it must at least have walls, and a fireplace, and a room in which to conduct interrogations.

"We'll put up in the inn," said the elder of the two.

I had certain reasons for avoiding that, but they were not reasons I could admit. I said, "Sir chevalier, another hour's riding at best will bring us to a place with stone walls; we'll have a roaring fire and we'll be able to sleep in real beds. And not have to pay," I added, for the execution of Gilles de Rais had made his lands temporarily forfeit to the church, until such time as all the rights and papers were sorted out.

"All very well for you to say, mon père," said the knight. "But think of us. And my squire's frightened; he's heard the stories."

The younger one turned around and I saw that he was, indeed, younger than I had thought from just seeing the back of his head for three days; but I had to hold to my word, lest authority be lost. It is in our training.

"We're not here to disrupt the village," I said. "The inquisition is not a circus. Let's get to the castle as quickly as possible, set up, and have the case brought to us properly."

"As you wish," said the knight.

But at that moment the inn door flew open. There were faces I knew; the innkeeper, even more grizzled than when last I saw him, some villagers who had given evidence in the matter of the Marshall of France; but I did not yet see the face I most dread to see, and so I breathed a sigh of relief. My traveling companions must have mistaken it for relief at seeing that this was not, after all, a village of ghosts.

"Father Lenclud," the innkeeper said, "it's best you came in."

I started to protest, "We are bound for Tiffauges," but he interrupted me. "What you want," he said, "is all in here."

The door opened wider. We saw tables inside, and we could smell a rabbit stew on the pot. There was a smoky light and the air heated up just a little; I could see the others were tired, and perhaps, perhaps the person I wished to avoid was no longer there. After all, it had been ten years; no, twelve. Perhaps I was safe after all. Perhaps she had gone away.

And in the grand scheme of things, it was, perhaps, a smallish sin, for which I had suffered seven painful penances already.

We piled inside, leaving our cart and our belongings unguarded; for who would steal from God? and we were offered benches inside; there were villagers there, and children, too, scurrying in the shadows; the walls were sooty and greasy; but the fire blazed, and the stew was filling.

The innkeeper said nothing while we ate, except to remind me of his name, which was Henri. I learned at supper that our knight was another Jean of Nantes; but this one we called Johan, because he had a Flemish mother.

It was only when we had eaten our fill that Henri was ready to tell us why the villagers had sent a letter to His Grace in Nantes.

"We've got him locked in the cellar," he said.

"And he is well rested, and has eaten?" It is true that we torture people, but we do love them; I never want to begin an investigation with threats and violence; that comes all too soon.

"Yes, he's eaten all right."

"Twelve fish," said a woman from the back. "I counted them myself. Raw. And all the bones. You've never heard such a crunching sound, mon père! Frightened out of our wits, we was."

"Bid her come out of the shadows," I said, "she seems to have a lot to say." And I regretted it as soon as I said it, because when she stepped into the light I recognized her, as I should have from the voice.

She knew me too. But she had the courtesy to lower her gaze, and gave no sign of it. In the firelight, in her grubby peasant shift, she was still beautiful, though. I looked longer than I ought to have. I was glad I had remembered to pack the flagellum.

"Your name?" I asked her, already knowing the answer.

"I am Alice, mon père. I am the innkeeper's wife."

So she had married. How much did the innkeeper know?

"Alice," I said softly, "tell me about the man in the cellar. If it is indeed a man; I have read the letter to the bishop, but we tend to view reports of devils in the flesh with a degree of cynicism."

The villagers looked at each other. Alice looked at me. Was there a hint of reproach? She did not reveal much. In the void in the conversations, all we could hear was the sizzle from the fireplace.

"Children, come out now," the innkeeper said at last, speaking at the shadows and at the space under the stairs. "The inquistor won't hurt you."

I realized then what it was that had subdued the noise. It was fear.

'You have to forgive us," Henri said, "they haven't trusted many people since ... you know."

Three children emerged. One was a little girl with stringy hair, perhaps seven; an older girl, on the cusp of womanhood, her shapeless smock belying an incipient voluptuousness. The two girls curtsied. Then there was the boy. He was perhaps eleven; he had long blonde hair, a dirty face, and clear blue eyes. He seemed so familiar ... I could not place him ... he did not look at me at all. But Alice did. At me and him. And in that awkward moment I understood everything, and I knew that her marriage must have been loveless, born from desperation.

"They saw him," the innkeeper said. "They'll tell you."

"We're not to tell him anything," said the boy, defiant. "They're going to burn him at the stake. He's our friend."

"Let the church be the judge of that now, Guillaume," Alice said. Was her voice not edged with cynicism?

"Guillaume, sit by me," I said, with all the gentleness I could muster. "Tell me of your friend." I reached out to touch his cheek. He flinched quite visibly, but overcame it, and sat on the bench. Meanwhile, the musician, the knight, and the torturer were already heavily into their ale. I called for Brother Pierre to take notes.

Guillaume kept his distance from me. I did not yet dare think the unthinkable: that I should acknowledge him, that he should have my name, that I could, in this peasant village, live on; that I had a son.

He said, "I'm sorry about the mud, mon père; that was my idea. Not any of the others'."

I remembered that the strange man was reportedly coated in mud. I waited for him to go on.

"It was a week ago. I wouldn't have seen the fire, but there was this noise, first. It was a rustling sound. I thought it might be a wolf, and we've only the one cow. I took a knife. When I stepped out of our hut it was almost as bright as day. When I looked up it was like the sun was in the sky, only bigger and more blue."

"Our Guillaume is prone to fancifying," the innkeeper said. "You tell mon père the truth now, you hear, don't exaggerate." To me he grumbled, "The boy should have been whelped in a castle, not a hut, the way he carries on."

"Go on, Guillaume."

"I'm not making it up," he said. "I can show you where the fire fell."

"An accursed spot!" said Henri. "No one has gone there save the boy since it happened. A whole circle of forest seared into a blackened clearing. If it isn't the devil's work, I don't know what is."

"Me and my sisters," said Guillaume, "we wanted to keep him as a pet. But someone saw him and denounced us to the inquisition. Are you going to torture him, mon père? Are you going to torture *me?"*

I would have embraced him then and there. But I knew that the pleasure of having him in my arms, the warmth of human love, was not for me; I am married only to Christ. And so I only said, "Guillaume, take me to that place."

"By the all the saints!" said the innkeeper. "Can you not burn the demon and be done with it?"

"I'll say this only once," I said. "Please listen. The men of the village could have handled this matter by themselves. They could have clubbed the stranger to death, hacked him up, buried him in an unmarked grave; without a feudal lord nearby, with the village's legal status still under negotiation, such a crime would almost certainly not have been noticed by anyone. But you chose to involve the Church. That was the right and honorable thing to do. But the Church is here now, and things will be done according to procedure. If a trial is necessary it will be a fair trial. If torture is demanded it will be strictly in accordance with the Papal Bull *Ad Exstirpanda*, which set appropriate guidelines over a century ago. If execution is required, it will be carried out by the secular arm in Nantes. We are not barbarians, Henri, and we shall not fall prey to peasant superstitions."

And that, it was to be hoped, was that.

And so I went out again into the cold, not yet having had a moment in private with Alice — for I dreaded that possibility — accompanied by Guillaume, by Brother Paolo, who fears nothing, and by Chevalier Johan and his squire, who held aloft a burning torch.

We entered the woods. Guillaume walked swiftly, knowing the location of every tree. We reached the clearing in only an hour, and when I stood there, with the bright moon shining down on every charred stalk, and the wind howling, I saw many hallmarks of the devil's work.

For example, the clearing was completely and perfectly circular. No random falling object, no hand of man could have made it so. The snow had melted and refrozen into a glassy shield, from whose center there projected a strange metal artifact. I say metal, but it had a purplish sheen unlike any steel or bronze I had ever looked upon.

Guillaume took me by the hand. "I'll show you the spaceship," he said. "Come, mon père. There's nothing living; it's just twisted metal."

"Spaceship?" said Johan the knight.

"That's the word *he* used," Guillaume said.

He tugged at my hand again, and, all in innocence, he tugged at my heart, too. I followed him, bold as he was, for he knew nothing of the dark powers, and I could not afford to show fear. The artfact was mostly concealed under the ice; we were seeing only the tip of it. It was a thing of delicate needles, of twists and twirls of metal, of gossamer webs no mortal hand could have woven. When I saw it my heart sank, for I knew that whatever was in the cellar of the inn was no lost village idiot. I prayed in my heart to the Blessed Virgin, and there sprang unbidden into my mind the image of Alice, Alice with unbound hair in the spring breeze, Alice of the ample breasts; and I trembled, knowing that the Dark One must have sent me that vision to divert me from my contemplation of all that is immaculate. I knew that tonight I was in for a long session with the knout, and that my hairshirt would be blooded come morning.

Now, I was truly afraid. But the boy was not. These infernal shards were just a new kind of toy for him, and the demon, perhaps, a new kind of pet. That is what is must be like, I thought, to grow up in the shadow of Tiffauges, in a world where evil, hanged and burned at the stake, still would not loose its grip. He bent down, stared at the metal with a natural curiosity, tried to pry the pieces from the ice, but they would not budge.

I looked at the boy, and past him, into the barren trees; beyond them I could see where the two rivers met, and I could see the castle as well; that is how bright the moon was, and how glistening the ice. The wind whistled. The chateau was a black and shapeless mass; one tower had already crumbled. Evil can rot even stone, rot it from within.

"We will turn back," I said curtly. The squire with the torch turned immediately. He sensed it too. Brother Paolo had been taking notes, even sketching the diabolical device on a scrap of vellum.

'Come, mon père," Guillaume said, "I'll take you to him now."

And on the way back to the village, the boy sang, in a hearty voice, the war-song *L'homme armé,* and because we were all afraid of the gathering dark, we followed his lead, and it was a raucous chorus; but as soon as we reentered the village something dampened our spirit and the singing petered out.

But Brother Paolo whispered in my ear, "That boy has a sweet voice, though untrained; he could really be something. I'll have him for the morning mass; he will brighten the gloom."

And so, with the others all fast asleep, or turning in, Guillaume led me down to the cellar. Always, our dour chevalier followed, his hand never leaving his sword-hilt. Brother Paolo had joined our friend the torturer in a room for six. I was to sleep alone.

He unlocked the door, lit a few more candles, and showed me what manner of creature had arrived at Tiffauges in a ball of flame.

Completely covered from head to toe in mud, as they said he would be. He was naked, a state permitted only before the Fall. Hunched over, chained to the wall by his ankles. Perhaps this room had served as a holding pen for Gilles de Rais' victims; for they were slender chains, such as might be used to subjugate a child.

Guillaume lit yet more candles, and now I could see the face clearly. The eyes were large and round, haunting, oddly beautiful.

"Len ... clud," he said. A sweet, small voice. It chilled me.

"Have you ever told it my name?" I said to Guillaume.

"No, mon père. He just knows things. He plucks them from people's heads, I think."

The eyes peered at me. Yes. I could feel something invading my thoughts. An alien presence. I tried to block it by thinking the words of the rosary over and over.

"Are you a demon?" I asked the stranger. When properly bound to answer by an emissary of the Church, a demon must speak the truth; for hell is ever subject to the will of heaven.

Suddenly, images filled my thoughts. I tried reciting the rosary aloud as though to drown them out. There were creatures with goats' horns, forked tails, hideous leering faces. He was answering me after all, in pictures if not in words.

"Stay back, Guillaume! Thiis creature has just shown me ... terrifying things."

"Mon père," Guillaume said, "he is only showing you what's in your own heart."

"It's a monster!" I cried, and I leaped to shield the child from its gaze.

And it said, "I not a monster."

Tears rolled down its cheeks. They dug great chasms in the mud. And now I could see what lay beneath all that mire. It was something green. The squamous, reptilian skin that was a certain mark of the dark powers.

"My son," I said, "you tried to hide his skin from us?"

"They would have killed him," said Guillaume.

"There are worse things than death," I said, and more images sprang into my head ... flames and bright red devil eyes, and I could almost smell the brimstone. "Tomorrow you will douse him with water, and we will see the extent of his monstrosity."

"I am not a monster."

His speech was much clearer than before. Before, he seemed to speak like the village idiot I had once thought him to be; now he had the more sophisticated accent of the city.

Guillaume said, "Mon père, he first learned to talk from us, but now he's getting it from you."

I stared into the monster's eyes and saw within them such a great despair that I knew he must be among those, once blessed by divine light, who were now eternally deprived of the presence of God.

"Perditus es," I said, for I knew that the devil must speak Latin.

"Per - di - tus." *Lost.* I did not know whether he understood, or if he was merely aping me; but then he continued: "Do - mum." He wanted to return home. He had even used the correct accusative of motion towards, so he could not have been simply copying my words.

"Ubi est domus tua?" I asked him where his home might be.

In response, he looked up at the dank ceiling. The candlelight flicked on old grime.

"In caelo," he said softly.

My home is in the sky.

Like Lucifer himself, he dared to claim heaven as his patrimony!

The cellar was cold, but the chill I felt was not from natural causes. I called for Chevalier Johan. "Sir Knight," I said, "the secular arm must have arrived by now. You must ride out quickly and tell them not to pitch their tents, but to ride straight to the chateau. They must clean out a few rooms and they must prepare a dungeon, and tell Brother Paolo to asperge the rooms with holy water, and celebrate mass in the chapel at dawn so as to purge the taint that hangs over it and over this village. Tell them to tie the accused up firmly and admit him there as the Church's ward. Ask them to clean the mud from the accused and to clothe him so that we do not have to be shamed in the sight of God with his nakedness."

The boy looked at me with alarm. "You'll burn him!" he said. "Our friend. He played with us."

"He is not your friend, my child. Go now."

I dismissed them all and told them to make fast the door of the cellar behind us.

And the stranger said, so quietly that indeed I was not sure whether he spoke aloud at all, or whether the words did not simply sound within the confines of my mind, "I am not a monster. I am from another world. I am lost. I beg of you, send me home."

I hoped for a few hours' peace before going to the chateau to say mass, but it was not to be. In the little cell they gave me, which was behind the kitchen, I scoured, by candlelight, the books I had brought with me, trying to glean some knowledge of just what this creature might be. Was he a denizen of hell who had somehow escaped the confines of the Dark One, and by saying "Send me home" was he actually begging for some kind of salvation, some reconciliation with God? Was there a village idiot underneath this skin, who had been possessed by a devil, who could yet be cured, if the devil could only be driven from the flesh? Was it a devious impostor, come to tempt me?

These were all possibilities. That was why a fair trial was essential.

In the brief hour of twilight, before the sunrise, I knelt down to pray. Before I did so, I stripped off my habit and my hair shirt, took the bloodstained knout from my satchel, and vigorously flagellated myself. To no avail. I had barely begun the paternoster when Alice, unbidden, entered the room. It was almost as though my penance had conjured up a further test.

"Mon père," she said. And then, again, "Oh Jean, my love."

I shook. My back was still bloody and it was perhaps the pain that convulsed me, though I should have been used to it by now; but no, it was the spiritual turmoil. "That was years ago. That was weakness. We can never think of it."

"That's easy for you to say, mon père," Alice said. "I've paid for it every day since then. I haven't come to reprove you. I know you scourge yourself. But there are other kinds of pain, too. Guillaume should not be growing up here, in this dreadful, desolate place. He's part of you. Can you not acknowledge that?"

"It's a lot to take in in a single day. Does he know?"

"Perhaps. I don't know. I've seen you look at each other. He must have guessed. And he has your eyes. I love him most for that."

"Alice," I said, "there are cardinals who have sired children, and popes who have made their bastards cardinals. But the Bishop of Nantes doesn't have a very modern mind. And I'm a Dominican. A *teacher*. How if it is seen that I do not follow my own preachings? Shall I give up even my vows to God?"

"Did you not do so already, Jean?"

And there she had me. But I had done penance. God forgives, even if the Bishop of Nantes would not. "What do you want me to do?"

"Take your son with you. You don't have to acknowledge him. Make him your servant. He could learn to read and write. He has a beautiful voice. He could have a future life as a singer."

"But they would have to cut him for that," I said. "And some boys do die under the barber's knife."

She has never seen what they do, I can tell. Oh, I have seen fine chanteurs with the voices of angels. The timeless melancholy of their songs comes, I think, from the wound to their manhood, which even when it has healed leaves a longing that can never be fulfilled.

"I don't understand those things. All know is that you have resources. You sleep in castles. You can call soldiers to throw people into dungeons. Your son has a grudging stepfather who doesn't want to spare the food to fill his belly, and he is the most powerless person in a village that men say is already damned. You must take him. Whipping yourself is all very well, but can't you see that you're also punishing *him?*"

I had come to Tiffauges to investigate a crime against God. But was I myself also to be subjected to the Question?

Alice kissed me. My flesh hardened, but I could not harden my heart. I turned away. I needed a pure heart for tomorrow.

"I'm sorry, mon père." She curtsied and left the room. Her scent remained. And so did the wound.

Why the wound, what wound? There was no wound. Should I not have followed the example of almost-martyred Origen and made myself a eunuch for the sake of the Kingdom of Heaven? Obviously a vow to God was an empty promise. Only the slice of a knife held truth.

Both Brother Paolo and Alice had told me Guillaume could sing; I only knew how well that morning, when I said mass in the chapel. Brother Paolo had found an old psaltery, and he had badgered the boy into coming up to the chateau and had taught him, neume by neume, a short chanson by Dufay, the Burgundian; and during the offertorium they contrived to perform it, with the brother playing the tenor on the psaltery and essaying the contratenor himself, while Guillaume took the upper part, with the high notes that seem to hover in the air....

I should say first that, at breakfast, over a loaf of black bread and a beaker of wine, the Chevalier Johan told me that all had been done as I had asked. They had requisitioned some of the peasants to dust and mop some of the rooms in the chateau; for they feared the soldiers more than they feared the curse of Bluebeard.

The chapel, wherein the Marshall of France had permitted the most repulsive abominations, had been scoured of dirt by dawn. The peasants who had been commanded to do the work stayed for mass, but several from the village came, too. Perhaps they thought that the touch of the host upon their tongues could take away the lingering taste of terror.

It was during the offertorium that Brother Paolo's ad hoc consort performed. The peasants had, of course, little to offer but a few loaves and cheeses; yet our torturer went among them, gracefully taking the gifts with a smile. They could never have guessed his normal profession.

The music was a setting of a holy sonnet by Francesco Petrarca; I knew this must be Brother Paolo's doing, for though the composer was Flemish, he had been in service in Italy, and the chanson had an Italian lilt to it, for the Italians have the fashion of giving a soaring melody to the highest voice, reducing the others to little more than accompaniment.

When I heard the words, I ached; for Petrarca speaks of the beautiful virgin cloaked in the sun and the stars, and then the poem goes on to say, "I want to offer you my prayers, but I cannot even begin to pray without your help. ..."

And it was the issue of my loins who sang those words, and he made the notes linger in the chill air as they climbed, note piling upon note, like a stairway to the sky —

In caelo.

That pitiful creature claimed to reside in the sky! And now he had put a curse on me, and I could not see the face of the Blessed Virgin with the raiment of starlight, but instead, a more earthly woman, a woman whose earthy scent and moist lips cried out for me to sin, whose every gesture was derived from the temptation of Eve and the wiles of the Serpent. I stood there, sweat pouring down my face even though the chapel was cold.

And my son's voice rose above the turmoil ... and there came dawn. A ray of light burst through the east window and illuminated the altar. And my son's voice was in that light. It lifted me out of darkness. In that melody was the voice of God himself.

And I saw the beauty in his eyes, my eyes....

I knew now how I had to redeem my sinful past. I had to rescue my son. Woman though she was, Alice had been a messenger. Those sweet sounds must not perish. He must be cut; surely the Lord would guide the knife Hmself, for the saving of so perfect a voice. My son was not to know the sins of the flesh. He could not fall as I had fallen. I knew then why God had sent me back to Tiffauges.

But for now, I kept this knowledge in my heart.

The papal regulations allow for only two sessions of Question; it is therefore the custom never to declare a session ended, so that the prescribed methods of ferreting out the truth may be applied until the truth is actually obtained.

The first session, which is intended to proceed without torture, I always like to stage in a well-lit room, without a threatening atmosphere. So we used the largest room in the chateau. Apart from a minimal chaining of the ankles, the prisoner was given free rein to stand or sit as he chose, and given a stool. I myself occupied what must have once been the Marshall's magisterial chair; flanking me were Brother Paolo, with his quill, ink, and parchment, and Jean the Barber; that, and our Chevalier and a few of the soldiers, were all that the huge council chamber held.

Now that I saw him in broad daylight, I knew why the children had covered him with mud. He was green. Oh, not *obviously* green, like grass or an emerald, but he had a gray-green cast to him. With a tunic, belt, and shoes, it was less noticeable, because the eyes were what held you most about him. But I did not fail to notice what I did not see in the dim light of the innkeeper's cellar; his hands were webbed, like the feet of a duck.

Once in a while, one hears of a child with webbed feet and hands being born in some remote village, and the peasants do not hesitate to kill it, for to dispose of a monster is not deemed murder. I had never heard of one surviving to adulthood.

Still, save for the odd coloration, the scales, the webbed hands, the creature did not exude an aura of evil. Not in this light, at least. I thought him more pitiful than terrifying.

Although I knew that he could speak Latin, I decided to begin the interrogation in the vulgar tongue.

"What is your name?" I asked.

"We have no names," he said. "We are all fragments of an All. Names are bad. They fracture us from the One." It was nonsense.

"But you must have a name," I said. It was a bureaucrat's nightmare; you have the papers, and you cannot even begin, because such things are filed away by name, and there is no name, how can one begin?

"We shall give you a name," I said. I turned to Brother Paolo. "Pick any name. We shall not fumble this case over some trickery."

"Call me Guillaume," said the creature.

Like Jean, Guillaume is one of the commonest names in France. But I could not help thinking that he took that name to taunt me with my sin. I was about to stop Brother Paolo, but he had already written it down.

"No, you are wrong," said Guillaume the Monster. "I honor him, he my first friend in this world." His French comes and goes; sometimes it is perfect; sometimes it is disjointed, as though he were stringing the sentences together from a heap of words.

"Why do you say this world? Know you another world?"

"I am lost. My world is far."

"Where is your world?"

Guillaume the Monster points only at the ceiling.

"Are you an angel?"

"Angel? ... Oh." He seems perplexed. He looks as though he is searching through some store of information to retrieve the word. "Oh. You mean Αγγελος." Then he says in French, "Messenger. Yes. I messenger."

"So you claim to be a member of the heavenly host."

"I fall from sky."

Brother Paolo cries out, "Listen! He condemns himself from his own lips. He is a fallen angel."

This was an outlandish claim; why would such an apparition not appear in some royal court, or before His Holiness himself? Why would a fallen angel choose an obscure village to bring his message to the world? But the answer was obvious when I thought about it. It was clear that the foul rites practices by Gilles de Rais had left a sort of spiritual chasm here. When a man murders hundreds of children to satiate his sexual appetites, all the while invoking the names of the Dark Powers, there are surely consequences to the natural order. For the tiniest sin is a hideous affront to God, and these were monstrous. It was as though Bluebeard had dug a well straight through to the heart of hell. Why not, then, a fiend shooting forth from the infernal depths, cloaked in fiery brimstone, to tempt the mind of an innocent?

Still, there were some elementary tests. "Can you say the Lord's Prayer?" I asked him.

The monster said, "How can I know these things? I come from the sky."

Jean the Torturer said, "I'm afraid that there's very little we can do about this." I knew he was not anxious to get out all his instruments, but like all of us he understood the meaning of duty.

I said, "Let's not be in a rush to be cruel. I suggest we try an exorcism first."

As was the custom, I declared, and entered into the record, that the session was adjourned; and we took our midday break, after leaving the prisoner more securely chained up in the council chamber, and well guarded.

The innkeeper sent up a brace of duck to the chateau; it was my son who brought the food, for though we had dismissed him after the morning mass, he had begged for some excuse to return.

We ate quickly and prepared our vestments as well as an aspergillum and a large cauldron of holy water. I asked the Chevalier to send a swift rider to Nantes; I suspected that reinforcements were going to be needed; not more soldiers, but more expert demonologists. Reverently, I kissed the violet stola before placing it over my surplice. I have never taken exorcism lightly.

But when I returned to the council chamber, I found the two Guillaumes alone together.

"What are you doing?" I shouted.

My Guillaume backed away. He had been bent over the prisoner; he had a cup in his hand.

"I'm sorry, mon père. I was giving him water."

I said, "You, of all people, need to stay away from him. He has invaded your mind more than anyone. He has plucked things out and will use them against us — against you in particular. Your immortal soul is in grave peril."

He looked at me and I could sense — defiance. And then, with bowed head, my Guillaume slunk away.

"Do you know what I am going to do?" I asked the monster.

For normally, when one is about to perform an exorcism, the demon has foreknowledge. When the holy water is brought into the room, he begins to howl. He hurls obscenities at the priest, and malodorous fumes begin to rise, which are best counteracted by the liberal use of frankincense. To that end I had already prepared two censers and the sweet fragrance was already seeping into the room. But Guillaume the monster did not respond at all.

I began the asperging, dipping the aspergillum and calling on the Father, the Son and the Holy Ghost, the Blessed Virgin, St. Peter, St. Michael, St. Denis and all the company of heaven to witness. Brother Paolo held up the crucifix to the prisoner's face, but the creature did not flinch; he merely stared at it curiously, blinking.

I started the preparatory incantations and then, summoning up all my inner strength, I bellowed out the words of exorcism: *Exorcizo te, immundissime spiritus, omnis incusio adversarii, omne phantasma, omnis legio, in nomini domini nostri Jesu Christi eradicare...* and with each sign of the cross I swung the aspergillum, knowing full well that the power that resided in the water would burn the devil from the being's flesh ...

But Guillaume the monster sat there.

And when the ritual was done, he spoke to me. "That was an interesting ceremony, Father Lenclud. What does it mean? May I see a repetition, so that I can play back the recorded memory to my companions in the sky?"

There arose in me a terrible anger. He was mocking me. He was mocking the Almighty. I knew that this blind fury was a sin. I went outside to get some fresh air. I was panting and my heart was beating fast. In the courtyard, I saw my Guillaume, sitting by a well.

My son pulled a fresh bucket of water, and gave me to drink. Though the noonday sun was brilliant, there were still piles of snow among the cobblestones. He held out the bowl for me, and the sun was behind him and the wind stirred his hair and I saw in his face all that I once wished to be, but could no longer, for that I had long descended into tainted ways of sin. I wanted to tell him right then and there, but perhaps it was not the moment. I drank deeply and the water cooled my choler.

"How is he?" my son said. "Is he in pain?"

I saw in his face a profound compassion and I thought to myself, "Guillaume, my son, you are good to feel such Christian love for even such a creature as this." I wanted so much to embrace him. But we are taught to avoid the warmth of human closeness, for darker dangers may lurk behind an innocuous caress. The mere touch of a boy's hand has aroused unnatural passion in many a cleric. It were better not to risk it. Love is best experienced solely in the spirit. I cursed myself for a hypocrite to think such things when only last night Alice had flung herself at me and I had released myself only with reluctance from temptation. I only said, "We are not torturing him at the moment, my son. It is possible that he will reveal all without recourse to the second stage of the Question. And we will all be spared much grief."

All afternoon, I wielded the aspergillum with a will. I shouted out the words of the ritual. Three times we commanded the devil to depart. Three times I flung the water and shouted out those puissant words, words composed to make Satan himself quake in the bowels in hell; yet the prisoner did not yield, did not even show fear; if he evinced any emotion at all, it was curiosity. Exhausted and exasperated beyond all measure, I finally hurled the entire basin at him. It struck him in the head. The water scattered and clouds of steam rose up. And at this unexpected turn, he slumped over and I was immediately concerned, for it is not a priest's duty to inflict pain. But then, when I looked about him, I saw that the pools of water were all boiling, and that there poured from a gash in his forehead a thick green rheum; and the creature began to vibrate as though he had the falling sickness, so that the chains clanked and made a racket that should have woken the very dead. A blast of heat emanated from him, and unearthly sounds poured from his throat; at last, I could see the symptoms of possession.

And, as I gaped, the wound in his brow knit itself together, and the pools of water ceased seething, and the room was as icy cold as before.

And he sat there, unperturbed.

I sank back on my inquisitorial chair. I was sweating. I called for wine. Slowly, the creature seemed to regain his senses, and sat up as before.

I folded my palms and began to pray. "God," I whispered, "I am already worn out. The demon will not budge. Oh God, give me strength. My faith is sorely tested." These words I spoke for myself alone.

So I was surprised when an answer seemed to come, not from heaven, but from my green-skinned adversary. "You know, Father," he said, "there is another possibility."

We are warned never to engage in conversation with the devil, for it leads only to despair. But before I could think of that, I had already said, "And that is?"

"Is it not possible," he said, "that I am *not* in fact possessed, and that I am simply what I say I am?"

I dared not respond for fear of further temptation. For I knew then that we were in the presence of a very powerful force indeed; that this was a stubborn being and that the light of truth would reach him only with the utmost difficulty. If the creature were not inhabited by a demon, he must be making those impious statements out of his own free will; which meant that he must be a heretic.

I took another gulp of the wine, and I commanded that he be removed to the dungeon. This investigation was inexorably moving down a path I did not wish for. Nonetheless, I reflected, *thy will be done.*

I rode down to the village because I could not bear to sleep in the vicinity of that being. Of course, in the village I faced demons as well, but at least they were my own.

At the inn, I supped on boiled leeks and a bit of pigeon meat. I sat alone, long after the others had retired, nursing a warm ale. Perhaps I dozed a little. I was startled awake, perhaps by the sound of the embers collapsing, for the fire was dying. I saw that my Guillaume was in the room, and that he was standing over me, gazing down at my face.

"My son," I said. A priest would say that to any boy. Yet I immediately feared to have revealed to much.

"Mon père, I would speak to you alone."

"Shall I take your confession?"

"It's not that. Mon père, Brother Paolo has been speaking to me. He says I should leave the village and seek my fortune as a singer. He told me that a voice like mine could gladden the hearts of prelates and of kings. He told me about cities and places I'll never see if I'm stuck here minding the pigs until I die. My mother told me the same thing. But they also say I will have to give up something. I don't want that."

"Did they explain it to you?"

"Yes. They said that if I undergo the cutting, I'll never become a man. But I'll never lose this voice, either. They say it's a sacrifice I must make. Otherwise I'll always be a peasant, and I'll always be a bastard. But I know it'll hurt and I know people die, sometimes."

"What did you say to your mother?" I asked him.

"I said, I really don't want to do it. I'm scared. I don't like pain. The innkeeper ..." He hesitated. "Well, I am a bastard," he said. He turned his back to me and lowered his tunic a little, and I could see scars in the firelight. And I burned with anger, but I held back that anger, for anger is one of the seven deadly sins. Truly, my sin was being visited on the next generation. If my son was willing to be cut, I reflected, at least the cycle of penance would end. "It's all right, really. I don't mind pain that much. I get it often enough. It's like I can't do anything right for him."

"Sit here beside me, Guillaume of Tiffauges," I said. He obeyed. His closeness terrified me. "Did your mother say that you should undergo this operation?"

"She said that it was entirely my decision."

"And what is your decision?" I dared to caress his hair for a brief moment.

"I told her that I will do it if you command it, mon père."

"Why me?"

"Because you are my father," he said.

And I saw that he knew, he knew it with utter certitude, as I knew of the existence of heaven and hell. "Who told you this?" I said. "Your mother swore to me she would never speak of our —"

"She didn't betray you, mon père. I found out for myself."

"But how?

"He told me, mon père."

Should I now say that the boy wept, and told me how he had dreamed for so many years of knowing his father, that he had imagined him a crusader, a warrior, a hunter, a prince, a troubadour, a sorceror, but never in his wildest dreams a priest? Should I tell how his tears broke down my reserve at last, and how I embraced him and felt at long last the joy of an untainted love?

But I may not say these things. Because, at that time, they did not happen. Rather I answered him very simply, "Then I do command it."

And he said, "I will do what you tell me, father." And he got up, and planted a single dry kiss upon my tearless cheek, and he left me.

I thought of the pain I was about to inflict upon him. But I thought also of God the Father, who must have known full well what pain our Lord his Son would have to undergo; I thought also of Isaac, consenting to the knife with joy because it was his father's will; and only then, only when there was no one to see me, did I give way to tears. I cried myself to oblivion, and before dawn they found me there, and woke me for the trek back up to the chateau, so I could say mass.

As the "gentle persuasion" portion of the investigation was now over, it seemed more appropriate to continue in the dungeons. The use of torture is never to be undertaken without proper reflection. After all, anxious as they were to obtain a conviction, the Inquisition did not torture Joan of Arc.

The dungeons were the dark heart of Tiffauges. It was there that Bluebeard once made a pile of the decapitated heads of the children he had murdered, so that he could compare them to see which was the most beautiful. It was here that the Marshall of France kept his captives, lured to the castle by the promise of a place in the chapel choir or a position as page in the great lord's estate. It was here that he sated his lusts with all manner of vice, culminating always in erotically charged slaughter.

No torture unto death would of course, be practiced by us. Indeed, the papal instructions are very specific, for we may not even shed one drop of blood during the Question. Bloodletting is the domain of the secular arm; our concern is only with the soul.

Only a single session of torture is permitted by church law, though one can extend that session over many periods if need be.

I entered the dungeon they had selected, one with no light but torchlight, and an odious damp, with vermin underfoot — for it is important to produce in the Questioned person the feeling of utter hopelessness, so as to hasten his confession. Jean the Torturer had already set up the strappado. The Inquisitorial chair had been brought down, and a rich rug placed to receive it and the desk, at which Brother Paolo already sat, with his notebook and quill at hand, making the initial entry by candlelight.

Guillaume the Monster had been stripped of his clothing, for the shame of public nakedness is often enough to induce a confession. Naturally, I averted my eyes, for it is not seemly for a spiritual man to behold such things; but curiosity made me look anyway, and when I did I could not help but stare.

The greenish cast of the skin was of made more reptilian in the dungeon's smoky light. They had already tied the cords to the shoulders, and attached the weights to his feet, but the torturer was waiting for my signal before beginning the actual excruciation.

As I grew used to the dimness, I stood up to examine him more closely, hoping for some sign that would allow me to avoid torture. For example, a clear supernumerary nipple could indicate his involvement in witchcraft; a circumcised *membrum virile* would signify that he was a Jew. We could have proceeded straight to the conviction.

But this monstrosity possessed no nipples at all, nor anything resembling the organ in question. His chest was a pattern of scales. Below his waist, his legs began. The scale pattern continued straight down.

He said, "You seem surprised, mon père."

"You are ... you are a natural eunuch! And without even vestigial nipples ... you are neither male nor female ... were you female, you could not suckle a child ... were you male, you could not engender a child ... you are an abomination!" The horror of it was unbearable. It was a prodigy.

"Perhaps my kind does not require this type of reproduction," said Guillaume the monster.

"So you claim to be without original sin?" I said.

"What is sin?" said the monster.

"Do you not honor God?"

"Who is God?" he asked me.

I could listen no more. I gave Jean the signal to hoist him up. As the weights left the ground I could hear the crack of the shoulder joints dislocating. "You deny God?" I shouted. "You claim to be in a state of grace?"

He writhed, and a serpentine hissing escaped his lips.

"More weights!" I screamed. "You will confess!"

"To what shall I confess?"

"That you are a heretic! That you claim to be free of sin, a state the Church alone is empowered to bestow through the holy rite of confession and absolution! Confess!"

"I am not a heretic. I am from another world. I am lost. Send me home."

"And how shall that be, when you claim that your home is in heaven?"

"I have already told your son how I may go home! There are two ways; the first is for me to communicate with the mother ship. The device is under the ice! You have but to wait until the spring thaw is complete and —"

At the mention of my Guillaume, I became more furious. With what corruptions had he been feeding my son? I commanded the torturer to add more weights, while every croak, every hiss was carefully noted down by Brother Paolo. The arms were already quite out of their sockets; the muscles were tearing; the monster's eyes bulged and he appeared to gasp. But what I did not hear were cries of pain. And so I hardened my heart and told Jean the Torturer to add weights until there were far more weights than any human could bear, which proved that Satan was behind his unnatural resistance, and which inflamed my rage still more.

"Confess that you have denied the sacraments! That you're a Jew! A witch! That you have had carnal knowledge of Satan! That you're a Cathar! A Waldensian! You have but to admit to a single heresy and I will cease tormenting you!"

It was at that moment, with my emotions aroused to fever pitch, that our captive's arms tore loose and he fell to the floor with a crash. It was horrible. A greenish sap began to ooze from sockets. The arms flailed back and forth as though independently alive.

"We're spilling blood!" I gasped, horrified that we had broken the papal regulations. "Jean, you must stanch it quickly!"

"I don't understand," said the torturer. "I haven't applied enough pressure to rip off any limbs." He was upset; a professional should know his craft better than to make such a bungle of things; I could tell that he was utterly appalled at himself. Quickly he found some rags so that he could prevent too much blood from touching the ground, which is the actual letter of the law we were violating. There was some straw in the dungeon — it was the prisoner's bedding — and he threw it over the heretic to try to absorb some of the gore.

But Brother Paolo said, "It is green, Father Lenclud. It is not blood."

The severed arms swung back and forth and now began to sizzle and chair, and an acrid green smoke began to fill the dungeon. I ordered more torches to be lit. We had to see what we were doing. A foul green fluid was spurting over our faces. I saw that Brother Paolo was right. This was not blood. It had neither the stickiness nor the characteristic scent. Jean the Torturer had not broken the law.

Meanwhile, Jean the Monster was writhing on the stone floor. A cacophonous babble issued from his lips. Doubtless it was some appalling witchery such as the Lord's prayer backwards. Indeed, clearly there was necromancy afoot, because the creature's shoulder sockets were quivering, vibrating, and small green stalks were pushing their way out through the flesh ... he was growing a new pair of arms, as though they were the tails of a lizard! I simply stared. The babble resolved itself once more into words:

"I am not a heretic. I am from another world. I beg you, send me home. I can wait until the spring thaw is complete. Or you can set off my internal monitor to signal the ship...."

Words they may have been, but it was still nonsense.

"His body magically repairs itself," said Jean the Torturer, and I was reminded of the tale of the hydra, who grew more heads whenever one was chopped off.

"But," said Brother Paolo as he finished a sentence of his trial transcript with a flourish of his quill, "the regeneration the flesh, and the fact that his body contains no blood to be spilled, opens up, by the legal constraints imposed by the papacy, a loophole in the process of excruciation...."

I understood at once. Without blood, without any permanent destruction of the flesh, there was no legal limit to the violence that could be inflicted upon this monster in the interests of perhaps saving his immortal soul.

Jean immediately strung him up again and, secure in the knowledge that he was committing no excommunicable crime, brought out more extreme instruments of pain. The scourgings, lashings, and burnings made us all wince, but the creature's stubbornness continued to inflame me, and by late afternoon I had almost taken complete leave of my senses. His stubbornness caused almost a reversal in our roles; for where normally the accused would be pleading for mercy after a few hours' torment, it was Brother Paolo and I who were so worn out by the monster's equanimity that we were beginning, pleading, cajoling the creature to try to get even the vaguest confession.

Half a dozen pairs of arms hang from the rafters. Straw on the floor was soaking up puddles of greenish phlegm.

Jean's art had punctured the monster's skin in several places. There were holes through which we could see the foul workings of his innards, and now, as he lay, his skin pulsating, yet another pair of arms pushing forth out of his sockets, his words were hoarse and accompanied by a bizarre whistling as breath passed through the many extra channels through his flesh. And he continued his talk of coming from the sky, and returning there, and incomprehensible mumbo-jumbo about his mission and about his internal sensors. We must have made some kind of an impression, surely! For his voice wheezed, and it seemed to me that I saw some weariness in his eyes.

I was about to declare an official continuation of the session until the next day, when the door of the dungeon creaked open, and my son Guillaume entered the tortured chamber.

"Church business is not to be interrupted!" Brother Paolo shouted, and threw a cape over the monster. But I knew that Guillaume had already seen.

"Mon père," he said, "I have come as you commanded, to receive the operation."

There was a dead silence. Under the cloak, the monster twitched and fibrillated. Guillaume looked up at the ceiling, where the creature's many pairs of severed arms still dangled. The cloak slid off the monster's face and we could all see his eyes, peering back and forth with a discomfiting watchfulness.

Guillaume looked at me and raised his arms in a gesture of remonstrance, and I said simply, "What can I do, Guillaume? He won't confess."

"Mon père," Guillaume said, "You could have asked me. I know what will make him confess."

"Child, there is a manual of instruction composed by His Holiness himself about these matters. We deviate from it on pain of eternal damnation. Leave these things to us. Come upstairs, now, into the light. We'll talk of your operation and of your future. Forget what you've seen."

"But mon père," he said, "my mother tells you have an expert, who will wield the knife deftly and who will give me as little pain as he can. Who is he?"

"I," said Jean the Torturer, who in an ideal world would have preferred to be known only as Jean the Barber.

And he held out hands of welcome, hands oozing with the monster's green rheum.

The torturer had not, of course, brought a gelding knife. He had to do with an instrument that had that same day sliced leeks in the castle kitchens. But I wanted the cutting to occur in a room as distant as possible from the squalor of Guillaume's former life. The peasants looked askance when I requisitioned the Marshall's own bedchamber, and commanded that clean linens be set out, and a goose-down pillow; but they could not argue with me, for I represented the Church, and the Church had jurisdiction over the chateau for the present.

I had them gather plenty of wood for the fireplace. I even went so far as to order Jean the Barber to bathe, so that my son would not see the traces of the monster's excruciation upon his hands. And I had extra candles brought in so that he would not wake up in the dark, and be frightened. The finest silver basins were brought in to catch the blood and to hold water to lave the wound.

Guillaume was terribly afraid. We held him down, I by the arms and Brother Paolo by the legs. I gave him a twig to bite on. I could not look into his eyes, could not gaze on the terror which was being inflicted by my wioll alone. The barber lifted the boy's tunic and sliced and Guillaume started screaming almost before the knife touched flesh, and he went on screaming. We held him fast. I did not realize there would be this much blood. I squeezed my eyes shut as the boy screamed and the torturer turned barber sliced, steadily and methodically, until the boy's scrotum was completely severed. Then, working as swiftly as he could, he applied linen bandages and a salve, wrapping as Guillaume screamed himself into a frenzy and, at last, exhausted from it all, sunk back onto the bloody sheets.

"You can let go of him," said the barber. "It is done."

I realized I was still gripping the lad's arms tight. I relaxed, but he clung to my wrists and murmured, "Papa, papa." And then he fainted.

The others looked away. I knew then that they must have already known. "I will sit with him," I said.

"Yes, you must," said Jean. "The first hours are critical. He is in so much pain that his soul cannot decide whether to depart his body. It isn't only the physical pain, mon père; it's the feeling of eternal loss. He doesn't even *want* to come back ... but you can give him something to hope for, to live for."

And all of them left me, and I sat alone, by the side of the bed, listening to him moan. I could not sleep. I did not know whether Guillaume slept; he twisted and turned, and sometimes his eyes opened; he never let go of my hand. The one Guillaume I had meant to hurt, and not the other; somehow I had reversed them. I prayed; how I did pray. "I'll give my immortal soul," I whispered, "if he will only pull through."

Towards midnight, he seemed to quieten. I wiped the sweat from his brow. He stirred. At last, he opened his eyes. He said, very softly, "Don't you want to know how to get him to confess?"

I said, "Don't think of it, my son."

"You hurt me," he said.

"I know," I said. And squeezed his hand.

"I don't mind," he said. "It's what you wanted."

I said, "The pain will go away."

He said, "I did what you wanted. So now, I'm going to ask you to do something I want."

"Anything," I said softly.

"He will confess if you promise that you will burn him at the stake," Guillaume said.

"Don't say such things," I said. "There's no need for you to become involved in —"

"No, Papa, please listen. I will tell it to you exactly as I heard it, because I don't understand it, but he's made me memorize it many times. He doesn't appear to be in pain, but he is desperate. He can wait until the thaw to retrieve his communication device, but there is another way for him to go home, another, more desperate way. He has a transmitter embedded deep inside him. It's not a machine, it's a part of him because he's connected to all the others. If his vital signs suggest that he's in imminent danger of death, it will start to transmit ... he told me they're cold-blooded. Extreme heat will set it off."

"You are delirious," I said. "You're speaking nonsense."

"But promise me that you will tell him you'll burn him at the stake."

The boy was clearly maddened by his agony, but I knew I had to promise. I did so. He squeezed my hand again, and finally drifted into slumber.

In the morning, I did what my Guillaume had asked me, and the monster immediately, to my astonishment, confessed to an entire litany of heresies. I fell to my knees and thanked God that I no longer needed to have recourse to torture. I swore then that, though I had promised to burn the creature, I would give him a final chance to repent and accept the mercy of strangulation; I owed him that much at least, for it was because of him that I had learned what it is to love a child.

And in the afternoon, we put the heretic's cap and robes on our prisoner and shut him up in a cage, as one would a circus animal, and hitched the cage to an ox; and I wrapped my son up in many layers of blankets and loaded his pallet onto my cart for the drive back to Nantes.

Alice and the innkeeper came to see us off; but I did not say a word to them.

And for the burning itself, Guillaume would not leave the house, though he was hale enough to have started his singing lessons.

There are not so many heretic burnings as there used to be; and so it was that by the time enough heretics had been delivered to the secular arm that a reasonable spectacle could be had on market day, the days had lengthened and there was no more snow to be seen. And each day, my son grew stronger, and we never spoke of the night of his delirium.

But I had made a vow to God that I would personally try to urge Guillaume the Monster towards an eleventh hour repentance. And thus it was I found myself standing beside him at the stake, holding up a cross to him and urging him to turn to God.

"Who is God?" he asked me.

Around us, they were already burning. The crowd was festive; they laughed, they sang, music played, sausages were being grilled; church bells rang. But it all seemed irrelevant. What transpired now was between the two of us alone.

In my whole life, I have made love only once, and that was in shame. And yet I have heard, in the confessional, enough to know what it is like for laypersons. Lovemaking is not permitted to men who have given themselves wholly to Christ, and yet, to us inquisitors, there is an alternative. For the process of the Question is not unlike carnal knowledge of a woman. That may seem twisted, even obscene, but there is truth in it.

First, you see, there comes the foreplay, the teasing, the flirting; that is the first stage, where we try to extract the confession swiftly; yet if we succeed, it is somehow not entirely fulfilling. Then there is the physical part; the writhing, the flailing; that, you see, is the torture, and that can lead only to one thing: the final explosion of passion, the spurting of the seed; that is the confession, you see. And at least, with the violent emotions spent, comes the afterglow, the gentle conversation, the quiet descent into slumber.

And this was the manner of conversation now, at the ultimate hour. There was no going back. He had asked me who God is, and I was bound to tell him: "God is the one who made us all, who loves us, who knows us inside out; and he dwells in Heaven. He who does not seek God is bound forever to the darkness."

"If that is true," said Guillaume the Monster, his scaly face utterly serene, "then I already know God. And I am going to him now. For the being of which I am a part does dwell in the sky, and when I am cut off from him I am utterly desolate."

"You have rejected him," I said.

"And what sane sentient being," said the monster, "would *not* reject your God? You have made a mockery of compassion. You have twisted the truth in a thousand ways."

"Repent," I cried out, and I held the cross right up to his face. It cast a cruciform shadow on his alien features.

"It is because you humans are all islands, because you are not part of some greater consciousness, that you have invented these fanciful stories about gods and demons," he said. "If you only knew how alone each one of you was, how incapable you are of the weakest psychic communion, you would despair. You would not care to live."

A soldier of the Secular Arm called up to me. "Come down, Father Lenclud! We need to get going, this is the last one."

"For the last time," I cried out. "You can be saved if you only say a few words of repentance. You can become a dwell in Him, in the unity of the holy spirit —"

"Then I am already God, for I already dwell in Him," he said.

And the fire began to blaze. I knew that I myself would be consumed if I did not leave. The piles of kindling crackled. The flames hissed. Already, the creature's extremities were beginning to char.

At that moment, the sky abruptly darkened. A monstrous dark *thing* descended and blotted out the sun. A shaft of brilliant blue light hit shot out of the heaves and struck the heretic, and he immediately vaporized. And then it was over, and the sun shone as before.

I looked wildly about. The revelers in the streets still danced and sang. Hawkers sold wine and food. Had no one seen what I had seen? And was the creature not gone? There were only the chains. Had my eyes played tricks on me?

I was troubled that night. I could not reconcile what I had seen with all that I knew and believed. And yet, as time passed, I grew to believe that it may have only been an illusion. For to believe the alternative made me far too uneasy. And I had to be steadfast in faith, for I had a child to raise.

In the bedchamber of the new King Louis XI of France, my son Guillaume is singing. I am not permitted to enter; it is a performance for the most intimate circle of the King's friends.

But as I wait for my son behind the arras, I realize that the song is another by that Burgundian, Dufay, whose song to the Blessed Virgin once moved Brother Paolo to demand the boy's emasculation. This is a secular song, *Donnes l'Assault,* in which the poet compares his lady to an impregnable castle to which he has lain siege. He speaks of battering down the gate to enjoy the treasure within. It is a bawdy song, turning images of war into double entendres. There is laughter in the bedroom; men's laughter, the high-pitched silvery laugh of a loose woman.

I wait for the song to end. It is a tawdry song, but haunting, too. And the wounded innocence of my son's voice transforms the song from a jest to a thing of vaunting beauty.

Was it for this that my Guillaume gave up becoming a man?

He will be wealthy, I know; he will be a courtier. But he did not do it to become rich. He did it as a proof his love. He did it because I demanded it of him.

Yet who was I to play God?

I too have become powerful. I too have become rich. But something in me has died. Or perhaps was plucked from my soul and has ascended into the sky along with the body of my heretical monster.

I too have been transformed by that fire. I have sent many more to the flames since that day. I have signed many death-warrants. I have consented to innumerable sessions of savage torture, and always with the knowledge that my scruples have ineluctably eroded until the act of condemning a man to an agonizing death has become but a figment of bureaucracy. I have come to believe that I am evil. I have come to accept that, because my becoming evil is the price of being allowed to love my son.

For though the heretic from another world has incontrovertibly proved to me that Satan exists, I am no longer certain of the existence of God.

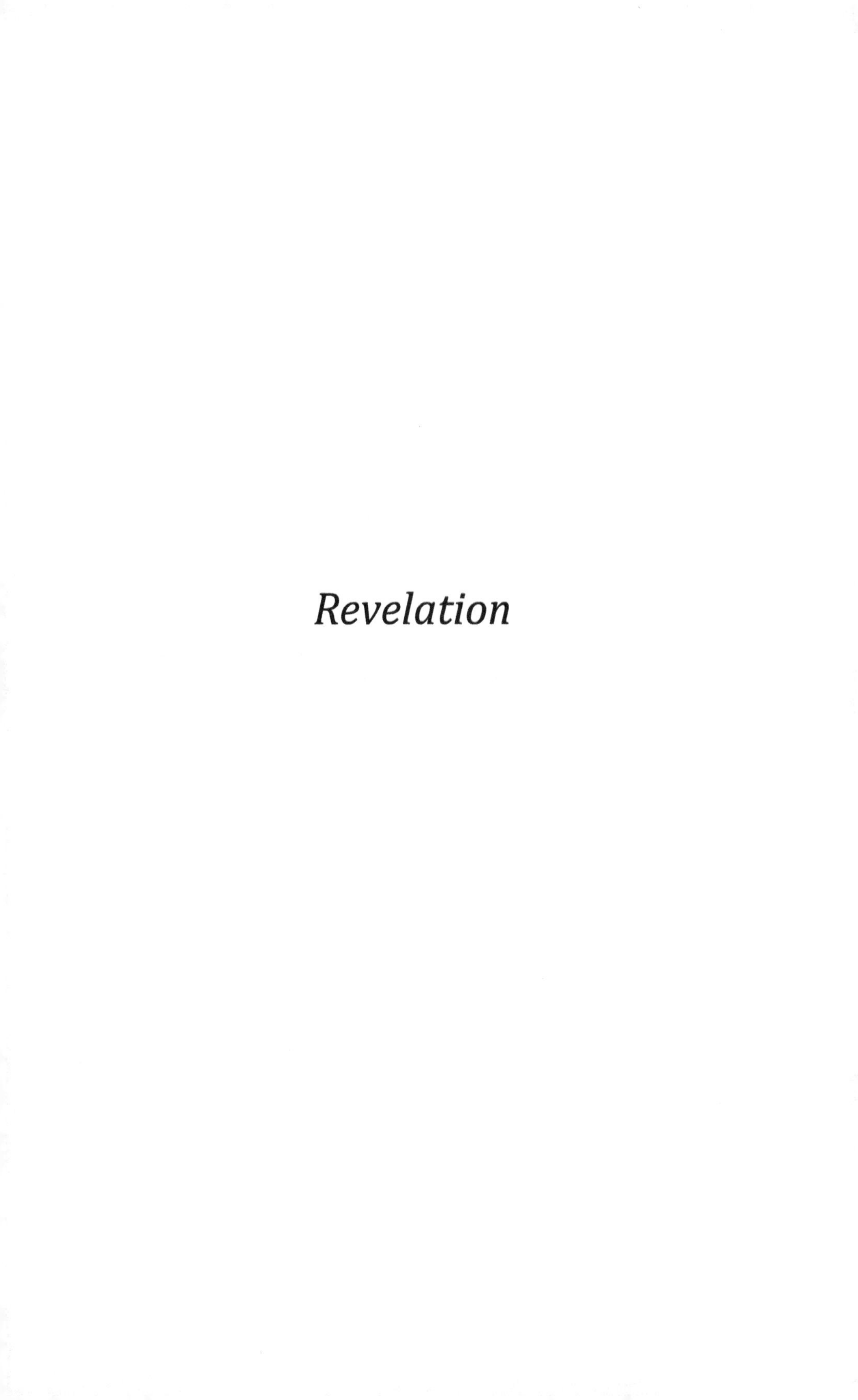

Revelation

This story was nominated for a number of awards. both in this form and in its later incarnation as a labyrinthine novel. Zombies appear again ... as elsewhere in this collection ... because they are the dark side of resurrection. I lived in Virginia for seven years and think about it often. The story was originally written for Confederacy of the Dead, *a Civil War anthology.*

I couldn't let go of the story and in the end it gave birth to the most convoluted novel I ever wrote, created in the Arabian Nights *style of naration in which stories are nested inside other stories, at times up to seven layers deep.*

Darker Angels

One day there'll be historians who can name all the battles and number the dead. They'll study the tactics of the generals and they'll see it all clear as crystal, like they was watching with the eyes of the angels.

But it warn't like that for me. I can't for the life of me put a name to one blame battle we fought. I had no time to number the dead nor could I see them clearly through the haze of red that swam before my eyes. And when the gore-drenched mist settled into dew, when the dead became visible in their stinking, wormy multitudes, I still could not tell one from another; it was a very sea of torsos, heads, and twisted limbs; the dead was wrapped around one another so close and intimate they was like lovers; didn't matter no more iffen they was ours or theirs.

I do not recollect what made me stay behind. Could be it was losing my last shinplaster on the cockroach races. Could have been the coffee which warn't real coffee at all but parched acorns roasted with bacon fat and ground up with a touch of chicory. Could be it was that my shoes was so wore out from marching that every step I took was like walking acrosst a field of brimstone.

More likely it was just because I was a running away kind of a boy. Running was in my blood. My pa and me, we done our share of running, and I reckon that even after I done run away from *him* and gone to war, the running fever was still inside of me and couldn't be let go.

And then, after I lagged behind, I knowed that if I went back they'd shoot me dead, and if they shot me why then I'd go straight on to the everlasting fire, because we was fighting to protect the laws of God. I just warn't ready for hell yet, not after a mere fourteen years on this mortal earth.

That's why I was tarrying amongst the dead, and that's how I come to meet that old darkie that used to work down at the Anderson place.

The sun was about setting and the place was right rank, because the carrion had had the whole day to bloat up and rot and to call out for the birds and the worms and the flies. But it felt good to walk on dead people because they was softer on my wounded feet. The bodies stretched acrosst a shallow creek and all the way up to the edge of a wood. I didn't know where I was nor where I was going. There warn't much light remaining and I wanted to get somewhere, anywhere, before nightfall. It was getting cold. I took a jacket off of one dead man and a pair of new boots from another but I couldn't get the boots on past them open sores.

You might think it a sin to steal from the dead, but the dead don't have no use for gold and silver. There was scant daylight left for me to rifle through their pockets looking for coins. Warn't much in the way of money on that battlefield. It's usually only us poor folks which gets killed in battle.

It was slippery work wading through the corpses, keeping an eye for something shiny amongst the ripped-up torsos and the sightless heads and the coiling guts. I was near choking to death from the reek of it, and the coat I stole warn't much proof against the cold. I was hungry and I had no notion of where to find provender. And the mist was coming back, and I thought to myself, I'll just take myself a few more coppers and then I'll cross over into the wood and build me a shelter and mayhap a fire. Won't nobody see me, thin as a sapling, quiet as a shadow.

So I started to wade over the creek, which warn't no trouble because there was plenty of bodies to use as stepping stones. I was half way acrosst when I spotted the old nigger under a cottonwood tree, in a circle which was clear of carrion. He had a little fire going and something a-roasting over it. I could hear the crackling above the buzz of the flies and I could smell the cooking fat somewhere behind the stench of putrefying men.

I moved nearer to where he sat. I was blame near fainting by then and ready to kill a body for my supper. He was squatting with his arms around his knees and he was a-rocking back and forth and I thought I could hear him crooning some song to himself, like a lullaby, in a language more kin to French than nigger talk. Odd thing was, I had heard the song before. Mayhap my momma done sung it to me onc't, for she was born out Louisiana way. The more I listened the less I was fixing to kill the old man.

He was old all right. As I crept closer I seen he warn't no threat to me. I still couldn't see his face, because he was turned away from me and looking straight into the setting sun. But I could see he was withered and white-haired and black as the coming night, and seemed like he couldn't even hear me approaching, for he never pricked up his ears though I stood nary a yard or two behind his back, in the shadow of the cottonwood.

That was when he said to me, never looking back, "Why, *bonjour,* Marse Jimmy Lee; I never did think I'd look upon you face again."

And then he turned, and I knew him by the black patch over his right eye.

Lord, it was strange to see him there, in the middle of the valley of the dead. It had been ten years since my pa and me gone up to the Anderson place. Warn't never any call to go back, since it burned to the ground a week after, and old man Anderson died, and his slaves was all sold.

"How did you know it was me?" I asked him. "I was but four years old last time you laid eyes on me."

"Your daddy still a itinerant preacher, Marse Jimmy Lee?" he says.

"I reckon," said I, for I warn't about ready to tell him the truth yet. "I ain't with my pa no more."

"You was always a running away sort of a boy," he said, and offered me a piece of what he was roasting.

"What is it?"

"I don't reckon I ought to tell you."

"I've had possum before. I've had field rat. I'm no stranger to strange flesh." I took a bite of the meat and it was right tasty. But I hadn't had solid food for two days and soon I was a-heaving all over the nearest corpse.

He went back to his crooning song, and I remembered then that I had heard it last from his own lips, that day pa shot momma in the back because she wanted to go with the Choctaw farmer. I can't say I blamed her because leastways the man was a landowner and had four slaves besides. Pa let her pack her bags and walk halfway acrosst the bridge afore he blew her to kingdom come. Then he took my hand and set me up on his horse and took me to the Anderson place, and went I started to squall he slapped me in the face until it were purple and black, saying, between his blows, "She don't deserve your tears. She is a woman taken in adultery; such a woman should be stoned to death, according to the scriptures; a bullet were too good for her. I have exercised my rights according to the law, and iffen I hear one more sob out of you I shall take a hickory to you, for he who spareth the rod loveth not his child." And he drained a flask of bug juice and burped, I did not hear the name of Mary Cox from his lips again for ten long years.

Pa was not a ordained minister but plantation folks reckoned him book-learned enough to preach to their darkies, which is what he done every Sunday, a different estate each week, then luncheon with the master and mistress of the house or sometimes, if they was particular about eating with white trash, then in the kitchen amongst the house niggers. The niggers called him the Reverend Cox, but to the white folks he was just Cox, or Bug-juice Cox, or Blame-Fuckster Cox, or wretched, pitiable Cox, so low that his wife done left him for a Injun.

At the Anderson place he preached in a barn, and he took for his subject adultery; and as there was no one to notice, I stole away to a field and sat me down in a thicket of sugar cane and hollered and carried on like the end of the world was nigh, and me just four years old.

Then it was that I heard the selfsame song I was hearing now, and I looked up and saw this ancient nigger with a patch over one eye, and he says to me, "Oh, honey, it be a terrible thing to be without a mother." I remember the smell of him, a pungent smell like fresh crushed herbs. "I still remembers the day my *mamman* was took from me. Oh, do not grieve alone, white child."

"How'd you come to lose that eye?"

"It the price of knowledge, honey," he said softly.

Choking back my sobs, a mite embarrassed because someone had seen me in my loneliness, I said to him, "You shouldn't be here. You should be in that barn listening to my father's preaching, lessen you want to get yourself a whupping."

He smiled sadly and said, "They done given up on whupping old Joseph."

I said, "Is your momma dead too, Joseph?"

"Yes. She be dead, oh, nigh on sixty year now. She died in the revolution."

"Oh, come," I said, "even I know that the revolution was almost a hundred years ago, and I know you ain't that old, because a white man's time is threescore years and ten, and a nigger's time is shorter still." Now I wasn't comprehending anything I was saying; this was all things I heard my pa say, over and over again, in his sermons.

"Oh," said old Joseph, "I ain't talking about the white man's revolution, but the colored folks' revolt which happened on a island name of Haiti. The French, they tortured my *mamman,* but she wouldn't betray her friends, so they killed her and sold me to a slaver, and the ship set sail one day before independence; so sixty years after my kinfolk was set free, I's still in bondage in a foreign country."

I knew that niggers was always full of stories about magic and distant countries, and they couldn't always see truth from fantasy; my daddy told me that truth is a hard, solid thing to us white folks, as easy to grasp as a stone or a horseshoe, but to them it was slippery, it was like a phantom. That was why I didn't take exception to the old man's lies. I just sat there quietly, listening to the music of his voice, and it soothed me and seemed like it helped to salve the pain I was feeling, for pretty soon when I thought of momma lying on the bridge choking on her own blood I felt I could remember the things I loved about her too, like the way she called my name, the way her nipples tasted on my lips, for she had lost my newborn sister and she was bursting with milk and she would sometimes let me suckle, for all that I was four years old.

And then I was crying again but this time they was healing tears.

Then old Joseph, he said, "You listen to me, Marse Jimmy Lee. I ain't always gone be with you when you needs to open up your heart." Now this surprised me because I didn't recollect telling him none of what was going through my mind. "I's gone give you a gift," he said, and he pulls out a bottle from his sleeve, a vial, only a inch high, and in that bottle was a doll that was woven out of cornstalks. It were cunningly wrought, for the head of the doll was bigger than the neck of the bottle, and it must have taken somebody many hours to make, and somebody with keen eyesight at that. "Now this be a problem doll. It can listen to you when no man will listen. It a powerful magic from the island where I was born."

He held it out to me and it made me smile, for I had oftentimes been told that darkies are simple people and believe in all kinds of magic. I clutched it in my hands but mayhap he saw the disbelief in my face, for he said to me with the utmost gravity, "Do not mock this magic, white child. Among the colored people which still fears the old gods, they calls me a *houngan,* a man of power."

"The old gods?" I said.

"Shangó," he said, and he done a curious sort of a genuflecting hop when he said the name, "Obatala; Ogun; Babalu Ayé...."

The names churned round and round in my head as I stared into his good eye. I don't recollect what followed next or how my pa found me. But everything else I remembered just as though the ten years that followed, the years of wandering, pa's worsening cruelty and drunkenness, hadn't never even happened.

It was as though I had circled back to that same place and time. Only instead of the burning sunlight of that summer's day there was the gathering cold and the night. Instead of the tall cane sticky with syrup, we was keeping company with the slain. And I warn't a child no more, although I warn't a man yet, neither.

"The *poupée* I give you," old Joseph said as I sat myself down beside him, "does you still got it?"

"My pa found it the next day. He said he didn't want no hoodoo devil dolls in his house. He done smashed it and throwed it in the fire, and then he done wore me out with his hickory."

"And you a soldier now."

"I run away."

"Lordy, honey, you a sight to see. Old Joseph don't got no more dolls for you now. Old Joseph got no time for he be making dolls. There be a monstrous magic abroad now in this universe. This magic it the onliest reason old Joseph still living in this world. Old Joseph hears the magic summoning him. Old Joseph he stay behind to hear what the magic it have to tell him."

Like a fool, I thought him simple when I heard him speak of magic. It made me smile. It was the first time I had smiled in many months. I smiled to keep from crying, for weeping ill becomes a man of fourteen years who has carried his rifle into battle to defend his country.

"You poor lost child," said Joseph, "you should be a-waking up mornings to the song of the larks, not the whistle of miniés nor the thunder of cannon. You at the end of the road now, ain't nowhere left for you to go; that's why us has been called here to this valley of the shadow of death. It was written from the moment we met, Marse Jimmy Lee. Ten years I wandered alone in the wilderness. Now the darker angels has sent you to me."

"I don't know what you mean."

"Be not afraid," he said, "for I bring you glad tidings of great joy." I marveled that he knew the words of the evangelist, for this was the man who would not go hear my father's preaching.

He nibbled at the charred meat. For a moment I entertained the suspicion that it were human flesh. But it smelled good. I ate my fill and drank from the bloody stream and fell asleep beside the fire to the lilt of the old man's lullaby.

I had not told old Joseph all the truth. It warn't only the need to run that forced me from my father's house. Pa was a hard man and a drinking man and a man which had visions, and in those visions he saw other worlds. He was unmerciful to me, and oftentimes he would set to whipping the demons out of me, but everything he did to me was in keeping with holy scripture, which tells a father that love ain't always a sweet thing, but can also come with bitterness and blows.

I had visions too, but they warn't heavenly the way his was. I would not wear my shoes. I played with the nigger children of the town, shaming him. I ran wild and I never went to no school. But I could read some, for that my pa set me to studying the scriptures whenever he could tie be down.

This is how I come to join the regiment:

We was living in a shack in back of the Jackson place, right next to the nigger burial plot. Young Master Jackson had all his darkies assembled in the graveyard to hear a special sermon from my pa, because the rumors of the 'mancipation proclamation was rife amongst the slaves. There was maybe thirty or forty of them, and a scattering of pickaninnies underfoot, sitting on the grass, leaning against the wooden markers.

I was sitting in the shack, minding a kettle of stew. Through the open window I could hear my pa preaching. "Now don't you darkies pay this emancipation proclamation no mind," came his voice, ringing and resonant. "It is an evil trickery. There are trying to fool you innocent souls into running away and joining up with those butchers who come down to rape and pillage our land, and they hold out freedom as a reward for treachery. But the true reward is death, for if a nigger is captured in the uniform of a Yankee it has been decreed by our government that he shall be shot without trial. No, this is no road to freedom! There is only one way there for those born into bondage, and that is through the blood of our savior Jesus Christ, and your freedom is not for this world, but for the next, for is it not written, 'In my father's house there are many mansions?' There is a mansion for you, and you, and you, and you, iffen you will obey your master in this life and accept the yoke of lowliness and the lash of repentance; for is it not written, 'By his stripes we are healed' and 'Blessed are the meek'? It's not for the colored people, freedom in this world. But the wicked, compassionless Yankees would prey on your simplicity. They would let you mistake the kingdom of heaven for a rebellious kingdom on earth. 'To everything there is a season.' Yes, there will be mansions for you all. Mansions with white stone columns and porticoes sheltered from the sun. The place of healing is beyond the valley of the shadow of death...."

My pa could talk mighty proper when he had a mind to, and he had a chapter and verse for everything. I didn't pay no heed to his words, though, because there is different chapters and verses for niggers, and when they are quoted for white folks they do not always mean the same thing. No, I was busy stirring the stew and hiding the whisky, for pa had always had a powerful thirst after he was done preaching, and with the quenching of thirst came violence.

After the preaching the darkies all starts singing with a passion. They done sung *All God's Chillun Got Wings* and *Swing Low, Sweet Chariot.* Pa didn't stay for the singing but come into the shack calling for his food. It warn't ready so he throwed a few pots and pans around, with me scurrying out of the way to avoid being knocked about, and then he finally found where I had hidden the bottle and he lumbered into the inner room to drink.

Presently the stew bubbled up and I ladled out some in a tin cup and took it to the room. This was the room me and him slept in, on a straw pallet on the floor, a bare room with nothing but a chest of drawers, a chair with one leg missing, and a hunting rifle. He kept his hickories there too, for to chastise me with.

I should have knocked, because pa warn't expecting me.

He was sitting in the chair with this britches about his ankles. He didn't see me. He was holding in one hand a locket which had a picture of momma. In the other hand he was holding his bony cocker, and he was strenuously indulging in the vice of Onan.

I was right horrified when I saw this. I was full of shame to see my father unclothed, for was that not the shame of the sons of Noah? And I was angered, because in my mind's eye I seen my momma go down on that bridge, fold up and topple over, something I hadn't thought on for nigh on ten year. I stood there blushing scarlet and full of fury and grieving for my dead mother, and then I heard him a-murmuring, "Oh, sweet Jehovah, Oh, sweet Lord, I see you, I see the company of the heavenly host, I see you, my sweet Mary, standing on a cloud with your arms stretched out to me, naked as Eve in the Garden of Eden. Oh, oh, oh, I'm a-looking on the face of the Almighty and a–listening to the song of the angels."

Something broke inside me all at once when I heard him talk that way about momma. Warn't it enough that she was dead, withouten him blasphemously lusting after her departed soul? I dropped the tin of stew and he saw me and I could see the rage burning in his eyes, and I tried to force myself to obey the fifth commandment, but words just came pouring out of me. "Shame on you, pa, pounding your cocker for a woman you done gunned down in cold blood. Don't you think I don't remember the way you kilt her, shot her in the back whilst she were crossing that bridge, and the Choctaw watching on t'other side in his top hat and morning dress, with his four slaves behind him, waiting to take her home."

My pa was silent for a few moments, and the room was filled with the caterwauling of the niggers from the graveyard. We stood there staring each other down. Then he grabbed me by the scruff of the neck and dragged me over to the chair, lurching and stumbling because he hadn't even bothered to pull his britches back up, and I could smell the liquor on him; and he murmured, "You are right; I have sinned; I have sinned; but it is for the son to take on the sins of the world; the paschal lamb; you, Jimmy Lee; oh, God, but you do resemble her; you do remind me of her; oh, it is a heavy burden for you, my son, to take on the sins of the world, but I know that you do it for love," and suchlike, and he reached for the hickory and stripped the shirt off of my back and began to lay to with a will, all the while crying out, "Oh, Mary, oh, my Mary, I am so sorry that you left me ... oh, my son, you shall bear thirty-nine stripes on your back in memory of our savior ... oh, you shall redeem me ..." and the hickory sang and I cried out, not so much from the pain, for that my back was become like leather from long abuse, and warn't much feeling left in it ... I gritted my teeth and try to bear it like I borne it so many times before, but this time it was not to be borne, and when the thirty-ninth stripe was inflicted I tore myself loose from the chair and I screamed, "You ain't hurting me no more, because I ain't no paschal lamb and your sins is *your* sins, not mine," and I pushed him aside with all my strength.

"God, God," he says in a whisper, "I see God." And he rolls his eyes heavenward, excepting that heaven were a leaky roof made from a few planks left over from the slaves' quarters.

Then I took the rifle from the wall and pounded him in the head with the stock, three, four, five, six times until he done slumped onto the straw.

Oh, I was raging and afeared, and I run away right then and there, without even making sure iffen he was kilt or not. I run right through them darkies, who was a-singing and a-carrying on to wake the very dead; they did not see a scrawny boy, small for his age, slip through them and out toward the woods.

I run and run with three dimes in my pocket and a sheaf of shinplasters that I stole from the chest of drawers, I run and I don't even recollect iffen I put out the fire on the stove.

And that was how I come to be with the regiment, tramping through blood and mud and shitting my bowels away with the flux each day; and that was how I come to be sleeping next to old Joseph, the hoodoo doctor, who become another father to me.

I did not confess to old Joseph or even to myself that I had done my father in. Mayhap he was still alive. I tried not to think on him. My old life was dead. Surely I could not go back to the Jackson place, nor the army, nor any other place from which I run. There was just me and the old nigger now, scavengers, carrion birds, eaters of the dead.

Yes, and sure it was human flesh old Joseph fed me that night, and again that morning. He showed me the manner of taking it, for there was certain corpses that cried out to be let be, whilst others craved to be consumed. We followed the army a a safe distance, and when they moved on we took possession of the slain. He could always sniff out where a battle was going to be. He never carried nothing with him excepting a human skull, painted black, that was full of herbs, the same herbs that he always smelled of.

Oh, it was God's country we done passed through, hills, forests, meadows, creeks, and all this beauty marred by the handiwork of men. Old Joseph showed me not to drink from the bloodied streams but to lick the dew from flower petals and cupped leaves of a morning. As his trust of me grew, he became more bold. We went into encampments and sat amongst the soldiers, and they never seen us, not once.

"We is invisible," old Joseph told me.

And then it struck me, for we stood in broad daylight beside a willow tree, and on the other side of the brook was mayhap fifty tents and behind them a dense wood. The air was moist and thick. I could see members of my old company, with their skull faces too small for their gray coats, barely able to lift their bayonets off the ground, and they was sitting there huddled together waiting for gruel, but there I was, nourished by the dead, my flesh starting to fill out and the redness back in my cheeks; it struck me that they couldn't see me even though I was a-jumping up and down on the other side of the stream; and I said to old Joseph, "I don't think we are invisible. I think ... oh, old Joseph, I think we have been dead ever since the day we met."

Old Joseph laughed; it were a dry laugh, like the wind stirring the leaves in autumn; and he said, "You ain't dead yet, honey; feel the flesh on them bones; no, your *beau-père* he nurturing you back to life."

"Then why don't they see us? Even when we walk amongst them?"

"Because I has cast a cloak of darkness about us. We be wearing the face of a dark god over our own."

"I don't trust God. Whenever my pa seen God, he hurt me."

Smiling, he said, "You daddy warn't a true preacher, honey; he just a *houngan macoute,* a man which *use* the name of God to adorn hisself."

And taking my hand he led me acrosst that branch and we was right amongst the soldiers, and still they did not see me. We helped ourselves to hardtack and coffee right out of the kettle. In the distance I heard the screams of a man whose leg they was fixing to hack off. Around us men lay moaning. There is a sick-sweet body smell that starving men give off when they are burning up their last shreds of flesh to fuel their final days. That's how I knew they was near death. They was shivering with cold, even though it were broad daylight. Lord, many of them was just children, and some still younger than myself. I knew that the war was lost, or soon would be. I had no country, and no father save for a darkie witch doctor from Haiti.

There come a bugle call and a few men looked up, though most of them just goes on laying in their misery. Old Joseph and I saw soldiers come into the camp. They had a passel of niggers with them, niggers in blue uniforms, all chained up in a long row behind a wagon that was piled high with confiscated arms. They was as starved and miserable as our own men. They stared ahead as they trudged out of the wood and into the clearing. There was one or two white men with them two, officers I reckoned.

A pause, and the bugle sounded again. Then a captain come out of a tent and addressed the captives. He said, in a lugubrious voice, as though he were weary of making this announcement: "According to the orders given me by the congress of the Confederate States of America, all Negroes apprehended while in the uniform of the North are not to be considered prisoners of war, but shall be returned instantly to a condition of slavery or shot. Any white officer arrested while in command of such Negroes shall be considered to be inciting rebellion and also shot." He turned and went back into his tent, and the convoy moved onward, past the camp, upstream, toward another part of the woods.

"Oba kosó!" the old man whispered. "They gone kill them."

"Let's go away," I said.

"No," said old Joseph, "I feels the wind of the gods blowing down upon me. I feels the breath of the loa. I is standing on the coils of Koulèv, the earth-serpent. Oh, no, Marse Jimmy Lee, I don't be going nowhere, but you free to come and go as you pleases of course, being white."

"You know that ain't so," I said. "I'm less free than you. And I know if I leave you I will leave the shelter of your invisibility spell." For that I gazed right into the eyes of the prisoners, and tasted their rancid breath, and smelled the pus of their wounds, and seen no sign of recognition. There was something to his magic, though that I was sure it come of the dark places, and not of God.

So I followed him alongside the creek as the captives were led into the wood, followed them uphill a ways until we reached the edge of a shallow gully, and there was already niggers there, digging to make it deeper, and I seen what was going to happen and I didn't want to look, because this warn't a battle, this were butchery pure and simple.

Our soldiers didn't mock the prisoners and didn't call them no names. They were too tired and too hungry. The blacks and the whites, they didn't show no passion in their faces. They just wanted it to end. Our men done lined the niggers and their officers up all along the edge of the ditch, and searched through their pockets for any coins or crumbs, and they turned them so they faced the gully and they done shot them in the back, one by one, until the pit was filled; then the Southerners turned and filed back to the camp. Oh, God! As the first shots rung out it put me in mind of my mother Mary, halfway across the bridge, with her old life behind her and her new life ahead of her, dead on her face, and the bloodstain spreading from her back on to the lace and calico.

And old Joseph said, "Honey, I seen what I must do. And it a dark journey that I must take, and maybe you don't be strong enough to come with me. But I hates to journey alone. Old Joseph afraid too, betimes, spite of his 'leventyleven years upon this earth. I calls the powers to witness, *ni ayé àti ni òrun."*

"What does that mean, old Joseph?"

"In heaven as it is in earth."

I saw the way his eye glowed and I was powerful afraid. He had become more than a shrunken old man. Seemed like he drew the sun's light into his face and shone brighter than the summer sky. He set his cauldron-skull down on the ground and said, again and again, *"Koulèv, Koulèv-O! Damballah Wedo, Papa! Koulèv, Koulèv-O! Damballah Wedo, Papa!"*

And then he says, in a raspy voice, "Watch out, Marse Jimmy Lee, the god gone come down and mount my body now ... stand clear less you wants to swept away by the breath of the serpent!" And he mutters to hisself, "Oh, *dieux puissants,* why you axing me to make biggest magic, me a old magician without no *poudre* and no herbs? Oh, take this cup from me, take, take this bitter poison from he lips, for old Joseph he don't study life and death no more."

And his old body started to shake, and he ripped off his patch and threw it onto the mud, and I looked into the empty eye-socket and saw an inner eye, blood-red and shiny as a ruby. And he sank down on his knees in front of the pit of dead men and he went on a-mumbling and a-rocking, back and forth, back and forth, and seemed like he was a-speaking in tongues. And his good eye rolled right up into its socket.

"Why, old Joseph," I says to him, "what are you fixing to do?"

But he paid me no mind. He just went on a-shimmying and a-shaking, and presently he rose up from where he was and started to dance a curious hopping sort of dance, and with every hop he cried, *"Shangó! Shangó!"* in a voice that was steadily losing its human qualities. And soon his voice was rolling like thunder, and presently it *was* the thunder, for the sky was lowering and lightning was lancing the cloud-peaks.

Oh, the sky became dark. The cauldron seethed and glowed, though he hadn't even touched it. I knew he were sure possessed. The dark angels he done told me of, they was speaking to him out of the mouth of hell.

I reckoned I was not long for this world, for the old man was a-hollering at the top of his lungs and we warn't far from the encampment; but no one came looking for us. Mayhap they was huddled in their tents hiding from the thunder. Presently it began to rain, it pelted us and soaked us, that rain; it were a hot rain, scalding to my skin. And when the lightning flashed I looked into the pit and I thought I saw something moving. Mayhap it were just the rushing waters, throwing the corpses one against t'other. I crept closer to the edge of the gully. I didn't heed old Joseph's warning. I peered over the edge and in the next flash of lightning I saw them a-writhing and a-shaking their arms and legs, and their necks a-craning this way and that, and I thought to myself, old Joseph he is raising the dead.

Old Joseph just went on screaming out those African words and leaping up and waving his arms. The rain battered my body and I was near fainting from it, for the water flooded my nostrils and drenched my lungs and when I gasped for air I swallowed more and more water; I don't know how the old man kept on dancing; in the lightning flashes I saw him, dark and lithe, and the sluicing rain made him glisten and made his chest and arms to look like the scales of a great black serpent; I looked on him and breathed in the burning water, and the pit of dead niggers quook as iffen the very earth were opening up, and there come a blue light from the mass grave, so blinding that I could see no more; and so, at last, I passed out from the terror of it.

When I done opened my eyes the rain was just a memory; the sun was rising; the forest was silent and shrouded in mist. And I thought to myself, I have been dreaming, and I am still beside the creek where the dead bodies lay, and I never did see no old Joseph out of my past; but then I saw him frying up a bit of salt pork he done salvaged from the camp. Warn't no morning bugle calls, and I reckon the company done up and gone in the middle of the night, soon as the storm subsided.

Old Joseph, the patch was over his eye again, and he was singing to hisself, that song I heard as a child. And when he saw me stir, he said, "Marse Jimmy Lee, you awake now."

"What is that song?" I asked him.

"It called *Au Claire de la Lune,* honey; 'by the light of the moon.'"

I sat up. "Joseph?"

"What, Marse Jimmy Lee?"

"Last night I had the strangest dream ... more like a vision. I dreamed you were possessed, and you pranced about and waved your arms and sang songs in a African language, and you raised up nigger soldiers from the grave."

"Life is a dream, honey," he says, "we calls them *les zombis.* It from a Kikongo word nzambi that mean a dead man that walk the earth."

The fog began to clear a little and I saw their feet. Black feet, still shackled, still covered with chafing sores. We was surrounded by them. And as the sunlight began to dissipate the mist, I could see their faces; it was them which had been kilt and buried in the pit; I knew some of their faces. For though they stirred, they moved, they looked about them, there were no fire in their eyes, and didn't have no breath in their nostrils. Mayhap they wasn't dead, but they wasn't alive, neither.

The stood there, looming over us. Each one with a wound clean through him. Each one smelling of old Joseph's herbs.

"The magic still in me," old Joseph said, "even without the *coup poudre.*"

I reckon I have never been more scared than I was then. My skin was crawling and my blood was racing.

"I never thought that old magic still in me," said Joseph again. There was wonderment in his voice. No fear. The dead men surrounded us, waiting; seemed like they had no mind of their own.

"Oh, Joseph, what are we going to do?"

"Don't know, white child. I's still in the dark. The vision don't come as clear to me no more; old Joseph he old, he old."

He fed me and gave me genuine coffee to drink, for the slain Yankees had carried some with them. I rose and went over to the pit, and it were sure enough empty save for the two white officers. "Why didn't you raise them too?" I said.

"Warn't no sense in it, Marse Jimmy Lee; for white folks there is a heaven and a hell; there ain't no middle ground; best to forget them."

So we threw dirt over them and we marched on, and the column of undead darkies followed us. I could not name the places that we passed, but old Joseph knew where he was going. It was toward the rising sun so I guessed it was south.

At nightfall we rested. We found a farmhouse. There warn't no people and the animals was all took away, but I found a ham a-hanging in the larder, and I feasted. In the night I slept in a real bed. Old Joseph sat out on the porch. The *zombis* did not sleep. The stood in a ring outside the house and the swayed softly to the sound of Joseph's singing; as I looked out of the smashed window I could see them in the moonlight, and there was still no fire in their eyes; and I recollected that they hadn't partaken of no victuals. What was it like to be a *zombi?* Iffen that the eyes are the windows of the soul, then surely there warn't no souls inside those fleshy shells.

We found plenty of gold in the abandoned house, they done hid it in a well, which was surrounded by dead Yankees; I reckon they done poisoned it so that the northerners wouldn't be able to drink their water. But poison means naught to the dead.

And we walked on; and the passel of walking dead became a company, for wherever we went we found niggers that had been kilt, not just the ones in Yankee uniform but sometimes a woman lying dead in a ditch, or a young buck chained to a tree that was just abandoned and let starve to death when his masters fled from the enemy, and one time we found seven high-yaller children dead in a cage, with gunshot wounds to their heads; for they was frenzied times, and men were driven to acts not thought upon in times of peace. It was amongst the dead children that I found another cornstalk *poupée* like the one old Joseph gave me ten years before, a-sitting in a vial in the clenched fist of a dead little girl; after we done wakened them, she held it out to me, and I thought there were a glimmer in her eye, but mayhap it were only my imagination.

"Get up and walk," old Joseph said. And they walked.

And I said over and over to him, "Old Joseph, where are we going?"

And he said, "Towards freedom."

"But freedom is in the north, ain't it?"

"Freedom in the heart, honey."

We marched. For many days we didn't see no white folks at all. We saw burned hulks of farms, and stray dogs hunting in packs. We passed other great battlefields, and them that was worth reviving, that still had enough flesh on them to be able to march, old Joseph raised up. He was growing in power. It got so he would just wave his hands, and say one or two words, and the dead man would climb right out of the ground. And I took to repeating the words to myself, soundlessly at first, just moving my lips; then softly, then — for when he were a-concentrating on his magic, he couldn't see nothing of the world — I would shout out those words along with him, I would wrap my tongue around them twisted and barbarian sounds, and I would tell myself, 'twas I which raised them, I which reached into the abyss and drawed them out.

Still we encountered no sign of human life. The summer sun streamed down on us by day and seemed like I sweat blood. It warn't at all certain to me that we was still alive and on this earth, for the land was a waste land, spite of the verdant meadows and the mountains blanketed with purple flowers, spite of the rich-smelling earth and the warm rain. Sometimes I think that the country we was wandering in was an illusion, a false Eden. Or that we was somehow half in, half out of the world.

Though I didn't know where the road was leading, yet I was happy. I trusted old Joseph, and I didn't have no one else left in the world. The only times I become sad was thinking on my pa and momma's death, and wondering iffen my pa was with God now, for he said he done seen the face of God before I smashed his head. Sometimes I dreamed about coming home to see him well again. But they was only dreams. I knew that I had kilt him.

On the seventh day we come onc't more into the sight of men.

The road become wider and we was coming into the vicinity of a town. I knew this was a port, maybe Charleston. There warn't no signs to tell us, but pa and I had been booted out of Charleston once, I remembered the way the wind smelt, wet and tangy. A few miles outside town our road joined up with a wider road that come in a straight line from due north. On the other road, straggling down to meet us, we saw a company of graycoats.

Not many of them, maybe three dozen. They warn't exactly marching. Some was leaning on each other, some hobbling, and one, a slip of a boy, tapped on the side of a skinless drum. Their clothes was in tatters and most of them didn't have no rifles. They was just old men and boys, for the able-bodied had long since fallen.

They seen us and one of them cried out, "Nigger soldiers!" They fell into a pathetic semblance of a formation, and them which had rifles aimed them and them which had crutches brandished them at us.

I shouted out, "Let us pass ... we don't have no quarrel with you." For they were wretched creatures, these remnants of the Southern army, and I was sure that the war was already lost, and they was coming back to what was left of their homes.

But one boy, mayhap their leader, screamed at me, "Nigger lover! Traitor!" I looked in his eyes and saw we were just alike, poor trash fighting a rich man's war, him and me; and I pitied the deluded soul. Because I knew now that there warn't no justice in this war, and that neither side had foughten for God, but only for hisself.

"It's no use!" I shouted at the boy who was so like myself. "These darkies ain't even alive; they're shadows marching to the sea; they ain't got souls to kill."

And old Joseph said, "March on, my children."

They commenced to fire on us.

This was the terriblest thing which I did witness on that journey. For the nigger soldiers marched and marched, and not a bullet could stop them. The miniés flew and the white boys shrieked out a ghostly echo of a rebel yell, and *les zombis* kept right on coming and coming, and me and old Joseph with them, untouched by the bullets, for his magic still shielded our mortal flesh. The niggers marched. Their faces was ripped asunder and still they marched. Their brains came oozing from their skulls, their guts came writhing from their bellies, and still they marched. They marched until they were too close for bullets. Then the white boys flung themselves at us, and they was ripped to pieces. They was tore limb from limb by dead men which stared with glazed and vacant eyes. It took but a few minutes, this final skirmish of the war. Their yells died in their throats. The *zombis* broke their necks and flung them to the ground. Their strength warn't a human kind of strength. They'd shove their hands into an old man's belly and snap his spine and pull out the intestines like a coil of rope. They'd take a rifle and break the barrel in two.

There was no anger in what the *zombis* done. And they didn't make no noise whilst they was killing. They done it the way you might darn a sock or feed the chickens; it were just something which had to be done.

And we marched onward, leaving the bodies to rot; it was getting on toward sunset now.

Oh, I was angry. The boys we kilt warn't no strangers from the north; they could have been my brothers. Oh, I screamed in rage at old Joseph; I didn't trust him no more; the happiness had left me.

"Did you hear what he called me?" I shouted. "A traitor to my people. A nigger lover. And it's God's plain truth. If you wanted freedom why didn't you go north into the arms of the Yankees? You spoke to me of a big magic, and of the coils of the serpent Koulèv, and the wind of the gods, and the voices of darker angels ... to what end? It were Satan's magic, magic to give the dead an illusion of life, so you could kill more of my people!"

"Be still," he said to me, as the church spires of the port town rose up in the distance. "Your war don't be my war. You think the Yankees got theyselfs kilt to set old Joseph free? You think the 'mancipation proclamation was wrote to give the nigger back he soul? I say to you, white child, that a piece of paper don't make men free. The black man in this land he ain't gone be free tomorrow nor in a hundred years nor in a thousand. I didn't bring men back from the outer darkness so they could shine you shoes and wipe you butts. The army I lead, he kingdom don't be of this earth."

"You are mad, old Joseph," I said, and I wept, for he was no longer a father to me.

We marched into the town. Children peered from behind empty beer kegs with solemn eyes. Horses reared up and whinnied. Women stared sullenly at us. The Yankees had already took the town, and half the houses was smoldering, and we didn't see no grown men. The stars and stripes flew over the ruint courthouse. I reckon folks thought we was just another company of the conquering army.

We reached the harbor. There was one or two sailing ships docked there; rickety ships with tattered sails. The army of dead men stood at attention and old Joseph said to me: "Now I understands why you come with me so far. There a higher purpose to everything, *ni ayé àti ni òrun."*

I didn't want to stay with him any more. When I seen the way *les zombis* plowed down my countrymen, I had been moved to a powerful rage, and the rage would not die away. "What higher purpose?" I said. And the salt wind chafed my lips.

"You think," said old Joseph, "that old Joseph done tricked you, he done magicked you with mirrors and smoke; but I never told you we was fighting on the same side. But we come far together, and I wants you to do me one last favor afore we parts for all eternity."

"And what sort of favor would that be, old sorcerer? I thought you could do anything."

"Anything. But not this thing. You see, old Joseph a nigger. Nigger he can't go into no portside bar to offer gold for to buy him a ship."

"You want a ship now? Where are you fixing to go? Back to Haiti, where the white man rules no more?"

Old Joseph said, "Mayhap it a kind of Haiti where we go." He laughed. "Haiti, yes, Haiti! And I gone see my dear *mamman,* though she be cold in her grave sixty year past. Or mayhap it mother Africa herself we go to. *Oba kosó!"*

And I remembered that he had told me: *My kingdom is not of this earth.* He had used the words of our savior and our Lord. Oh, the ocean wind were warm, and it howled, and the torn sails clattered against the masts. The air fair dripped with moisture. And the niggers stood like statues, all-unseeing.

"I'll do as you ask," I said, and I took the sack of gold we had gathered from the poisoned well, and I walked along the harbor until I found a bar and ship's captain for hire, which was not hard, for the embargo had starved their business. And presently I come back and told old Joseph everything was ready. And the niggers lined up, ready to embark. Night was falling.

But as they prepared themselves to board that ship, I could hold my tongue no more. "Old Joseph," I said, "your kingdom is founded on a lie. You have waked these bodies from the earth, but where are their souls? You may dream of leading these creatures to a mystic land acrosst the sea, and you may dream of freeing them forever from the bonds of servitude, but how can you free what can't be freed? How can you free a rock, a tree, a piece of earth? Dust they were and dust they ever shall be, world without end."

And the zombi warriors stood, unmoving and unblinking, and not a breath passed their lips, though that the wind was rising and whipping at our faces.

And old Joseph looked at me long and hard, and I knew that I had said the thing that must be said. He whispered, "Out of the mouths of babes and sucklings hast thou ordained strength, O Lord." He fell down on his knees before me and said, "And all this time I thought that *I* the wise one and you the student! Oh, Marse Jimmy Lee, you done spoke right. There be no life in *les zombis* because I daresn't pay the final price. But now I's *gone* make that sacrifice. Onc't I done gave my eye in exchange for knowledge. But there be *two* trees in Eden, Marse Jimmy Lee; there be the tree of knowledge, and there be the tree of life."

So saying he covered his face with his hands. He plunged his thumb into the socket of his good eye and he plucked it out, screaming to almighty God with the pain of it. His agony was real. His shrieking curdled my blood. It brought back my pa's chastisements and my momma's dying and the tramping of my bare feet on sharp stones and the sight of all my comrades, pierced through by bayonets, cloven by cannon, their limbs ripped off, their bellies torn asunder, their lives gushing hot and young and crimson into the stream. Oh, but I craved to carry his pain, but he were the one that were chosen to bear it, and I was the one which brung him to the understanding of it.

And now his eye were in his hand, a round, white, glistening pearl, and he cries out in a thunderous voice, "If thine eye offend thee, pluck it out!" and he takes blind aim and hurls the eye with all his might into the mighty sea.

I clenched the *poupée* in my hand.

Then came lightning, for old Joseph had summoned the power of the serpent Koulèv, whose coils were entwined about the earth. Then did he unleash the rain. Then did he turn to me, with the gore gushing from the yawning socket, and cry to me, a good-for-nothing white trash boy which kilt his own father and stole from the dead, "Thou hast redeemed me."

Then, and only then, did I see the *zombis* smile. Then, as the rain softened, as the sky did glow with a cold blue light that didn't come from no sun nor moon, then did hear the laughter of the dead, and the fire of life begin to flicker in their eyes. But they was already trooping up the gangplank, and presently there was only the old man, purblind now, and like to die I thought.

"Farewell," he says to me.

And I said, "No, old Joseph. You are blind now. You need a boy to hold your hand and guide you, to be your eyes against the wild blue sea."

"Not blind," he said. "I *chooses* not to see. I gone evermore be looking inward, at the glory and the majesty of eternal light."

"But what have I?" Where can I go, excepting that I go with you?"

"Honey, you has lived but fourteen of your threescore and ten. It don't be written that you's to follow a old man acrosst the sea to a land that maybe don't even *be* a land save in that old man's dream. Go now. But first you gone kiss your *beau-père* goodbye, for I loves you."

My tears were brine and his were blood. As I kissed his cheek the salt did run together with the crimson. I saw him no more; I did not see the ship sail from the port; for my eyes was blinded with weeping.

So I walked and walked and walked until I come back to the Jackson place. The mansion were a cinder, and even the fields was all burnt up, and the animals was dead. The place was looted good and thorough; warn't one thing of value in the vicinity, not a gold piece nor a silver spoon nor even the rugs that the Jacksons done bought from a French merchant.

I walked up the low knoll to where the nigger graveyard was and where our shack onc't stood. The wooden markers was all charred, and here and there was a shred of homespun clinging to them; and I thought to myself, mayhap the Yankees come down to the Jackson place not an hour after I done run away, whilst the slaves was still a-singing their spirituals. That cloth was surely torn off some of the slave women, for the Yankees loved to have their way with darkies. And I thought, mayhap my pa is still laying inside that shack, in the inner room, beside the locket with mamma's picture, with his hickory in his fist, with his britches down about his ankles.

And so it was I found him.

He warn't rank no more. It had been many months since I run off. Warn't much left of his face that the worms hadn't ate. At his naked loins, the bone poked through the papery hide, and there was a swarm of ants. It was a miracle there was this much left of him, for there was wild dogs roaming the fields.

I set down the *poupée* on the chair and got to wondering what I should do. What I wanted most in life were a new beginning. I spoke to that doll, for I knew that old Joseph's spirit was in it somehow, and I said, "I don't know where you come from, and I don't know where you are. But oh, give me the strength to begin onc't more, oh, carry me back from the land of the dead."

Without thinking I started to murmur the words of power, the African words I done mimicked when I watched him raise the dead. I knelt down beside the corpse of my pa and waited for the breath of serpent. I whispered them words over and over until my mind emptied itself and was filled with the souls of darker angels.

I reckon I knelt all night long, or mayhap many nights. But when I opened my eyes again there was flesh on my father's bones, and he was beginning to rouse himself; and his eyes had the fire of life, for that old Joseph had sacrificed his second eye.

"You sure have growed, son," he says softly. "You ain't a sapling no more; you're a mighty tree."

"Yes, pa," says I.

"Oh, son, you have carried me back from a terrible dream. In that dream I abandoned you, and I practiced all manner of cruelty upon you, and a dark angel came to you and became your new pa; and you followed him to the edge of the river that divides the quick from the dead."

"Yes, pa. But I stopped at the river bank and watched him sail away. And I come back to you."

"Oh, Jimmy Lee, my son, I have seen hell. I have been down into the fire of damnation, and I've felt the loneliness of perdition. And the cruelest torture was being cut off from you, my flesh and blood. Oh, sweet Jesus, Jimmy Lee, it were only that you made me think on her so much, she which I killed, she which I never loved more even as I sent the bullet flying into her back."

And this was strange, for in the old days my pa had only spoke of heaven, and of seeing the face of God, and when he done seen God he would wear me out, calling on His holy name to witness his infamy and my sacrifice. But now he had seen hell and he was full of gentleness.

And then he said to me, "My son, I craves your forgiveness."

"Ain't nothing to forgive."

"Then give me your love," says he, "for you are tall and strong, and I have become old; and it is now for you to be the father, and I the child."

It were time to cross the bridge. It were time to heal the hurting.

"My love you have always had, pa."

So saying, I embraced him; and thus it was our war came to an end.

Zombies are back in this present-day story as well, which is the first story I wrote to be nominated for the Bram Stoker Award. Finding and resurrecting the story proved to be quite difficult as the only file I had was composed in MacWrite 1.0, a software so ancient that even by the late 80s it wasn't compatible with much. I had to send the file halfway across the world to be resurrected by a High Priestess of sorts, one who keeps ancient machines in a state of well-maintained splendor and is therefore able to make these texts come back to life.

ResurrecTech™

Owen Gallenkamp suffered a peculiarly unpleasant mishap while mowing the postage-stamp-sized front lawn of his townhouse in a middle income Washington suburb. He had been cursing ferociously at the power mower, much to the amusement of the kids next door, who had, as usual, been playing hooky. At long last, the confounded device whirred into action; and Gallenkamp, returning to his labors, was forced to swerve suddenly to avoid an encounter with a monstrous turd that glistened on the unkempt grass like a baroque jewel.

He could not have known, alas, that this was no piece of squishy excrement, but a lump of painted and varnished plaster of paris that the hooky-playing neighbors had planted there for the express purpose of arousing his ire. But so offensive was the spectacle to his refined sensibilities that Gallenkamp lost control of his mower. The coprous simulacrum caught in its mechanism. Pieces of plaster began to shrapnel the lawn, and one such shard was propelled through Gallenkamp's left eye with such force that it invaded his brain, killing him almost instantly.

He fell forward, arms outstretched, against the mower's handles, and it was in this position, a sort of hybrid of Christ and scarecrow, that his wife Elayne (having returned from the drugstore with a fresh supply of sanitary napkins) found him ten minutes later.

She sighed, went inside, and telephoned my office.

Although it took me only twenty minutes to arrive, the house was already swarming with sycophants and leeches when I stepped inside.

"Oh, there you are, Whitey," Elayne said, wringing her hands in a convincingly distraught manner. "Gentlemen, this is Whitey Jefferson, our attorney."

A row of earnest-looking, cadaverous men in dark suits was standing against the far wall, from which depended several tomahawks and painted Plains Indian shields. A veritable aviary of war bonnets graced the lid of the Steinway grand piano that blocked the stairway to the second floor. Another wall sported a futuristic poster with the legend *ResurrecTech™* in embossed chrome letters. The significance of that poster was at that time known only to me. Apart from the undertakers, then, the room was precisely as I had last seen it. Except, of course, that Elayne had not been wearing that half-zippered black dress. She had been naked.

I said, "How could there be so many undertakers so soon?"

"Mr. Gallenkamp had a device that monitored his heartbeat," said one of the undertakers with his nose in the air, "designed by the Sargnagel Corporation. It outputted directly to the Morticians' Union headquarters."

Before I had time to gape, they all started talking in turn. "Mr. Jefferson," said another of the undertakers, "I represent the firm of Mortworth, Mortworth and Mortworth, specializing in the expeditious beautification of the Loved One's remains and offering a choice of three easy payment plans—"

"Shut up, Mortworth!" a second interrupted. "I was here first. My dear, dear Mrs. Gallenkamp! Forgive my colleague's untimely and insensitive sales pitch. I am Mr. Ruddigore, president of Ruddigore's Rapturous Havens. Wouldn't your husband have loved to lie in gentle repose amongst others of his breeding, listening to the strains of Mozart on our twenty-four hour string quartet service? We also have easy listening."

"That's nothing!" crowed a third. "Surely, Mrs. Gallenkamp, a woman of your sensibilities must understand the importance of racial purity! I represent Sampson's Segregated Cemeteries. Our motto is, 'Paradise or bussed!' Get it? Har, har."

Elayne looked at me imploringly.

Suddenly the undertaker stopped gabbing. "Look! Outside!" another one screeched.

"It's him!" said Ruddigore.

They ran to the open front door. I and Elayne followed. We saw an elderly gentleman in a top hat and tails, busily directing two lackeys, who were about to lift Gallenkamp off the mower.

The other undertakers were clustered around the body, protesting their right of precedence. The one in the top hat, spying us, came over and pulled out a business card.

I took it and read, "Lord Texas-Chainsaw, President, Olde Worlde Funeral Services."

"That's *Tanshawe*," he said stiffly.

"What are you talking about?"

"My name," he said, and I noticed the British accent, perhaps fake. "It's *spelt* Texas-Chainsaw, pronounced *Tanshawe.* We are a very ancient family."

"I think I'm going to puke," Elayne said, as we both noticed the viscous rheum dripping from Gallenkamp's jellying eye socket.

"Go ahead, dear madam," said Texas-Chainsaw suavely. "A little regurgitation is nothing to be ashamed of in this hour of ultimate bereavement."

"I think I'm going to scream!"

"I suppose I'd better do something," I said. "I mean, to repel the invasion of the body snatchers."

"Get them out of here already!" Elayne screamed.

"Leave at once!" I said in my most majestic voice.

"But—the body—" said Mortworth.

"As Mrs. Gallenkamp's attorney, *I* shall inform you of her final decision in the matter of the disposition of the body."

I waved grandly, in my most Perry Masonesque manner, and the morticians fled like a herd of kine down the gentle incline of the front yard into their waiting limousines. All but this Texas-Chainsaw, that is, who stood scrutinizing me for some moments (as a biologist might peruse a microbe) before he shambled off. As he left, I knew him—as though by a sudden prescience—for my mortal enemy.

Elayne followed me into the house. I slammed the door shut. Then I embraced her, and we kissed passionately.

"What a stroke of luck!" Elayne said when our ardor had abated somewhat, steering me toward the very couch where we had last made love.

"Yes," I said, "it seems that dear Owen will be out to lunch more frequently from now on."

"And dinner," Elayne panted.

"And breakfast!" I said, anticipating the wild abandon of the night to come.

"Though I rather regret," Elayne said, "that we won't have to murder him. That was so thrilling . . . the whispered plans over the lunch breaks . . . the debates over the most appropriate murder weapon. . . ."

"Darling!"

Just then, we heard voices squawking outside: "Totally awesome! Icky! Ooooh, gross! Daddy's dead!"

"C'mon, it's just a rubber corpse. Don't you remember, he brought one down from the studio when he was doing the novelization of *The Beast that Decapitated Nuns?*"

"Crap, you can tell from the stink, stupid. Like, he's totally dead."

I opened the door and saw two dirty identical ten-year-old girls with braces and freckles. "Oh, shit!" I said. "It's Heckle and Jeckle."

"Oh, Uncle Whitey! Is he really dead, I mean, *dead* dead?"

"Come in, kids," I said, "I suppose you'd better hear the will."

"Then I'll have to decide on which of those creeps to hire for the funeral," Elayne said.

"I don't think so," I said. "Not after you hear what's in the will."

The moment of truth had finally come, and it was with a heavy heart that I pulled the sealed document from an inner pocket of my gray three-piece suit.

"So," Elayne said at last. "It's worse than we ever imagined."

"I'm afraid so."

"Want a drink?"

"Scotch." One of the twins went into the kitchen to fix it, and Elayne and I sat down and pored over the document again.

"God! Look at that part!" she said.

I read: *I know you've been screwing that scumbag of a lawyer, Elayne darling. At first, I thought I would make the inheritance contingent on your never seeing him again, but I've thought of a worse plan.*

"Oh, God, the plan, the plan," Elayne moaned.

"Now, the Sioux used to leave their dead on platforms on the premises. I see no reason why you should not do so. If I die, I must insist that you leave my body precisely at the place

of death undisturbed. Especially if I die at home. My grisly, rotting corpse will haunt you daily as you rut with that shyster, you tacky, disloyal slut. How wonderful the Sioux were! They were never tainted by your petit bourgeous *sensibilities. As for those hideous children I sired, the continuous presence of a* memento mori *in their home will be a salutary exposure to the human condition. No one is to perform any embalming or anything else on my carcass except Dr. Sargnagel."*

"Sargnagel . . . who's he?" Elayne said.

"My, he's certainly kept his life a secret from you, hasn't he? Owen owned 46% of the Sargnagel Corporation, a holding corporation which includes *ResurrecTech™*—I glanced at the poster on the wall."

"I thought that was just a movie he was novelizing," Elayne said.

"It could almost be one. *Resurrectech™* specializes in mad scientist sort of experiments. . . ."

"How are we going to get out of this?" Elayne wailed.

"I don't see how we can. I drew it up myself. I was humoring him, really. Didn't expect him to croak before I had a chance to monkey with it. Look at this part: *If my instructions are not obeyed to the letter, my entire estate will be bequeathed to the Sioux Nation. The corpse is not to be moved more than twelve feet from the scene of my death, and only for the purpose of cleaning or cosmetic decoration or effecting a more aesthetic arrangement."*

"What does he mean, the Sioux Nation?" Elayne said. "He's never even met an Indian in his life."

"Our mutual friend was even more eccentric than I thought."

"Can't we just let the Indians have it? How much can there have been, anyway?"

"About eight million."

"What!" The screeches came simultaneously from the woman and the two little girls.

"My dear, it appears that dear Owen, whose literary works were critical and commercial failures, who appeared to be just struggling along in this decidedly unsumptuous condominium, acually amassed a vast fortune by shrewd investment of the royalties from the novelizations of *The Beast that Decapitated Nuns* and *Gangbanged on Ganymede.* A computer error at Stupendous Publishing, you see, apportioned *his* share of the royalties to the studio, and the studio's to him. In fact, I've known this for some time; that's why I agreed to become executor of the estate."

"My God . . . you've always known . . . do you mean to say that you've inveigled yourself into my bed for purely materialistic purposes, that you've been—"

"Using you? I hardly think you're in a position to make that accusation, darling, considering you've been guilty of adultery for the past eleven years. By the way, who *is* the father of those hideous twins?"

"You parasite!"

"Elayne darling, I *know* what I am. You have yet to learn."

"How dare you—"

"Now, you wouldn't want to upset the executor of the estate, would you?"

"So what's the plan?"

We were interrupted by a scurrying sound outside. "Let's go and see," I said, anxious for any diversion, for I dreaded having to call Sargnagel's office. The sun was setting over the kiddie playground across the street. I got a whiff of Gallenkamp, and didn't terribly much care for the smell. Two figures were hulking over the corpse; a police car was parked on the curb, and farther up the service road was a limousine I recognized as belonging to Lord Texas-Chainsaw's body shop. The lord himself was there, attired in a sort of Dracula cape, and he was grimly orchestrating the theft of Owen's corpse.

"There, there," he was saying. "We don't want to take

away the handle of the mower, would we? That would be stealing."

"And what do you think *this* is?" I said. "Trespassing. Stealing the personal effects of the owner, no less!"

"My dear fellow—"

"I, Whitey Jefferson of Jefferson, Shapiro and Tablecloth, happen to be the executor of this estate. Since no formal transfer has taken place, you are stealing the late lamented's property."

As though in agreement, Gallenkamp's head craned forward on its neck. Assorted fluids drooled from his nose and mouth. A dog ran by, sniffing longingly at the cadaver's brain-besmirched buttocks until I shooed it away.

"But I am leaving the mower intact!" Texas-Chainsaw said.

"The mower? Who cares about the mower? It's the body I'm concerned with. If a man doesn't own his own body, what *can* he call his own?"

"I see I shall have to call upon the law for assistance, Mr. Jefferson," Texas-Chainsaw said imperturbably. "I say, officer!"

From behind one of the parked police cars emerged a grotesquely blubbery policewoman brandishing a badge. "I'm officer Heartfelt," she said.

"Stay where you are!" I said. "The sidewalk may be public, but the grass isn't. Got a warrant?"

"Sir," the officer said, "It is illegal in this state of ours to leave a body lying around rotting for more than twenty-four hours without having it removed by a licensed undertaker."

"So what are you going to do?" I said. "Give it a ticket?"

"Well—" She pulled out a notebook, fished a pencil from her pocket, and began scribbling.

"Furthermore, I demand the immediate extradition of Lord Texas-Chainsaw from the premises."

"Oh, I say, I object, what. I was only doing my duty as a citizen. Why, if I didn't report your shameful neglect of the deceased, I'd be an accessory after the fact, wouldn't I?"

"Ah—" said the officer, patting her paunch thoughtfully while Elayne did a passable imitation of a grief-stricken widow.

"In any case," I said, "it isn't even twenty-four hours yet. Now will you get this idiot off the Gallenkamp turf before I call the police?"

"I am the police," said Officer Heartfelt. "I suppose you'd better come with me," she said to Texas-Chainsaw.

"Foiled again!" said the twins, who had come from the house and were nibbling between them a leviathan hunk of amaretto cheesecake. "Nyah, nyah, nyah! Gash me with a ginsu! Totally radical!"

"Go to bed!" said their mother.

"But it's not our bedtime yet," said Heckle. By the way, these are not their real names. In my years of involvement with the Gallenkamps, I had yet to learn to tell them apart. Nor would I have wanted to.

"Uncle Whitey and I have important business matters to discuss."

"You mean," said Jeckle, "that you're getting rid of us so you can fuck."

"The things these children are saying nowadays!" Texas-Chainsaw said. "Simply appalling!"

"Get him out of here," I said, and there was a concerted exeunt that left me alone with Elayne on the front lawn in the suburban sunset, about to cuckold the corpse of my best friend.

I patted the old fellow on the head. A hank of hair, matted with brain tissue, clung to my fingers. "I can see, my dear," I said, "that we must be prepared to fight a legal battle of epic proportions. But never fear! Whitey Jefferson's never lost a case yet!"

Inexplicably, Elayne began to cry. I guess it was all too much to take in, having me all to herself and all that.

When I climbed into bed with Elayne I was anticipating a night of rapturous and continuous orgasm. Instead, I was surprised to find her rather frigid. I was expecting a long and tender lay-in in the morning; indeed, I'd even left word at the office that we would be working over the details of the will and that they were to start without me on *Hobson vs. Hobbes.* Instead, we were awakened at the crack of dawn by the shrieking of the children.

I started. She moaned. I said, "So this is what actually living with a woman is like."

"Go for it, baby."

"I think I'm starting to feel nostalgic about the lunch break arrangement," I said, casually stroking one of her breasts.

"Come quickly!" one of the kids screamed from somewhere outside the house. "The storm troopers are back!"

I heard sirens, crowd noises, and various *ughs* and *ooohs* and other ejaculations of repugnance, as I helped myself to one of Owen's shirts from the closet. I even wore his underwear. I felt particularly evil doing that. It was a superb sensation. Grabbing a sheaf of papers from the living room to make it look like I had been burning the midnight oil, I flung the front door open. Elayne followed in a floral nightgown.

The sight that assailed me can only be described as a spectacle of insensate and unmitigated horror, equal to if not exceeding the notorious crowd scene from Owen Gallenkamp's *The Beast that Decapitated Nuns,* a scene which, I hasten to add, was not in the movie.

It seemed as though the entire population of Rattlesnake Junior High had played hooky that morning. My hapless friend's corpse—whose head was swarming with ants and centipedes—was completely surrounded by jeering children. Officer Heartfelt was protecting the corpse with one arm and waving a nightstick with the other. Lord Texas-Chainsaw and a gang of henchmen, all dressed in dark suits and wearing dark glasses, were beating back the children as he tried to make his way through to the corpse. Heckle and Jeckle were bombarding them with spitballs. Old Mrs. Snodgrass from across the street was standing on the doorstep, obliviously telling me the latest gossip. A Hare Krishna was selling everyone flowers.

"All right, all right," I said.

"Twenty-four hours is up," Officer Heartfelt said imposingly. "I'm now empowered to authorize the removal of the corpse."

"Over my dead body!" I shouted, gesticulating wildly. My hand smashed into Gallenkamp's decomposing face. I snatched it back. Several gloppy maggots adhered to my hand. The grim comedy of the situation was coming home to me. "Bring me the phone!" I shouted at the twins. One of them rushed into the house and emerged with the patio cordless. I dialed furiously as the maggots crawled from my hand to the mouthpiece. "Give me Judge Strickland," I said. "Now, this minute." To Texas-Chainsaw and Heartfelt I said, "Your asses are about to be in deep, deep, deep, deep shit."

"The law—" the officer began.

"—is the handmaiden of the well-heeled," I said, as I heard Judge Strickland's phthisic voice wheezing away at the other end. "Courtney? It's Whitey. I want a court order." It would hard be to go much higher that Courtney Strickland, who was head of the president's judiciary advisory commission or something. The crowd of truants was hemming us in tight now, and I had to kick away one intrepid child who, mayonaise jar in hand, had been trying to scrape off a memento of the dear departed. "It's the Gallenkamp case—"

"Oh, is the old bugger dead?" the judge rasped. "Wonderful news. I'll have a rehoboam of Moët Chandon shipped over right away."

"Hold the booze," I said. "There's trouble. The will. He picked the front lawn to die in. . . ." Of course, the judge had known all about Gallenkamp's will. It had been the talk of his chambers for some months now. "They're trying to take him away."

"The rotters!" the judge said. He probably hadn't had this much fun since his triple bypass. "But of course, the state law clearly states—"

"You want me to reveal"—I cupped my hands and whispered into the phone—"your part in the seminary brownie molestation coverup?"

"Oh, I, ah—"

"I knew you could be reasonable, your honor." I turned to Officer Heartfelt. "The court order should be here in a half hour. Get out."

She drew herself up. "Until it appears, Mr. Jefferson, I am still the law around here. We'll bring the body back when we see the document."

It was at that dramatic juncture that an enormous van pulled up in front of the townhouse. It was a sleek, streamlined thing, all black and chrome, with a futuristic hood ornament. The sides were blazoned with the legend

ResurrechTech™ and beneath that, in tiny letters, the words "Sargnagel Enterprises." Help had arrived at last! I thought. For Sargnagel Enterprises was, of course, one of Owen's own little projects, and Dr. Sargnagel had been mentioned in the will as the only person authorized to tinker with the corpse.

"I believed that the morticians specified in the deceased's will have finally arrived," I said.

Officer Heartfelt gave them no more than a cursory examination. Relieved that she no longer had to duel with me, she and her squad car departed; and I thumbed my nose at the unsavory Texas-Chainsaw as he and his cohorts drove away. It was only then that I turned my attention to the labcoated technicians who were piling out of the car, all carrying some high-tech device, each one more outlandish-looking than the last.

A tiny man, with dark glasses, was directing them. Were he not bald, I would have pegged him as about fourteen years old. I recognized him from the photo in the dossier I had in my office—his was the thinnest file in the cabinet. In all my years as a dirt-digger I had uncovered almost no information about this fellow at all. He didn't even seem to have a birth certificate or a social security number— if he did, they were well hidden even from the prying computers at Jefferson, Shapiro and Tablecloth.

"Dr. Sargnagel," I said.

He ignored me. "No, stupid!" he barked at one of the assistants. "He'll need at least a hundred feet radius circumambulation field. Plant the ROM module"—he stalked out into the middle of the lawn and pointed at a patch of ground a couple of yards away from the rotting cadaver and the power mower—"right here."

The assistant started digging immediately, while another began attaching electrodes to the body.

"Totally radical!" the twins screeched. "Can we help?"

"Hold this," Dr. Sargnagel said, thrusting wires and switches into their hands. He then advanced toward the body of my late friend and began to drill a hole in his skull with some kind of laser device. Brains spattered his head, but he didn't seem to notice. Then he gave a signal, and one of his assistants poked a sort of computer cable into Owen's cranium.

Owen fluttered his eyelids.

"Ah, good," Sargnagel said.

"Just what the hell do you think you're doing?" I said.

"What the—oh, you must be that Jefferson dude," Sargnagel said. "Well, we have like this gigabyte ROM module, kind of a simulacrum of Gallenkamp's brain processes, and we're like installing this like interface that will like function as a digital-to-analog coprocessor. Thing is, like there's virtually no RAM, so the loved one can't learn anything new, and so like it guarantees that his character doesn't like change, and aborts the Jekyll-and-Hyde complex, you know?"

"Awesome!" Heckle crooned, while her sister placed her hand to her forehead and pretended to swoon. "You're turning daddy's body into a robot!"

I must admit that that was not at all how I had translated Sargnagel's sentiments to myself. But the young are always much more knowledgeable about scientific jargon. It was clear that my dear friend had, in effect, donated his body to some bizarre experiment. Perhaps the interests of science were being served; perhaps not. Well, I would not let it deter me from the embraces of Elayne. Or from the eight million.

I went back inside, leaving the twins to help the mad doctor. Elayne was still in bed, whinnying and heaving like a steam locomotive. Exhilarated by my victory over Officer Heartfelt and Lord Texas-Chainsaw, and by the ease with which I had blackmailed Judge Strickland, I leaped eagerly into the fray. Then we watched daytime soaps for a few hours, consumed TV dinners, and resumed our feverish fornication. By midnight I was exhausted. Flattered though I was by Elayne's continued ardor, I decided to sleep on the couch downstairs. My rest was fitful, for it was continually punctuated by sounds of hammering and by electronic beeps and buzzes from the high-tech crew on the lawn. Eventually I went back upstairs. Mercifully, Elayne had fallen asleep; I did so too. My last thoughts before I passed out were of millions upon millions of greenbacks raining down from the sky.

I was awakened by the fragrance of hot coffee. I rubbed my eyes. "You needn't have, darling," I said. Then I noticed that Elayne was snoring away beside me. Could Heckle and Jeckle undergone so dramatic a transformation as to bring us our morning coffee in bed? "Thank you, children," I murmured.

"You're welcome." A rasping, buzzing voice. I opened my eyes wide. A tray was being held out at me. "I thought you and my harlot wife would like a little something for breakfast."

There was an odor of putrescence behind the smell of coffee, and the tray was covered with slime.

The bearer of the tray was none other than the corpse of my old friend. He stood, quite still, stinking up the bedroom. An electronic cable led from an opening in his back (through which the spinal chord glistened with beads of coagulated blood) all the way out the bedroom door, from behind which came the diabolical giggling of the twins. Such was my astonishment that the horror of having my friend's zombie resurrection did not register at first.

"Enjoying my wife, are you?" Owen said. He gaped wide and I saw the glint of some metal device implanted in his throat. I was reminded of the prosthetics certain laryngectomy patients use to simulate speech. Owen leered. I noticed that there was a trail of slime leading to the door and presumably all the way downstairs and into the lawn.

At that moment, Elayne stirred. "Coffee? How thoughtful of you, darling," she said.

She opened her eyes and saw the rotting animated corpse of her late husband, who attempted a sheepish grin through lips stained with blood, pus, and decaying vomit.

Elayne screamed.

The television crews had been gathering since dawn. When Elayne had calmed down enough, I made her make herself up nicely and put on a moderately yuppie dress. Then I carefully waved a sliced onion in front of her face for a few minutes, so that the tears would streak the mascara so as to suggest a woman heroically struggling with her grief.

Meanwhile, the corpse puttered around the living room. It had a go at vacuuming, but the power cord became hopelessly entangled in Owen's own I/O cables, so that he tripped and made a gloppy mess out of that nice pseudo-Persian carpet Elayne had purchased from Bloomingdale's. The sight of her dead husband jerkily attempting to rise from the floor and to disentangle his entrails from the various wires and cables set off another screaming fit.

"Shut up!" I said. "They'll hear you outside. We've got to act as though this is all perfectly normal."

"I want that corpse out of my house!"

"That's a fine thing to say," the cadaver riposted. "The three of us should have a threesome sometime. I used to fantasize about that over my word-processor when I was alive." It managed to straighten itself out; it then proceeded to shamble to the sofa.

"Are we ready to meet the public?" I said.

Numbly Elayne nodded.

"Think of the money," I said.

We opened the door.

Sargnagel was already holding forth from the front steps. All the networks were there. "Well like none of the hardware is really new, but like there are whole areas in applications that we haven't had the imagination to like effectuate. I'd say the *ResurrecTech™* process should be like totally available within like maybe a couple months. The subject's memory is downloaded from the brain like before death and cut down to fit the gigabyte ROM module and there's like this hierarchical memory banking file-management user-independent operating system. We're totally backed up with orders though."

"Are you saying that we'll soon be seeing a plethora of zombies, Dr. Sargnagel?" a reporter said, nervously eyeing Owen, who had come outside. The cables that controlled him emanated from a machine buried in the lawn; a spooling device kept them taut, sort of like fishing tackle.

"I wouldn't exactly call them zombies," Sargnagel continued, "I just think of them as computer-enhanced cadavers —CECs for short."

To my horror I saw that the Texas-Chainsaw limo had arrived. Moreover, this time Lord Texas-Chainsaw had brought with him about half a dozen Plains Indians in war-bonnets, and they were dancing up a storm on the sidewalk.

"This is the most awesome spectacle since the Philippine election!" one reporter rhapsodized, as the videocameras turned and the microphone booms swivelled, causing a hardware traffic jam above our heads.

"Why are they dancing?" Elayne said.

"These representatives of the Sioux Nation have been flown in to collect their ten-million dollar windfall," an earnest woman reporter was declaiming into one camera. "But will they get it or not? Will Elayne Gallenkamp and ace legal expert Whitey Jefferson be able to keep the body of Owen Gallenkamp in defiance of city ordinances about proper removal of the dead?"

Texas Chainsaw was waving a document. "I have here a court order from Judge Strickland—"

"Wait a minute!" I said. I ran back into the house and returned with my own court order. I brandished it, pushing Texas-Chainsaw out of camera range. He rearranged his Dracula cape and came bouncing back. The cameras reshuffled themselves as Owen's computer-enhanced cadaver came back into view. It was socializing with the Indians, joining in the dance. I took the opportunity to look at Texas-Chainsaw's paper. *Expeditious removal of the deceased...* Astonished, I said, "How did you manage to get Judge Strickland—"

"My dear Mr. Jefferson! How could you be so naïve as to suppose that you have a monopoly on Judge Strickland's little, ah, foibles? I don't know which one you used on him, but one teeny dropped hint of his involvement in the Boy

Scout heroin scandal was enough to render him *most* cooperative."

Even *I* hadn't known about that.

"Well," I said, "we do seem to have two conflicting court orders—"

Texas-Chainsaw stepped in front of the nearest camera and began to speak in doleful, dulcet tones: "What we have here, ladies and gentlemen of the media, is a clear case of environmental pollution . . . corrupt lawyers . . . poor, deprived Native Americans being cheated of their inheritance to satisfy the craven lusts of—"

He went on in this vein for sometime. If there's anything I hate, it's one of these bleeding heart appeals, whether it's whales or Indians or anything else. I was getting steadily angrier. Elayne, who stood beside me, was weakening, though. I could see that she was not relishing the prospect of sharing life with her husband's corpse. "Please, let's just give up the whole thing," she whispered. "We'll go away somewhere . . . at least we have each other. . . ."

That was precisely what I was afraid of. I saw a vision of ten million smackers swirling down the toilet bowl . . . and only a supply of mediocre free pussy to show for it. "Are you kidding?" I said. "This means war!"

"Totally rad!" said the twins. "Get 'em, Rambo!"

Texas-Chainsaw was saying, ". . . the sad state of contemporary culture . . . when a man is deprived of a decent burial and made into a monster . . ."

Suddenly I had an inspiration. I shoved him onto the lawn. "This is a constitutional issue," I said. "The man wants to be able to rot on his own private turf, and these henchmen of the state would deprive him of that right! I say just because a man is dead doesn't abrogate his civil rights—let alone his human rights! You, Lord Texas-Chainsaw, and you, Officer Heartfelt, are Big Brother personified! Communists! Fascist pigs!"

Texas-Chainsaw's face was becoming steadily more livid in hue. "I fail to see how you can accuse me of being both," he said.

"We've passed laws to stop discrimination against blacks and women and homosexuals," I said. "Well, I say there's one more barrier of prejudice to be overcome—our discriminatory practices against the deceased! We'll get another restraining order"—I was going to play my trump card, the fact that Judge Strickland had been getting kickbacks from the mafia—"and we'll resist this un-American living/dead apartheid all the way to the Supreme Court . . . all the way to the President of the United States!"

I paused to take a breath. That was when the applause began. How sweet that applause was! As a lawyer I well knew that the content of a speech doesn't matter, only its rhetoric, its tone, its fervor. I had delivered a classic speech, on national television; my words were going to echo through the land.

That evening, Sargnagel's crew were making adjustments to Owen: spraying him with a fixative that hardened into sort of a Saran Wrap around him, so he would ooze and leak all over the place; fine-tuning his interfaces and cables; and—so help me—brushing and flossing his teeth.

The phone rang. It was the Reverend Obadiah Crackerjack, a popular TV evangelist. Oh, no, I thought. He's going to berate me for not allowing people their proper Christian burial. I sat down on the sofa, carefully wiping off Owen's slime, and tried to decide on the least actionable brushoff.

"Mister Jefferson, sir, I'm a-telling you, the Lord has touched you, sir, he has chosen you to bear his word."

"What?" I said, not quite believing my ears.

"I mean, I heard you on the news today, sir, and it is my belief that you have been singled out to bear a divine revelation. I got to thinking about all you said—about discriminating against the souls and wishes of the dear departed—and I think this whole sick thing is just another example of the sin and degradation that's tainting this Christian country of ours. One moment they're telling us that the right to life is only applicable after the wee, pathetic embryo has been delivered . . . and now these sodomitic sinners are saying that the right to life stops at the moment of death!"

"That's very interesting," I said noncommitally, wishing I could hand this lunatic over to my secretary. "Quite a paradox you've—ah—uncovered, reverend."

"—when everyone knows that the soul is immortal and the death of the flesh is but the beginning of life eternal—of the glories of hell or the fires of damnation! That's why I'm a-fixing to hold a special telethon for your cause—"

Horrified, I realized that I had been sucked into an unholy alliance with the forces of excruciating moral rectitude.

The reverend continued (obviously rehearsing his sermon for later that night), "I'm a-galvanizing my congregation for a march on Washington. They'll come, believe me! Dead or alive, they'll come! Should the earthly forms of some members of my church have succumbed to the corruption of the body, I intend to be raising enough capital to purchase CEC units for all! Sargagel's ResurrecTech™ process is the Lord's plan to prepare us for the more perfect resurrection of the life to come! Now, won't you say a few rousing words to my flock?"

"You're on TV again!" squealed Heckle or Jeckle from upstairs. "On some religious voodoo nut show! You're gonna be totally famous!"

So the reverend wasn't rehearsing. This was live. I had better make it good. But I didn't believe in any of this bullshit! And yet . . . ten million dollars . . . the computer-enhanced cadaver of my ex-best-friend hunkered in the hallway. He didn't smell bad anymore; they'd installed a couple of time-release fragrance ampoules in his armpits. Surely having him around couldn't be that bad. I mean, he might walk and talk, but he *was* dead. Dead and harmless. It was all psychological. Just your typical Owen Gallenkampian emotional blackmail.

"Well, Mister Jefferson? Do you believe?" Jeckle had come in and turned on the living room TV, so I saw the Lord's ambassador in all his porcine splendor.

"Ahem," I said. I had to say something fast. "Ah—the constitution of the United States—the—ah—habeas corpus —human rights—can't descend to the level of the Soviet Union—" I knew that one would get them. I went on in that vein for a while, being careful to mention apple pie at least once per paragraph.

"That," Obadiah Crackerjack, "has got to be the most moving speech we've ever heard on Heavenly Hour. And now, a word from our sponsor—"

Their sponsor! It was the Sargnagel Corporation . . . with an ad for a bible quotation PROM module, implantable in the computer-enhanced cadaver of your favorite atheist! *Why allow your beloved friends and relatives to die unsaved? Technology comes to the service of His word . . . give your dead friends a second chance to accept Him into their hearts. . . .* It was sickening. PROMS—EPROMS would be next, whatever they were. The twins would know.

But it *was* pouring money into the coffers of Elayne and me . . . as long as that talking corpse remained with us. If they took it away . . . there'd be a new string of condos on the reservation.

"Hi, Owen," I said, smiling as he shambled in and sat down beside me. "Make yourself at home. Have a drink?"

"Don't be ridiculous. I'm dead."

At night, during our desultory lovemaking, I became conscious of someone else lying in bed with me and Elayne.

Someone thrusting wildly and hapharzardly away at the sheets. In the half dark I saw who it was.

"Jesus Christ," I said.

Elayne, eyes closed and transported by ecstacy, had failed to notice that she was participating in a particularly unusual act.

"You were never like this when you were alive," I muttered. "If you had been, Elayne would never have turned to me."

"Being a cyborg does have its advantages," he said, as Elayne heaved and panted passionately and obliviously.

Owen neither panted nor heaved. He didn't even breathe. Maybe that was the secret of his newfound sexual prowess—he didn't have to worry about his heart, his cholesterol, or his ulcers.

At last, he rolled away. There wasn't much slime; the plastic sheath was holding up quite well. Elayne cried, "Oh, not yet, not yet, darling."

"Want to finish her off?" he said.

Sighing, I returned to the ramparts of love. But somehow it wasn't the same with Owen sitting there, rotting away. I just couldn't . . . well, I just couldn't. I had to let old Roy Rogers back into the saddle. I had never felt more stupid in my life.

"That was wonderful, darling," Elayne whispered, as the zombie slunk back into the shadows.

To be honest, I was not displeased at this turn of events. Without the element of furtiveness, my relationship with Elayne had been reduced to the level of bourgeois adultery. Let him have her, I thought. After all, what else does he have to live for?

Contributions from Obadiah Crackerjack's church started to arrive the very next morning. I began to realize that we could never pull out now. The ten million was nothing compared to this new racket. Elayne bought several fur coats. I didn't go into the office for the fourth day running. I considered quitting the law firm altogether in order to give my full attention to this great constitutional issue. Yes, I still had qualms about aligning myself with the Crackerjack Morality Squad; but how could I resist the checks that were flooding in through the mailbox?

One day later, a group of raving religious fanatics exhumed the entire contents of a local cemetery and loaded the coffins onto Sargnagel trucks.

Three days later, zombies were spotted in nearby Springfield Mall. Their leashes were attached to mobile processor units. The zombies purchased some new wave clothing at J.C.Penneys. There were some problems with expired credit cards, and the police were called in. A battle ensued between right-to-computer-enhanced-lifers and members of the morticians' solidarity group.

That evening, Lord Texas-Chainsaw and I were guests on CNN's *Crossfire*. He called me a environmental polluter; I called him a communist. It degenerated into a fistfight. Luckily, I had learned kung fu; in my line of work it's always good to be able to fend off some angry client. I climbed atop the heap of debaters' bodies and—to the nation at large—I announced that we were going to march on the White House. "Zombies out of the closet!" I screamed at the top of my lungs. "Corpses of the world unite!"

A whirlwind talk-show tour followed. Mornings I spoke to studio audiences of earnest housewives. Evenings I had spots on news hours. Late nights I did the call-in circuit . . . "Mr. Jefferson, my mother has been dead for ten years and I was wondering whether computer-enhancement would be feasible." . . . "Sure. Get a good plastics engineer to reconstruct the body on the old frame. But if you haven't had the ROM-dump done, you probably can't be helped—although you might consider redesigning her personality entirely and creating a character-simulacrum for the frame." "Great show! Whitey, my uncle was cremated last week, and—" . . . "Forget it! They might be able to build a plastic body, though. Did you do the dump?" . . . "Do you think I could get my kids embalmed *before* they die?" . . . "Most experts consider it inadvisable, but I'd make sure they sign a release first. If they're minors, you can of course do it on their behalf." . . . "What happens to my IRA if I try to draw on it and I'm already dead?" . . . "Call your local tax advisor." Etcetera, etcetera. I found a ready answer for almost any question they could throw at me.

Excitement grew. My best friend's right to rot had become a *cause cél`ebre*, and all the sickos were coming out of the woodwork . . . I mean, all the Norman Bates types with their stuffed mothers in their fruit cellars . . . you'd be surprised how many of them there were . . . every one of them fighting mad and militant as hell.

I finally did quit the job. Actually, they fired me after the firm was retained by the morticians' solidarity caucus. I didn't even notice.

Owen started filling in for me every night now; the task of sevicing Elayne had become onerous to me. Elayne had found a man—or whatever—who could match her tireless passion thrust for thrust. At first she found it rather distasteful; but with the lights off, and with the perfume ampoule set on high, she hardly seemed to notice after a while.

And me? Only the good fight mattered now. I was a man possessed. I had a vision. I had a dream. I also had millions of dollars.

The day of the great march on the White House finally dawned. It was a fine summer's day. The stench of putrescence filled the street as Elayne and I emerged from the house. We were followed by Heckle and Jeckle, who carried between them a stripped-down version of the CPU that animated Owen's corpse.

Sargnagel and Crackerjack were there to greet us. The

former was surrounded by a crowd of techie nerds; the latter was at the head of a motley assortment of people and corpses. The corpses were what had been stinking up the street. There were hundreds of them. Many of them had not been as smoothly animated as that of my friend Owen; for several fly-by-night CEC outfits had appeared in the past few weeks, each one seeking to bypass Sargnagel's patented microchips with bug-filled Taiwanese imitations. The corpses jerked, flailed and gibbered.

"My God," Elayne whispered, tripping over a human hand that had fallen by the wayside.

Then a fervent chanting arose from the gathered throng: "I'd rather be dead than dead! I'd rather be dead than dead!"

"What a singularly inspired slogan," I said. "It doesn't mean anything."

"Ah, Jefferson, my son," Crackerjack said expansively, "that's because you haven't yet come to a complete understanding of the mysterious ways of the Lord. It don't matter *what* they're chanting. The important thing is that they're chanting. The second coming is at hand . . . the dead shall be raised incorruptible!"

"I don't know," I said, wrinkling my nose at a maggot-ridden liver that had landed at my feet. "Looks pretty corruptible to me."

"Believe."

"Yeah." I was in too deep now. It was my face on all those talk shows. I was the one most prominently identified with this latest extension of the right-to-life concept. I tried to keep a straight face as our contingent began to lead the marchers down the street toward the highway. After a while I got into the rhythm of it, and it seemed like no time at all before the gathering—now grown to perhaps a hundred thousand people, and a thousand or so dead bodies—reached Pennsylvania Avenue.

The corpses were a big hit. Two teenage corpse

breakdanced frantically out front; one of them actually removed his own head and begun juggling with it. Not to be undone, the other unzipped his legs from his torso and executed some bizarre maneuvers, such as doing a handstand ten yards away from his tapping feet, for example. As a consequence of the fine summer's day, however, the crowd was becoming increasingly rank, some of Sargnagel's shock troops moved in with hoses that sprayed embalming fluid over the celebrants.

Wellwishers lined the sidewalks, many of them waving frayed copies of *The Beast that Decapitated Nuns.* My heart swelled with pride. Here I was—I, Whitey Jefferson, a shyster from a second-rate law firm—elevated to a champion of the constitution— possibly even sainthood, at the rate the Reverend Crackerjack was carrying on!

The crowd marched on. Already we had reached Fifteenth Street; just ahead was the White House, splendid in the sunlight. The corpses began to sing, their raspy, electronic voices drowning out the sounds of traffic and police sirens.

We paused in front of the gates. The Reverend Obadiah Crackerjack gave a rousing sermon, although I had to admit that the biblical references went right over my head. I suppose that finding the right biblical quote is sort of like looking up obscure legal precedents in order to flummox the opposing attorney. As Crackerjack got into his stride, I admired him more and more. His ability to prove that black is white was equalled only by my own. I wish I'd had him with me on Hobson vs. Hobbes.

Then it was my turn. Crackerjack had just been warming up the crowd.

Nervously, I got up in front of the cameras and the throng. I cleared my throat a couple of times. What was I supposed to say? "Friends, Romans and countrymen"? Before I could begin the shouting began. Cheers, whistles, slogans, and above it all the song of the corpses bursting forth from thousands of computer-enhanced throats. . . .

At that moment—

Cries of "Sabotage! What an outrage!" I turned to see that fighting had broken out. Hundreds upon hundreds of Sioux Indians were leaping from Seventeenth Street office buildings, and, with bloodcurdling screams of "Hoka hey!", were hurling themselves upon the chanting dead.

"Like, I think there's trouble," Sargnagel said, and the Reverend Crackerjack made a dive for the public address system to try to restore order.

I knew who was behind it. I just knew. And there he was, his limousine thrusting through the throng and mowing down corpses like bowling pins. The street resounded with the crack of bone and hardware. There was a whole fleet of Texas-Chainsaw hearses. More Indians, in all all the feathered finery of war, were squatting on the hoods, tomahwaks upraised. Others were dancing on the roofs and leaping from hearse to hearse, shooting rifles and fire arrows at the mob. Flaming zombies ran amok, sending up a stink of formaldehyde-marinated steak. Texas-Chainsaw's limo made a swath through the carnage and screeched to a halt in front of my podium. No sooner had the lord leapt out than he and Sargnagel were at each other's throats.

"You sold out!" Texas-Chainsaw was screaming. "The world was supposed to be divided into three parts—and you and Crackerjack want it all to yourselves!"

I stood there, feeling helpless, as I realized that mine was by no means the first unholy triumvirate that Owen Gallenkamp caused to come into existence . . . that the entire edifice of my newfound wealth had been built upon the ruins of some previous entrepreneurial disaster. . . .

"The money," I heard Elayne whimpering. "We'll lose it all unless you do something!"

I seized the microphone from the reverend and began to speak. It wasn't a good, logical speech, one point after another. It was a direct appeal to apple pie, motherhood, and the American flag. But no one heard me, because as I started, there came the whirring thunder of overhead gunships. . . .

In a few moments it was all in shambles. Texas-Chainsaw, bleeding, a microphone stand draped around his neck, was shambling off into his limousine, whose windscreen was completely covered with flailing corpses. What kind of power had Gallenkamp held over him? What bargain had he made with Sargnagel? I struggled to make sense of it all as the Reverend Crackerjack blessed the throng.

Amid the chaos, the gates of the presidential mansion opened.

Silence fell.

"The president will see you now." A man in a black suit had come to escort me inside.

The crowd was hushed. Slowly I followed him inside.

"First I'd like to thank you, Mr. Jefferson. You've done a lot of the dirty work for us. You've established the right . . . ah . . . atmosphere, you see."

The familiar face, so full of sincerity and concern, watched me from the other side of the great desk. I noticed that Dr. Sargnagel had come in and was standing by the door. Some of Sargnagel's laboratory technicians were wheeling in a familiar looking apparatus.

"Thank you, Mr. President," I said. "But why—"

Suddenly I saw it. A cable that emerged from the back of the president's head and wound its way into an outlet in the wall. The presidential desk was covered with bloodstains and slime—sights familiar from the Gallenkamp livingroom.

"Jesus!" I said. "You're dead."

"An astute observation," he said. "But one which the rest of the populace has, as yet, failed to make—thanks to good makeup and tasteful camera angles."

I am, of course, well trained to adjust instantly to, for instance, startling new pieces of evidence in the courtroom, surprise witnesses, what have you. I looked around me and saw that I wouldn't get anywhere by agreeing . . . after all, I was supposed to be here to espouse the rights of dead people, wasn't I? . . . so I switched to my most ingratiating voice. "I must say, Mr. President, you've really kept in shape . . . I've seen people alive who looked more moribund than you, sir. How long has this—ah—state of affairs been going on?"

"Thanks a lot for your compliments," said the president. "I don't recall my death that well—I think they edited out of the ROM—it was a while back. But enough small talk. The reason I brought you here is simple. You, miserable worm that you are, are the chosen instrument of God, I don't know why. The dead have clearly arisen, and the second coming is evidently at had, although not quite the way we'd imagined it. It took a rare man of God—the Reverend Crackerjack—to see the full implications of all this. But you're not . . . a believer, you see. That's the trouble."

"Oh, I believe, I believe," I said, looking around anxiously.

"Maybe. But we must be quite certain of it."

"I'll do anything."

"Anything?"

Too late! Secret servicemen had rushed in and pinned my arms behind my back. More machinery was being carted into the office.

"We need a good man to fill the post just vacated by Judge Strickland," he said. "Oh, you didn't know? He's dead."

"Can't you just . . . bring him back?"

"Shot himself in the head. Like, no time to do a brain dump beforehand," Sargnagel said as he fiddled with various knobs and levers on his equipment. An oscilloscope started to beep. It was just like a scene from *Gangbanged on Ganymede.*

"Poor Strickland," I said, shaking my head.

"Well, the media were threatening to reveal his AIDS test results," the president said. "That, coupled with his part in the brownie molestation coverup and the Boy Scout cocaine ring and the SPCA's pending investigation of his animal pornography business. . . ."

"I guess it's better this way," I said. "Oh, and . . . the morticians and the Indians, sir? What is their place in the new order?"

"My dear Jefferson, surely you have heard of manifest destiny?"

"Well, yes, but—"

"Che sera, sera," the president said. "Anyway, welcome to the government of the dead."

"I'm honored, sir," I said. But I didn't see why the guards were holding on to me so tightly.

"As well you should be! We stand on the threshold of utopia! In a CEC-controlled nation, no one need suffer again. Poverty will be abolished. By carefully monitoring brain dumps, we can ascertain that only desirable emotions and truths are transmitted to the people. Sargnagel is a genius . . . and Owen Gallenkamp, whose sleazy novelizations funded his research, is the greatest humanitarian benefactor of all time. Isn't it wonderful?" The president said, trembling at the vastness of his concept. "Wonderful . . . wonderful!"

He shook his finger at an imaginary TV camera—preparing a speech, obviously. The finger flew into the air and hit me in the face. My hands bound, I could not wipe off the smear of putrescent bodily fluids that were now oozing down my cheek into the corner of my mouth. "I'm terribly sorry," he said. "Now if I'd been alive, that would have hurt like hell. Now . . . one can always get another finger glued on. Finger, schminger!"

"Of course, sir," I said uneasily. The stench was flooding my nostrils, but I couldn't show my anxiety.

"You see," the president continued, "the genius of Dr. Sargnagel is that he has made life itself obsolete. Life is no longer necessary . . . life is . . . a liability!"

"I couldn't agree more, Mr. President," I said, nodding enthusiastically.

Someone opened the window. The singing of corpses wafted into the room. Choral hallelujahs filled the air. Dr. Sargnagel and his assistants assumed a beatific expression. The president fumbled around in a drawer and pulled out a revolver.

"I'm so glad you feel that way, Mr. Jefferson," he said, pointing it at my chest. "I'm sure that you are going to be a stalwart ally in our fight to bring about the kingdom of heaven. And now, Dr. Sargnagel, if you could initialize the brain dumping hardware. . . ."

I froze, terrified. I felt something cold at the base of my skull.

The president paused. "Oh, darn! I've lost that trigger finger again! Sargnagel, next time try glue. Er—would someone else care to do the honors?"

I don't remember dying. The brain dump was over seconds before the guard killed me. It's just as well. I wouldn't want any unpleasant memories to taint the new age.

Elayne and I were married the other day. She's thinking of having it done herself. Heckle and Jeckle want to wait for puberty. Owen and Elayne and I have a lot of fun together, although I don't really have that much time for sex and other light entertainments.

For one thing, there's this counterrevolution going on somewhere in Latin America. Rumor has it that the leader is none other than Lord Texas-Chainsaw, who fled there with a group of angry Indians after the collapse of the morticians' solidarity caucus. He has vowed to return, so they say, and "run every last zombie back into the grave."

I don't care. I'm too busy dealing with the present and preparing for our shining future. After all, I'm an important man now . . . the official prophet of the millenium. As long as they don't turn the power off on me.

Apocrypha

This story must *have been inspired by the strange sect that killed itself when the comet went by, believing they would fly straight to heaven on futuristic wings. It occurred to me that the early martyrs were just as deluded, only because millennia have passed rather than a few years, their folly has become blurred by nostalgia and worship.*

The other side of the coin is, what if it's true? What if martyrs do get spirited away to another world ... only it's another real *world, not something in a fantasy?*

This is the first appearance in print of this science fiction story.

Avoiding Close Encounters

"I think they're back, Ma," said Jason, bursting in on her dream of a warm blue sea. Helen had thought the wine would help, but her son's urgent tone was enough to break through any reverie.

The room was windowless. And chilly, of course; it took all of the village's resources to render the place even tolerably above freezing. The wine still sat there, half-drunk, gone bad by now; pity, thought Helen, since it's the last of this year's.

Jason pulled his mother up from her pallet. He was a thin little thing. "You shouldn't run around so much up there," said Helen. "Look, I'm going to have to mend your tunic —"

"And there aren't any more where that came from," he said, knowing her only too well. "You'd better hurry. I think there's even less time than usual."

"Do you know for a fact?" she asked him. "How do you know. Did you get Cassandra to double-check?"

"Yes, yes, Ma," Jason said. Kept tugging at her while she took out her frayed himation from the ancient chest.

Laughed. It was only his second time, that was why. If only he knew how deadly serious it all was. If only he knew how much was at stake.

She decided to drink the wine, soured as it was. Every year the crop was thinner, stranger. It was becoming more and more a product of this place. As she left the room, she began buckling herself in. They walked past the vineyards, kept in bloom by an artificial sun, hurried down the corridor where the machines thrummed as they manufactured air from rock, reached the first of many flights of steps, stopped at the first of many landings to sip at the trickle from the water-maker.

At the last level before the outside, Helen found several elders already sitting in their niches, fretting. Especially Cassandra, true to her name, who was always ready to predict the worst.

"Don't worry, people," Helen said, trying to stay as matter-of-fact as she could. "We'll handle it; we always have."

"It's worse this time," said Cassandra. "I think it's an actual person this time. Not a machine."

"We'll deal with it." She sent Jason to fetch the watchman so we could have a real report, not rumors. "They were bound to send a person sooner or later."

"But why now?" It was Clement who spoke. "Now, when we're so helpless, so undefended?"

"I don't know," Helen said. "I'll have to think about it." These were the times when she sometimes wished we were back home. When her kind of people stayed in the back of the house, and had no say at all, let alone being a hereditary leader.

When Jason came back, he had Marcus with him. "It's bad," the watchman said. "We've got a day, maybe half a day. And their trajectory puts them within two miles of the entrance."

"Well, we'll clear everything, of course, as usual," Helen

said. "Call everyone in. Do a head count. Make sure there aren't any stragglers. Or people like my son here, kids who don't understand the danger, who are liable to walk right into one of them."

"Ma," Jason began, "if I hadn't been on the surface, you wouldn't have gotten this warning for another hour. No one knows where you go away to dream, 'cept me."

"All right. I'll decide your fate after the crisis is over." She wasn't inclined to punish him, really; theirs was not a community of harshness, after all.

"Why do we always have to make the decisions?" Cassandra wailed. "Why can't they come down and help us? They brought us here — they ought at least to look in on us from time to time —"

"They're not gonna," Jason said.

Helen said, "Let's be practical, Cassandra. The last angel to come was in our grandparents' time."

"My god, my god," Clement murmured, "why hast thou forsaken me?"

Three of them went up to take a look — three was all that could squeeze into the ground chariot. It was a vehicle enclosed completely in a thick, clear glass, a gift from an angel naturally, powered by the same machines that made the air. Helen took the rudder; Marcus read the coordinates in the frosty screen that showed word and images; Jason should not have been there, but Helen knew that he would torment her about it for weeks afterward.

By Jesus, she thought, the world is beautiful. The blue-gray sky, the brooding crags, the whorls of rust-red dust ... the mountains that bisected the horizon, anguished, angular; the lakes of ruddy sand, the ancient craters, craters within craters ... so beautiful, and all I've ever known, she thought ... so why do I always dream of oceans?

"Look," cried Jason. "There's the first one —"

Yes. Like a spider, on its back, its metal legs curled

around its stomach. That one had been easy enough to sabotage, years ago. Not much of a brain, and it ran aground against the first big rock, and never budged again; the later ones were harder to deal with, since they could see in all directions; they had gotten more and more cunning; Helen knew they were determined to come.

"Two stades north of Parnassus," Marcus said. "That's what the sensors tell us. They mean to land here."

It was a nice-sized plain without too many craters. Along its perimeter ran the bed of long-dead river. Behind that, mountains. wine-red at ground level, easing into a muddy, dried-blood color at the tips. Here and there, a spear of rock cast a mile-long shadow.

"Any of us been out this way lately?" Helen asked him.

"Not to my knowledge. Except ... I think ... Paulina. The gravid one. Some children were playing, but I made sure they gathered all their toys."

"Looks clean to me," Helen said. "And sunset is in an hour."

"Wait," Jason said. "Over there."

He had sharp eyes, that one. A glint of bronze. Marcus brought the chariot closer. We slid into our pressure skins ... no need for a cumbersome air maker, we'd only be a few moments ... and ran out there, Jason leading the way.

Breathless, he held up his prize. You can't hear much up here, the air is so thin, but the pressure skins have a way of projecting voices; she heard him right in her ear. "It's a rattle," he said. "That won't do at all, will it?"

His mother took it from him. Why would someone leave a thing like that out in the open, knowing the danger? She shook it. No amplifier on it, of course; she heard only a dry distant whisper, like sand in an hourglass ... it was a beautiful thing, with a horse's head with one ear broken off, a priceless bauble from back home, a piece of an unreachable past.

"Better stow it," she told her son.

He ran back to the chariot. Meanwhile, Marcus was finding an inconspicuous place to plant the seeing-stone. Murmuring a brief prayer to the Savior, he placed the stone among a thousand other stones, and it blended perfectly.

Helen didn't have to worry long about the rattle. The baby lay only a few paces away. She could have kicked herself for not realizing it early. "Marcus, Jason," she called out, "there's been an exposing."

Jason ran back. "Look at that thing!"

It was stiff. Helen couldn't feel the cold outside her pressure skin, but she saw it in the baby's eyes. They shone like polar ice beneath the winter starlight. Everything else had ruptured, of course; the veins had crystallized outside the burst skin.

"Thought Paulina was planning to keep this one," Marcus said. "Well, I hope she remembered to baptize it first."

Exposing was a time-honored custom, of course; without it there'd be no village at all; life beneath this world's dead skin was a perpetual war against the most unforgiving of elements. The machines could only do so much. And angels had not come down in a generation. She must have loved it, Helen thought. To leave the rattle, there's undying love. She held the shattered little corpse in her arms, and rocked it a little, crying to herself. And night fell. In this place, night fell in an instant; even though she'd never known the lingering sunsets of legend, she knew that this sudden night was an alien thing, that this home was not her home.

She didn't mention it to Paulina that night, as they sat in the vineyard, watching the images from the seeing-stone projected against one cavern wall. They huddled, the villagers, after their nightly love-feast, trying to get as close to the warming-stone as they could.

"Back it up again," Clement said. Now that there were

pictures, he seemed less fearful, Helen thought. "No, no," he said at last, watching the figures lope across the plain, utterly encased in shielding suits. "Angels would not need such cumbersome pressure skins. They would breathe the empty air as easily as we breathe the air down here." He was something of an eschatologist. "This doesn't fulfill any of the known prophecies."

Helen watched. Her pulse pounded. They were getting close to the place where ... she wondered if Paulina knew that her child had already returned to the resurrection tank, that the village had already consumed her flesh and her blood, baked into the bread of the love-feast; Paulina had not eaten with them that evening. Exposing a child is something that always gnaws at you, that never leaves you alone; Helen's first-born tormented her even now, twenty years later.

Where was Paulina anyway? She shouldn't be alone, Helen thought. They were replaying it again and again, the ungainly men shambling across the sand, their features stark in the moons' harsh light. Ugly creatures. Ugly and damned. Yet they too came from God. Didn't they? Had the kingdom come after all, and left this distant village in the cold? Was this place hell, after all, and not some waystation on the road to paradise.

"Jesus, but they're ugly," Cassandra said.

That, in truth, they were. After the twentieth repetition Helen could not take any more; she left to find Paulina, stopping off at the storeroom to pick up the rattle. She was in the spinning-room, where the cave walls were of a fibrous mineral that could be coerced into a kind of homespun. Paulina was spinning and weeping, and weeping and spinning, and now and then she would prick herself, and dye the thread red. Helen put her arm around the younger woman. Paulina pushed her away. "I've had enough," she said. "I want to give myself up."

"Give up?" said Helen.

"I watched her die!" said Paulina. "She exploded."

"I've killed seven of them myself," said Helen. "You have to have faith."

"Faith? It's been two thousand years since our ancestors put on their winding-sheets and sipped the laurel wine and lay down in the catacombs with silver obols in their mouths to pay the angel who bore them away in a fiery chariot ... what a rescue it proved to be ... I would rather have burned up like a torch at a banquet ... I would rather have perished in the fire that engulfed the world."

"Faith," Helen said, and softly, calmly, she stroked the young woman's hair. "You can't give up now. Be strong. Why, my own grandmother saw the angel who came to warn us, who gave us the seeing-stones so we could stay hidden. And who told us that one would come in our generation, to show us the next stage. And who told us to keep the faith and be strong."

"You don't know how hard it is," Paulina said, sucking at her bloodstained finger.

"Oh yes," said Helen, "oh yes, oh yes." How could Paulina really understand. It's worse for me, she thought. I'm always bottling it up, hiding from my own despair, because I've got all these others who look to me ... I always have to think of them, of shoring up up their faith ... but what about mine?

Helen pulled the rattle from the bosom of her tunic and set it down beside the spinning wheel. "Look," she said. "I brought this back for you. You shouldn't be abandoning bits of the past up there; the past belongs to all of us."

Paulina took the rattle and clasped it to her chest and went into a paroxysm of grief. Now, at last, she allowed Helen to embrace her. Helen held her and let her cry. But suddenly Paulina stiffened and let out a shriek. "It's missing an ear," she said.

"It's two thousand years old," Helen said.

"No. You don't understand. The bronze was cracked there, the ear was coming off ... it's still up there ... Oh, God, I've put the whole village in mortal danger...."

No time for tears now. The two women ran down the corridor to the vineyard, where many of the villagers had gone to sleep; only Marcus, and Jason, rubbing his eyes, and Clement the eschatologist were still staring at the images from the seeing-stone.

"Run it back," Helen said, "to where we found the rattle."

The blur of the rewind. The ugly demons in their monstrous suits, striding backwards over the sand. The movements of the seeing-stone, jittery and jarring in the high-speed mode. Now there was something she had missed ... a giant glowing bubble next to their landing chariot ... living quarters! How long were they going to stay? Were they going to remain there until they had rooted out all the humans in the world, capture them, send them all back to the slaughter? Could they really be so vindictive? Yet Helen's grandmother had been absolutely clear: the angel had told them to protect the village's secrecy at all costs ... even if it meant shedding blood ... what did a few lives matter when the kingdom of heaven was at risk?

And Helen, just a girl then, had asked her grandmother, in the very same chamber where she often went to dream her private dreams, "Is this the kingdom of heaven then, Grandma, these rooms, these machines, the vineyard, the great red world above?"

And her grandmother said, "Just a waystation, Helen. A wilderness where we must wait, and pray, and have faith."

She remembered then: Lowering her grandparents into the resurrection tank. The love-feast. The sharing of the bread and wine. The image was fleeting, quickly pushed back into the ocean of memory. Now she concentrated on the seeing-stone's recording. The life-sized image on the wall shifted, back and forth, back and forth.

"Again," she said. "Slower."

Back again. Forth again. I should stop worrying, Helen thought. Paulina's distracted, imagining things ... the loss of a newborn child makes a woman go crazy, she knew that. And yet —

Bloated from the love-feast, her companions had all drifted off. The visitors, too, had retired into their bubble-dwelling; like other men, they had a cycle of sleep and wakefulness. That was why they were clearly not angels.

The vineyard was the warmest room; the grapes needed all the heat the machines could generate. She too was getting tired. This was needlessly obsessive, wasn't it? And yet —

No. There it was all right. She had rewound the record all the way past it four or five times. How could she have missed it? There was the bronze ear, sandwiched between two jagged rocks, as clear to the seeing-stone as it must be to the instruments of the visitors.

I mustn't panic the whole village, Helen thought. I'll deal with it now, alone, while they're all asleep.

She left the room and walked briskly toward the stairwell that led to the surface of the world.

"I'm coming," Jason said.

There were many passageways to the staging level. She was surprised, though, that he'd gotten there so quickly, that he'd managed to do it so quietly. He was already taking one of the child-sized pressure skins off the rack.

Helen said, "You'll be a lot safer here," but she already knew that he would get his own way. He was that kind of child. How could she deny him this taste of adventure, when the whole world comprised but a few corridors and a vast inhospitable desert?

At the last minute, Helen decided to take a thunderbolt. A weapon had not been fired here in a thousand years, but she was scared. The exploded baby ... the fact that the visitors kept coming, kept sending their seeing-creatures, had kept the whole village on edge for a generation ...

The thunderbolt fit in the palm of her hand. Just a squeeze could send death, seeking out the victim's heartbeat, ripping him apart. She had only seen it in the records of a seeing-stone. She shuddered, stuck it in the belt of the pressure skin.

Then they slipped on their skins and took the chariot up through the trapdoors, camouflaged by boulders. It was normally an hour's drive to Parnassus; this time it would take longer, because the chariot needed to take long detours and send out jamming-specters to confuse the visitors.

Helen leaned back in the seat. Jason rapped his fingers against the clear walls. "Ma," he said, "me and the other kids talk about giving ourselves up."

Helen said, "But the angels — the commandments —"

"No one living's seen an angel. Maybe it's all wrong. Maybe they've forgiven us and they've come to fetch us home."

"Home is the Kingdom of Heaven, Jason, not some Roman catacomb."

"Yeah. Ever think about oceans, Ma?"

Helen looked. The plain, frozen, stretched to the far horizon. What if it were all in motion? What if the very sand were to liquefy, and the hard rock become a sea of blood? The eschatologists always spoke of such things ... but the ocean of her dream was a different thing ... a warm and living thing ... full of comfort ... an end to pain.

"Yes, son," she said softly. "In dreams. But this world is not a dream."

"Sometimes I think it is a dream," said her boy, "and we'll wake up to a green world, a watery world. Sometimes I think the visitors will lead me there."

"That's Satan speaking, son," she said softly. "You must

always tell him to get behind you."

"Don't believe in that crap," he said.

That disturbed her profoundly, and she began telling him the story of the Exodus all over again — as much for herself as him, for she was sure that repeating the familiar incidents would soothe her, lessen her apprehension. It was what her mother had told her, and her mother's mother.

They were persecuting us. Burning us alive. Feeding us to lions. Slashing, sawing, slicing, and impaling us. And still we kept the faith. They took us from our houses. They took us from the catacombs. They burned us out of the forests and the caves. And still we kept the faith. Death did not matter; it was the gateway to paradise.

It was whispered that, just before dying, we would be caught up in a great white light, and taken in golden chariots through the clouds, to the bosom of the Anointed One....

One group of the Christianoi was specially favored of God. It was a terrible night. They were taking us to be dipped in pitch and set ablaze to illuminate the Emperor's midnight banquet. We were waiting, chained up, in an anteroom of the palace. We knew we would die soon ... that the very world would end in fire. We tried not to be afraid. We remembered what we had been told; that we would be caught up, transfigured, enveloped in the eternal warmth of God's love. The screaming was terrible to hear, and many turned their backs on God and agreed to worship Caesar. But to those that remained in that terrible chamber, there came an angel of the lord....

Clothed in light he was, and his face shone like the sun. He said, "O Christianoi, I have heard your cries. Have faith. This very night, a ship is prepared that will carry you into the sky."

"Will we be with Jesus?" said the first Helen, in whose honor the firstborn girl of our line has always been named

Helen.

"Not in the flesh," said the angel. "I go to prepare a place for you ... you are not yet ready for union with the ultimate. You shall live there forty generations, and then, perhaps, your people will be ready to join God's other chosen peoples."

The angel's lips never moved when he spoke; the voice came from a speaking-stone that he held in an outstretched hand. His shape also shimmered against the light; at times we could see right through him to the bloodstained walls of the holding cell. He lifted the stone to his lips and uttered words from his mouth for the first time, words in a guttural, primal language that must have been the very language of creation, for the room began to shake and one by one the Christianoi's chains shattered, and we were gathered up into a ship that sailed the sky, and passed through the night like a comet, straight upward to the star that astrologers call Ares, or, in the Roman tongue, Mars.

And so we lived, in the place prepared for us, carefully conserving our resources, carefully controlling our population so that we did not soil the pristine splendor of this Ares, which was a world, not a star, and a world that mortals are not equipped to live in without the aid of the angels' gifts: the machines that make air, the seeing-stones, the chariots that move by themselves.

But there was young Jason, bright-eyed, sullen, and all he could say was "Don't believe in that crap." He said it several times, and then added, "Besides, it was a long time ago. And we can't stay here forever. I have dreams, too, Ma. I want to touch the visitors. I want to speak to them."

"Not so long ago," Helen said. "Your great-grandmother saw an angel. I took his commandments from her: secrecy at all costs, even unto the shedding of blood. You think my grandmother would have lied to me?"

"I can't keep the faith. Maybe you should have had a daughter, another Helen, to carry on. Maybe you should have exposed me."

"Don't carry on so," Helen said. "I love you."

They had reached the vicinity of Parnassus now, and they needed to find the horse's ear quickly, and eradicate all traces of their coming, before the visitors broke their cycle of sleep.

Finding it was not hard. The seeing-stones were all connected to one another, and each could track the seeings of all the others. A huge outcropping concealed the chariot in its shadow. Mother and son went out, Jason carrying a pair of tongs to gather up the ear with, Helen a brush to smooth the sand back down. They walked in a patterned sequence, covering the tracks from one foot with dust thrown by the other; an angel had taught them that generations before. Knowing where to go, they discovered the horse's ear quickly enough; Jason picked it up, and Helen got on her hands and knees to eradicate their traces.

Tall, pointy boulders surrounded them. Carefully, she worked the dust back over the little gully that the ear had dug. It took her a moment to realize that she was no longer in Jason's shadow. She could still hear his shallow breathing through her pressure skin, but —

She looked up through the a V-shaped gap in the boulders. Her heart almost stopped beating. A man had emerged from the bubble. He was coming their way, slowly, bending over frequently to collect samples of the dust. And there was Jason, still in the boulders' shadow.

"Get back," she said. "He'll see you."

"I don't care," he said. There was a desperation in him she'd never heard before. The same feeling she'd seen in Paulina. The hopelessness.

"Despair is the devil's doing," she said. "Don't be tempted, son."

"I have to, Ma!" he said.

He began to walk toward the visitor. The visitor was still far away, had not seen him, doubtless was expecting nothing.

She heard him whisper the ancient words of greeting: "Rejoice, stranger. Our home is your home." But he was only talking to himself, practicing, perhaps, for the encounter.

But then her son began to shout. "Take me home!" he screamed. "I want to see the ocean!" The visitor did not hear it. She hoped he could not hear it. They did not have the voice-sending pressure skins, did they? And yet ... though the air was thin ... there was some air here. A shout might become a pale thin cry —

"Forgive me," she whispered. She drew her thunderbolt and shot him. He crumpled. The visitor had turned in another direction, hadn't even seen. She ran to her dead boy. Death from a thunderbolt is instantaneous. The puncture was clean and the skin had already sealed back up by the time she got to him, but inside that skin was death.

"In the name of the Father, the Son, and the Sacred Paraclete," she said, and pushed down on the filmy fabric of the pressure skin to close his eyes.

Only later, in the resurrection room, waiting for the tank to fill up so that she could lower the body into it and cycle the flesh and blood back into bread and wine, only then did Helen weep. Only then did she feel that ultimate despair she now knew the others had felt. Her son lay on a stone slab. Death hadn't marred him; thunderbolts killed invisibly, and the pressure skin had seared shut before the boy could explode.

Thirty years of faith and prayer, and now she was left with a gaping why, a chasm in her heart ... a chasm she had never confronted, only dimly knew about. She had nurtured a doubter in her own bosom, and in the end she, the one whose duty was never to doubt, had been unable to allay his doubts.

He was dead.

As Helen sat weeping, there came to her an angel....

He had been in the room a long time, perhaps; the light and warmth had come gradually. Warmth was a rare commodity in this place. At first it was only a tingling. Then it began to penetrate beneath her skin. She thought it must be some interior heat generated by her grief ... but no, there was a kind of joy in it. And finally she looked up to see the angel standing next to the corpse of her son.

He was just as her grandmother had described. Winged, shimmery, wreathed in light. She could see the ocean in his eyes. "Helen," said the angel, "don't be afraid. I've come to tell you the experiment is being dismantled."

"What does that mean?" Helen said. "Are we entering the Kingdom of Heaven?"

"I'm not here to tell you about that, Helen. Just to say that the tests have all been done, and you are free to make contact."

"Make contact? ... with the Romans?"

"There are no more Romans."

"Then the world has ended."

"In a sense. You are the last people to think, to feel, to dream like the people of that ancient world; soon you will have to learn the ways of another world."

"No Romans?" Helen said again. But the world was Rome.

"Helen," said the angel, "there have been some changes in oversight. There was a fear in certain quarters that the revelation of our ... meddling might be too inflammatory to the delicate balance of your home world, and so a last-minute effort was made to conceal the evidence; but there's been ... well, a change of government. I won't bore you with details, but ... well, we won't be coming back."

"A change of government! Then Armageddon has been fought — and lost?" It was going to be hard to adapt to a universe where Satan was king. Her dead child was proof of that.

"There's so little I can tell you. We are not supposed to reveal anything. But alas, no experiment is flawless when the subject is sentient. That's why we shall not return."

"And God? And the resurrection of the body? And the flaming chariots that are to carry us into the sky? And the redemption?"

"You are human," the angel said. "When faith goes, there first comes a terrible despair. Yet after such despair, you still persist. I can't answer you questions. In my own way — from the vantage of a vastly superior science, I suppose — I am still trying to ask them."

"But, but —" Helen cried, anguished, "I killed my son!"

"That, at least, I can remedy."

The angel gazed solemnly at Jason's pitiful body. He waved his hand — a casual thing, dismissive almost. And all at once Jason opened his eyes. The sourceless light in the chamber was so painful that Helen had to squint, and tears spurted from her eyes.

He sat up, and, seeing he was not alone, coyly covered his nakedness with one hand. "Ma, Ma," he said. "I think I died."

Helen went to embrace him. "Baby," she said, "you did, you did."

She wanted to ask the angel so much more — wanted to spit out that noisome why that was now stuck in her craw and would perhaps never be dislodged — but as she turned from kissing her warm son, the angel vanished.

No time for more despair. She knew she would never hurt her son again. No truth was worth killing one's child for. Abraham had been wrong to agree to kill Isaac. This discovery — and this second chance — was a greater miracle than anything in the ancient tales of Jesus' life. No time to lose. "Get your clothes back on. We're going back to Parnassus," she told him.

He looked at her. Questioning at first. But then — with the sureness of one who has harrowed hell, and returned to the living world — he said, "And when we've greeted them, they'll take us to the ocean, won't they?"

Helen wept. She could almost hear the crash of the waves. "Yes," she said She closed her eyes and savored the remembrance of her dream of the warm blue sea. "Yes, Jason, yes, they will."

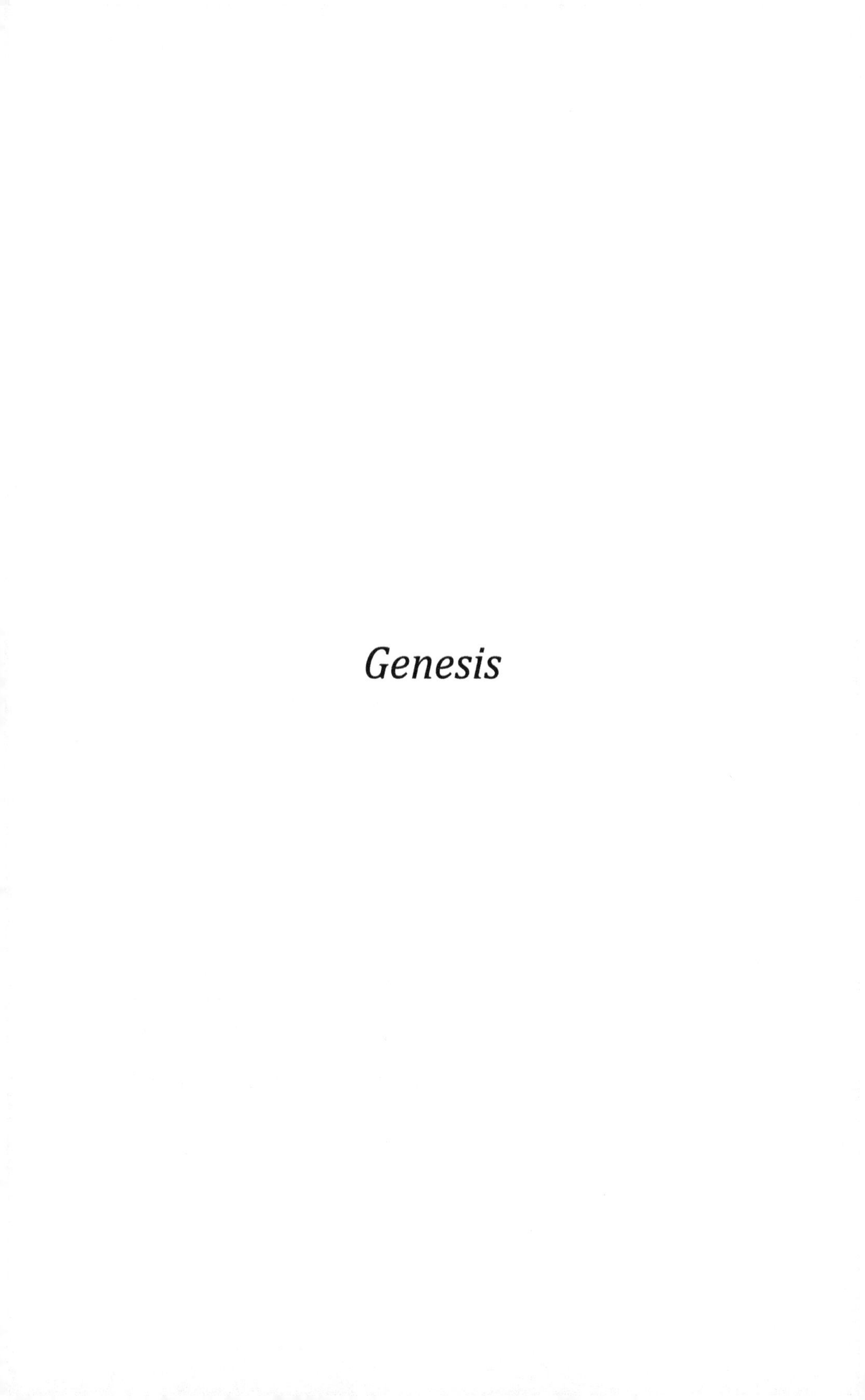

Genesis

Wrote this piece for an anthology that Peter Beagle was spearheading. I think it leads us nicely back to the beginning of our journey.

Our journey has been through dark passagewaysand obscure readings from the penumbra of scripture, but it has led us back to the problem of evil and the central problem of religion: if God exists, why is the world such a lousy place? *This sentiment was stated much more poetically be writers far greater than myself, such as Euripides.*

The thesis in this last story, stated in words attributed to the Antichrist, is I think the "secular humanist" answer to the question of original sin .

It was wonderful and scary to look back over about thirty years of my life and put together this road map through hell. I see that there's a certain philosophical evolution here. In my life I have been dramatically converted several times, and I've been a serious Buddhist monk as well as a hokey Beatitude of the Universal Life Church.

I would like to propose an alternative question: If humanity is so evil, why isn't the world even lousier than it is? *I think the question is equally valid, and I think that the answer may lie in those parts of our psyche that defy logic. It may even suggest, after all, that God exists.*

Wishful thinking, perhaps, but I am evolving toward that conclusion.

A Thief in the Night

It's tough to be the Antichrist. Nobody ever feels for the villain.

Without the eternal dark, they can never shine, those messiahs with their gentle smiles and their compassionate eyes and their profound and stirring messages.

Without me, they have no purpose.

And I'm older than they are; I'm the thing that was before the billion-stranded web of falsehoods that they call the cosmos was even a flicker in some god's imagining ... some *dark* god's.

In a house by the sea in Venice Beach, California, I wait for the second coming. Not really the second, of course; there have been many more than one. But the millennium is drawing near, and one tends to make use of the tropes of the culture one has immersed oneself in; *ergo:* in a house, a white house, by the sea, a placid but polluted sea, I wait, by a sliding glass door that opens to a redwood deck with shiny steps that leads down to the beach, for the second coming.

A unicorn led me here.

I can tell that the unicorn is very near. I can't see him directly, of course; I don't have the kind of stultifying purity that allows that. But we've achieved a kind of symbiosis over the eons. He works for me. What he does for me is very obvious, and very concrete. He leads me to purity so that I can destroy it.

What *he* gets out of this I do not know.

Today, a summer day, a cloudless sky, an endless parade of rollerbladers down the concrete strip that runs beneath my window. I feel him more than ever. When they breathe, there's a kind of tingling in the air. Sometimes you see the air waver, as in a heat-haze. Today the shimmering hangs beside the refrigerator as I pour myself a shot of cheap Chardonnay.

"Where is he?" I ask the air.

I hear him pawing the carpet. I turn in his direction. But already, he's just beyond my peripheral vision. I don't know how he manages it. One day I'll be too quick for him. it it hasn't happened in three billion years.

I hear him again. To my right. I slide the doors open. I squat against the redwood railings. I look to my right.

Against the slender trunk of a palm tree, the sharp shadow of a horn. Only a moment, but it is disquieting. A shadow is all I can normally see, or sometimes a hoofprint in the sand, or sometimes a piercing aroma that is neither horse nor man. The one who is purity personified is very close. Like an arrow on the freeway, the horn's shadow points me home.

He is a youth with long blond hair. He is rollerblading up and down the pathway. He wears only cutoffs and shades. I've seen many messiahs. This one does not seem that promising.

Sex is usually their downfall. I think that's how it's going to be this time. I go to my closet and pick out what I'm going to wear. I'm going to be as much like him as I can. His type. I select a skimpy halter top, and as I slip into it my breasts start morphing to strain against the cotton. I squeeze myself into Spandex leggings, strategically ripped; in the back of the closet, which after all does stretch all the way to the beginning of time, I find a pair of rollerblades.

In the mirror, I am beautiful. Too beautiful to be true. I am California herself. The sandy beaches are in my hair. The redwoods are my supple arms and torso. My breasts are the mountain lakes and in my eyes is a hint of the snow on the summits of the Sierras. My scent is the sea, the forest, and the sage. I am ready to go to the new messiah and fuck him into oblivion.

Outside: I follow the hoofprints which linger but a moment before dissolving in the fabric of reality. I glide along concrete. The wind gathers my hair into a golden sail. I pass him. I don't think he recognizes me. His eyes are childlike, curious, wide. I whip around a palm tree, cross paths with him again; he looks longer, wondering if we've ever met before, perhaps; then, a three-sixty around the public toilets, a quick whiff of old piss and semen, passing him for the third time, calling out to him with my mind, stop, stop, stop, at the palm tree tottering, slipping, slamming down hard against the pavement, have to make it look good now, me, the mother of all illusion.

I look up. Shade my eyes. The shadow of the unicorn crosses his face. You can tell; the sun is blazing, there's no shade, but his countenance darkens and then, moving up and down his face, the telltale stripe that shows the unicorn is standing between us somewhere, bobbing his head up and down, pawing at the sand perhaps, for there's a flurry of yellow dust about his heels.

Oh, he is beautiful.

Now, sensing something wrong, he shimmies across the concrete, smooth as the wind,

Bends over me, I groan.

"Are you hurt?"

"Only a scratch."

I look up with what I know to be a dazzling smile, one that has toppled empires. It's not a glad smile; it's a smile that knows all the sadness of the world. But he counters my smile with a smile of his own, a smile like sunlight, a smile like the sea. Takes off his shades, lets them dangle around his neck on a gold chain.

"Let me heal you," he says softly.

"Nothing can heal me," I say.

"It's. gift," he says.

He touches me where it hurts. I have made sure to be hurt only in the most strategic places; where he touches, I murmur arousal. He only smiles again. His hand wavers over my breast, just scabbing over, and the wound closes in on itself.

"How did you do that?" I ask him.

"It can only be temporary," he says. I know now that he must be the one I'm seeking. He has the long view. He really knows that the cosmos will crumble to nothing one day, and it grieves him. He has compassion.

I moan again. "What's your name?" I say.

"I don't know," he says. "I just live here."

"You just popped into existence?"

"No, I do remember some things. Parents kind of a blur, I guess. Social worker talked to me once, took me to McDonald's. I ordered a bag of fries. Everyone had some. It was cool how long those fries lasted, you coulda sworn there was five thousand people in that restaurant. Okay, so the social worker, she's totally trying to dig some kind of trauma out of me, you know, drugs. molested by daddy, whatever, but she made me remember a couple of things."

"Like?"

"Dunno, like, prices of a jigsaw. Can't see the whole picture. There's a dove over my head. Keep thinking it's going to shit. That's good luck, isn't it? My mother ... I only remember her a little. Kissing me goodbye at the bus station. I don't know who my dad is."

“Do you sometimes think he came down from above?”

“Oh, like an alien? Sure. But that don’t make sense either, bad genetics—I ain’t so dumb.”

"I feel a lot ebtter." The air is so chill; it's the unicorn breathing down our necks. He's impatient, maybe, He doesn't like to work for me that much. He is a slave, in a way. His shadow crosses the boy's face.

How old? I still can't tell. So blond, you don't know if there's hair in his pits. "Old enough," he says, "if that's what you're thinking."

I'm thinking: what are you telling me, you stupid beast? After all these eons, you're coming down with Alzheimer's? This is the purest heart in the world, and he's staring at me with knowing eyes, and his smile turns into an earthy grin and I don't think he's any stranger to sexuality? I remember the one that got away, two thousand years ago. Now there was purity. Is this the best you can do? I cry to the unicorn in my mind; but though he hears me, he seldom answers.

But I might as well see this through. The Antichrist can leave no stone unturned.

"You made me feel, I don't snow, so *healed*," I tell him. "All warm and tingly." I'm not even lying. "Is there something I can do for you?"

"Is that's your condo over there?"

"Yeah."

"Maybe Coke?"

"I'm all out. I might have enough for a couple lines."

"You're so funny. I mean Coke as in pop."

A smidgin of purity at least. I laugh. "Come on over," I say. That are possibilities in this after all.

So we are standing in the room by the glass door that leads to the dock with the stairway down to the sand and he has his soda in his hand and then, always smiling, he sort of drifts over to where I'm standing, almost as if he has still his rollerblades on, that's how he moves. He kisses me; his lips are very sweet as if they been brushed with cherry lip gloss; his kiss draws the pain from me, each nugget of pain almost more painful to clock out than it was when it lay festering inside me. I feel myself respond. It's a strange thing. I don't feel passion over what I do, but now, oddly, I'm vibrating like a tuning fork, and he hasn't even taken off his clothes, although I have, of course, temptress that I am, and yeah, there's a dick down there somewhere straining against those frayed cutoffs. But what's happening to me? Aren't I supposed to be sucking his purity out of him? Aren't I the vampire darkness that encircles, poisons, and consumes? I might into sweat and sand. He laughs. It's like hugging a tree. I yank down on the denim, no underwear, put him into the jungle chaos that seethes inside, I just I are closed and I think yes, yes, yes, you see now, I am killing the god-child in you, killing the future, closing the circle of the world, shoving the serpent's tail into his jaws. Oh, I cry out in an ecstasy of conquest. I exult. One more that didn't get away. It's child's play, I tell myself, as I let him empty himself into me. I feel a fire down there. I've never felt that before. It's never been so good to destroy.

But then he opens his eyes and I know something has gone wrong. Because he doesn't seem to have lost his purity at all. What I see is not the dullness of a flame extinguished. I see compassion. We're still standing there, flesh to flesh. Perhaps I was not detached enough. Perhaps he is actually caused me to have an orgasm. I am not sure. My thighs are throbbing.

Gently he leads me to the futon. It's black, naturally, L.A.'s most fashionable color. The pine frame is glazed black, too. He sits me down. And he says, very softly, "sex is a beautiful thing, you know. Sometimes, when I'm with a stranger, I feel I'm giving away all of myself, and yet there always seems to be more to give."

I stare at him dumbly. Have men evolved that much, then? Have I given them too much freedom of thought? It has only been the blink of an eye since St. Augustine equated original sin with filthy sexuality. In his purity, this boy is completely innocent of such an idea. To me, what has transpired has been a once in reveling in flesh and fluids; to him, I realize in astonishment, it has been an act of love, even though it was consummated with a stranger.

"You needed me," he says. "I heal people."

And turned away from me, and whistles, and I see the pointed shadow on the wall, and he walks away in his cutoffs with his blades slung over his shoulder, and the shadow follows him, and I wonder who the unicorn works for, and what he is getting out of all this, after all.

At the sliding door he said, "oh, later. And I'm Jess. I don't know *his* name." He can see the creature as clearly as I see him, and he assumes everyone else can. A sure sign all a prophet, the ability to see such things. In the 90s they also call it schizophrenia. I don't look up. I hear him slipping the blades back on and thudding down the wooden stairs.

I work myself into a frenzy. He has to be destroyed. I sit by the sliding door and gaze down onto the sand, and I see him whooshing past, a can of soda and his hand, and his hair streaming.

Sex is still the answer, I tell myself. That's still what the Garden of Eden thing means, isn't it? Though he seems to have found a way out of the Augustinian dilemma. He's found a way of imbuing sex with the attributes of Divinity. There's deep theology here somewhere, but what do I know of theology? I am not God. The rules of the game keep changing. How was I to know you could have sex and still retain your purity?

Sex. But somehow it's got to be made more potent. And keep love out of it. And make it so I can't be healed.

I think I have an idea.

Evening.

It's easier to follow the unicorn in the night, in a crowded wharf, on a narrow walkway crammed with vendors of beachwear and hot dogs and incense and sunglasses and car shades. In a sea of faces, an equine shadow stands out. Practice it sometime. Watch the dark patches that ripple across walls, past people's gray complexions.

I follow. But I'm not a beautiful woman anymore. I'm a man old before my time. Too thin for the wrinkled Armani that sags on my skin and bones.

He's squatting between two trash cans; above his head, two dope dealers are squabbling. He looks up at me; I'm not sure if he recognizes me or not. He's mumbling something to the unicorn. The crack dealers hunch together over him and I realize that, shoulder to shoulder, they make the outline of a unicorn.

But the moment the image gels in my mind, the two men break apart. The one with the mohawk that seemed to be the horn of the beast, that one goes north while the other goes south, toward a hotdog stand. All that remains of the unicorn is the shadow of a torso in a pile of trash, flickering between the moonlight as a strident neon of a coffee house.

Does he recognize me? I think not. "Hi," I say.

"You forgot 'sailor'," he says.

"Am I that obvious?"

"Do you need to be healed?"

"No."

"I think maybe you do."

"A drink somewhere?"

"A drink? But you're dying."

"Is it that obvious?"

"Yes," he says.

We go to a bar. It's another bar, sleazy as shit. I have a glass of Scotch, and he asks for a glass of Evian. "Nothing stronger?" I say.

"It's a strong as it feels," he says, and waves a hand over the longstemmed goblet. I wonder if he's turned it into wine. "Do I know you? You remind me of someone I met once."

"I remind a lot of people of people."

The waiter leaders at us. And why not? A dirty old man and a beautiful youth. Actually I thought he was going to get carded. But no. We sits on the right stools, swimming in smoke. It's grim. I'll be waiting forever if I don't charge ahead. "Do you know what I want?" I ask him.

I make my eyes still and cold. The way people imagine a serial killer's eyes to be, though in reality they are sad people, lost on the fringes of fantasy. "You want to fuck me?" He says. Ingenuous. He smiles again as if to say, sure, anything, because I'm here to make you whole, I'm the caulk that will bind your soul.

"I want to kill you," I say. "I've got it. You know."

"I know." Still the smile. He always knew and yet he followed me. Was that a swizzle stick in the bartender's tray, or was it the horn of the unicorn? The smoke swirls like the tail of the beast.

"I'm riddled with Kaposi's. I have lesions on my lesions. If I fuck you, you will die. But I don't want to play safe. I'm bitter. I'm angry. I want to kill the world. I want to kill God."

If sex is not enough, I think, then sex and death together should do it. They are the twin pillars of the human condition. The error in making the Word flesh is that flesh is necessarily flesh.

"Will it be enough," he says, "to kill me?"

"I don't know. I'm raging. I don't know if you'll be enough. I could pretend you're the world. I could pretend you're God. Maybe that's what it will take."

"I don't like to say that I'm God."

"Are you?"

"People have said it."

"What people?"

"Little girl that the one-eyed man was pimping said it. I healed her up inside, totally. She closed her eyes and said, *God, God.* The social worker found her on the beach. She was staring up at the sun. I think she's blind now. But when I visit her in the group home, she says she can see. I don't know what kind of seeing it is because she's always walking into walls and tripping over coffee tables. I know she sees me okay, she never bumped into me. Except when she needs to be held."

"Is that a parable?"

"You mean, did it really happen? When I say a thing, somehow it gets to be true. But I've never said who my father is."

He is a profound enigma, this youth with the flowing hair and the deep, unfathomable eyes. "But you mean it," I say. "You *will* consent to die." I know that he cannot lie to me. "You will yourself to die."

"If that's what it takes to heal your rage."

I take his cup from him. I drink it in one gulp. It *is* wine, one of the faceless California whites.

I take Jess back to where I found him earlier, the trash cans, the sea; now there is no one there at all. Behind us, the unicorn hunters; I can hear the hoofclacks on the concrete, not a clippety-clop of an ironshod horse, but a softer sound. It is almost the sound of raindrops on the leaves of a banana tree. And then, with alarming suddenness, it *is* the sound of rain.

He been over, spread his arms across the garbage can lids, and I pull down his cutoffs. There is no love here. There is no compassion.

There is no desire save the need to kill. There is no passion except fury. The rain is our only lubricant. I am the battering ram with the horned head. I am all anger. I squeeze the disease into him, a billion viruses, in every spurt of semen. If I can't suck the purity out of you, I think, I'll fill you to bursting with my own impurity. I'll soil you with sin. Sex may no longer be the ultimate crime, but surely I have tricked him into seeking out death, and that is a mortal sin. Surely, surely. The rules of the universe do not change that much.

The rain pours down. I feel the exultation of victory. I pull away, kick the trash cans, send them rolling down the pavement and Jess slumping to the concrete, facing the sea. I didn't just give him AIDS, it's a kind of mega-AIDS and it works right away. The lesions sprout up in a hundred places on that bronzed flesh, and they spread with every raindrop; he shits blood; he vomits; he writhes; he is in utmost torment.

He crumbles. The rain washes them down to the sand and sea.

I go back to the condo and make myself a double espresso.

In three days, he is back.

It's not by the sea I see him, but down in Beverly Center, uppermost level, food court, me coming out of one of those artsy Zhang Yimao movies, iced cappuccino in hand. He's standing in the window of Waldenbooks, at the foot of the escalator I'm about to go down. Rollerblades slung across the shoulder, black T-shirt blazoned with the logo of some Gothic band.

Why hasn't he gone away?

He's coming up and I'm going down, we're crossing paths, I look at him, he looks at me, perhaps he knows me; I reached over, a glancing, electric touch of hand on hand for split-second, and I say, "Aren't you supposed to be dead?"

And he says, "I heard a rumor about that."

And passes out of earshot.

I go back up the escalator. I catch him coming down again, this time in more of a hurry. "I know you," he says, grabbing onto me; I am not sure what he sees, because I have not had time to change my shape. I run down the escalator the wrong way. We reach Waldenbooks, and the unicorn's shadow crosses the entrance. "But I don't seem to know anything else anymore."

I stop. I'm getting an idea. "You lost your memory?"

"It's more than that. Sure, like, I wandered into a homeless shelter this morning and I don't know my own name. They thought it was maybe I was off my medication. But they didn't have anyone with authority to dole out Xanax or whatever it is, flavor of the week. So like, I'm here."

"I can tell you who you are."

"Do I want to know?"

"You know the answer to that."

He looks at me. He is disoriented. I have no shape, and he has just awoken from the sleep from which there is no awaking. But behind his confusion I can see that that demon compassion is about to come to life. I don't have much time. I have to do it soon, or it will be like that fiasco in Jerusalem. But I need to prepare myself.

I tell him I'll pick him up where Venice meets the sea, tonight, Friday the thirteenth.

Moonrise. I go to him as myself. I can hear the unicorn's breath above the whisper of the Pacific. His rollerblades are stashed against the wall of the public men's room, and he is squatting on an old recycle bin, speaking to a withered hooker. For a while, I stand beyond the periphery of his vision, listening to what he has to say.

"Tell you a story," he's saying to her. "Because you think you've thrown away your youth, lost your beauty, and now you're this mangy old bitch yapping at tourists for a ten-dollar handjob. I knew this rich dude back east, and one day his daughter runs away from home, and she ends up somewhere around Sunset and Cahuenga, turning tricks, not cheap drinks at first, but later when she's totally lost her looks and been around the block too many times to count, they do get cheap and like, she's doing crack and everything. And she starts to miss her dad, so one day when she's completely bottomed out, she checks out of the women's shelter and hitches all the way back. And thirty-nine blowjobs later she walks in the front gate of the estate, and her dad's all sitting at the dining room table with her brothers and sisters, and her mom's dishing out this putting which is all flaming in brandy, because it's Christmas. And everyone's crying and saying, you walked out on us, see how much you made us suffer, what did we ever do to make you do this to us." I can't help smiling. The homespun stories never change. He goes on, "But the dad says, it's okay, honey, I'm not going to ask what you've been through. I'm just going to say I love you, and welcome you home." He plants a chaste kiss on the prostitute's brow, and says, "That's what you have to do, babe. Go home to your dad."

"My dad's dead."

"There's a dad in your heart. That's the dad you have to go home too."

She weeps, and I interrupt them. "Another true story?" I ask him. She takes one look at me, stifles a scream, scurries away across the sand. He looks at me too. I don't know if he is afraid; if he has, he hides it well.

"True story?" he says.

"Oh, I remember now. When you say a thing, somehow it gets to be true."

"That sounds familiar."

"This morning, before the sun came up, Jess, you were still dead."'

"I knew it had to be something like that! I woke up and it was like I'd been in a dark place, fighting monsters. The whole place was on fire but the fire gave no light. Was that hell?"

"Yes, Jess. You harrowed hell."

"No kidding."

"I tell stories too, you know. You'll have to tell me if you think they're true. I've been called the father of lies, but that's kind of a sexist thing to say; I'd rather be the mother of invention."

The tide is coming in.

"You keep changing the rules on me," I tell him. "First I thought sex would do the trick; it's worked every time for a couple of thousand years. And then that was death. I was your death would work, because to seek death is the ultimate sin. Death and sex together. But you screwed me over by letting your death purge me of the cancerous anger that I'd worked up inside myself."

"I don't remember," Jess says. "I can't even see you too clearly. I look at you and all I see is a void. I know you're there because I can hear you inside my head. Does that mean I'm a schizophrenic?"

"Most people like you are."

"Don't I know it."

"Alright. Are you hungry? I'll take you out somewhere."

We go to a Mongolian barbecue on Wilshire because he seems a bit hungry. It's a no shirt no shoes no service kind of a place but I happen to have an old lumberjack shirt in the backseat of the Porsche that has my name written on it in the Venice Beach parking lot, don't ask me how, probably just another of this world's whimsical illusions.

Jess eats a lot: a lot of meat, a lot of vegetables, about five ladles of sauce, and a triple order of rice. I watching. Sipping my water, I detect a hint of the vintner; it's still him all right, and he's still full of the power that comes from his ultimate innocence.

"I'm starting to remember a bit more," he says. "I guess seeing you was, what do they call it, a catalyst."

"What do you remember?"

"I'm a healer."

"How do you heal?"

"Sometimes with love. Sometimes by letting the world fuck me. Sometimes by telling stories. The stories just come to me, but I know they are true. I've got a direct line to the source of the world dreams. Don't I? That's who I am."

He's starting to know. He's coming out of living dead mode. I toy with a piece of celery, flicking it up and down the side of my bowl with my chopsticks. "Did the unicorn tell you this?" I say, not looking into his eyes.

"No," he says, "we don't talk much. He doesn't, you know. He's not people. I do all the talking."

The shadow of the chopstick; the horn of the beast. In the distance waitresses gibber in Chinese. But maybe it's Spanish. I say, "there is something you really need to know. You're dying to know. but you can't know it because you're not fully human. The thing that you want to know is a wall that separates you from the human race."

After sex and after death, there is only knowledge.

Knowledge is the greatest of all tempters.

"You know," he says, "you're right. Maybe."

He smiles. Is he humoring me, or does he already see it? The breath of the unicorn hands in the air; it's not cigarette smoke, because it's illegal to smoke in restaurants in LA. for a moment, his eyes lose that I-will-heal-you look. "But if I tell you what it is," I say, "then everything is going to change."

"How?" he says. "You might be lying. Tomorrow you'll still find me rollerblading up and down the beach, putting lost souls out of the fire. One day I'll rescue every soul in the whole world, and everyone will shine like the sun, and the sea will part for us and will go into it and we'll see a crystal stairway and it'll lead all of us into the arms of our father."

"Whose father?"

Your father is not my father, I think. I pop a wafer-thin slice of lamb into my mouth.

"So tell me your story," he says.

But first he gets up, filled up of food bowl with goodies, and hands it to them to cook. The restaurant is emptied out. When he comes back, I could see the doorman switching the sign to *closed*, but they don't seem to be kicking us out. Jess waits.

"Once upon a time," I say, "there was a perfect place."

"Like paradise?"

"Kind of. You can imagine it is regarding if you want, but I'd like to think of it as a big mansion with hundreds of rooms. Super Nintendo. Videos. Entertainment. Roller coasters. Discovery and laughter everywhere you turned. And that were two children who lived in the house, a boy and a girl. They were like brother and sister. Their father was a weird old man with a long white beard, and he lived on the top floor, and he had a lab where he experimented with creating life. Every time he made a new creature, the kids got to name it. Every day was an adventure, but the estate was surrounded by a stone wall, and there was no gate. The father loved them so much that he wanted them to stay with him forever. He knew that there was only one thing that would cause them to leave. He shut that thing up in a room in the basement of the house. They weren't allowed to go into that room. Not that it was locked or anything. That would have been too easy.

"The kids played in the house for a million years. It wasn't boring. It wasn't that they lacked things to do. But somehow they started to get fidgety. It was time for me to come to them. And I did. 'Adam,' I said, 'why haven't you gone into that room yet?' And he said, 'it's against the rules.' And I said, 'if your father had really wanted you not to go into that room, he would have locked it and throw away the key.' So the boy talked it over with his sister for a long time, and eventually I took them all the way down there, slithering down the clammy stone steps, I watched them go in, and I watched the door close behind them, and I waited.

"Sex and death were in that room, Jess."

"I remember now!" He's exhilarated. "They were kicked out of the house, and I've come to fetch them home."

"Oh, Jess," I say, "that's the illusion I've come to strip away; that's the one piece of knowledge in *your* dark basement room – we all have them, those basement rooms – and I've come to give it to you."

"Oh," says the boy, and the light begins to drain from his eyes.

"You see, the boy and the girl went upstairs to tell their father they'd broken the rule. The old man was very sad. He said, 'you can stay if you want. We can work this out. I don't want to lose you.' Adam and Eve looked at each other. Strange and grand new feelings was searching through that bodies. At last, Eve said, 'we have to go, Dad. You know we do. That's why you didn't lock the door.' And the old man said, 'Yes. You're human beings. It's human to defy your parents. It's human to strive, to seek new worlds, to leave the nest, earn a living, make love and babies, filter back into the earth so that it can nourish more human beings. You're dust and you must turn to dust again one day. It's a sad thing. But it's not without joy. Look how dust dances in the light. You are beautiful because you are not immortal. I'm the one who can't change. I'm the one who has to go on forever. Pity me, children. Pity your poor old father.'

"The knowledge the children gained with the gateway through the stone walls and into the world outside. They lived in the real world after that. Not always happily, and not ever after.

"And paradise became an empty nest, and the old man realized that the perfect place yet built with a private hell from which he could never escape."

Jess doesn't speak for a long time. They are turning out the lights, but a different light suffuses us, the light from the unicorn's eyes. At last he screams out, "Oh, God! Why did you send me here? Fuck you - you told me I was here to love them and redeem them and really you want me to change them up and throw the key into the ocean and —"

"You're talking to the unicorn?"

"Sometimes I think the unicorn is my father."

That's never occurred to me in all those years.

"Goodbye," Jess says softly, and he's not speaking to me. I've robbed him of his innocence at last. And now, for a few brief seconds, it is I who am pure: I am all the goodness that was once in the boy, I am his hopes and dreams, I am his sacrifice, I am his redeeming love. Only in that moment, as his vision leaves him, do I see the unicorn.

The restaurant has dissolved into thin air and the great beast is running toward the waves. The sea splashes against his moon-sheened withers. His horn listens. The wind from the Pacific whips Jess's hair across his bare shoulders. He looks down at the sand. "I'm naked," he says at last. "Can't you hold me?"

The unicorn has dissipated into mist.

I cradle Jess in my arms, and he weeps. In that embrace, without sex and without death, I drain the last dregs of Divinity from him. We love each other.

Maybe God *is* their father. But they are my children too, and I'm a lot older than God. Because of darkness is the mother of light.

I love them just as much as he does. More. My nest is empty too. But *he* just won't learn to let go. He just won't let them be. He always wants to meddle in their affairs. But he always lets me have my three temptations.

They think they want to live forever. They think they want eternal bliss. But what they really want is to love and to die. That is their real nature. That is the truth that God can never face, and that's why the war has to go on, why there'll always be an Antichrist.

Yesterday he was the savior of the world, but today, Jess is just another lost boy. Tomorrow I'll give him the keys to the Porsche and the title deed to the house by the sea, so at least he can go rollerblading to his heart's content, and have somewhere to come home to when he falls in love and raises a family and forgets that he ever had the power to mend broken souls.

I'm not the villain in this war.

Tomorrow I'll go someplace far away and I'll sit and wait for a hundred years until one day I'll hear the leaves rustling and see the hoofprints in the sand, or the snow, or the forest floor. It's always been this way and it always will be.

World without end.

Amen.

About the Author

Once referred to by the *International Herald Tribune* as "the most well-known expatriate Thai in the world," Somtow Sucharitkul is no longer an expatriate, since he has returned to Thailand after five decades of wandering the world. He is best known as an award-winning novelist and a composer of operas.

Born in Bangkok, Somtow grew up in Europe and was educated at Eton and Cambridge. His first career was in music and in the 1970s he acquired a reputation as a revolutionary composer, the first to combine Thai and Western instruments in radical new sonorities. Conditions in the arts in the region at the time proved so traumatic for the young composer that he suffered a major burnout, emigrated to the United States, and reinvented himself as a novelist.

His earliest novels were in the science fiction field but he soon began to cross into other genres. In his 1984 novel Vampire Junction, he injected a new literary inventiveness into the horror genre, in the words of Robert Bloch, author of Psycho, "skillfully combining the styles of Stephen King, William Burroughs, and the author of the Revelation to John." Vampire Junction was voted one of the forty all-time greatest horror books by the Horror Writers' Association, joining established classics like Frankenstein and Dracula.

In the 1990s Somtow became increasingly identified as a uniquely Asian writer with novels such as the semi-autobiographical Jasmine Nights. He won the World

Fantasy Award, the highest accolade given in the world of fantastic literature, for his novella The Bird Catcher. His fifty-three books have sold about two million copies world-wide.

After becoming a Buddhist monk for a period in 2001, Somtow decided to refocus his attention on the country of his birth, founding Bangkok's first international opera company and returning to music, where he again reinvented himself, this time as a neo-Asian neo-Romantic composer. The Norwegian government commissioned his song cycle Songs Before Dawn for the 100th Anniversary of the Nobel Peace Prize, and he composed at the request of the government of Thailand his Requiem: In Memoriam 9/11 which was dedicated to the victims of the 9/11 tragedy.

According to London's Opera magazine, "in just five years, Somtow has made Bangkok into the operatic hub of Southeast Asia." His operas on Thai themes, Madana, Mae Naak, and Ayodhya,have been well received by international critics. His most recent opera, The Silent Prince, was premiered in 2010 in Houston, and a fifth opera, Dan no Ura, will premiere in Thailand in the 2013 season. His sixth opera, Midsummer, will premiere in the UK in 2014.

He is increasingly in demand as a conductor specializing in opera and in the late-romantic composers like Mahler. His repertoire runs the entire gamut from Monteverdi to Wagner. His work has been especially lauded for its stylistic authenticity and its lyricism. The orchestra he founded in Bangkok, the Siam Philharmonic, is mounting the first complete Mahler cycle in the region.

He is the first recipient of Thailand's "Distinguished Silpathorn" award, given for an artist who has made and continues to make a major impact on the region's culture, from Thailand's Ministry of Culture.

Books by S.P. Somtow

General Fiction

The Shattered Horse
Jasmine Nights
Forgetting Places
The Other City of Angels (Bluebeard's Castle)
The Stone Buddha's Tears

Dark Fantasy

The Timmy Valentine Series:
Vampire Junction
Valentine
Vanitas

Moon Dance
Darker Angels
The Vampire's Beautiful Daughter

Science Fiction

Starship & Haiku
Mallworld
The Ultimate Mallworld

Chronicles of the High Inquest:
Light on the Sound
The Darkling Wind
The Throne of Madness
Utopia Hunters
Chroniques de l'Inquisition - Volume 1 (omnibus)
Chroniques de l'Inquisition - Volume 2 (omnibus)

The Aquiliad Series:
Aquila in the New World
Aquila and the iron Horse
Aquila and the Sphinx

Fantasy

The Riverrun Trilogy:

Riverrun
Armorica
Yestern
The Riverrun Trilogy (omnibus)

The Fallen Country
Wizard's Apprentice

Media Tie-in

The Alien Swordmaster
Symphony of Terror
The Crow - Temple of Night
Star Trek: Do Comets Dream?

Chapbooks

Fiddling for Waterbuffaloes
I Wake from a Dream of a Drowned Star City
A Lap Dance with the Lobster Lady
Compassion: Two Perspectives

Libretti

Mae Naak
Ayodhya
Madana
The Silent Prince
Dan no Ura
Helena Citronová

Collections

My Cold Mad Father
Fire from the Wine Dark Sea
Chui Chai (Thai)
Nova (Thai)
The Pavilion of Frozen Women
Dragon's Fin Soup
Tagging the Moon
Face of Death (Thai)
Other Edens
S.P. Somtow's The Great Tales (Thai)
Bible Stories for Secular Humanists

Essays, Poetry and Miscellanies

Opus Fifty
A Certain Slant of "I"
Sonnets about Serial Killers
Opera East
Victory in Vienna
Nirvana Express

www.ingramcontent.com/pod-product-compliance
Lightning Source LLC
Chambersburg PA
CBHW020935310726
48980CB00007B/784/J

* 9 7 8 0 9 8 6 0 5 3 3 6 8 *